Stealing

Ali

Based on a true story

A Novel by William & Daisy Serle

Since this book is fiction, names, businesses, and
incidents have been made up by the authors.
Real organizations and places are used fictitiously.
Resemblance to actual persons and events is coincidental.
The story is based on actual events.

ISBN: 1456560670
ISBN-13: 9781456560676

There are Angels among us
doing good through
kindness to strangers

There are people we need to thank for their help with this story. Family, friends, professionals and strangers; too many to name.

It's the kind strangers we'd like to thank most, if only we could. They were Muslims, Jews, Christians, men, women, black, white and brown. Rich and poor. Americans, Europeans, Africans and Middle Easterners.

Some gave us shelter. Some offered escape, hope or protection. None sought reward.

Special thanks to Amy Garza, friend, editor and advisor.

Cover and Interior Design by CreateSpace

Table of Contents

PROLOGUE – THE PERSIAN GULF

Hot and humid. Midsummer. Maggie's face was rigid with fear and tension. She was trying to be brave to protect her precious little girl.

With the speedboat on plane, they headed for their rendezvous at sea. The decisive action made their pulses race. After the long period of frustrating inactivity, it was exciting to be masters of their own fate again. The rush of air cooled them.

Impulsively, head back and lungs full, Lee flung up his arms and screamed a victory cheer, "Yeaaaah!!!!"

"Lee! For God's sake!" Maggie's look told Lee that this was half a jesting rebuke and half an agreement that she'd always remember this moment of her life.

Maggie struggled. There were no seats in the back of the little runabout, so they balanced by kneeling to absorb the shocks as the boat sped through the light chop. She had to hold on to tiny Ali, balance herself and manage her own drink, all at the same time.

The low lying land soon dropped out of view. No other vessels were in sight as the sky became darker. There were distant dots of light on the sea each time the boat rose on a wave. Out to sea blazing fires could be seen far away atop the many oil rigs.

Ali didn't really need to be held. Her five-year old body adjusted to the motion better than the adults. Lee reached over and pulled Ali to him to give Maggie some relief; her little body wedged between his chest and arms.

The Scotsman rode in front, sitting next to the driver. He had given them the cold beer to toast their freedom. To them it was as good as champagne.

The wind tore through Lee's clothing, blowing away the stink of sweat and fear. His beer dribbled down his chin whiskers. He shook the can in the air and some foam bubbled out blew in Maggie's hair.

"Don't do that." She grinned. Maggie really didn't care. He sensed her excitement. The soaring moment of escape was on them and they laughed at her words.

Their celebration spread to the front of the boat. Even the boy at the wheel was whooping it up. Their emotional responses were heightened by the escape after so many defeats. They had been like animals in a trap, gnawing their own bones. Now they felt free.

The western sky was a sailor's-delight, draining the color from the departed sun. The waves were bigger now that the boat was away from land's shelter. Abdul slowed the boat to ease the pounding. Without warning he cut the motor. When the boat stopped he stood up, legs spread wide, one hand on the windscreen. He began to scan the horizon, looking for their ship.

Their moods changed as the boat slowed. The roar of the outboard motor and the speed had shut out the possibility of thought or conversation. The boat quietly lifted and fell with the rhythm of the sea. The air became oppressive now; hot again and full of moisture wrung from the salty sea.

"Oh God Lee," said Maggie nervously, "What if we can't find our boat?" Her face was twisted, revealing dark thoughts. "It would be awful if..."

"Ah come on. We'll find it." Lee steadied her by putting his hand on her shoulder and giving it a gentle squeeze.

"Abdul. How soon should we see them?" Lee asked their young driver. His voice was normal, but he shared Maggie's concern. He thought, "She's right. It'd be awful to go back. If Joe catches up to us he'll have the police force with him and we wouldn't have a chance." His mind drifted back over the events that had elapsed over the course of their marriage. The stealing of Ali....

LEE ELRES

Maggie's husband, a Brooklyn boy, was transplanted to steamy South Florida in 1956. Miami's Cuban migration had not yet begun in earnest. Sleepy South Florida, along with its newly acquired college sophomore, never dreamed of the human wealth that was about to reach its shores.

Lee was a quiet guy. He was strong and fit but not quite sure that he was in the right time or place. Miami seemed small time to him compared to fabulous New York; he thought of himself as a dreamer. Passive. He thought his life was like swimming at an ocean beach at the breaker line, with waves breaking all around.

He liked the feel of the wave surge when it pulled, lifted and then swept toward the sandy beach. Lee usually went with the flow, floating over the waves, enjoying the sunshine, the breezes and the palm lined beach.

There was one exception. Wooing and wedding Maggie was like catching a big wave just right. He swept along famously, reaching for the shore as fast as he could go.

Maggie became a Goddess for him, but her history was very human.

They met at work in 1967 when he started at the large weight-reduction clinic where Maggie was a medical assistant. He acted as the general manager but given the title of Administrator.

The owner, Dr. Burt Arnold, had a major weight reduction practice with a staff of physicians to help him. In addition to fourteen clinics in South Florida cities, there were six clinics in Colombia and Mexico. Lee was very involved in the creation of this little empire and the Latin American expansion.

Lee had a banking background and a B.B.A. He had lots of management and leadership training and experience courtesy of the U.S. Army. He was an Army Reserve first lieutenant when he began working for Dr. Arnold.

MAGGIE ALVAREZ

Maggie was a pistol! Boisterous. Flighty. Sensuous. Loving. Beautiful. Enthusiastic. Scary. Fun to be with.

At five foot-four inches, Maggie was a sight to behold. She had a voluptuous figure and an angel's face with dark hair, a narrow nose and a clear light Mediterranean complexion. She was a hottie.

When Lee first noticed Maggie, she was making fun of him. He was making a speech at his first staff meeting at the main clinic in Hialeah, Florida. It was his first day at work.

What he noticed first was her impish grin. Then her long, sleek black hair that cascaded below her waist. She made funny gestures and faces behind his back. A quick glance over his shoulder and he caught her in the act.

Her whole package was a little incongruous. She wore a demure white nurse's uniform with a very short skirt. "How in hell can that gal sit down?" he wondered as he smiled at her joke. Later on, after a little study, he came to appreciate her great figure and boldly rounded derriere.

Stylish and feminine, she had no need to compete with men. Males tended to worship her. She was lightning in a bottle. Maggie's extreme side was cunningly hidden most of the time. But it could pop out when least expected. Sometimes as anger, sometimes as humor, and sometimes as deep sadness.

She often acted on impulse and thought things over later.

Quick to love and quick to loathe. Maggie was not always easy to really know. Her hidden thoughts require a long relationship to decipher.

She communicated well whether using words or not. Maggie could let people know exactly how things stood with a glance or a simple gesture.

Her hands, face, arms and body were always in motion when she talked. She spoke her mind. When an idea came to her the thoughts seemed to blaze out of her brown eyes. She was passionate about life.

Maggie was fully bilingual, at ease in her native Spanish or in the English she had to use since she was nine. This was just one aspect of her unique personality. She had an adolescent confusion about whether she was a Cuban or an American.

She spoke perfect, colloquial, unaccented, American English. Hardly anyone ever suspected that she was not U.S.A. to the core.

As she graduated from high school, she was in rebellion and desperate to escape her father's overzealous supervision. Her family was just one source of her distress. Her dad, Alfredo, and her mom, Caridad, moved to the U.S. in 1948. Maggie remained in Cuba with her grandparents for school and spent her summer vacations in Miami.

At age five, Maggie was a handful for her grandparents in Cuba. At eight she went to a boarding school where her grandparents hoped the nuns could deal with her better. She felt abandoned by her parents.

Her time in boarding school was a disaster. Her anger and rebellion escalated against the excessive number of rules. She felt isolated from friends and family.

One of the rules at the American Dominican Academy allowed the girls an opportunity to go home for weekends if they did their homework, made their beds, were on time for meals and said their prayers. Margarita, as the nuns called her, didn't make that trip to Havana very often.

Her parents split and divorced. Maggie moved to Miami Beach to live with her dad. When Caridad moved back to Cuba Maggie felt abandoned by her mother again. Alfredo, convincingly, placed the blame on Caridad and Maggie bought into the story.

Then the shit hit the fan! Alfredo showed up one day married to Elizabeth. Maggie, at thirteen, suddenly had a step-mom and a blond stepsister to share her room. She was mad at everyone!

Her father had betrayed her. This betrayal combined with her screaming teen hormones kicked her further out of the frying pan.

She couldn't wait to slip away into adulthood.

Her needs for love and support forced her into marriage three times.

Maggie was 29 years old and in full bloom in 1973. She was a beautiful Cuban American woman with dark eyes and midnight-black hair.

Trouble, however, seemed to follow her everywhere. Like a middle name. Always lurking. Seldom spoken.

Maggie married big George Mathews, her high school sweetheart, in her eighteenth year. That adventure involved four years in the Air Force and a cross country relocation to Seattle, Washington where her first daughter Jackie came into the world.

When George's hitch in the air force ended the little family returned to Miami. Maggie had her second baby. Scott.

Things were not going well for Maggie and George. Times were hard as they lived from paycheck to paycheck.

He was an office machine salesman and did not earn big money. He began to drink and soon became unreliable and resentful. Maggie fumed. The marriage became so difficult that Maggie had to leave.

Separated from George, penniless, with two small children to feed and care for, Maggie went to work at Dr. Arnold's clinic at minimum wages. She struggled to make ends meet with little support from George. She couldn't afford hair salons so her hair grew longer and longer. She could sit on it. It looked great.

She lived in a one-bedroom Hialeah apartment with her children. It was close to work. She had to be within walking distance because she didn't have a car.

Maggie earned her rent and grocery money but not much more. Her folks tried to help but her pride pushed her to try to make it by herself.

Motherhood had become Maggie's central issue in life. Her two children were on her mind and in her heart when the sun came up and when the moon rose. Circumstances forced her to have a job but she would rather have stayed home to care for the kids.

Then tragedy struck with an iron fist.

Precious little Scott died in the care of his baby-sitter while Maggie was at work. She thought that he had bronchitis but it suddenly turned into pneumonia and he passed away while he was napping.

The death of baby Scott was the final straw for the young couple. It pushed George into alcoholism and the couple into divorce court. Maggie hovered on the edge of a breakdown. At this point in her life she really went into a deep depression.

This terrible event in Maggie's life soured everything. She couldn't cope in her emotional tailspin.

That's how things stood when Joe Zayyat came along a few months after her separation from George.

Maggie was like a magnet and Joe like an iron bar. He had money and time to spend on winning the heartbroken girl. He paid for her to hide out from her life at a resort in the Bahamas. She went to recuperate there in the sunshine with little Jackie.

Joe flew over on Chalk's Ocean Airlines every weekend for a month. They bonded.

Love happens. Divorce happens. Exit George. Fast forward. Joe and Maggie married.

She had been struggling and Joe was her rescuer. Joe was a Lebanese immigrant to the U.S. and had traveled a lot. He seemed worldly and supremely self-confident. Joe spoke fluent French, Arabic, Italian and confident Spanish, He knew a smattering of phrases in several other languages.

Their union started strong and well but, as always, lovers really begin to know each other after the ceremony.

Joe wanted Maggie to stay home but she continued to work, partly out of a need for self-reliance, and partly because Joe let her fully share the financial burden of supporting the household.

He was about to start a new business, providing hydraulic services to Miami's burgeoning Cuban fishing fleet. He needed to use his funds to rent a shop on the Miami River. He said, "Maggie, I'm not gonna get rich on day one, but there's a lot of money to be made there. I'm going to specialize in fixing the hydraulic systems on those commercial fishing boats." Maggie's job paid the bills.

Maggie continued to work throughout her marriage to Joe except for maternity leave when Ali came along in 1969.

JOSEPH ZAYYAT

One would call Joe a hardworking, smart, good looking guy. Even charming if you met him socially. His mild mid-eastern accent made him interesting.   Think of young Omar Sharif. He was thirty years old when he spotted Maggie at a friend's Halloween party.

He had a complicated history of work and adventure on several continents after his departure from Lebanon.

Stocky and dark-haired, Joe claimed to be a champion bodybuilder and told Maggie that he had once held the body building title of "Mr. Lebanon."   At various times he told Maggie that he had been a mercenary soldier in Africa, a ship's captain and a trained engineer.

As years passed Maggie had a hard time discerning Joe's truth from fiction.   She did know that he held a U.S. Coast Guard Masters License, valid, it said, for any vessel in any waters.

When Joe met Maggie he was the chief engineer on the University of Miami's tall, square-rigged oceanographic re-search ship.   The highlight of his time on the ship was a transatlantic voyage to Italy.   He had just returned from Italy when Scotty died.

Joe had a cruel streak.   On several occasions he brought cute puppies home as a gift to the family.   This seemed fine on the surface but he would go into a rage when the dogs peed or pooped on the floor and beat them mercilessly.   They never lasted long.   He'd give them away complaining that the mutts didn't live up to his standards.

Six year old Jackie longed for Joe's attention.   She had no contact with George who was bitterly angry at Maggie. George stayed away because he regarded Maggie as the one who had abandoned him, never giving any weight to his own misdemeanors.

Joe was tolerant of Jackie but never as warm as the little girl wanted. When Ali was born Joe became Ali's doting daddy leaving Jackie out in the cold.

To Maggie's horror she had to step between Joe and Jackie when Joe wanted to beat her with his belt for minor infractions. He did hit Jackie on occasion and sometimes locked her in the bathroom when she was naughty, threatening to beat her if she dared to come out before he was ready.

He was preoccupied by his new business and sometimes went missing without warning. Business was first with Joe.

Joe was secretive about money matters and about his business activities. He looked down at his Cuban clients and was critical of everyone.

His business prospered and he bought a house with the money he'd saved by letting Maggie pay the rent and buy the groceries for five years.

He was cruel to the dogs and Maggie, too tough with Jackie and not attentive to his family's emotional needs. Despite his promises to do better when Maggie complained, the nice new lakefront house became an arena for bitter fights.

The marriage was too painful for her. Maggie moved out in January 1973 while Joe was at work. She took the furniture, pots, pans and clothing and, when Joe begged, refused to come back. She felt that her life had to change.

Joe had several wealthy clients with big expensive yachts. Maggie found out that he was having an affair with an owner's "arm-candy" wife. And Maggie knew them! The two couples sometimes had dinner together.

Carol was tall and voluptuous. She showed off her assets with short shorts and revealing tops.

When Maggie moved out, Carol moved in. Maggie heard some of the details when Carol telephoned her for help in the summer of 1974. Carol was stuck, without transportation or funds. Joe was abusive and she had to get away to the airport to pick up a ticket her husband in Oklahoma had bought for her.

"Come now Maggie. Now!" she croaked. Carol's voice was urgent. "He's at work and I don't know when he's coming back. Just a ride to the airport. I don't have cab fare and I don't know anybody else to call. He'll kill me if he catches me trying to get away. Hurry. Please!!!"

When Maggie picked Carol up she looked a wreck. She was without makeup and wore a wrinkled tee shirt over Bermuda shorts. She was waiting in the driveway with two suitcases.

Carol poured out her woes. Apparently Joe paid little attention to her except for sex and meals.

"Joe never hit me but I was scared all the time. He gets so mad. When I ask for something he ignores me. He even goes to the grocery with me. He tells me what to buy and pays the bill. Right now I have just $3.00 in my purse."

"We had no social life. Never went to a movie or talked to the neighbors. He thinks everyone in the neighborhood is nosey and stupid."

"He was so nice at first. I can't believe this has happened to me."

Maggie gave Carol the $45.00 she had in her purse and wished her well.

In 1974 Joe was in shock and denial over the separation and subsequent divorce from Maggie. He wanted her back and was willing to pay a price. He couldn't believe that Maggie would ever marry someone else. In his twisted head the demise of his marriage to Maggie was someone else's fault. Never his own. Joe was mad as hell.

CHAPTER 1 - 1974 - MIAMI

Maggie and Lee were married on August 22, 1974, survivors of unhappy marriages that had gone on the rocks. They had vowed to love, honor and keep each other, until death did them part. Their lives together were to be a symphony of love and accomplishment in modern America.

Their bliss lasted thirteen days. The length of the honeymoon. Joe was a vengeful person and he still wanted Maggie as his wife. He gave them a wedding present that almost blew them apart. It was a terrible gift that aged them, scarred them, and in the end, caused them all to blunder about.

As the wedding preparations and pre-ceremony activities were finalizing, Joe became more aggressive. He declared that he still loved Maggie and he wanted her back.

While the new furniture was being moved into their house and as they learned the intricacies of the swimming pool plumbing, dishwasher and so forth, Joe began to badger Maggie with menacing telephone calls.

"You know that you love me. Why are you marrying him? Because I wasn't nice to Jackie? I'll be good to her this time. No man is going to raise my daughter." Meaning Ali of course. "I'll put out a contract on Lee. They'll cut him up before they stick a gun in his mouth and pull the trigger." Joe was not showing his nice side.

"Tell me you don't love me. You are sacrificing yourself for Jackie and your parents." He couldn't tolerate Maggie's parents, friends or relatives.

"Maggie please I'm asking you on my knees. I'll make it all up to you." He had been living with another man's wife in the house that Maggie had tried to turn into a home for him until she was forced to leave him. "We'll take a grand tour of Europe. Paris, Rome. The Riviera! Wherever you want to go. First class all the way." He had been somewhat parsimonious during their marriage.

"That bastard. He bought you with that house. Didn't he?" Joe refused to believe that Maggie could have a relationship with another man which was not based on money.

"I'll buy you a better house. You name it and I'll make a twenty-five thousand dollar deposit on it tomorrow." He named several houses which he had heard Maggie admire.

"You tell Lee that I know where his sons live." His nasal voice gravely and evil on the telephone. He gave Lee's former wife's address. "Tell him that they'll never walk again when I get done with them. Then I'll have Lee killed."

Maggie recorded the conversation and played it for Lee. "My God Lee. What can we do?"

Lee said. "Maggie. Don't worry. He's just trying to scare you. He's a bully and he is used to getting his way.

"Look. If he seems serious I'll get a gun and take care of him."

Lee tended to be introspective. A little nerdy, reading fiction about far away places and adventure. He was always the most peaceful guy in any gathering. Lee was six foot four inches tall and a fit two hundred and twenty pounds. Never a violent man, he was scared enough by the recorded threat to threaten murder.

"I'm an expert shot and I even have medals to prove it." He showed Maggie his collection of army medals and awards. Sharpshooter. Marksman. Expert. He was a lieutenant in his reserve unit.

Joe's threats and Lee's talk about shooting guns shook Maggie. If their wedding arrangements hadn't been so advanced, she might have delayed until Joe cooled off. They could have waited until her fears and misgivings, so cruelly raked to the surface, had quieted. Have you ever known a bride, or groom, without misgivings?

Lee took action. The baseball bat he kept near his bed wasn't enough anymore. He bought a Titan Tiger 32-caliber revolver for $95.00 and planned to defend himself. Trouble was, the threat was today and there was a one-week waiting period before he could actually get the gun.

Lee tried to borrow a gun from their boss, Dr. Arnold. "Lee. I can't let you have it. I'm afraid you'll do something foolish - something you'll regret."

A friend, lawyer Stan Schulman was in the room. He said, "Lee. I have a gun in the car. You can have it as long as you need." So Lee now had a fine semiautomatic pistol and pondered. What to do?

Early mornings, weekends and after work he went to the river front neighborhood of Joe's marine hydraulic business and learned the layout of the neighborhood. He sat in his car a half block away and had a pretty good view of Joe's comings and goings. "What if I just go in at a quiet time and kill him? How can I get away with it. Even if I'm not seen, I'll be a suspect. I'll spend years in jail. What good would that do for the kids and Maggie?"

Lee was able to take possession of his new gun after the week was over and he returned Stan's gun with thanks.

Lee stalked Joe but couldn't figure a way to kill him that made any sense. And what about killing him? That would sit heavily on his soul. He was just not cut out to be an assassin. He never told anyone about his thoughts of murder.

Despite their difficulties with Joe, Maggie and Lee plunged ahead becoming obligated for thousands of dollars for a leased house and new furniture. Their wedding reception was all arranged and, of course, of supreme importance, driving them onward, was their love for each other. They wanted to be united! Maggie and Lee were married on a brilliant August day.

When their determination became clear, the threats ceased and a smoother and calmer Joe emerged.

Joe wanted to take Ali to visit her grandparents in Lebanon for three weeks during the honeymoon. He indicated, at last, that he was resigned to her marriage. He said that he would wait and that when she came to her senses he would be ready to take her back.

Joe begged Maggie, "Please let me take Ali to Lebanon to meet her grandmother. Mami is getting old and she's dying to see Ali. Please?"

Maggie couldn't say no and that's how things were while the newlyweds honeymooned in Mexico. Joe and Ali went to Lebanon.

At first Maggie voiced many objections to the proposed trip. School began in early September. She told him she was afraid that he would try to take Ali away from her. He assured her that he would never do anything to harm his own daughter. He promised to return Ali in time for her to begin kindergarten school; without fail. He swore on the grave of his sainted older brother - David, who had been killed in an Israeli border clash. So Maggie consented and Ali went to Lebanon to see the grandmother, aunts and uncles that she had not met before.

The wedding was the most exhilarating celebration they'd ever experienced. The ceremony took place in a tropical garden. It was remembered through a pink and blue cloud. A beautiful and dear friend performed a ceremony full of tender and meaningful sentiments before relations and close friends. Lee's father was the best man.

That night became a champagne whirl of dining and dancing.

They honeymooned in Mexico City and Acapulco. They had a glorious time. The extent of their downfall was almost classical in scope. Those who fly too high, too fast, have a long way to fall.

They returned to Miami on September second and eagerly awaited Ali.

Joe did not bring Ali back. After two days of anxious waiting, Maggie began a series of frantic telephone calls to Lebanon. She could not locate Joe. Known relatives in Lebanon refused to accept her calls or were conveniently out.

Joe was being too cruel. Given Maggie's history of already losing one child, losing another was the worst thing that could ever happen to her - a new disaster piled on the old disaster.

Joe's mother Adele was called "Mami." She lived in a mountain village near Beirut. She reacted very emotionally when, after many attempts, Maggie finally managed to get her on the phone. The woman carried on unintelligibly. Clearly, Joe was back to his evil ways.

Lee and Maggie contacted the Welfare and Whereabouts Section of the U.S. Department of State in Washington and asked for help in locating Ali.

They got a prompt telephone response and, later, copies of wire traffic between the State Department and the Embassy in Lebanon. This led nowhere.

E.O. 11652: N/A
TAGS: CASC (ZAYYAT, ALLISON ADELE)
SUBJECT: W/S ABOVE MENTIONED

SUBJECT DPOB AUGUST 9, 1969 MIAMI PASSPORT NO, E029704
TRAVELED WITH FATHER JOSEPH ZAYYAT AUGUST AND WAS DUE RETURN US SEPTEMBER 4. MRS ELRES, SUBJECT'S MOTHER RECEIVED TELEGRAM SEPTEMBER 9 FROM FATHER STATING SHE HAD CONTRACTED EAR INFECTION AND RESTRICTED FROM FLYING. HE WAS, THEREFORE, OBLIGATED TO RETURN TO U.S. WITHOUT SUBJECT. Mr. ZAYYAT HAS NOT YET RETURNED NOR CAN HE BE CONTACTED AT BEIRUT. MRS ELRES STATES SHE HAS CALLED FORMER HUSBAND'S FAMILY MANY TIMES, HOWEVER, THEY HAVE BEEN UNCOOPERATIVE IN PROVIDING INFO. REQUEST POST ATTEMPT CONTACT Mr. ZAYYAT C/O BROTHER, WADI ZAYYAT O.G.D.R.O. P.O. BOX 1226 BEIRUT TEL: 581022/115314/170059 OR MOTHER AT BKASSINE (TEL 46) AND ATTEMPT OBTAIN INFO RE SUBJ'S HEALTH AND PLANS FOR RET. US. INTERESTED PARTY. UNCLASSIFIED   SCS94

PAGE 01BEIRUT 11451 1435Z

7

53
ACTION SCSEAPP

INFO OCT-01   /001 W

— 089689

P 1230Z SEP74
FM AMEMBASSY BEIRUT
TO SECSTATE WASHDC PRIORITY 402

UNCLAS BEIRUT 11451

EO 11652: NA
TAGW: CASC: (ZAYYAT, Allison ADELE)
SUBJ: W/W Allison ADELE ZAYYAT
REFERENCE STATE 6310

SUBJECT'S GRANDMOTHER CONTACTED AND REPORTS
THAT SUBJ LEFT LEBANON WITH FATHER AUG 18 ON
9 AM FLIGHT FOR U S. GRANDMOTHER DOES NOT
KNOW FUTURE ADDRESS IN U S AND EMBASSY UNABLE
TO CONTACT OTHER RELATIVES. SUBJ IS REPORTED IN
GOOD CONDITION AND RECOVERED FROM INFECTION.
EMB WILL ATTEMPT TO VERIFY DEPARTURE AND
FLIGHT INFO FROM LOCAL AUTHORITIES. INTERESTED
PARTY.
GODLEY.
UNCLASSIFIED

When Maggie heard the contents of the wires she knew
immediately that Joe's mother told the investigator that Ali

was fine and had departed with her father. Neither Maggie or Lee realized that she had lied until much later. A sharp reader will notice discrepancies in the dates but Lee and Maggie could not tell, and did not care much, afterwards, to know if this was a result of typos or deception.

Maggie made a desperate telephone call to her cousin Vincent's ex-wife, Chloe, who had handled the sale of their townhouse. Maggie had learned in the months since she'd left Joe, that Chloe had been having an affair with him but Maggie figured that Chloe was probably pissed off at him by this time.

"Chloe. It's me. Maggie. How are things?"

"Good." Chloe was a little reserved, not knowing what was coming or if Maggie was mad at her.

"Good."

"How are you Maggie?"

"Not good Chloe..." Maggie burst into tears and couldn't talk for a bit. Lee handed her a tissue.

"Oh god! What's wrong honey?" Chloe's heart went out to her friend.

"That shit head stole Ali, Chloe." Maggie groaned. Her breathing was so heavy that she could hardly talk. "He has her in Lebanon and isn't bringing her back..." More weeping.

"Maggie. That's awful! How could Joe do such a thing? What can I do to help?"

"I don't know Chloe. I just had a thought about the settlement on the townhouse. I'm going to go to court and maybe the judge can hold it up to give us some leverage."

"Maggie." Chloe's voice was conspirital. "Don't ever tell anyone what I'm about to tell you. I'll get in trouble and could lose my job or even my license, but, Joe hasn't been paid yet. The money will be his on the 15th." She gave Maggie a lot of information. The name of the bank Joe used and his account number. The name of the lawyer handling the sale and his bank information too.

"Thank you Chloe. I swear I'll never, never tell. I love you!" A glimmer of hope arose.

"Lee. We have got to go to court now. Maybe we can hold up his money." Maggie and Lee went right to work.

They sought legal help on the thirteenth of September. The situation deeply depressed Maggie.

Their attorney and friend, Stan, recommended Maurice Gelb as the best lawyer in the state when it came to family matters.

Maggie and Lee called Mr. Gelb, got an appointment to meet with him immediately.

They learned that things happened fast around Mr. Gelb. He was the soul of efficiency and very smart. His practice was located in a expensive suite of offices in a Brickell Avenue tower with long views of Biscayne Bay.

A dapper man with short steel-gray hair, he wore custom-made, boldly striped shirts under his beautiful suits. His imported silk ties seemed worth a week's paycheck for the average guy.

His fees were high but he gave them confidence that he could get any job done.

The very next day there was an emergency hearing in front of Judge Silverman who'd granted Maggie's divorce. She was awarded an Arrest Warrant, and an "Order of Sequester" which froze the twenty thousand dollars due to Joe from the sale of their home. They also got a court order demanding the return of Allison to her mother.

Maurice Gelb seemed like Superman in a silk suit.

Judge Silverman was clearly outraged by the situation. He demanded of Joe's attorney that he return immediately with Ali.

At the time of the divorce Joe had closed his business and supposedly moved to Louisiana to work for an oil company. Maggie had abandoned her share of the home proceeds in an effort to placate Joe in his rage over the divorce. Obviously it had not worked. Ali was still lost in Lebanon.

Joe sat on the shady front porch of his mother's house watching Ali play with her cousins. Allison was learning Arabic. She was singing songs with the neighborhood kids and she refused to speak Spanish which was her primary language when they left Miami.

He couldn't believe how dumb Maggie was. She'd believed him when he said he would bring Ali back. Maggie said she wanted Ali to have a relationship with him. Well, the relationship was going to be there all right because he was not going to take Allison back to the States, no matter how much Maggie begged.

Adele, Joe's mother, came out to sit with Joe. She spoke in Arabic with a liberal Italian vocabulary mixed in. It was almost a private family language.

She looked at him closer and asked, "Why did Maggie give up her daughter?" She had been asking the same question for the last week. Joe's answer was the same each time.

"Mami," that's what the children called Adele, "When Maggie got married again, Ali was in her way. All she wanted was her new husband. I couldn't let Allison live under those circumstances, anyway Ali wanted to come and live with me."

"But Joe, you're traveling all the time, how are you going to take care of Ali by yourself?"

"Don't worry Mami I've already made arrangements to put her in a boarding school, I'll be with her on holidays and vacations."

"How is a life in a boarding school going to be better for the child? Allison needs her mother." Mami looked at her son with tearful eyes.

"I've told Ali that Maggie doesn't want her anymore and she's ok with that," Joe muttered.

Joe turned to Adele with rage in his eyes and said. "No other man is going to raise my child, you are not to talk to Maggie when she calls or tell her where Allison is. Is that clear?"

"My son, I see such hatred in your eyes, that part of you is not a part Ali should see." "I will do what you ask, but my heart breaks for Maggie every time I hear her crying on the phone when she calls. She doesn't sound like she doesn't want Allison."

Mother and son sat in glum silence for a long time watching the children play.

The telephone rang early in the morning in Joe's mother's Bkassine house. Adele didn't want to answer it in case it was Maggie again, so Joelle, Joe's sister answered the call.

It was a man's voice asking for Mr. Zayyat in English. Joelle went to Joe's room to wake him.

"Hello."

"Hello Joe, it's Mark." Mark Goodman was Joe's attorney in Miami.

"What's wrong Mark, why are you calling?"

"I've got bad news and you're not going to like it."

"What is it man, spill it out."

"Well it seems your ex has sequestered the twenty thousand dollars from the sale of the house and you've got to appear in court ASAP to answer the charges she's brought against you."

"What charges?"

"Kidnapping. You are to bring Allison back to the states immediately and there's an arrest warrant for you. If you do not appear in court at the appointed time, Maggie will get the money from the sale of the house."

"How can she get away with this Mark? She signed the house over to me, I'm the sole owner now."

"She's done it Joe, you took Allison out of the country and didn't bring her back on the date you agreed with Maggie."

"I'm not bringing Ali back Mark."

"If you don't bring her back, Maggie will get the money and they'll be an arrest warrant for you as soon as you touch American soil."

"What is my time line for this?"

"ASAP buddy, tell me when you can get here and I'll call the judge and set up a court date."

"I'm not bringing Ali back, besides she's sick and can't travel."

"You'd better have a Doctor to verify this. I'm sure the judge will ask for verification."

"Ok, I'll take the first flight out tomorrow, but Ali stays here. She's sick."

"Call me as soon as you get in."

"Will do."

Joe slammed the phone down. Ali was standing right next to him.

Daddy I'm not sick, why did you tell that man I was sick?" "Daddy where are you going? I want to go home to mommy."

"I've already told you Ali, your mother doesn't want you anymore. She married that man and now she doesn't want you anymore."

"But Daddy Lee loves me. He tells me all the time and plays with me and we swim in the pool all the time. Tell mommy I'll be a good girl, I'll pick up my toys and eat my vegetables."

Joe scowled.

"Allison! Go to your room, I don't want to talk about this any more."

"But Daddy..."

14

"I said go to your room, right now."

Ali ran to her room sobbing.

"And stop that crying, it won't do you any good."

Joe picked up the telephone and said "Operator, I'd like to send a telegram to the states..."

The consequences of freezing Joe's funds was almost magical to Maggie and Lee. On the fourteenth of September a telegram came:

Allison is ill and cannot travel.
I am obliged to return
without her. Joe

A few days later there was a phone message at the office. Joe left a local number to call back. He was back in the U.S. But where was Ali?

Lee and Maggie did some sleuthing. They got the street boundaries for the three-digit exchange from the phone company. Maggie and Lee immediately set out to drive the neighborhood together, trying to locate any apartment building that might be suitable for Joe.

There were very few apartment buildings in the industrial area. Most of them were shabby. There proved to be only one that might be suitable. It was a large complex surrounded by a wrought iron fence. The cars in the parking area were clean models of recent vintage. Coincidentally a friend of theirs once lived in the same building complex following his divorce.

They knocked on a door near the parking area and hit pay dirt. The man who came to the door said he knew Joe and described his car. He said that Joe had been living there for about a year. He gave them the apartment number.

Joe's car was not there and there was no response to the knock on his door. It seemed to them that Joe was still living and working in Miami. Maggie drove to the apartment building again early the next day before work, but she had a fender bender on the drive over and was unable to complete her mission. Frustration, confusion and anger mounted.

Joe was back and appeared in court as Judge Silverman had instructed. This had mixed results. Joe claimed that Ali had an ear infection and was too ill to fly. The judge directed Joe to tell his family, in writing, to release Ali to Maggie.

Joe looked contrite and said, "Your Honor. I want to bring her back to her mother but she's been sick and her physician has advised me to not let her fly." His story was not believable.

At a second hearing in Judge Silverman's chambers Joe arranged for Lee's and Maggie's employer Doctor Burt Arnold to talk to Ali's physician in Lebanon on the speaker phone from Miami - a Dr. Karim Massaad at the Military Hospital in Beirut. He found out that she was taking penicillin and valium. Judge Silverman listened with his hands interlaced under his chin. Joe was stoney faced and grim.

They were gathered around a boat-shaped wooden conference table. Tension filled the air. Maggie listened in tears and Lee was still, his face pale, his right leg jumpy. Joe wore a face of stone. The lawyers listened intently and made notes on their yellow legal pads.

The connection was made by Mr. Gelb's secretary. Dr. Massed came on the line.

Massaad: "This is Doctor Massaad." His English was accented.

Arnold: "Why are you giving a five-year-old child Valium?" said Dr. Arnold.

Massaad: With a heavy accent. "Well. Because she's been very agitated."

Arnold: "Why has she been agitated?"

Massaad: "Well it seems the mother abandoned her and the father had to go back to the states for court hearing."

Arnold: "The mother did not abandon her. That's what this hearing is all about. Can we talk to Allison?" He always called her by her full name.

Massaad: "No. she's sedated right now and can't come to the telephone."

A loud dial tone ended the call abruptly. Every one was surprised. It seemed that Dr. Massaad was done talking.

Joe presented a handwritten letter from Dr. Massaad in French. There was an English translation attached. It was on the doctor's hospital stationery with little documentary stamps and a Arabic inscription apparently attesting to its authenticity.

Dr. Karim MASSAAD
MEDECIN A L'HOSPITAL MILITARE
DOMICILE CLINIQUE

(The printed parts of the stationery with the name, addresses and telephone numbers were in both french and arabic)

(The english translation read)

> I the undersigned Karim Massaad hereby certify that I examined Miss Allison Adéle Zayyat who is suffering of a general anemia and an intermediate socket with head-noises.
>
> Her health condition does not allow her to fly. She still is under my control. Her Health condition requires a treatment of at list six months as from 2.9.74.
>
> In virtue of I delivered this certificate.

Seal and Signature
of the Physician

Dated: September 2 1974

Dr. Arnold told Judge Silverman that he felt that the diagnosis and letter were suspect. He used the word "Bullshit" several times.

The judge and the attorneys went into the judge's private office to decide what to do.

The judge sternly told Joe that he was ordered to stay in Miami and that the money would not be released until Maggie and Ali were back in Miami together.

Joe turned to his attorney in disbelief. His evidence was being disdainfully ignored. The attorney whispered something in his ear. An admonishment to be quiet no doubt. He turned to glare at Maggie with his face screwed up in hate. Maggie almost looked away but then forced herself to glare back at him.

She thought, "Not this time you bastard. You've gone too far. This is my daughter you're hurting!" She kept her eyes on him.

Lee took her hand and squeezed it.

Judge Silverman told Maggie to go to Lebanon and to return with Ali as soon as she ascertained that Ali's health would permit travel. A legal writ was produced with relevant orders. Joe was to remain in Miami and provide Maggie with round-trip plane tickets. Joe presented the following letter, with his signature on his attornney's letterhead:

September 22, 1974

Mr. Wadi Zayyat
Lebanon

Dear Wadi,

You remember that the last thing I said was that no one was to touch my daughter without me being present. I must change these instructions NOW.

This letter is being given to you by Maggie and she believes that I do not want Ali to return to the U.S.A. Please help me convince Maggie that I want Ali back home as soon as medically possible.

Help Maggie make her independent choice of a doctor to examine Ali and confirm whether our daughter should travel. It would help for Maggie's doctor to be in consultation with Dr. Massaad.

Under no circumstances should you decide the doctor for Maggie as her choice must be her own.

Love to all

Joseph Zayyet

Attached to the letter was a notarized Authorization for Ali to travel with Maggie.

The events that followed were nightmarish. Lee learned the real story much later. Maggie left for Lebanon on Wednesday, September 25th. There followed a gloomy period in his life and a low point in the lives of all concerned.

Joe called his brother Wadi in Lebanon.

"Wadi, we went to court today and the judge said my money will be held until Maggie goes to Lebanon and picks up Allison and brings her back to the states."

"Joe, Ali is crying all the time. She wants her mother."

"Just make sure you keep on telling her that her mother doesn't want her, and keep talking to her in Arabic. I want her to forget her Spanish. That should really get to Maggie."

"Ok Joe, I'll do what you want."

"Good! I'll give you the information about Maggie's flight when I have it.

Goodbye brother."

The first step in going to Lebanon is to apply for a visa at a Lebanese consulate. Maggie wanted to go to N.Y.C. to get her visa quickly. She just could not wait for the mail. The tickets were waiting for her at the Miami airport for her journey to Lebanon via New York City.

Maggie flew to New York intending to proceed to Beirut directly from New York. She was refused a visa because the consulate had had reports that she was a "Zionist and in league with the Jews." Untrue, of course. Not that Maggie or Lee were against Israel – it is just not their cause.

Maggie called Joe in Florida and he smirked, "I told you so!" She could see no other solution so she promised him anything if he returned her precious four-year-old girl.

He immediately flew to New York, disobeying the court's orders, and cleared the way for her visa. He was parading his pull with the Lebanese government. He had demonstrated his invincibility and her inability to fight him. She was sick with dread.

At the airport. Joe walked her to the departure gate. She stiffly let him kiss her cheek as he said good bye.

21

"I'll see you when you get back. We'll have time to talk then."

CHAPTER 2 - LEBANON

Joe stood scowling by the airport's huge bank of public telephones. He was mad and worried. In the few minutes it took the international operator to connect him, he was thinking dark thoughts.

"Wadi, Maggie is on her way. I just put her on flight 705. She'll get into Beirut on Friday. Pick her up but don't give her Ali's passport and see if you can get her passport. That will scare her and show her who is in charge."

"Ok Joe, I'll pick her up. Shall I take Ali with me to the airport?"

After a thoughtful pause, "Yes, go ahead and take her with you."

Maggie arrived at the Beirut Airport midmorning. Standing in the baggage area she was anxiously looking for Wadi, Joe's brother. She was trying hard to remember what he looked like, but she'd only seen blurry photos of him and his family. He held a high executive position with the official Lebanese government radio station, according to Joe. She expected a man in a suit leading Ali by the hand.

"Oh!" She thought. "I think I see him. No...that's not him."

She continued to scan the crowd. "Yes I do see him." He wore the same sunglasses in all his photos. He wore a short-sleeved, white sports shirt which was not tucked into his pants.

But where was Ali? "Keep calm," she lectured herself. "She's here. I know she's here!"

Wadi walked toward Maggie holding a little boy's hand. "Is that his son?" she mused. "I thought he and Amale had two girls."

As he drew closer she suddenly realized it was Ali. "Oh my God. She looks like a boy! What happened to her long curly hair?"

"Calm Down. Don't cry." Maggie lectured herself again. "Keep your cool."

They came face to face.

"Hello Maggie." Wadi greeted her.

"Hello Wadi," she said. But her eyes were locked on Ali. "Hello Sweetie."

Ali looked up at her mother and said, "What are you doing here? Daddy told me you didn't want me now because you have Daddy Lee and Jackie."

Maggie felt lightheaded. Her heart dropped to her feet. "Keep calm. Don't panic. You can do this," she kept saying to herself.

She knelt and tried to take Ali in her arms. "Ali. Mi vida. Mami te adora. Yo no te abandone."

Ali, her life and love, looked away from her mother. Eyes down. "Don't talk to me en Espanole. I only speak English and Arabic now. I don't know what you're saying."

Six weeks ago Ali mostly spoke Spanish. "Oh my God. She doesn't want anything to do with me or even my language." Maggie whimpered to herself. She thought, "Joe's family has brainwashed her."

Wadi said, "Is this your suitcase?"

Maggie nodded, while trying to fight back the tears. She was both angry and frightened. He picked it up and walked off holding Ali with his other hand. Heartsick, Maggie followed.

Wadi's car was a little 4-door European model. Ali rode in front with Wadi. Fuming, Maggie sat in back.

"I'll take you to your hotel so you can check in and then we'll go to my house. Amale is making lunch for us."

The streets of Beirut were crowded. Many women wore traditional Islamic hijab and others were in European styles. Men wore both Middle Eastern robes and western suits. The mix of style and culture seemed very foreign and exotic to Maggie.

There were grand boulevards and mysterious little streets and avenues going off in all directions. Tall palm trees graced the street corners and parks they passed.

Army tanks were positioned on major intersections with sand bags piled around them. "What a strange, scary city," Maggie thought to herself.

Food shops had barrels of pistachios, olives and herbs lined up in front of their doors. Women were carrying small plastic sacks filled with exotic groceries.

The drivers seemed rough. Traffic was fast and aggressive.

Wadi quickly maneuvered through the crowded streets ignoring traffic lights and stop signs. He pulled into the St. George Hotel and handed Maggie her suitcase from the trunk. She followed him to the reception desk. Ali again held Wadi's hand. It gave Maggie a sinking feeling in her heart that Ali was walking with Wadi and not her.

The desk manager had her registered as Maggie Zayyat, even though the name on her passport was Elres. Wadi seemed to know the manager and even greeted several other employees by name.

"Here are your keys," said Wadi helpfully. "You can take your suitcase to your room and Ali and I will wait here."

Maggie was desperate to talk to Ali by herself. She seized the chance and said, "Ali honey. Would you like to come to Mommy's room?"

Ali looked to Wadi for his approval. He said, "You can go. Go ahead and I'll wait here." She gave him a little gap-toothed smile. She was still six front teeth shy of a perfect toothy smile.

Wadi stepped into the hotel office and got permission to make an international call by the office secretary.

"Hello Joe. Maggie's here at the St. George. Ali won't talk to her." They spoke in Italian.

"Good! Maybe Maggie will see we mean business and come around."

"I don't know why you don't just forget about this woman, she's more trouble than she's worth."

"Right now, little brother, she's worth twenty thousand dollars to me. We'll see what happens when I get my money back."

"Ok Joe, I'll call you in a couple of days. I'm taking them to Bkassine tomorrow to see Mami."

Joe hung up and looked around his apartment. "How did this all happen? How did Maggie and I drift apart? Well whatever happens I'm not letting another man raise my child. It won't happen."

Ali was a little reluctant and hesitant in the elevator but she seemed glad to be with her mother as they walked the hallway.

The room was just ordinary with a queen-size bed, a table, two club chairs and a bathroom.

"I need to go potty." Those were the first words out of Ali. She always checked out the bathroom first in any new house or restaurant.

"Of course darling. You don't need to ask permission."

Six weeks ago this little waif had never asked permission to use the bathroom. Six weeks ago this little girl kissed and hugged Maggie at every chance and called her Mommy. Maggie was waiting for Ali to say Mommy again.

"Keep calm. Don't cry. You will win her over," Maggie said to herself over and over. "She loves me. She loves me."

As Ali emerged through the bathroom door Maggie was unpacking some of Ali's favorite things and toys. "Oh Mommy." she exclaimed. "Those are my toys. Look at all of these things."

With tears rolling down her face Maggie said, "Yes darling. Jackie sent you the doll. Grandma and Grandpa Alvarez sent you the book and Grandma Carrie sent you this toy for your bath time."

"What did you bring me Mommy?" Maggie was happy now.

"Here. I brought you this outfit." Ali loved new clothes. "And this barrette for your..."

Maggie stopped talking and looked at Ali.

Ali began to cry. "Uncle Wadi had my hair cut so I would look like a boy because I was going to a school way, away from here. Mommy, I don't want to go away to any school. I want to come home with you. Why did you leave me?"

"I didn't leave you honey. Daddy wanted you to come here to meet his family and then he was supposed to bring you back. It just didn't work out that way and it took Mommy a little while to come and get you."

"Mommy. Don't leave me any more. I want to go home!" she wailed.

"Oh my love. Mommy will be with you forever. Don't worry."

Maggie held Ali for quite a while, rocking her and saying a little Spanish lullaby she sang every night at bedtime. She ran her fingers through Ali's short curly hair.

They were startled by the telephone ringing. Maggie picked it up. "Hello?"

"What are you doing up there?" Wadi asked. "We need to go to the house for lunch."

"OK. We'll be right down."

Maggie smiled at her daughter and said, "Ali honey. Let's wash our faces and fix our hair so we can go with your Uncle Wadi."

Ali squeezed her mother's hand on the ride down. She held it so tight that Maggie worried about hurting her hand. At the car, mother and daughter climbed in back. Maggie saw that Wadi seemed surprised, and even dismayed at this, but Ali sat close and hugged Maggie around the middle.

"Mommy came to get me." Ali announced proudly.

Maggie felt Wadi's eyes on her in the mirror even though he wore his sunglasses. She closed her eyes as she thought of the heartache and tears she and the whole family at home had been going through. She thought about the sleepless nights and the endless hours in courtrooms during the long six weeks since she'd been without Ali. She was so happy to be with her baby again.

Maggie dozed off. Jet lagged and content. She woke suddenly when Wadi stopped the car.

They were in front of a large apartment building. "This is it," he said. "We're here."

The drab gray building had arabic graffiti scrawled on the front door. Maggie wanted to ask what it said but she was feeling down and stayed silent.

The old-fashioned elevator creaked up to the sixth floor. It was really the seventh floor by Maggie's count so she knew that they were using the European convention for counting floors.

Amale waited in the dark apartment. There was an awkward moment before her eyes softened and she stepped in to give Maggie a sisterly hug.

Amale spoke to Ali in a musical voice but in Arabic. Ali shook her head and came closer to Maggie.

"What did she say Ali?" Asked Maggie.

Ali looked up at her mom with big eyes and whispered, "She told me to let go of your hand and go inside."

Maggie tensed up, kept tight hold on Ali's little hand and said, "Stay with Mommy honey." She turned to Amale and said, "It's very nice of you to invite us to stay for lunch."

Amale gestured the way and they stepped inside. The apartment was furnished with older furniture. Not antiques; just worn and somewhat shabby. Everything was dark in hue. The room had a large blue sofa and a dark mahogany wooden table that was set for lunch. The rooms seemed small and claustrophobic to Maggie.

The women made small talk about Maggie's flight and hotel accommodations. Wadi sat and read his paper until Amale called them to the table for lunch.

The Lebanese food was familiar to Maggie: hummus, baba ghanoujh, black olives, pita bread and salad. Maggie was famished and ate eagerly. Ali ate little and mostly stood quietly next to Maggie's chair.

During lunch Amale told her to sit straight in her own chair and give Maggie some room to eat her lunch. This was said kindly but Ali just shook her head and stood her ground.

Amale and Wadi seemed unhappy about this behavior and her refusal to obey. Maggie surmised that her brother and sister-in-law ran a tight ship insofar as Ali was concerned and that there was a little power struggle that she was upsetting. She didn't care and hoped that her ex-in laws were damned uncomfortable about the whole situation.

Maggie turned to her hostess and said, "Amale, I was very surprised that you cut Ali's hair. She had such beautiful curls."

Amale looked embarrassed. "It was getting hard for me to comb her hair every morning. So I had it cut."

"It had nothing to do with a Catholic convent school?"

"No, no, no. That had nothing to do with her attending any school."

Maggie thought that Amale was protesting too much and took the haircut as another assault on her world and resented it very much. She gave Amale a dark look to leave no doubt about her disapproval. The meal was finished in silence and everyone went to the living room to drink coffee. Ali stayed by Maggie's side.

Wadi announced the plan for the rest of Maggie's visit. "I'll drive you and Ali to Bkassine to visit Mami tomorrow. This will be a half a day's drive. It's just about a hundred kilometers from here. But the roads are narrow and mountainous. It can be a slow drive with the checkpoints and all."

"Checkpoints!" Maggie thought. "What the heck is that about?"

Unbeknownst to Maggie, Lebanon was on the verge of a civil war with conflicts on every side; Muslim and

Christian minorities were feuding. Syria, Israel, Jordan and Palestinians, fighting for a homeland, were also involved.

Maggie, like most Americans, had been insulated from all this with just a vague awareness that there were problems in Lebanon. The U.N., Europe and the U.S. also had vested interests here and the presence of these other interests added to the confusion. Political and criminal kidnappings were a daily event. Banks were even being robbed by militiamen.

"Ali can go back to the hotel with you if she wishes and we'll leave from there early in the morning."

Ali looked at Maggie. "Please Mommy. Let me stay with you. Please."

Maggie knelt on the floor and hugged Ali. "Of course you're staying with Mommy darling.

"By the way Wadi. I'll take Ali's passport please."

"That will be impossible." he said imperiously. "I'll give it to you when Joe tells me I can."

"And when," Maggie asked warily, "will that be?"

"When he's good and ready." said Wadi arrogantly.

The gloves were coming off and Maggie was getting mad. Joe had anticipated what she might do because she was already thinking how to get out of Beirut that night. But without the passport she felt trapped. She had to acquiesce.

Ali showed her mother the cot where she shared a bedroom with her cousins. Her overnight bag was quickly packed.

Mother and daughter were reunited and alone in the hotel room. They ordered room service for dinner, played games, talked and spent time snuggling. They went to sleep early. Travel, fatigue, and emotional events of the day were having an effect. Maggie escaped into a deep sleep.

Lebanon, Maggie later learned, with four million inhabitants living on about 10,000 square kilometers, has always been a densely populated country. Beirut was busy, stylish and always in trouble. The city's one-and-a-half million residents were divided between Muslims and Christians.

Only a few hundred people lived in rural Bkassine. At one thousand meters above sea level, the climate was mild in the summer and cold in the winter. It was known for its dense pine forest. There were few shops and public facilities.

The phone rang early, waking Maggie and Ali. Wadi's voice was neutral. Businesslike. "I've checked you out of your room. So bring your suitcases and we'll be on our way. Mami is waiting for us in Bkassine."

Maggie took her time, wanting to look put-together for her former mother-in-law.

They found Wadi waiting in the lobby. He took her suitcase and started to walk out the door. "Wait a minute!" Maggie called. "My passport. The front desk has it."

"I have your passport." Wadi announced. "I'll keep it with Ali's until you leave."

"I'm not comfortable with you having my passport, or, for that matter, Ali's." Maggie declared. "I'll keep them both thank you." They stood just outside the lobby glaring at each other. Ali was in the car by this time.

"I have orders from Joe to keep both of your passports until you leave. Besides they're safer with me." He played his macho trump card.

Maggie fumed. Joe was still pulling strings from the states. Her voice became loud and strident. Ali stared at them fearfully through the car window just a few feet away. "Wadi. You have no right! We are American citizens and our passports are very important to us!"

"Maggie. You seem to forget. Ali has dual citizenship and I'm her guardian here in Lebanon. If you make a scene and the police come, who do you think will walk away with Ali." Maggie was frightened now.

Ali ran back out of the car and began to wail, "Mommy, Mommy. Don't bring the police. I want to stay with you!"

"Oh my baby. I'm sorry I upset you. OK? I won't bring the police. We're all right." She gathered her daughter into her arms and held her close.

Wadi walked to the car with a grin on his face. "Oh God" Maggie prayed silently, "Give me strength to bring my baby home."

The morning traffic was horrendous. It seemed to take an inordinately long time to get out of the city and reach country roads and mountains, and the roads were not smooth.

Wadi had to stop a few times for herds of sheep on the road. Once he was halted while a camel driver moved a wooly herd of camels across the road.

Ali seemed right at home and not at all surprised to see the camels. "Ali. Have you been up to Grandma's house before?"

"Yes Mommy. When daddy was here he took me up to Grandma's and Uncle Wadi took me once."

"No wonder the camels didn't impress her." Maggie thought. "She's an old hand at this."

After a while Ali asked Maggie to read her a story. Maggie mused how she used to take the child for granted. Now she was worried about losing her. She gave her a squeeze.

"Ow Mommy. Don't squeeze me so hard!" They giggled at each other and sat close watching the little houses and trees pass by.

They stopped for lunch at an open air roadside restaurant. Wadi ordered several dishes. Maggie was famished and devoured her shish kebab and a lamb stew. Ali did not order but the adults shared bits from their plates. Maggie cut the meat for Ali as she always did at home.

Wadi bought Ali a ride on a huge camel tended by a shabby looking guy in Arab robes and head cloths. He was giving local children rides for a few coins. He took Ali around the field a few times under Wadi's watchful eyes.

Maggie knew that the currency was in Lebanese pounds but did not recognize the coins Wadi used and had no idea of their value. She felt lost and isolated from her world.

Ali ran up to Maggie saying, "I can't wait to tell Laura and Sandy I rode a camel!

"Mommy. Do you think Laura and Sandy miss me?" Neighboring sisters Laura and Sandy were Ali's best friends back home in Miami even though she had just recently met them.

"Yes. I'm sure of it. They asked me to tell you they miss you."

Characteristically, Ali soon went to sleep in the car and Maggie gazed at the passing houses, people, and especially the children playing by the side of the road.

The car slowed as it entered a little town with red roofs. The road was very narrow. Locals waved at Wadi and stared into the car at Maggie clearly wondering who she was.

Ali perked up and began to wave and call to some of the children her age. "There are my friends Rambebe and Estrella." She used the strange names easily.

Wadi parked in front of a small stone house. He got out and called out, "Hello!"

A short woman emerged from the open front door. She seemed powerful, as if she was used to hard, physical labor. Her gray hair was covered by a black kerchief. She wore a gray dress and a work-stained white apron. Maggie saw a pained expression on her face and thought she looked old and worried.

She took Maggie's hands in both of her own and gave her a little peck on each cheek, speaking in Arabic.

"Mami." said Wadi. And then began an explanation of some kind which Maggie took to mean "The American doesn't speak Arabic. She's not one of us."

Mami looked even more pained. Like a child that had just been told "No!"

Maggie spoke in Spanish. "Mami. Joe told me you speak Italian. Maybe we can understand each other this way."

Mami smiled at last. "It has been a long time that I wanted to meet Joe's wife." She spoke in Italian. Maggie understood.

She kissed Maggie's cheeks again, pulled back to hold her shoulders at arm's length. She looked at Maggie's face and said, "Bellisima. Multo bella."

Ali was pulling at her grandmother's dress to get her share of the attention. Adele turned and pulled her up to her bosom to give her hugs and kisses.

The two spoke to each other in Arabic but Maggie knew it was simply grandmother to grandchild conversation.

Maggie spotted a young woman standing shyly in the door. She instantly knew the girl was Joe's sister, Joelle.

Joelle was tall and slender with beautiful, long, black hair. She had large, dark brown eyes and beautifully arched eyebrows. She wore a white blouse with a long full black skirt. Peasant style. "Fresh and clean." Maggie thought. Then, on second thought, "No. More like a school uniform." She approached Maggie and said, "Welcome to Bkassine," in English. She too gave Maggie a little peck on each cheek, mimicking her mother exactly.

Her English accent was perfect and clear. "Good." thought Maggie. "She can help me translate for her mother."

"Thank you Joelle. I just wish I could have met you and Mami under better circumstances."

Joelle lowered her eyes; she seemed embarrassed by the situation.

The entry to the house had wooden benches on two sides. It put Maggie in mind of a mud room used for removing shoes in wet weather. Maggie was given a tour with Ali tagging along to give her approval of the proceedings.

Wadi carried the suitcases to the back bedroom. It had a twin bed and a dresser. Joelle's room. Joelle showed Maggie drawers that she had emptied to make room.

"I feel bad taking your room," Maggie told her.

"No problem. Mami has a big bed. Anyway you're our family."

The small galley kitchen seemed to be a well-used work room. Maggie thought Adele must spend a lot of time in this part of the house.

On the left was a door that led to two bedrooms and a bathroom. Beyond the door was the sitting room furnished with the same dowdy style as Wadi's apartment. The wood was dark and Maggie thought that some of the pieces must be antiques.

The large dining room was beautiful. It contained an elegantly carved table, eight chairs nestled up to it and an ornate, matching wooden buffet.

That night Maggie and Ali slept in the twin bed holding each other. Maggie woke during the night to make sure that Ali was still next to her. Actually, Ali wouldn't even let her mother go anywhere without her. Not even the bathroom. Whenever Maggie went anywhere Ali would say, "Mommy. I'll go with you."

Maggie woke the next morning to an awful, rotten fruit smell wafting into the window, along with strange squishing noises. "Am I hearing right?" she muttered.

Squish. Squish. Squish. Squish. The unfamiliar sound came in through the open window. She peeked out to find

Joelle in a large wood trough stomping and shuffling. Her feet furiously going up and down.

Joelle spotted Maggie as she turned and called out, "Good morning. I'm almost finished. I'll come in and we can have breakfast."

"What are you doing in that thing?" Maggie asked.

"I'm just smashing grapes for Mami to make her arak."

"Oh my God!" Maggie hissed under her breath. "Moonshine!"

Evidently it was not against the law here. The squashing went on in daylight right in the back yard.

Breakfast consisted of freshly baked bread with garlic and olive oil and a delicious, strong coffee.

"This is great," Maggie told Mami. My grandmother in Cuba often made this kind of breakfast for me when I was a little girl." Ali was munching away on her bread, listening and taking in everything her mother said as if it was the gospel.

"Mami grows her own garlic and makes her own olive oil," Joelle said proudly. "I'll show you the garden after breakfast. The olive press is out back in the house next door."

Maggie contemplated these women who she was camping out with. "What different lives they lead," she thought. "In the states at this time of morning, my house is in chaos. Lee would be getting ready for work and I would be getting the girls ready for school. Here, in this sleepy mountain village there was no rush to go anywhere."

A knock on the door interrupted her reverie.

Mami went to answer the door and greeted an older man with his hat in his hands. He handed her an empty green bottle. He wore heavy boots and working clothes and eyed Maggie warily. He greeted Mami quietly.

Mami went to the cupboard and filled the bottle with a clear liquid, pouring from a large pitcher. She took some bank notes from him in exchange and smiled at him. He bowed slightly and left, glancing at Maggie with a nod. Maggie smiled at him as he left.

"They come from all over to buy Mami's arak. She makes the best you will find anywhere in the mountains," said Joelle. "Come on Maggie, I'll show you the garden."

Ali and Maggie followed Joelle outside. Ali dragged a jumping rope and played a few feet away.

The garden was beautiful; huge red grapes hung from their vines on an arbor. The vineyard looked very old and healthy. Olive trees were scattered about and flowed into the yard in back of the house next door.

It was one large garden. Chickens pecked at the earth here and there. Maggie recognized garlic, tomatoes and other vegetables growing in neat rows.

"Doesn't your neighbor mind that Mami's garden is on her land?" Maggie asked.

"Oh no. That was my grandmother's house. She left it to Joe. I guess it belongs to you and Ali now. That's where the olive press is."

CHAPTER 3 - BKASSINE

Maggie dreaded this conversation. She didn't want to be too overtly critical of Joe and thus lose Joelle as a potential ally.

"Joelle. I'm not sure what Joe has told you and Mami but Joe and I are divorced. I'm remarried. This house belongs to Joe and Ali maybe. But not to me."

Joelle looked Maggie in the face searching for the right words. She said, "Joe told Mami you had married again and that you didn't want Ali any more because she was in your way and that your new husband didn't want her."

Maggie suspected that Joe had already told his family that story from the things Ali had said and from the initial coldness of Wadi and Amale. She was surprised that Mami and Joelle were at all friendly considering the character assassination that had been performed on her.

"He said that Ali was going to go to the same convent school that I attended and that when you realized what you had done you would come back to him." Her face was contorted and a tear came to her eye.

Maggie felt like she was going to pass out. She walked to a bench and sat down. Maggie felt exhausted. Drained. Dizzy. "How in hell did my life get so complicated?" she thought. Ever since she met Joe she knew that she was riding a roller coaster.

"Did I say something wrong? I'm sorry. I didn't mean to upset you," Joelle said kindly.

"You're only repeating what your brother told you. Mami must think I'm an awful person." She paused, then continued, "Listen Joelle. You must help me explain to your mother what really happened. She must believe that I could never abandon Ali. I've come halfway around the world to get her because Joe is trying to harm me in every way he can. He has been so awful! Lee, my new husband, loves Ali. Her sister adores her. My parents are distraught over this."

Joelle nodded in understanding, her face and posture changing as she reevaluated everything she had heard. Now, sitting with Maggie in person, she was learning the true story.

"Ali is loved and wanted. Your brother just doesn't want to face the fact that we're divorced. He has done everything in his power to make our lives miserable. The worst thing he knew to do was to take Ali."

Maggie was feeling sick. "Joelle. Please help me inside. I feel faint and my stomach is queasy."

Ali was jumping rope nearby. As soon as she saw them moving she came and took her mother's hand.

"Maggie. You're very pale. Are you all right?" Joelle said with great concern in her voice.

"No. I feel ill. I have to go inside."

"Mommy. Mommy," Ali clamored. "What's wrong?"

"I'm not feeling well honey. I'm going to lay down for a little while."

They entered the house and Maggie went to her bed. Her stomach was churning and her legs were weak. She wondered if it was just food poisoning or a mental breakdown. Mami brought her tea to sip and she drifted off to sleep.

For the next five days Maggie moved only between her bed and the bathroom and ate only a little bread with cups of tea to wash it down. Whenever she woke up Ali would be curled up next to her.

A doctor came to check on her. He took her temperature, felt her stomach and glands but, since he could not talk directly to Maggie because he didn't speak English, he told Mami and Joelle that he thought that Maggie had some sort of stomach virus. Maggie speculated that it may have been that big meal at the roadside restaurant enroute to Bkassine.

The illness took a toll on Maggie. She knew that she was loosing weight and she continued to feel very weak in the days that followed.

Ali spent a lot of time reading with her mother and sometimes colored in the books that Maggie had brought her. She loved to use her crayons and would be bent over her work with a peaceful expression on her face.

On the sixth day Joelle came into the bedroom and said brightly, "You're looking better today. Can you go for a walk?"

Maggie did feel better. "That would be really nice. I need to get out of the house." She wanted to see the sun and feel its warmth on her skin.

The anticipation and excitement perked her up. Finally she would get to explore Bkassine. In the early afternoon Joelle, Ali and Maggie set out for a walk. Maggie inhaled deeply and felt well at last. It was a glorious, cool day with brilliant sunshine. A light breeze riffled the leaves.

They walked the main street of the town. There was a tiny bakery with a wood-fired clay oven. Delicious baking aromas met the walkers upon their approach.

Several women were outside the shop apparently waiting to be served. The women stopped talking and turned their attention to the threesome.

They spoke with Joelle in Arabic but Maggie heard the word "American," so she deduced that she was the topic.

Ali tugged at Maggie's sleeve. "Mommy. They wanted to know if you are Daddy Joseph's wife." She pronounced Joseph the same way the women chatting with Joelle did.

"What did Joelle say Ali?"

"She said you are here visiting the family."

They continued their walk up the mountain and soon were out of the sun in the shade of a pine forest. Maggie missed the sun but she enjoyed the gentle stir of the wind that was blowing on her face.

Ali skipped ahead and was playing with a stick. Joelle glanced at Maggie and said, "Do you mind if I ask you a question?"

"No. Go ahead and ask."

"Why did you and my brother divorce?'

How to explain? Maggie chose her words carefully, afraid to say what a bastard her brother had been. How he had mistreated Ali's sister, Jackie.

"Joelle. There are several reasons I divorced your brother. You're too young to understand. Maybe when you marry and have a family you'll understand better."

"Everybody says I'm too young but I'm not. Mami and I see how much Ali loves you and how much you love her. He probably lied about a lot of other things. You're not going back with him when you go back to the states. Are you?"

"Is that what he told you?"

"Yes if you want Ali you'll come back to him..." she faltered. "Mami says a daughter should be with her mother."

"Mami is right. Ali needs to be with me. Your brother and I will have to work things out without hurting Ali."

It was getting cooler as the threesome turned back to town. They stopped at the bakery for fresh bread and then went home.

Maggie was thinking about Bkassine as home. Joe sometimes talked about building a house here where she and the girls could live while he worked out of the country.

That was the arrangement his parents had. Adele lived in Bkassine while Joe's father lived and worked in Egypt. He came home for his sixty day vacation once a year.

Joe said his mother liked the arrangement because she couldn't stand his father for more than two months a year.

Maggie now believed that Joe wanted to keep her isolated from her family and friends and from Jackie.

Thirteen-year-old Jackie's only sin with Joe was that she wanted to have a father figure. A dad. Joe wouldn't or maybe wasn't able to give her this. He frequently said "Let's send her to a boarding school. It'll be good for her."

This was not a possibility for Maggie. Her own boarding school days were a painful memory. Jackie needed Maggie's love just as much as Ali. Joe's hopes were out of the question. She'd never live in Bkassine! "This is not home; now or ever," she thought.

Her resolve to leave strengthened as she walked into the house.

She had Joelle get Wadi on the phone and said to him, "I'm feeling better. I'd like you to come pick me up and take me to the airport so I can go home."

Wadi said, "That's impossible right now. I haven't gotten the permission from Joe to do this."

"I'm not looking for permission. I need to go home now!" Maggie's voice rose an octave.

Mami stood by and Joelle translated while Ali held onto Maggie's leg.

Maggie despaired. How could this be happening to her. Joe was controlling her life from the states. She must try harder.

"Wadi." She shouted into the phone, "Is Joe planning to just leave us here?"

"I don't know when Joe will give me permission to give you back the passports. One of the conditions might be for you to divorce that man you married and marry him again."

"Has he told you this in those words?"

"We've discussed this. Yes." His voice was flat. He was clearly upset.

"What else have you discussed?" she said through clenched teeth.

"Well there's the money the court is holding."

Maggie thought, "Money, money money. With Joe its always money. He wants to be sure to get back the twenty thousand dollars from the sale of the townhouse."

"What about the money Wadi?"

"Well. If you were to release the money maybe I could give you your passports back."

This, Maggie realized, was a negotiation. She thought, "Am I buying our freedom for twenty thousand dollars? Is the money so important? Calm down. Think before you speak."

"Maggie." He said. "Are you there?"

"Yes I'm here Wadi. OK. Here's what I'll do. You come and take us to Beirut, give us the tickets to the states and I'll release the money."

"What about promising Joe you'll divorce and remarry him?"

"Wadi. That is between Joe and me. How do you expect me to discuss my life, my future and my children's future with you?"

"Well then. I'll have Joe call you so you can talk about it."

Wadi was done talking. He hung up suddenly and Maggie was left with just a buzz in her ear.

She closed her eyes to keep them from leaking tears. "Damn it!" she thought, "How did I get here? How did I let Joe take over my life? I always thought I was a strong woman. Heaven knows I had a hard childhood, I went through a divorce and I suffered the death of a child. The loss of Scott alone could of done me in, but I had to be strong for Jackie. It took time but I was able to move on.

"How was I so blind with Joe? I guess I thought he was my knight in shinning armor, coming to rescue me on a white horse. It didn't take long after Ali was born that I realized Joe wasn't capable of loving Jackie *and* his child.

"So, what to do? A life with Joe watching him mistreat Jackie, or a life alone with both my girls. There was no other choice for me, and Joe should of known that. He could not understand the love a mother has for all her children. I guess he'll never get over the fact that I left him. No, not Joe Zayyat!"

Ali was still glued to her leg. "Mommy. Mommy. When are we going home?"

"Very soon honey. I have to talk to your daddy first."

Maggie had forgotten about Joelle and Mami standing there, just a few feet away, listening to everything. Mami's eyes were swollen and red. She was crying. Joelle wore a wan look.

Maggie went to them and gave them hugs. In Spanish she said. "Mami. No te preocupes. Todo se va a resolucionar." "It's all right Mami. We'll work it out."

They spoke in a funny, made up, mixture of Spanish and Italian but they seemed to understand each other.

In Italian, "What has happened to my son. How can he do this to his bambina?"

In Spanish, "I don't know Mami what's happened to him. But the sad thing is that he's hurting Ali more than anybody."

"Si. Si. Correcto."

Meanwhile, Joe had a few projects he was working on but he was not so busy that he couldn't keep thinking about Maggie and Ali.

The fishermen on the river were elated he was back. They depended on Joe for their livelihoods. If their boats weren't running their catches were small. Joe never lacked for work during the season. Off-season, the fishermen updated their engines and winches. Joe was always busy. But right now he was only looking for a few jobs to keep his mind occupied.

The phone rang, it was Wadi.

"Hello Joe."

"Hello Wadi." Joe's deep voice rumbled.

"Joe, I just spoke with Maggie, she is anxious to go home. She says that if you give her the tickets and the passports to go home, she'll release the money. I think she needs to release the money first. What do you think?"

"Yes, I think you're right. I'll call her and let her know she has to release the money first."

"Joe, I asked her about divorcing that other guy and coming back to you."

"Wadi, that's between Maggie and me."

"Yeah that's what she told me too."

"Ok so drop that subject. I'll talk to you later." No other family questions came up. They were totally focused on the awkward subject of Maggie and Ali.

The brothers hung up and Joe sat in his chair, put his head back and for the first time since all this trouble with Maggie, he felt tears running down his face.

Maggie woke early the next morning when the phone rang. She heard Adele yelling into the phone. First in Arabic. Then French and then Arabic again. It was Joe. She heard her name. Then Joelle, Wadi's and Ali's names too.

Adele spoke on the phone for a few minutes and Maggie came into the room and stood by.

She could hardly breath. She was so afraid of this moment. Afraid of the strange man on the phone. She gave herself a pep talk. She couldn't be scared of him! This was not the same loving father who had held Ali in his arms with tears in his eyes on the day she was born.

She had to fight him. Now was the time to stand up for her future; who she wanted to be. Ali was at her side.

"Hello Joe." Her voice guarded.

"Hello Maggie."

Silence. A faint crackling on the line.

"Wadi tells me that if I release the money I can have our passports and the tickets back to the states."

"Yes. That's correct."

"OK. I agree to releasing the money if I get the passports and tickets."

"What about the second part of the deal?" He asked.

"Joe. How can you expect me to promise you I'll get a divorce and marry you again. I have another life now. A husband...I don't trust you anymore. Without trust a marriage isn't a marriage."

"I expect it because I promise you I'll be a father to Jackie and you will live like a queen. I never realized just how much I loved you and Ali until I lost you. I never thought you'd leave me."

"Come on Joe. Our marriage was going down the drain for two years. I kept hanging on because I thought you'd change. I thought you would realize how much a family meant. But it didn't happen. I had no more strength left to deal with the situation."

"That's why I signed everything over to you. I didn't want any money from you then and I don't want any now. All I want is to go home with Ali."

Pause. "Don't tell me you don't love me anymore," his voice was hoarse.

Maggie began again, "It's not easy to erase the years we were together but in the last couple of months you've made it easy to hate you and everything you've done."

"You'll have to promise you'll get a divorce."

"I'm not promising anything but I will promise to think about my life with you and my life now. If that's not good enough, then we're at a standstill." She was gasping for breath. Once again she felt like she was sliding into despair and depression.

Silence.

"Joe. Are you still there?"

"Yes. I'm thinking. OK. If you promise to think about it I'll give Wadi permission to give you your passports and buy the tickets."

Maggie sighed with relief. She was getting the passports at last. She pulled Ali close.

"When can I expect Wadi to pick me up?"

"Probably in a few days." Pause. "Can I talk to Ali?"

Maggie looked down. Ali was at her leg again. "Sweetie, daddy wants to talk to you."

Ali didn't react. Maggie felt wretched for her.

"It's Okay sweetie. Talk to daddy."

She took the phone. "Hello daddy." She said in her sweet little voice.

"Yes I like being here at grandma's. Yes. Mommy likes it too." She looked up at Maggie with sad eyes. Ali seemed about to cry. She was finished talking and handed the phone back to Maggie.

"I'm back."

Joe said, "Wadi will be calling you with information about your trip."

"Thank you Joe. Good bye."

"Goodbye Maggie. See you in the States."

Maggie's stomach was doing flip flops. She felt scared. She felt doomed. She tried to give herself a pep talk, "Get it together woman. You're almost there."

Joe's last words were echoing in her head. "See you in the states." What was he planning?

The phone rang again right after breakfast. Wadi said, "You have to release Joe's money before I can release your passports." Maggie thought, "He sounded so "arrogant and so hateful".

"Yes. I know. I have to wait for my attorney's office to open at nine a.m. Miami time." She just then realized that Joe's call had been made in the wee hours of the morning. She thought that he must not be sleeping, which she took as a good sign.

When morning came Maggie called her Miami attorney. Mr. Gelb came to the phone quickly. "Very good to hear from you Maggie. Where are you? Are you all right?"

"Hi. As well as can be expected under the circumstances."

"What can I do for you?"

"I need for you to release the sequestered money."

"Are you sure you want to do that? That's the only leverage we have with Zayyat."

"Mr. Gelb, believe me, I have no choice. I have to do this."

"Have you spoken to your husband about this?"

"No. This is my decision and mine alone. Now, what do I have to do to make this happen?"

"Your word on the phone is good enough Maggie. Is anyone there with you making you do this?"

Maggie wanted to tell him that Joe was still pulling strings, even from Miami but, she thought better of it. "No sir. No one here is making me do this. I'm doing it on my own."

"All right. I'll call the Judge and get it done. I hope you know what you're doing Maggie."

"I do too." Maggie said with a sigh. "Bye Mr. Gelb. Thank you."

She called Wadi and said, "Okay Wadi. I've released the funds."

"OK Maggie," he responded. "I'll wait a few days to make sure and then I'll come and get you."

"All right Wadi. And, uh, Wadi, just bring the passports!"

On the home front weeks had passed with no word from Maggie. Lee was worried and when the lawyer called to tell him about Maggie's request to release the funds, he couldn't believe it. "Mr. Gelb," he said, "please wait a bit until I talk to Maggie to find out what this is about. I'll try to call Maggie now."

Lee dialed the number in Bkassine. Several operators were involved for the call to be placed. He waited on the line until the connection was made.

"Allo." A strange female voice.

"Allo." said Lee back. "Could I speak to Maggie please?"

A hesitation. "Who is this please?" The voice said in good English with a slight British accent.

"This is her husband Lee."

A pause. "Yes. Please hold." The line was silent for a while.

"Hello." Maggie's voice sounded weak and stressed.

"Hi honey. It's Lee. How are you? What's goin' on? Jackie and your mom miss you dreadfully. Oh, and me too!"

Pause.

"Lee. I'm all right and Ali's fine." Her voice was flat. Lee felt that she was angry.

"Joe said Ali was too sick to travel. Was she? Is she better?"

"She's fine now. Look it is really hard for me to talk now." Joelle and Mami were standing nearby "I'll tell you later what's going on. How's Jackie doing?"

"She's fine baby. She misses you. We all do and folks ask me about you every day Maggie. Mr. Gelb told me that you told him to release the $20,000. What is that about?" He was feeling a little hurt that she hadn't asked him how he was.

"Lee. I have to do it. Please trust me and don't do anything that will slow it up. I can't leave here until the money is released."

"But..."

She cut him off. "Lee! Just release the damn money!" She hissed into the phone. "Please! I've gotta go now. I'll see you soon."

They said good bye.

Maggie stumbled into her room weeping. She whispered to herself, "Oh my love. Forgive me for speaking to you like that. I'm so angry at Joe and Wadi but I'm taking it out on you."

Stunned, Lee didn't know what to do. He called their attorney back and said "Let's just do what Maggie says."

Lee went back to waiting mode; taking care of Jackie and the house, working and answering a dozen queries about Maggie and Ali every day. Friends, family and all of Maggie's coworkers missed her. But Lee missed her most of all.

Four days later, after a flurry of phone calls, their bags were packed and standing by the front door. Wadi was due to arrive soon.

Mami looked agitated today. She carried her rosary and was seen praying; her eyes were closed, her head bowed and her lips moved.

"What," Maggie wondered, "was she praying about? Should I worry?"

Ali was coloring with Joelle at the dining room table.

The phone rang and Joelle picked it up. She spoke in Arabic and then turned to Mami and delivered a message of some kind.

"Maggie," she said, "Mami's cousin Angelina just came back from Beirut and she's coming over to talk to you."

"Where does Angelina live?" Maggie asked.

"Just up the road. About a half a mile."

A tall, slender woman walked in a little while later without knocking. She had beautiful blond hair, fine features and didn't look Lebanese but more like a sophisticated Swede or Norwegian. She was dressed in long, billowing, bellbottomed slacks and a flowery top.

Two-cheek kisses were exchanged with Mami and Joelle and then she turned to Maggie and said, in perfect Spanish, "It's so nice to meet you. I'm sorry I could not get here sooner. I had business to take care of in Beirut.

"Adele wanted us to talk. Never mind. I'm here now." And with that she kissed Maggie too. "I'm Angelina."

Maggie noted that Angelina smelled wonderful and familiar. She realized that Angelina wore Channel, the same scent that her mom, Caridad, used.

"It's really nice to meet you too," said Maggie.

"Come here little one and let me see you." she said to Ali.

"Hello. Who are you?" she asked the newcomer who was giving her a hug.

"I'm your grandmothers cousin. I know I don't look like anyone from the family," she continued. "Its because my mother was a fair-haired Spaniard. From Spain. I look just like her."

Angelina clapped her hands quickly, like a schoolteacher. "Joelle. Get us some coffee then take Ali for a walk. Your mother and I need to talk to Maggie."

Angelina was definitely in charge. She seemed to be used to giving orders.

The three women sat in the living room as Joelle served the coffee and then departed with Ali.

"Well then. Mami wanted me to talk to you in Spanish so that she can finally get a straight story about what's happened between you and Joe."

Maggie began to tell the story to Angelina, musing that she was spilling the beans to someone she could have passed on the street a few minutes ago without a second glance. Now she was revealing intimate thoughts to this stranger. But she liked and trusted Angelina and wanted Adele to have her side of the story to analyze.

Maggie told about the many times Joe had deceived her with matters of his business and finances. She spoke about his extramarital affairs. How cruel he was to Jackie and how he punished her by putting her in the bathroom with the light off. How he shunned Jackie once Ali was born.

"Jackie was so hurt by all this. She was totally ignored by her father after we divorced. And then, just when her six year old heart had found a new father figure in Joe, he was so...indifferent. He pushed her aside. All she ever wanted was approval and love."

Angelina stopped Maggie every few minutes and translated for Adele in Arabic. Then she would turn to Maggie and say kindly, "Go ahead dear."

"I tried to understand Joe. It was very hard. I knew that we were from different cultures and I tried very hard to make things work. But when it came to my innocent children, I gave up trying to understand after a while.

"We fought over his treatment of the kids and the dogs. We fought over his hiding things from me. We separated several times and, each time, he made promises to treat us better but he disappointed me and always went back to his old ways and we'd split again.

"After many months I sought a divorce and found my new husband Lee. He loves me and my children.

"When Joe found out about my upcoming wedding he asked if he could take Ali to Lebanon to visit Adele. He wanted her to meet his family.

"I was reluctant to let her go but I did want her to meet her grandmother and learn about her heritage and her father's culture. To see where her father was born and to love his family too.

"I also wanted Adele to meet Ali.

"We agreed that he would bring her back on September second. Her kindergarten school started on the fifth.

"I guess you know the rest."

Angelina nodded.

"He never brought her back and told all of you that I abandoned her.

"The cruelest thing is, he is playing on the fact that I lost a two-year old son shortly before we met. He died." Maggie's voice was low. "It almost...almost destroyed me." Maggie broke down and sobbed. Angelina held her hand and squeezed it to let her know that she sympathized. She too was weeping.

After a while Maggie regained her composure enough to continue.

Maggie tried to tell everything. About the lawyers, the frantic phone calls to Adele and Wadi, the money and the misery visited on her parents and friends.

Angelina shook her head throughout Maggie's recitation. She glanced at Adele every so often with an expression indicating her total disapproval of Joe's misbehavior.

"Joseph has forced me to release the money and he asked me to promise to think about divorcing my brand new husband - the man I love so much. He's so good with the kids.

"Joseph wouldn't let Wadi give me my passport back until I did those two things. I'm so scared of ruining everyone's life." Maggie broke down again. She'd said enough-probably too much. She was emotionally exhausted.

Angelina spoke softly to Adele for some time. Then she turned to Maggie and said. "You poor child. What a tragedy for our family that we have lost you. I am so very sorry that Joe has acted in such a way.

"I have translated everything to Adele. She wants to say something to you."

Adele looked at Maggie with sad, red rimmed eyes. The saddest eyes, Maggie thought, that she had ever seen.

Angelina translated, "There are no words I could say to make the last few years go away. Deep in my heart I knew my sons, Joe and Wadi were lying to me but I had a hard time accepting it. I didn't want to believe it.

"As soon as I saw the way that you and Ali loved each other I knew that you couldn't have abandoned her.

"I am ashamed of my sons and I ask for your forgiveness."

Maggie sat thinking. What could she say to this woman who had lied to her on the telephone saying that Ali wasn't there.

She had called numerous times crying on the phone, hysterical-begging Adele to tell her where Ali was. Each phone call would end with a "hang-up." Adele leaving Maggie in anguish.

The worst thing was not knowing where Ali was. Adele knew but said nothing.

Maggie looked at Adele and realized how frail she looked. So sad and ashamed. She felt the forgiveness flood in.

Maggie took her former mother-in-law's hands and said, "I forgive you Adele. You didn't really know me before I came here. All you heard came from Joe and he's your son."

Angelina translated and Adele lowered her eyes and cried.

Maggie excused herself and stepped outside to sit on the bench in the garden for a breath of air; she needed to recover and try to get back to a normal state. She muttered to herself, "My God. Will this ever end?"

"What will end Mommy?" Ali was standing right behind her and Joelle was walking up the path towards them.

Bird songs played in the clear air and the sunlight felt warm on her skin.

"It's nothing sweetie. Don't worry. Mommy was just thinking out loud."

Joelle gave them a puzzled look not having heard what was said.

"Mami and Angelina are in the living room." Maggie told her former sister-in-law.

Joelle turned and went inside.

"Joelle took me for a walk and I didn't want to go without you." said Ali.

"I know honey-babe but mommy and grandma had to talk about some grown-up things."

"Oh, I know. You were talking about how Daddy took me away from you. Grandma has been very sad and she cries a lot."

"Oh baby. You are one sharp cookie."

"Mommy. Did you say cookie? I want some."

"Yes sweetie. There are some cookies in the kitchen. Let's go get 'em."

Ali skipped along holding her mother's hand.

Angelina was ready to leave upon their return from the kitchen. "I have to go my dear. It was a pleasure meeting you." She smiled.

Angelina knelt and said "Come here little one and give your auntie a hug."

Ali obliged and threw in a kiss as well.

"Thank you Angelina for helping me tell my story."

Angelina said. "I like your spunk. I wish we could have met under different circumstances."

"I hear a car," Joelle said. Maggie's heart skipped a beat, ready to go and anxious again.

Wadi arrived. He walked in and went straight to his mother for the usual hug and kiss. Mami stood very still not returning his hug.

"What has she been telling you?" he demanded. "Whatever it is, it's all lies."

Mami spoke in a very low and even tone for some little while and Maggie could see his face getting redder with each word. Maggie couldn't make out a single word so she looked at Joelle with a questioning glance.

"It's not good." She whispered. "I've never seen her so upset with the boys."

After a few more unintelligible sentences, Angelina turned to Maggie with a kind look and said, "What a tragedy for this family to lose you."

Wadi chimed in, in Italian, hoping to redeem himself, "Oh she's still going to be in the family. She's divorcing that man she married and she and Joe will marry again. Joe told me that he was going to bring her back to get married again. Here in Bkassine."

Adele kept her eyes on Maggie and Maggie saw that she knew that this was not going to happen. She opened her arms and Maggie stepped into them. She whispered into Maggie's ear. "Vaya con Dios mi hiya."

Ali was tugging on Maggie's skirt. "Mommy. Come on. Let's go. I want to go home and see Jackie and my friends."

Joelle and Maggie said goodbye sadly. Ali exchanged final goodbye hugs and kisses as Wadi put their suitcases in the trunk and Maggie took her last look around.

Maggie mused. "What a different world this is. Would I have married Joe if I'd understood his world? Could I give

up my life in America to come and live among these people. These Lebanese people seem to think differently about
so many things. I'd be just like Adele who only sees her husband a couple of months a year and is alone so much."

She thought, "The fear of ending up like this is one reason I'm able to keep pushing to get away. I love being independent. Joe expected me to be subservient and dependent
like his mother and sister. This is a different world."

"Wadi. Our passports please." Maggie wanted them
right away before he could get out from under his mothers
gaze. He handed them to Maggie without comment.

She hugged them to her breast and relief flooded in.

The car started to roll with a jerk and retraced their route
back to Beirut. The silence weighed heavy and Wadi did not
stop for food but the time sped by.

Maggie was ready to get home. She missed her family,
her daughter Jackie and Lee, her newly minted husband.

CHAPTER 4 - GOODBYE WADI

Maggie's mood was mixed. She was elated by the progress toward home but heartsick over all the troubles she'd seen and imagined. "Oh my aching life, Maggie thought. "I need a rest from everything."

Wadi dropped them off at the Saint George Hotel. He leaned out of the window and said, "I'll be here at eleven o'clock in the morning. The flight leaves at half-past one in the afternoon." He hurried off before Maggie could ask for her plane tickets. She thought that having the passports was the most important thing though. "I can always get to the airport on our own if he doesn't show." She considered just getting on a taxi and going to the airport at once and getting the first plane out. But she was so tired.

Maggie tossed and turned while Ali slept the night away. She rose early, showered, dressed and was ready to go by the time the sun was visible over the sea. She watched the sunrise from her little balcony and let Ali sleep as long as possible.

Ali woke at last and sat up rubbing her eyes. "Is this the day we go home Mommy?" She had a big smile showing off her toothless gums.

"Yes Sweetie. This is the big day!" Ali stood on the bed and began jumping up and down. She too was ready to go back to her life in America.

It was barely seven a.m. and Wadi would not arrive for hours.

"Ali. Would you like to go down, have breakfast and then go for a walk? Maybe we could find a present for Jackie."

"Okay mommy. Maybe Jackie would like to have a necklace or a bracelet. And I'm hungry too."

Maggie called for a bellman to collect and hold their bags as they prepared to go to breakfast. She felt peaceful for the first time in weeks.

The city was lively as Maggie and Ali ventured out to find souvenirs.

Men with briefcases were busy making their way to offices. Women were walking children to school and others were shopping for groceries.

They crossed the street and went to a little shop with colorful shawls and jewelry in the window.

A bracelet with little bells caught Maggie's eye and she picked it up and put it around her wrist. It was a little large.

The attentive shopkeeper said, "No, No madam. It is like this."

He took the bracelet and knelt at Maggie's feet. "Lift your foot," he ordered. When she complied he put the bracelet around her ankle.

He motioned for her to shake her leg and the bells jingled merrily.

Ali laughed, "Mommy, if you give this to Jackie you can hear her when she walks around the house."

"She is a very clever girl."

Maggie turned to see who spoke. A fashionably dressed woman stood there. She was stunning; tall and slender. Her eyes were an arresting green color.

"Definitely not a typical Lebanese woman," Maggie thought.

"The men like to see the women wear these bracelets. It helps them keep track of their wives. Personally I think it's archaic. Although I'm Lebanese, I don't follow the customs of my country."

She extended her hand. "My name is Nadia. I own this shop and a couple more down the street.

Maggie introduced herself and Ali. "We're looking for gifts to take back to the United States."

Nadia looked through the shop and pulled out a selection of bracelets which Maggie liked. "I'd also like a shawl. Can you make a recommendation?"

Nadia said, "Not here. These shawls here are not local. They're made in Singapore. Let's go to my other shop. I think I'll have something you'll like better." She waited while Maggie paid for her purchases.

The three walked a half block to another store. This one was more sophisticated and upscale in price. Three young girls were rushing around cleaning and setting out merchandise; they paused to speak with Ali.

Nadia took Maggie to the back of the store and pulled out a number of beautiful shawls. "Now these are what I think you'll like."

"Oh Nadia. How beautiful! These are exactly right."

She bought one for her mother, one for her stepmother and one for herself.

"Would you like to join me for a cup of coffee?" Nadia invited.

Maggie saw that it was only 9:30. Plenty of time before Wadi was due. Ali seemed content as she helped the girls fold clothes. "All right. That would be nice. Thank you."

Maggie felt relaxed as she watched Nadia pour. The two women sat in front of the shop at a little round sidewalk table. For the first time in weeks she could draw an unworried breath. She sat back with a sigh and watched the traffic and passersby.

Nadia looked at Maggie with a question forming on her lips.

"I hope you don't mind my asking, but what are you and Ali doing here in Beirut?"

"It's a long story and I'm sure you don't want to hear it."

"On the contrary. I would like to know about you."

Maggie spilled out her story yet again over two long cups of coffee. When she was done she remarked, "I can't believe that I just told a total stranger my story."

"You know Maggie. I've heard the name Zayyat. Was Joe's brother a Colonel in the Lebanese Army?"

Maggie sat forward, suddenly on her guard.

"Don't worry. I'm not friends with the family. I just know how influential the Zayyat's are here in Beirut."

"Yes. I've heard that too. I won't really relax until I'm back on U.S. soil."

Maggie stood to leave. Nadia said, "You know Maggie, these Lebanese men are not used to having women stand up to them or leave them. They're used to doing the leaving and most of them can't be trusted. Take it from a Lebanese woman who knows her men."

"Thanks for the advice Nadia. It was really nice meeting you."

Nadia pulled out her business card and handed it to Maggie. "I have a feeling that if you're ever in Beirut again, it will be against your will. Keep my card and call me if you ever need help."

Maggie carefully placed the card in her wallet.

Maggie and Ali walked back to the hotel with their packages. They sat in the lobby and waited for Wadi.

Wadi was right on time, wearing his trademark sunglasses. He loaded the car and drove in silence for a few minutes.

Maggie asked him for the tickets and sat studying the itinerary. The flights were from Beirut to Luxembourg, to New York and then to Miami.

"How come we're not flying straight to Miami?" Maggie asked.

"This is the itinerary Joe wanted you to follow," was the answer. And he didn't say another word during the remainder of the drive to the airport.

After putting their bags on the curb at the airport, Wadi said, "Come here Ali and give me a kiss good bye."

She complied and returned immediately to her mother's side.

Wadi turned his hostile eyes toward Maggie. "You've managed to turn Ali against me and more importantly you've managed to turn my mother against Joseph and me...I'll never forgive you for that."

"All I did with Ali and your mother was to tell them the truth Wadi." Maggie said in a level voice. "You and Joe, on the other hand, have been lying to her all this time. I can't help the way she feels now."

"You'd better get inside or you'll miss your flight. I don't know why my brother is so obsessed with you. He should just leave you alone."

"I wish he would Wadi. I wish he would."

They walked into the busy airport and when Maggie turned to look back, he was gone. The flight left on time. Ali slept most of the time while Maggie thought about her next encounter with Joe. The questions played over and over again in her mind. "Can he ever accept the fact that we can not be married again? How am I going to handle this?"

There was a two hour layover in Luxembourg. Maggie wanted to call home because Lee didn't know she was on her way. She worried about telling him that she had promised Joe to think about going back to him. How could she tell Jackie something like that? "My God. What have I done? Could I have gotten out of Bkassine any other way? I don't think so. Well, maybe. Oh I don't know." She was distraught and tired.

Ali brought Maggie back from her reverie.

"Mommy. I'm hungry. And I need to go to the bathroom."

"Okay honey. Let's go." They ate and walked around until the flight was called. She decided not to call home.

It was a long leg to New York. Ali colored, played with her doll and read her picture books.

Maggie tried to read magazines but mostly tortured herself with the same revolving questions.

When the plane finally landed, the waits for immigration, customs and luggage were long and tedious.

They had nothing to declare and pushed through the lines as quickly as possible. As the automatic door from customs opened to the lobby, she stopped dead in her tracks. Was she seeing things? Dreaming?

Joe stood at the gate with his arms opened for Ali to jump into.

She ran to her father saying, "Daddy! Daddy! Mommy came! Mommy came to get me!"

CHAPTER 5 - NEW YORK

Maggie was flabbergasted. "Hello Joe. What are you doing here? You're not supposed to leave Miami. If you do you could go to jail." Maggie had forgotten that Ali was right there listening to every word.

"Mommy. Mommy. Don't put Daddy in jail."

"No Honey. Mommy won't do that." Joe said.

"Come on. let me get your bags so we can get out of this place."

"Our flight for Miami leaves in two-and-a-half hours. We have to stay here."

"I changed the reservations. We're staying in New York for a couple of days." There are things we have to discuss."

"Joe," she argued, "we have to go home. I haven't seen Jackie and my family for almost four weeks."

"Two more days isn't going to kill them. Anyway you promised to talk about our future."

"We can talk in Miami."

"NO! Now. Don't make a scene. Let's go." Maggie could fight no longer. She was tired and confused.

Joe took the suitcases to the curb. There was a limo waiting.

Maggie was annoyed. "Why did you get one of these. A cab would have been fine."

"Nothing but the best for my girls."

Maggie thought about the twenty thousand dollars. "It must be burning a hole in his pocket," she thought.

Ali climbed in. "Mommy. Look at how big it is in here." Wadi's car had been very cramped.

The driver tipped his cap and said, "Good day madam and madamoiselle. My name is Fred."

Fred, pulled out and headed for Manhattan. Ali leaned through the little window to the front and talked his head off all the way to the hotel.

They pulled up to the Waldorf Astoria. "We're here." Joe announced.

Maggie looked at him and said, "Nothing but the best for your girls."

Joe scowled. He knew she was being sarcastic.

He checked them in and the bellman escorted them to a beautiful suite. The man enthusiastically showed them the amenities. "This is the bedroom for the little one. She has her own bathroom."

"Here is the master suite. You have a full kitchen with a private dining room." He went on and on. Ali followed him like a puppy, loving the attention.

"Mommy. I have my own television." she said proudly.

Maggie sat on the couch in a state of collapse.

"Do you want a drink? We have a full bar."

It sounded good. "Thanks Joe."

"Daddy." Ali placed her order. "I want an apple juice."

He complied and said, as he handed Maggie her glass, "Gin and tonic with a twist of lime. Just how you like it."

"Thanks," she mumbled. "I need this."

"What time is it? I'm all confused with the time zone changes."

"Nine p.m. Ready for some dinner?"

"Yes but I don't want to go to a restaurant. Can we just eat here? After all, we do have a private dining room."

Joe frowned. Maggie knew that her sarcasm was not lost on him. Maggie nursed her drink while Joe ordered dinner.

Ali and Joe sat in the dining room talking about her grandmother. Maggie dozed and was awakened by a bell.

"It's our dinner," Joe announced.

They made polite conversation during dinner. Maggie enjoyed the excellent cabernet but forced herself to stop half-way through the second glass. She was feeling a little tipsy.

Maggie gave Ali a bath and tucked her in bed.

"Mommy, stay with me until I go to sleep." Ali asked.

Maggie went into her bedroom and returned in her robe and nightgown. She lay down with Ali and whispered a lullaby.

Joe came in and kissed Ali goodnight. His face came close to Maggie's as she lay dozing and he whispered. "Don't take too long. We need to talk."

His lips brushed against hers, his tongue slightly parted her lips and she smelled his breath and tasted the brandy he'd been drinking. She pulled back just in time to see him smirk as he said, "That old feeling is still there."

Maggie said, "There's many feelings inside me just now. I just have to sort them out." She dozed in the grip of jet lag, wine, fear, and depression.

She woke up to feel Joe picking her up and carrying her to the master bedroom. He put her on the bed gently. "Here. I'll tuck you in."

"Joe. I can put myself to bed." She said archly.

"Maggie. I want you. You are the only woman that completes me. All of the women I've had since we divorced have meant nothing to me. When I'm inside you I feel the love we have."

"Had, Joe. Had. We've had this conversation many times. Sex is not the only thing that keeps a marriage together. There has to be more."

"What more do you want?"

"I want a partner. A father for Jackie. Someone I can trust. I can't trust you anymore."

They were getting nowhere again. Maggie's head was in a whirl.

Joe was all about sex. Maggie had always enjoyed the sexual side of a relationship and Joe was good at making a woman happy in bed. But that was where his relationship skills ended.

Joe said, "Look. You're very tired from your trip. Let's talk tomorrow."

"You're right. I'm beat."

With that she rose and went into the bathroom to brush her teeth.

She looked into the mirror and saw that Joe had followed her. "What? What are you doing in here?" She quailed. Her mind was racing. Why hadn't she just gotten on the plane to Miami? She knew what Joe had in mind when she saw him at the airport. Was his hold on her so strong that she could forget the vows she'd taken just a couple of months ago?

Tears were streaming down her face and she couldn't stop them. Lee. Sweet, kind, loving Lee. It was easy to fall in love with him. She saw him as the complete opposite of Joe. Their relationship was so different.

Lee was her partner, her lover, her friend, and a daddy to the girls. He was fun to be with and always made her laugh. She trusted him and could see herself growing old with him.

How could she even think about ending a marriage that hasn't had a chance to blossom yet. Joe had planned this assault well.

She saw Joe approach in the mirror. He was right behind her.

He put his arms around her and kissed her hair.

"Oh my God," Maggie thought. "All the old feelings are coming back."

Joe turned Maggie around and kissed her cheeks. Drying her tears with his lips. He raised her chin with his hand and kissed her. A deep kiss. His tongue explored the inside of her mouth. Maggie, in a trance, responded to his passionate embrace.

A strong man, Joe put his hands under her thighs and pulled her up on him. He dropped his pants and entered her in a moment.

Joe grunted like an animal in his passion and Maggie reciprocated his every move.

Maggie came with great force. Joe slowed down and started tickling her neck and breasts. He teased her mouth with his tongue. They kissed deeply. They panted and shuddered to a stop, both gasping for breath.

Joe began walking still hard inside Maggie.

He stopped when they reached the bed and lowered her onto the mattress.

Joe lay on top of Maggie and whispered, "No one can make me feel the way you do." He whispered as he dozed off, "I love you."

Maggie was wide awake under the covers. She was shaking like a leaf. She worried about Ali seeing her this way. Ali would be up soon.

Maggie rose quietly, went into the bathroom and closed the door silently. She stood under the hot shower for a very long time. The water came out hard from the faucet, it felt good on her body. "Maybe the water will wash away this guilt I'm feeling." thought Maggie. Maggie started to cry and shake uncontrollably, her legs felt weak and she slid down on the shower floor.

Holding her knees to her chest she stayed in that position until she heard the bathroom door open.

"Mommy, what are you doing on the floor?" asked Ali.

Seeing her little girl outside the shower door brought her back to reality. "Mommy dropped the soap honey, that's all." She stood and grabbed a towel.

"Daddy says we're going to see a play today, and go to the park, and ride a buggy, and go to a big toy store." Ali was excited, she had spent weeks up in Bkassine mostly in the house, now she saw her daddy as her pal taking her to all these exciting places.

"Wow, Ali those are a lot of things to do in one day. Let's talk about this over breakfast."

Ali chattered as Maggie dressed. She helped pick the clothes Maggie was going to wear. The dining room table was loaded with food. There was a fruit tray, bagels and cream cheese, pancakes, eggs, bacon, potatoes, orange juice, apple juice for Ali and a big pot of coffee.

"Joe, did you order everything on the menu?"

"I didn't know what you wanted so I guess I must of ordered a lot of food, but I'm starved. We worked hard last night so we need reinforcements." He smiled at Maggie.

"You and Mommy worked last night Daddy?" asked Ali.

"Daddy is just kidding honey, now let's eat before it gets cold."

They ate while Ali asked questions about what they were going to do next and where they were going. When Ali left the table to go to her room, Maggie looked at Joe and asked, "When are we going back to Miami Joe?"

"I told you at the airport, we're staying here for a couple of days. Now don't spoil this day for Ali."

They left the hotel to find Fred waiting with the limo to drive them around town.

"Mommy, Mommy there's Fred." She ran up to him. "Fred are you driving us today?" Ali was excited to see Fred and the limo. She remembered how attentive he'd been.

"Yes, I'm your driver for the day. Where are we going Miss Ali?" asked Fred. Ali sat towards the front of the Limo, opened the little window and said to Fred, "I'd like to go to the big toy store." Everyone laughed. Joe gave a nod to Fred, and the limo made its way to FAO Schwartz, the biggest toy store in Manhattan.

Joe was on a crusade to win Maggie back. He knew what children meant to Maggie so by keeping Ali happy, he was keeping Maggie happy.

The day passed with smiles from Ali at the toy store, a horse drawn buggy ride around Central Park, and a fashionably late lunch at Central Park's Tavern on the Green restaurant.

On the way back to the hotel Ali fell asleep on her mother's lap; the day and the jet lag had worn her out too. Maggie imagined that their bodies were still functioning on Beirut time.

As the limo was pulling into the hotel entrance, Joe said "Fred, we'll see you back here at eight tonight."

"Where are we going tonight Daddy?" Ali was rubbing her eyes.

"Tonight, Mommy and Daddy are going out, you have a fun baby sitter who will play with you and the toys you bought today."

Maggie started to say something but Fred had the limo door opened, ready to help them with the packages. "We'll talk about this upstairs," murmured Maggie under her breath.

After Maggie had settled Ali and her new things in her room, she came out to the living room and said to Joe, "I'm not comfortable leaving Ali here with someone I don't know."

"I hired a nanny from a reputable company the hotel uses all the time, they're bonded, she'll be fine."

"I'm still not comfortable. If I don't like her, Ali is coming with us."

The nanny's name was Annie. She was a plump five foot woman in her forties. She had brown hair, kind eyes, and a huge smile that lit the room as soon as she entered. She had an English accent and a high pitched voice. Ali immediately felt at ease with her and took her to her room to show her all her toys. Joe and Maggie waited until Ali came back out holding Annie's hand.

"Mommy, Daddy. I like Annie. We're going to play. Can I order ice cream with dinner?"

"Sure honey, order some for Annie also." said Joe.

Maggie looked at Joe and nodded. Joe smiled and said "Annie the concierge has our itinerary tonight. If you need us, he can find us."

He turned to his daughter and said, "Come give us a kiss goodnight." Ali ran to her father, gave him a big hug and kiss then reached for Maggie and did the same.

"Good night Mommy and Daddy, see you in the morning."

Fred was waiting downstairs with the limo.

"Where are we going?" asked Maggie.

"Don't ask so many questions, just relax and enjoy," said Joe as he reached into the ice bin and pulled out a bottle of Dom Perignon.

"Nothing but the best for your girls," remarked Maggie.

"Don't ruin this night by being sarcastic Maggie, let's just enjoy the present."

Joe poured the champagne and looked at Maggie. "You look beautiful tonight, but then, again, you always look beautiful after we make love. Your cheeks always get red and you look peaceful."

Joe held his glass up to Maggie and said, "To us." Maggie looked at Joe and reflexively held her glass up to his.

She wanted to keep peace. The champagne was savored in silence. Maggie noticed at that point that the limo was turning into Central Park.

Maggie looked out the window and felt her eyes water. "This is not reality," she thought. "This is a fantasy world that Joe is creating so I will come back. I wonder what Jackie and Lee are doing tonight? I have to call home, but what will I say? Lee, I'm not home yet because I'm spending a couple of days in a suite at the Waldorf making love to Joe and riding around in a limo drinking champagne. Here I go again, being sarcastic."

The limo stopped Fred opened the door to help Maggie out of the car. "Here you are Madam."

Maggie stepped onto the curb in front of a beautiful, old Venetian house. A small sign announced *Chez Joli*.

"What are we doing here?" asked Maggie.

"This is where we're having dinner. A friend of mine owns this restaurant. It's very quaint. Every table is in it's own little room so we'll be private and cozy."

Maggie almost said, "Nothing but the best for your girls." but thought better of it.

As Joe and Maggie approached the door, it was opened by a young man who could have been any one of the men Ali and Maggie had seen walking in Beirut. He was definitely Lebanese. His hair was black and curly, his dark eyes were big and his skin was olive. He spoke perfect English and greeted Joe with a kiss on both cheeks. "It's good to see you brother."

He turned to Maggie and said, "And you must be Maggie."

Joe said, "Maggie this is Ahmed, he's a friend from Beirut who is crazy enough to come to the states to open a restaurant."

Ahmed extended his hand to Maggie. He pulled her hand to his lips and kissed it.

"I couldn't have pulled this off without your help Joe," said Ahmed.

"Oh, and just how much help did Joe give you?" asked Maggie.

Maggie saw Joe become a little uncomfortable with this conversation but Ahmed was so happy to talk about his restaurant that he didn't notice.

"Well Maggie, Joe is a big investor in this place." Ahmed patted Joe's back. "I brought this deal to him a couple of years ago. That's how long it's taken to open the restaurant. Joe saw the potential; he knew my family owned restaurants in Beirut. The clincher was that my mother was going to be doing the cooking. Everything else is history."

Two years ago Maggie and Joe were husband and wife, however Maggie had no clue that Joe invested in a restaurant. That was typical of the way things had gone in their marriage.

Maggie's thoughts swam. "Too many secrets. Where is the trust? How can I trust him now? What else had he been into during our marriage that I don't know anything about?"

Maggie wanted to run out of this place. She felt cold all of a sudden, and a shiver went up her spine. Joe put his hand on her shoulder and she pulled away.

Joe knew Maggie was upset. He turned to Ahmed and said, "Please take us to our table."

Ahmed obliged, oblivious to or ignoring the tension between Maggie and Joe.

On the way to their table, Maggie noticed the decor, very tastefully done with a French flair. She saw that every room was occupied and lit with candles. She thought, *"Tres romantiqué.* This restaurant is a place for lovers to meet. For anniversaries. And for Joe, a place to try to regain my feelings for him." Some of the rooms accommodated a table for two, some a table for four and so on.

Their table was secluded near the back of the restaurant. A bottle of white wine was cooling and the table held appetizers and a bread basket.

"This is nice," allowed Maggie.

When Ahmed left them, Maggie said "I had no idea you owned a restaurant for two years."

"It's an investment Maggie, that's all."

Maggie leaned in so she could make her point, "An investment that you made while we were married...an investment you made while I was putting all the money I earned into our household expenses so you could get your business off the ground. And all the while you had enough money to invest in this place and who knows what else," Maggie said. "Trust Joe, that's a huge part of a relationship. That's what was missing from our marriage."

"You're making a big deal out of this Maggie. I did this for us," said Joe.

Maggie sat back in her chair and slumped. She felt defeated and spent. She was too exhausted to argue any more.

"Let's order," she said.

"I've already ordered for us. All the things you like," said Joe.

The waiter brought some of Maggie's favorites: escargot, caesar salad, filet mignon with béarnaise sauce and creme brulé for dessert. "The food is delicious Joe."

They made small talk about Bkassine, Adele and Joelle, and Wadi, and Ali. Joe confessed to Maggie that Ali had been very upset when she realized that she was going to be sent to a school in Lebanon; that is why she had to have the valium.

Maggie closed her eyes and breathed in, "You wanted to hurt me and ended up hurting Ali."

"I wanted our family back together. Keeping Ali was the only way I could get you back."

"Oh Joe, I'm afraid that Ali will be paying for what you did for the rest of her life."

Joe frowned. "You always make a big deal out of things, Ali will forget this happened by the time she gets back to Miami."

"We can only hope," said Maggie.

Joe and Maggie said their goodbyes to Ahmed and found Fred waiting at the curb. As Fred was pulling out of the curve Maggie looked back at the old Venetian house, she wanted to see the name of the restaurant again. "Chez Joli" was written on the sign. How apropos she thought. "'Jo' for Joe and 'Li' for Ali."

Maggie sat back and closed her eyes. "Joe, I'd like to go back to the hotel, maybe Ali will still be awake and I can tuck her in," said Maggie.

Joe pressed the button to talk to the driver, "Fred take us back to the hotel."

"Yes sir," Fred crisply answered.

Joe reached over and took Maggie's hand. "I hope you had a nice evening."

Maggie looked at him and smiled. "The food was delicious, I'm sure Chez Joli will be very successful."

Joe said. "That's part of our future Maggie, yours and mine."

Maggie put her head back on the seat and thought it over. "I would have never known about this place if we hadn't gone to dinner there. Who's future is Joe thinking about? Do I want to spend the rest of my life with a man that's secretive about everything he does? Isn't part of a relationship sharing? Joe's culture is so different than mine. Oh, my God, I'm so confused."

"Maggie? Are you ok?" You seem so far away," Joe said.

"Yes, very far away." said Maggie.

"Here we are sir," said Fred. "What time do you need me tomorrow?"

"I'll call you in the morning to let you know what we're doing," said Joe.

"Goodnight" said Fred.

"Goodnight" said Joe.

Maggie was already inside the lobby.

They took the elevator to their suite and found Ali already asleep in her bed.

"Ali is a delight, I really enjoyed being with her. We played with all her new toys. She named one of her dolls Jackie, she said that's her sister's name."

"Thank you Annie," Maggie said. "Did Ali eat all her dinner?"

"Yes Mrs. She also had ice cream." replied Annie.

Joe paid Annie for her services and saw her to the door. Maggie went to Ali's room to kiss her goodnight. As Maggie was standing by Ali's bed Joe came in and stood behind Maggie and whispered, "She's our angel and she's happy when we are together."

"Yes, she is an angel," said Maggie.

They walked out of Ali's room together and headed for the living room. "Would you like an after dinner drink?" asked Joe.

"That would be nice, thank you," said Maggie.

Joe made a drink for Maggie and sat next to her. She sipped in silence. "It's been a full day, hasn't it? said Joe.

"Very full, I'm very tired, I need some sleep."

Joe took Maggie's hand and guided her to the bedroom. He stood in front of Maggie and taking her face into his hands, gave her a long and passionate kiss. "You taste so good,"

"I thought I had forgotten this feeling," whispered Maggie.

"No way baby, you'll never forget this electricity we have."

"It's not electricity. It's lust Joe."

"I don't care what you call it, I've never felt this with any other woman."

In moments they were in bed tearing each others clothes off. Joe put his hand up Maggie's skirt and in one move he had her panties off. He ripped Maggie's blouse next. "I'll buy you ten more tomorrow," said Joe.

They lost track of time intertwined in each other. Joe turned Maggie around. "I want to see your face when you come," whispered Joe.

Joe entered Maggie again, looking into her eyes. When Maggie looked up Joe was coming. Maggie felt herself coming also. They came together like two animals, scratching, sweating and panting. Joe fell against Maggie's body kissing her face, neck, and shoulders.

"What is it with you? What do you have that drives me crazy?" said Joe.

"I don't know, it's just me," said Maggie.

They lay in each others arms until Joe fell asleep. Maggie nudged him off. He turned and kept on sleeping.

Maggie went into the bathroom, sat on the tub and turned the water on. When the tub was full she climbed in, put her head back and closed her eyes.

The hot water felt good. Maggie felt relaxed, but soon her thoughts went to her home in Miami. Jackie, Lee, and her mother didn't know when she was coming home, she had not called them. At that moment Maggie made up her mind. She and Ali were flying to Miami tomorrow, no matter what Joe said. She needed to get back home and put her life back together. She needed to make a choice.

She dried off and went quietly back to bed in her nightgown.

Maggie woke the next morning to Ali's kisses and hugs. "Mommy wake up, breakfast is here."

"I can't get up until you get off me, baby," said Maggie.

"Oh Mommy, you're funny. I'll wait for you in the dining room Mommy, hurry."

When Maggie came to the table, Joe and Ali were eating chocolate chip pancakes. "Good morning," said Joe with a smile on his face.

"I didn't hear you get up this morning," said Maggie.

"You looked so peaceful and satisfied I didn't want to disturb you," said Joe.

"Thank you, I needed the sleep."

After breakfast, Maggie asked Ali to go to her room so she could talk to Joe. She went to her room mumbling "Adult talk, always adult talk..."

"Joe, Ali and I are leaving today to go back to Miami."

"Not today Maggie, leave tomorrow. Give me one more day."

"I can't Joe. I shouldn't have stayed the time I did. Jackie needs me and in case you've forgotten, I have a husband waiting for me."

"You weren't thinking about your husband last night when you screwed your brains out with me," said Joe.

"You're right. I wasn't thinking about my husband. I wasn't thinking at all, but now I am. My place is at home in Miami."

Joe walked over to Maggie, put his hands on her shoulders and said, "Okay Maggie, we'll go back to Miami today. You'll go to a hotel, stay there and Jackie can come to you. I don't want you going back to that house."

"Impossible Joe. Jackie has a school close to home to attend. My mother is at my house. Sick. Ali needs to go back to her things, and most of all I have to face Lee and talk to him. I can't just walk out on him." Maggie was trying to stand her ground.

Joe put his arms down with disgust. "Have it your way Maggie, but I'm coming for you three days from now, you'd better be ready to start our new life together."

Maggie glared at Joe. "Or what? Or what Joe? It sounds like you're threatening me."

"No threat Maggie, a promise." With that Joe turned and said over his shoulder, "You'd better start packing."

Maggie packed while Joe made arrangements for tickets and the limo. Ali was excited to be going home to see her sister and her friends.

Joe and Maggie didn't say much to each other that day. During the flight Ali was very talkative, which took the pressure away from the adults to make conversation. Their flight arrived in Miami at nine-thirty p.m. and it took a while to get their bags. Maggie, still jet-lagged, was sagging with fatigue.

At the curb, after Joe hailed a taxi for them, he said, "Remember Maggie, I'm coming to get you three days from today."

Maggie looked at Joe, gave him a nod, and entered the cab. Joe picked Ali up kissed her, hugged her and said goodbye.

CHAPTER 6 - LEE

The cab ride was quiet in the late evening traffic. Ali was tired and eventually fell asleep in Maggie's arms.

As the taxi approached the house through quiet streets, Maggie woke Ali. "We're almost here honey, wake up." Ali rubbed her eyes and looked around. "Mommy, Mommy there's our house." She was exited, jumping up and down.

Maggie paid the driver picked up their suitcases and went up the driveway worrying and wondering, "What'll I say to Lee?"

There was no time for thinking because Lee was waiting. He opened the door while Maggie was fumbling for her key. He leaped out, and gave her a bear hug and a kiss on the lips. He then picked Ali up to hug her.

"Hello baby. We've missed you." said Lee.

"I missed you too Daddy. I thought I was never going to see you again."

"Mommy and I wouldn't let that happen honey," Lee whispered in Ali's ear.

Lee extended his hand to Maggie and squeezed her hand. "I was worried about you two. Are you all right? You look exhausted."

Maggie looked at Lee with weary eyes and said, "No, I'm not all right. And yes, I'm exhausted."

"Come on let's put Ali to bed and then we'll talk in our room." Lee carried the bags.

Maggie could not sleep with Lee that night, not with what had just happened in New York. Maggie said, "Lee, I would really like to sleep in Ali's bed tonight. Tomorrow we can talk."

Lee put Ali down came over to Maggie hugged her and said, "Okay honey. If that's what you want, we'll talk tomorrow."

As Lee went to walk away he felt Ali hugging his leg. He picked her up. He took her to her bedroom and helped her put on pajamas.

Maggie slipped into Jackie's room and looked at her first born.

"Jackie you're such an angel. I love you so very much. I want to see you happy." She whispered. "This is where you're happy darling, this is where you feel safe isn't it?"

Jackie stirred. Maggie pulled the covers over her daughter and kissed her lightly on the cheek.

"Mommy is that you?" Jackie was awake.

"Yes honey, it's Mommy."

Jackie sat up in bed, gave her mother a huge hug and kissed her all over her face. She was crying. "Mommy I missed you so very much."

Maggie and Jackie hugged each other until Jackie stopped crying. Maggie kissed her once more and said, "Honey, please go back to sleep, we'll talk tomorrow. Your sister is dying to see you but if she knows that you are awake she'll never go to sleep. Good night my love."

"Good night Mommy." Jackie said this with a big smile on her face. As Maggie walked out of the room she heard Jackie saying, "I love you Mommy, I missed you."

"I missed you too my darling."

Maggie woke very early. She was disoriented. How many different beds has she slept in since she last slept in Miami? She felt a familiar little arm on her. Ali was stirring.

"I need some coffee," thought Maggie. She carefully slipped out of bed, went to the kitchen and started the coffee.

Lee must of smelled the coffee because he was the next one up. He came into the kitchen and said, "Good morning darling, did you sleep well?" He kissed her and gave her a hug, wrapping his arms around her.

Maggie couldn't look at him. She felt ashamed.

With her back turned she said, "Not well, but I guess good enough." There hadn't been much room in Ali's bed for her.

Maggie poured coffee, handed Lee his cup and walked over to the kitchen table to sit down. Lee sat next to her. They drank their coffee in silence for a while.

Lee broke the silence, "You want to talk about it now?"

Maggie looked up at Lee and with tears in her eyes she said, "No I don't want to talk about it. I wish these last few weeks would just go away but that's wishful thinking."

Lee took Maggie's hand and squeezed it, "I really missed you."

They could hear laughter coming from the other side of the house.

"I guess the kids are up," said Lee. "We'd better put this off until we can be alone.

"I know your mother will want to talk to you and your Dad wants you to call him as soon as you get back. All of our friends call on a daily basis for an update."

The kids came into the kitchen, followed by Maggie's mother. Caridad came to the table to give Maggie a kiss and hug. "Como estas hija?" Maggie's mother reverts to Spanish every once in a while.

"I'm a little tired. Jet lagged. But I'll be fine. How are you feeling?" Carrie looked pale and tired.

"I'm all right. I was just worried about you and Ali. Lee thought you might be back a couple of days ago, did your trip get delayed?"

Lee whispered to Maggie, "I called Lebanon a while back and spoke with Joelle. She told me you were on your way back to the states. I was expecting you a couple of days ago."

This was a surprise to Maggie. She held her head with both hands.

"Do you have a headache, hija?" asked Carrie.

"No Mamita, I don't have a headache. I'm just tired." Maggie went to the fridge, pulled out the milk and orange juice and said "Who wants breakfast?"

"I do, I do!" said Ali.

"Me too," chorussed Jackie.

Caridad walked to the work counter and said, "I'll make some Cuban coffee. Lee, do you want some?"

"Yes Carrie, that would be great I need the caffein."

Maggie made breakfast with Jackie's help. Every once in a while, Jackie would stop cooking, look at Maggie and start crying. "Jackie darling, don't cry. I'm home now I'm not leaving you again, come here and give me a kiss."

Ali, realizing her sister was crying, said, "Mommy. Why is Jackie crying? Why is she sad?"

"Jackie is just happy to see us honey...they're happy tears," said Maggie. But Maggie sensed that Jackie was scared.

Breakfast took longer than usual to prepare this morning. Maggie felt awkward, she could feel Lee looking at her. "How am I going to tell him about New York? Worse yet, how am I going to tell Jackie I'm considering going back to Joe?"

They sat at the kitchen table to eat. Ali was talking so fast no one could understand her. "Thank God they tuned Ali out," Maggie thought, "because some of the things she was talking about happened in New York.

Jackie, however, was listening intently.

Ali jumped up from her chair and said, "Mommy, can we give presents now?"

"Yes Ali. Bring them in here," ordered Maggie."

Ali came bouncing back to the kitchen with her arms full. She loved giving presents. Everyone seemed to like the gifts. After more hugs and "thank you's" the dishes were cleared.

Maggie poured herself another cup of coffee and went to sit out by the pool. This was her favorite spot.

"This was the place," she thought, "that she and Lee would sit after work with a gin and tonic to talk about their days while Jackie, Ali and the rest of the neighborhood kids went swimming. A place the neighbors next door could amble by and have a drink with them and stay for one of Carrie's Cuban meals. My mother always made enough food for an army."

Lee gave Maggie time to be alone. Carrie tried to keep the kids busy in Jackie's room. Things were tense.

Maggie felt Jackie's hand on her shoulder. "Sit with me darling and tell me about school and what you've been doing," Maggie said.

Jackie told Maggie all about her new friends at her new school and about the boy down the street who had been coming by the house to talk to her and go swimming. And her dance lessons! Jackie loved the Jazz classes that she took twice a week.

Jackie stopped talking and looked at Maggie, "Mommy, at breakfast Ali was talking about being with you and Joe in New York, what was that all about?

"Did you spend time with Joe in New York?"

Maggie noticed that when Jackie talked about Lee she called him Daddy, when she talked about Joe, it was Joe.

Her bond with Lee had been very strong from the first day. It seemed even stronger now. "After all Lee has been her security here while I was gone," she thought, "and if there was anything Jackie needs it's security."

"Honey, please don't worry about what Ali said at breakfast, you know how she can talk."

"I do worry mommy. I worry you're going to leave Daddy and go back to Joe."

"Out of the mouths of babes..." Maggie thought.

"Oh sweetie, you've had to grow up fast, haven't you? Look at Mommy. I promise you I will do what is best for all of us, and the us definitely includes you."

Jackie looked at Maggie smiled and said "I'm so glad you're home. I missed you very much. We all missed you very much!"

"WAHOO! Maggie is that you?" Maggie and Jackie looked up to see their neighbor Kathy Garnet coming across the yard. Maggie and Lee had not lived in this house very long but they were already good friends with their neighbors. Kathy and Jim had two girls, Laura was the same age as Ali and Sandy was a year older. Ali had played with them when they were moving in but obviously had not seen them in a while.

"Come in Kathy. Yes, it's me finally," Maggie said.

Jackie went back into the house to let the women talk.

"We didn't expect you to be gone for so long. How was your trip?"

"I didn't expect to be gone that long either. But I had no choice. My trip was stressful and long, I'm very glad to be home."

"Lee was so worried about you," Kathy said. "He has been looking rough. Some nights we'd see him sitting out here for hours. We were really worried about him. Jim and I invited him out a few times but he refused. He wanted to be around in case you called."

"The girls will be happy to see Ali back. Do you think it would be all right to invite her over?"

"I think that's a great idea. She'll be thrilled. I'll get her dressed. I think she's still in her pajamas."

"Send her over when she's ready, and let's get together in the next few days," said Kathy.

"That would be great," said Maggie. Ali dressed in record time. She was going to play with Laura and Sandy and she couldn't be happier. Carrie was in her bedroom preparing her lesson plans for the next day and Jackie was listening to music and talking on the phone.

"I wonder if anyone is trying to call." Maggie wondered. She would have to get Jackie off the phone soon so she could call her father. But not now; Maggie was drained.

This seemed to be the perfect time to talk to Lee. Maggie found him sitting out by the pool where she had been sitting talking to Jackie and Kathy.

"Hi Lee," said Maggie.

"Hi yourself," said Lee. "It looks like we're alone, can we talk now?"

Maggie wasn't ready, but it wasn't right to keep Lee waiting. "Sure, this is a good time. Everybody is involved in their own things," said Maggie.

Maggie sat on the sofa next to Lee. Lee took her hand, and looked into Maggie's eyes. Maggie lowered her gaze. She was afraid to look at Lee after what had happened between her and Joe in New York.

"Look at me Maggie." said Lee. Maggie looked up. Her eyes glittered. "Tell me about your time in Lebanon with Joe's mother and brother."

Maggie was relieved to talk about Bkassine, so she relayed all the particulars of the trip to Lee.

When Maggie came to the New York part she said, "Lee when we arrived in New York, Joe was waiting for us at the airport and he put us up in a hotel for a couple of days."

Lee looked very sad but he went on. "Ok. Tell me what happened."

"Joe wants me to leave you and go back to him. He says if I do what he wants I won't have any more problems with him taking Ali, he will be a father to Jackie, and I will never have to work again, so I can concentrate on the girls and my mother."

"Maggie, do you actually believe what Joe tells you?"

"I don't know what to believe any more. When I'm with Joe I believe what he says, then when I'm with you I want to stay here. I don't know what to do. The thought of loosing Ali to Joe and having her live in the Middle East scares the hell out of me.

"Lee, I've already lost a child and that is the worst thing a mother can go through. I thought I was going to go crazy. If it wasn't for Jackie and the fact that she needed me, I would have been in a psych ward. I can't go through anything like that again."

"Maggie, I love you. Please don't leave me," Lee said. He knelt in front of her and embraced her. They clung together, their eyes streaming with tears.

Lee had known that something was wrong when Maggie didn't get back on Monday. He figured that the journey would not take more than thirty-six hours, even with terrible connections.

Tuesday afternoon, he sat on the couch in the living room that they'd never used. It gave the best view of the street where Maggie's taxi would appear.

He sat there until Carrie called him for dinner.

"Daddy. Are you all right?" asked Jackie when she spotted him sitting there.

"Sure. I'm okay honey. I think Ali and Mom are due today and I'm waiting for the cab." Off she went to hang out with her new school friends. She was very happy to know her mom's arrival was imminent but had plans.

Not Lee. He'd had difficulty concentrating on work, his Army Reserve duties and even taking care of things at home since the call to Joelle.

It wasn't clear to him just when Maggie had left Lebanon. He'd failed to ask the girl that simple question when he heard Maggie was on the way back.

Wednesday morning Lee rode his bicycle for exercise and went to the office late. Dr. Arnold was away for a week of Continuing Medical Education and Lee felt free to just stir things up on his desk, make a few phone calls and bail out.

"Mercy," he told his secretary, "Maggie is due back today and I'm not sure of her flight information. Beep me if you need me. I'm goin' home."

"Yes Mr. Elres. Wow! Today. How exciting! You must be happy."

Mercy and Maggie were very friendly. Both Cuban Americans. Both young mothers. Both had men problems.

"What should I tell Dr Arnold when he calls?" She was offering a cover-up if he wanted one.

"Not to worry. Just tell him Maggie's due." No need to excuse his absence today.

Once home, he was at loose ends. Carrie was at work and Jackie at school.

He worked on a bookcase he and his father-in-law were building for the master bedroom. Cutting and sanding the wood was soothing. There was a long way to go with this project which took up most of the space in the two-car garage.

When the mail came he was reminded that it was time to pay bills. He wrote checks but his interest was low.

Jackie and some of the neighboring children were taking an afternoon swim in the pool behind the house. He heard them faintly from his place on the couch on the far side of the house. He was on station by the window again.

He thought of all the possibilities. Accidents. Delays. He called Air France and BOA, the most likely carriers, and could learn nothing.

Then it hit him. "She's with Joe." A range of jealous emotions surged through him but he fought them and tried to sort it out.

He decided to keep quiet about his convictions when Maggie came back and see how things played out. He cared for her deeply and knew that she was in a place of hurt and pain. He was determined to try and help her through it. No matter what!

Two more long days had passed with Lee worrying away the hours before he finally heard the taxi pull in near midnight.

"Lee, I love you too, but my children are my priority. I have to make sure I do the right thing by them."

"Do you think going back to Joe is the right thing to do for Jackie?" asked Lee.

"I don't know, I don't know." Maggie was crying, the tears wouldn't stop. Maggie looked at Lee and he was crying too. They held each other for a long time.

"Maggie, while you were gone, Jackie was terrified that you wouldn't come back. More than once she asked me if I thought you would stay in Lebanon with Joe.

"Jackie loves me like a father and I love her like a daughter. We will have a happy marriage that includes both the girls, not just Ali. You know how Joe treated Jackie when you two were together. Do you honestly think he can change just like that?"

"I don't know what I think any more, I'm so confused."

Lee knelt in front of Maggie and held her hands. "I'm begging you Maggie. Stay with me, let's make a life together. We haven't had a chance to make things work."

"Lee was right." Maggie thought. "Two weeks after their marriage the world had been turned upside down. Joe knew just what he was doing. Damn him!"

"Maggie, Maggie, I love you with all my heart, I love the girls and I'll be a good father to them, please don't leave me. Give us a chance."

"Lee, you're breaking my heart. You are so very special, I love you very much, I don't want to lose you because I think I would regret it for the rest of my life. Oh my God, what can I do?" Maggie said this looking up at the sky as if she would be able to get an answer, but no one answered, all she heard were Lee's sobs.

"Lee, Joe is expecting me to call him so he can come and get me. He'll be furious with me if I don't go with him. He expects to come here to get me. I'm afraid of what he's going to do next."

"We'll deal with whatever he does together." said Lee. "He knows what a bad experience this was for Ali, he won't do anything like that to her again." Lee was recovering from his emotional state.

"I don't know Lee. He's very selfish. He doesn't think of the kids like you and I do. He thinks of himself first, and gets what he wants above all. And what he wants is me. What am I going to tell him?"

"Just tell him the truth. You love me and want to stay with me."

"It sounds so simple when you say it. But it won't be that simple with Joe, especially when he expects me to go back to him."

Maggie and Lee sat together by the pool holding each other and talking it out. Carrie came to the door to announce that lunch was ready.

"Mami, I'm not hungry right now I just want to lay down for a while, the time difference is still taking a toll on me. Lee, please have some lunch with the girls. I'll eat a little later. I have to take a nap."

Maggie woke from her nap to the sounds of laughter and splashing from the pool. When Maggie and Lee moved into this house they knew the pool was going to be a source of entertainment for the girls. She didn't realize that the whole neighborhood would join in the fun. That was fine with her. The more the merrier. She liked knowing where the girls were and who were their friends.

Maggie put her bathing suit on and joined the frolicking children and Lee.

Sandra and Laura from next door were there. Lee was letting the kids dive from his shoulders and they were loving it. Ali was shouting, "Me now Daddy. It's my turn."

Maggie jumped in. "This," she thought, "was a family. This is the way it's supposed to be."

Jackie was all smiles and came to stand by Maggie. "Did we wake you Mommy?" she asked.

"No honey, it was time to get up, besides I didn't want to miss this."

With that Maggie reached out to Jackie and dunked her. Jackie jumped up and dunked Maggie. When Maggie looked up she saw that Lee had a huge smile on his face. He was happy to have her home.

The neighborhood kids left to have their dinner, so it was just the four of them left swimming and splashing about.

They stayed in the pool until Carrie announced that food was on the table. "God bless my mother, I wouldn't even have thought about dinner."

"Ok gang let's get out, dry off and have dinner. I'm starved." Maggie realized she had not eaten lunch and her stomach was growling.

Carrie had made Maggie's favorite dinner, Arroz con Pollo – nice and moist, the chicken meat falling off the bones. Sweet plantains fried in olive oil. Perfectly browned and sugary. And a salad. When Maggie was a child she used to beg her mother to make this dinner. Most of the time Carrie was working so it was only on special occasions that she made this meal.

"Thank you Mamita for such a nice meal. You know how I love Arroz con Pollo. There's nothing like a Cuban meal," said Maggie.

"Amen," said Lee.

"Amen," imitated Ali with a grin. Everyone laughed.

Bedtime came early; Ali was exhausted. Jackie had school the next day and Carrie had to go to work.

When all the tucking in and book reading was over, Maggie knew where to find Lee. He was outside by the pool; their favorite place.

Lee had an after dinner drink ready for Maggie. Cointreau on the rocks. It tasted wonderful. Maggie loved the orange flavor.

"Lee, I'm scared," said Maggie.

"Are you scared that Joe will take Ali again?"

"Yes that, of course, and I'm scared to face him when I have to tell him I'm not going back with him. Joe will be furious.

"I don't know what I was thinking when I told him I would think about going back to him. It's just that when I'm with him, I feel overpowered, like I have to do what he wants. What kind of sick relationship is that?"

"Honey, some people have that power over others. Joe has a very strong personality and you probably feel submissive when you're with him," said Lee.

"I guess you're right. This afternoon when we were all together I knew that I could never have that kind of relationship with Joe. Children get in his way. All he wants to do with them is pat them on the head and have them in bed when he comes home.

"I can't picture Joe doing homework with Ali much less with Jackie. Or taking them to their dance lessons like you do. That's woman's work to him.

"I swear, if I didn't know better, I would of thought Joe grew up in Cuba. That's how my grandfather treated my grandmother.

"When I was a little girl, living with my grandparents, I used to think that's not how I want to be treated when I grew up and got married. The maids used to hide when my grandfather came home. They'd say, 'El caballero llego, el caballero llego.' and then run back into the kitchen. The gentleman is here! The gentleman is here!

"Those women were scared stiff of him, and I think my grandmother was scared of him also.

"That's the feeling Joe gives. Poor Jackie. She's scared of him too. I have to make certain I reassure her."

Maggie did not tell Lee the details of her time in New York with Joe. Lee did not ask but she felt certain that he knew. It was just too painful and frightening to talk about.

"Honey, let's go to bed, I haven't slept well since you left. Maybe tonight I'll get a full nights sleep," said Lee with a grin of anticipation at having his bride back again. He held her hand on the walk to the bedroom.

That night the love making between Lee and Maggie was magical. Maggie could feel the love Lee had for her, deep inside her soul as well as her body. It was a different kind of love making than what she had felt with Joe. This was sweet, easy, comfortable. It felt right.

Lee's eyes looked at her, soft with love. Before her next heartbeat his mouth was on hers.

Maggie's mouth, hands and body all responded. She kissed him hungrily as she worked his shirt over his head.

She dipped her head and kissed his chest, her lips brushed over it lightly.

Lee lifted her mouth up to his and made love to it. He pulled her top over her head and pulled her against his bare chest. Maggie's body was flushed; hot to his touch. His arms enveloped her, his hands caressed her.

As they stood and rocked together, Maggie removed his belt and pulled his zipper down. He walked her backward towards the bed, their lips locked in a kiss.

Lee lowered her to the bed and helped her wriggle her panties over her hips and tossed them on the floor. He lifted her hips and entered her easily.

Maggie slid her hands over his butt and drew him in deeper. "Maggie. Maggie," he murmured as he began to thrust. Her climax was sudden and strong. They came in a rush and moved together in the natural rhythm of mating.

Lee kissed her and his lips wandered over her nose, eyes and lips. His breath was sweet and warm on her skin as he lowered his lips to her breasts to suckle and tease. Her nipples were hard as he worked one with his lips and teeth and the other with his fingers.

Maggie moaned with pleasure and reached for him. He kissed her soft belly and continued to pinch her nipples and moved his mouth to her wet vagina and clitoris.

Maggie began to shudder with pleasure. "Lee, Lee..." she murmured his name and moaned again. He rose, entered her again, and she began pulsing, again and again, each thrust stronger than the last.

From a far-away-place she looked down on herself and Lee and knew that Lee would be with her for the rest of their lives. For better or for worse, for richer or for poorer, till death do them part - these were their vows and they would live by them.

They slept in each other's arms that night without much movement. Daylight came through the window early in the morning and they made love again. Kissing each other while their bodies writhed together. Arching her back, Maggie climaxed again and again. This time she shed no tears. She wore the smile of contentment.

110

The house woke presently. They got Jackie off to school and Caridad left for work. Ali was ready for kindergarten but they did not want to start her so soon after the trip. Lee stayed home from work. Maggie procrastinated about calling Joe.

"What are we going to do with Ali when Joe comes over?" asked Maggie.

"Let's call Kathy and see what she's doing today, maybe she can come and pick up Ali so she can play at her house," suggested Lee.

They called Kathy first to make sure Ali would be out of the house. "Of course I can keep her. As a matter of fact, I was going to the mall in a little while, I can take her with me. That way she'll be far away."

"Thank you Kathy, you're a life saver." replied Maggie.

When Ali left with Kathy, Maggie called Joe. He must of been right by the telephone because he answered on the first ring.

"Joe, can you come to the house now?"

"I'll be there in thirty minutes." Joe hung up.

Maggie paced the floor the whole time that they waited for Joe. Lee asked her to sit down several times but she wasn't listening.

Joe was at the house in record time. He knocked at the door and Maggie answered.

"Are you ready? Where are the suitcases? Where's Ali?" Then he saw Lee in the background.

"I would have thought you wouldn't want to be here when Maggie left," Joe said to Lee.

"Come in and sit down Joe. We have to talk," said Maggie.

"We've done all the talking already Maggie, now let's go."

Maggie looked scared. Lee came to stand next to her and said to Joe, "Please come in Joe."

Joe obliged, coming into the family room and sitting down stiffly at one end of the couch. Lee sat at the other end and Maggie sat in the middle.

"Good thing the couch is a sectional," Maggie thought, "or we would of been cramped. My goodness what a thing to think about, maybe I am going out of my mind."

"Joe," Maggie said quietly, "I've thought about what we discussed in New York and I can't do it."

Joe leaned forward and Maggie cringed. "What are you saying? I can't believe my ears. We talked about this...you told me you were going to leave him and come back to me."

"I was very confused in New York. I've come to my senses. I can't take Jackie and Ali away from here. They're happy here."

"And how about you, are you happy here?" asked Joe.

"Yes, I'm happy with Lee and the girls," said Maggie bravely.

"You're a liar!" Joe said hoarsely. "You're not happy. You're staying for Jackie. She'll be done with school in a few years, she's going to leave you, and then where will you be? You'll be without me and without her. You are sacrificing Ali for Jackie. Do you think that's fair?"

"Ali is happy here too," said Maggie. "Ali loves her sister. She loves being part of this family."

"Family? We had a family and you destroyed it," Joe's voice was getting louder and his face was getting red. Maggie knew this sign, he was ready to explode.

"What we had was not a family, Joe. What we had was very dysfunctional. All you wanted from me was to make sure the kids were in bed when you came home. I had to have dinner and a drink ready for you, and be ready for sex, whether I wanted it or not."

"As if you didn't want it all the time. She wanted me and enjoyed every minute of it." Joe glared at Lee.

"Look Joe, we could argue about this all day. The bottom line is that Maggie and the girls are staying here." Lee said this emphatically looking squarely at Joe.

Joe sat back on the couch and smiled bitterly with his lips tightly together. "Maggie sit next to me," he said.

Maggie looked at Joe and said, "I can't Joe." Maggie edged a little closer to Lee.

As soon as Maggie moved toward Lee, Joe jumped up. Standing in front of Maggie he snarled, "You're going to regret this day for the rest of your life. Nobody does this to me and gets away with it."

As Joe stalked out the door he looked back at Maggie and Lee and said, "You'll see. You'll see..."

They sat motionless on the couch. Maggie was shaking and crying. Lee was comforting her.

"Oh Lee, what have I done? I think I've unleashed a lion."

"Honey, his roar is worse than his bite. When he thinks about it he'll calm down. He's just using bully tactics."

"I've humiliated him Lee. I didn't mean to do that. I honestly thought I could go back to him when I was in New York. What was I thinking? I know he'll never change. I knew that in New York. Why didn't I just tell him this in New York?"

"Because he intimidated you, that's why. And because you have two daughters and you don't want to hurt either one of them. You saw Ali with her father and you probably thought you didn't want to take him away from her. I love both the girls and I will be the best father I can be to them."

"I know that Lee. I don't deserve you."

CHAPTER 7 - MIAMI

The next few months were hard for the family, but the holidays kept everyone distracted. Maggie's biggest fear was that Joe would steal Ali. Caridad and Jackie watched Ali like hawks while Maggie and Lee were at work.

When school started after the holidays, Ali proudly went off to Kindergarten. Ali spent a lot of time playing at the Garnet home next door. Maggie, Lee and Caridad provided most of the transportation. They absolutely did not want her walking to school.

Jackie and Ali began taking dance lessons two afternoons a week and Maggie alternated chauffeur duties with a friend to make it easier for her to work at the clinics. Lee pitched in too.

Joe spoke to Ali on the telephone on a weekly basis. He still badgered Maggie to come back to him and she still refused. Maggie didn't let him have visits with Ali unless she was present or he came to the house. These were awkward encounters for everyone, but Maggie was torn between refusing him contact and her desire to help Ali have a father's love from Joe.

George, Jackie's father totally ignored his daughter and was not even paying his small child support payments. Jackie worshiped Lee, but Maggie thought that some part of Jackie, deep inside, hungered for her birth father's love and acceptance. She didn't want Ali to experience this kind of rejection from her father.

There were a couple of really nasty scenes involving Joe at the house that summer. Once, Joe tried to drive off with Ali and Maggie was barely able to pull her out of the moving car, through an open window, before Joe roared away in his car. On another occasion Joe attacked Lee in the doorway to the house and Ali got cut by broken glass in the scuffle. She needed two stitches at the ER to close a little gash in her scalp.

Maggie was still, she thought, in a very difficult situation. None of her friends or acquaintances had these issues with ex-spouses. "Maybe it's punishment for my sins."

Things got better in January; Joe told Maggie that he was leaving the area for New Orleans. He closed his business on the Miami River and went to work, he said, as a hydraulics technician for a large firm who's boats transported workers to the Gulf of Mexico oil wells.

Joe's telephone calls became irregular and less frequent. He was nicer to Maggie. She hoped that her problems with Joe were over.

Worries cropped up again in May when Joe announced that he was moving to Fort Lauderdale. There was an opportunity to set up a shop on the New River there to service the many yachts there. But they scarcely heard from Joe.

Maggie thought that he must have a new love and that she was off the hook.

Joe called at the end of June and asked Maggie in the nicest way possible if he could have the fourth of July weekend with Ali. He said his apartment was small so he would take her to Disney World and have her home whenever Maggie wanted.

Maggie consented, feeling that they'd had enough warring. Their ordeal was finally over.

Joe picked her up at the house after school on July third. He promised to have her back by the sixth of July just in time for an important event.

Sunday, July 6, 1975

The suitcases were packed and were near the front door. Jackie, Grandma Carrie, and Maggie bustled around the house in the long process of dressing, makeup, hair curling, and such. Joe and Ali were late. "He promised to be on time," Maggie worried aloud.

Maggie had tickets for Ali, Jackie, Grandma and herself to go to Mexico City. Maggie was to work at the just-opened Mexico City Branch of Arnold Medical Center. She would work for just one week and then have a few days off.

Ali and Joe were due at three in the afternoon. They needed to be at the airport by five p.m.

Dr. Arnold's office staff in Mexico City needed training and organization. That was Maggie's mission. While Maggie worked, her mother and the girls would be on vacation. A "girls only" Mexican vacation. They were all wildly enthusiastic about the trip.

Lee, recovering from a hernia operation, was not going.

"Now Maggie, calm down. It's only two-thirty. There's plenty of time. Just get yourself ready so that you can concentrate on Ali when she gets here." Lee was worried too but he wanted to keep Maggie from getting more upset.

In addition to making sure that everyone packed the right clothing, Maggie had to make sure she had her notes and other materials for her training sessions. The telephone rang twice, but it was Dr. Arnold calling with last minute thoughts and instructions. Not Joe.

When Ali wasn't home by three, fear replaced worry.

"Lee." Maggie's words croaked out as her emotions eroded her control. "Have you seen the time? It's three thirty. Should I call Otto?"

Maggie's plane time for Mexico was six o'clock. Joe had told Maggie he would stay with his friend Otto, Ali's Godfather, on Wednesday night when he took Ali.

"I'll ask him what time Joe and Ali left."

"Yes. Call him." Lee too, was sick with fear of what would happen to Maggie if Ali was gone again.

"Hi Otto, it's Maggie. I'm calling to find out what time Joe left your house to bring Ali over?"

"Hi Maggie." Otto's rich Argentine accent gave his voice a lilt she loved. They reverted to Spanish and Otto said, "Joe left my house yesterday in a taxi."

"Yesterday?" Maggie protested. "I thought he was staying with you until today." Her tears were flowing.

"That's what I thought too, but he took off with Ali yesterday."

"Okay Otto. Thanks. If you talk to him or see him, tell him I called and to call me. Please."

She looked at her watch. "Lee. Now he's an hour late. I'm starting to panic!"

"Take it easy honey. Your plane leaves at six, so you have plenty of time."

"Oh Lee. He did it again. I just know it." She wailed. We went through this last year and he didn't bring her back. My motherly instinct tells me we have a problem."

They called Maggie's father, who lived near Otto, and he'd gone to Otto's apartment at about four-thirty in the afternoon. He learned nothing more.

The police and the F.B.I. were called but could not help other than to check taxicab companies' records to learn where the taxi had taken them. No record was found of a pick up at Otto's address.

They telephoned Joe's last address in Louisiana, a Holiday Inn, where he'd lived for several months. He was not there. The room clerk did not know him. Maggie was near collapse.

119

She sat on the couch and told Lee, "Let me think by myself for a while. There may be something Joe said that I've forgotten."

She sat with her head back and her swollen eyes shut against the lamp's glare. Lee sat quietly next to her, silently willing her to think hard.

"Lee," she muttered, half talking, half thinking-out-loud. "...last time Joe saw Ali...we were in the mall and he bought her some clothes then we went to an ice cream store. Ali wanted to draw and Joe gave her a...a pen!

"That's it. The pen Lee!"

"What do you mean?"

"Joe gave Ali a pen to draw with and then she gave it to me to hold for her when we left. It's in my purse. It has a company advertisement on it. Maybe that's where Joe's working."

Maggie jumped up to search her purse, dumping the contents on the floor to see better. There were three pens but not the one she wanted.

Maggie ran to the closet to look through six other purses. "Oh God. Help me find it," she said but no other pen was found. She sat in the dim closet weeping.

Jackie was standing by her crying. "Mommy. Will we see Ali again?"

"Honey. We're doing everything we can think of. Joe gave Ali a pen and I was just looking for it to give me the name of the company he's working for. But I can't find it."

"Oh. Did you look in Ali's room? She loves to play dress-up in your closet and play with your stuff. Maybe it's in her room."

Maggie jumped up and kissed Jackie. "You're brilliant my darling. Let's look together."

Maggie and Jackie searched Ali's room together. Maggie through the closet and Jackie looked in the toy box.

"Mommy. Here's your red and black beads. Your long slip and your red purse."

"Let me see it," Maggie cried out urgently as she reached for the slim pocketbook.

She dumped the bag and out fell a hair clip, a few coins and a pen. "Oh my God Jackie! This is the pen I was looking for!"

Mother and daughter hugged and hurried out of the room to find Lee.

The pen bore an ad for a construction company with two phone numbers. No city and no address. Maggie hoped fervently that this had something to do with Joe's employment.

They were totally out of ideas about what to do next so, in desperation, Maggie dialed the area code for New Orleans and the number on the pen. Lee listened on their extension.

The phone rang twice and a woman answered, "Hello?" No company name was given. It sounded like a home phone being answered.

"Hello. I'm calling for Joe Zayyat. Can he be reached at this number?"

After a moment of silence, the woman said, "Yes I know Mr. Zayyat, but he's not here. Who is calling please?" Her voice was puzzled and questioning.

"This is Maggie. Joe's ex-wife. It's important that I reach him. Can you help me?"

"I don't know. This is Lottie. Mr. Zayyat used to work here." There was obvious reluctance to give information freely. The tone of her voice was not unfriendly, but somehow she broadcasted her reservations about speaking to an unknown voice on the phone. "I usually don't answer the phone, in fact I was doing some rush typing today. My boss just returned from a trip. No one is ever here on a Sunday. I just picked up the phone on impulse."

Maggie thought rapidly. "Look, Joe took Ali, our five-year-old daughter, for the weekend and I forgot to give him her allergy pills. I need to tell him about the pills. She needs to take one now and I really need to speak to him. Is there any way that you can reach him to give him a message. He's supposed to be in Louisiana this weekend."

Again a short period of silence.

"But Mr. Zayyat can't be here," she said. "He's in Bahrain." A chill settled over Maggie's soul. "Where?"

"Bahrain. He was there ten days ago. John saw him there."

Maggie was stunned! "He's here because he picked up Ali on Thursday and I have to tell him about her medication. Do you think that you could try to reach him for me, with a message? Please!"

Lottie seemed to be troubled by the image of a little girl without her medicine. "Yes. I'll call around and see if I can find him. But I was sure that he was in Bahrain."

The opportunity, at last. "Where's Bahrain?" The question was asked in an offhand manner. Her voice did not quaver.

"BAH-RAIN," Lottie corrected Maggie's pronunciation. "It's an island in the Persian Gulf. He works there for Otis Engineering."

"My goodness," Maggie continued, pumping for more information. "I didn't know where it was!" She used her friendliest voice.

The conversation wound down for a few moments, then closed with Lottie agreeing to attempt to find a phone number and call Maggie back. She took their phone number.

"Oh my God! Lee! He's taken her again. We never should of let her go with him." She sobbed in Lee's arms.

Struggling to keep control, Maggie recalled that Joe had had a very dark suntan when he picked up Ali. She'd remarked that it looked like he'd been in the sun. He told her that he'd been in Bermuda taking a ride on a client's yacht. Since he was involved in Marine hydraulics, it seemed to be a natural explanation. Now his suntan took a more significant meaning.

He had been on an island in the Middle East. He was not getting ready to open a business in Fort Lauderdale at all. It was all lies.

Maggie remembered that he wore a gold pendant when he came for Ali. She speculated that it was the sort of ornament that could be bought in the Middle East. He was wearing a sleeveless, open vest for a shirt; a stylish and expensive looking garment that showed off his dark tan and his hairy, muscular body.

They immediately telephoned Bahrain through a maze of overseas operators. There was a seven hour time difference. It was nighttime there, and the number listed for Otis Engineering did not answer. No telephone was listed for Joseph Zayyat. The operator checked several hotels, but he was not registered in any of them.

123

There was no way to confirm Ali's whereabouts until after midnight, Miami time, when, presumably, businesses in Bahrain might start to open. Maggie and Lee were shaken by the situation.

Lee's atlas of the world enabled them to locate Bahrain, and the encyclopedia gave further information.

> Bahrain is an island ruled by an Arab Sheik. Its population is 145,000, and its chief city is Manama, with a population of 30,000. The island only 26 miles long. Its industries are oil, fishing and pearl diving. There is no link to the mainland so it can only be reached by air and sea.
>
> On 15 August 1971 Bahrain's full independence was proclaimed, a new treaty of friendship was signed with the UK, and Sheikh Isa took the title of Amir. A new constitution came into effect in 1973. Elections were held the following day.

So Bahrain was a newly minted Middle Eastern nation.

And their worst fears had been confirmed. Ali was gone from the United States!

Despite the fact that Ali was born in the United States to parents that were both American citizens, she had dual citizenship because her father was Lebanese.

What chance would Maggie have in the Arabian countries? "None!" she told herself. Not only would she be a foreigner but, as a woman she believed that her rights would be close to zero.

Maggie's entire world caved in. She lay in bed with tears streaming down her face. Mascara blackened her cheeks and stung her eyes. "Oh my baby! Oh my god! I'll never see her again!"

Lee stood by, helpless. No comfort could be given, although he tried. Maggie's traveling outfit was rumpled and creased. Finally she fell into a troubled sleep.

Grandma Carrie wept quietly in the family room, and Jackie, in shock, hid out in her bedroom behind closed doors. What to do? Lee prowled the house, paralyzed, frustrated. Their luggage in the living room, packed for Mexico, lay as a mocking memorial to spoiled plans.

The day passed and night came. The phone did not ring. Lee hoped and then prayed for it to ring. Joe would say, "We're on our way. Sorry about the delay, but the car broke down."

Lee kept the night watch while his three tormented women slept. He waited for Miami's midnight to announce Bahrain's morning.

At ten o'clock, desperate for constructive activity, Lee placed a call to the state department in Washington, D.C., to ask for advice. He knew from their previous experience that a "Welfare and Whereabouts" investigation could be done through the American embassy in Bahrain which would try to find her and determine her situation.

The duty officer heard the story and agreed to make inquiries by cable. She told Lee the Embassy in Bahrain would begin looking tomorrow morning, local time. Lee gave her all the required information.

"What can you tell me about Bahrain?" Lee asked.

"Not a great deal, I'm afraid. My book indicates that it is an independent country, formerly a British protectorate.

The country has a modern system of justice. It's based upon English law. Our Bahrain desk officer will be in at eight tomorrow morning, and he could give you more information."

Lee thanked the woman and hung up. Time passed slowly.

Lee called the F.B.I. and spoke with an agent. "The federal kidnapping laws specifically exempt the natural parents from this crime. We can't help you. I'm sorry."

Lee woke Maggie at half past eleven. She looked terrible. Her eyes were so swollen she could hardly see. She refused the soup Lee had warmed up for her but she did sip some cold milk.

"Oh my God! My head. Lee, I feel so bad." She sat at the edge of the bed holding her head in both hands.

"Honey, take a shower and I'll get you some aspirin. You have a half an hour before we can call." Lee had checked with the overseas operator and had been told there would be no delay.

Maggie agreed, reluctantly, and trudged off to the bathroom. Lee fetched the aspirin and then straightened out the bed. He brought pencils and a large tablet of paper for note taking.

After her shower Maggie looked somewhat better. Lee felt her heart's pain. He wanted to ease her mind, but there were no words.

Finally, at a few minutes before midnight, she placed the first call. The male overseas operator in Bahrain seemed to personify the expected of the male chauvinistic attitude of the Middle East. He called the American operator, "Dear," "Honey," "Sweetheart," "My love," in a patronizing manner.

Lee stayed close to the phone to overhear the complete conversation.

Otis Engineering finally answered at one in the morning, Miami Time. When asked for Joe Zayyat, the secretary said, "He's not here."

Maggie spoke directly to the woman, over the operator, to determine her exact meaning. "Is he in Bahrain? Is his daughter with him?"

The secretary clarified, "He's not yet here in the office. Yes, he is in Bahrain and the little girl is with him."

Joe had been found by luck, or perhaps God had smiled. He was expected in thirty minutes.

Maggie called again. "Joe," Her voice was unnaturally high. "Where is Ali?" Lee listened in.

"Oh. She's here with me." He spoke in a matter of fact voice.

"Joe!" Hysteria was near. She almost laughed. "What about Disney World? You said you were going to Disney World."

He was nasty. "Forget Ali. She's with me now and she is very happy. She doesn't need you. She decided that she'd rather be with me. Go ahead. Take your trip to Mexico and have a good time with Jackie and your mother. You have Lee now...that's what you wanted, isn't it?"

"That's all ruined now, Joe, thanks to you. Jackie and my mother, in addition to being worried to death about Ali, have had their vacation ruined. They've been in tears all afternoon." She was trying to make him feel guilty on all counts.

The conversation took Maggie over the brink of hysteria. She pleaded, begged, cried, and sobbed. "How could you do this to me?" How could you do this to Ali? I'm her mother and she needs me. Please, Joe, bring her back. Oh, Joe," she wailed. "I'll do anything! Tell me what you want?"

Joe thought about Maggie's broken promises to return to him if he facilitated Ali's return to her from Lebanon. He said, "Forget about her. You'll never see Ali again." He hung up with a bang.

Maggie called again, vainly attempting to keep her emotions in control. But the result was the same. He said that Ali was in Lebanon but refused to say where.

"Don't make an ass out of yourself by coming here. It won't do you any good. She's not here. Ali is happy. Don't you understand? She doesn't need you. She'll be all right. She hasn't even asked about you. She's well taken care of here.

At the end, he said, "Don't call me any more. I've said all I'm going to say. I'm too busy for these phone calls."

Joe looked around the office, everyone was looking at him, they had heard the whole conversation.

"Fuck them," he thought. "It doesn't matter what they think, I'm in control of Maggie's life again, and that's what's important."

How easy it had been for him to lie to her about the Disney trip. Maggie would learn not to cross him. Ali will get over her whining about her mother and her sister, then he'd send her away to school where Maggie couldn't find her. He'd make Maggie suffer like he had.

Joe's boss stuck his head out of his office and motioned for Joe to come in.

"What's this all about Joe? I couldn't help but to hear you on the phone. I thought you said your ex gave you the little girl, that she didn't want her any more. She isn't going to cause us any trouble here in Bahrain, is she?"

"No, she won't cause any trouble. She'll never have the guts to come here and face me. Besides she's married again and all she cares about is her new husband. She could care less about Allison."

"Ok buddy, if you say so."

Joe strode through the office, his brown face a stone mask, and left for the docks where he worked.

Grandma and Jackie stayed in their beds, petrified by Maggie's cries. At two in the morning, emotionally and physically exhausted, there were decisions to be made. Maggie would go to Bahrain and Jackie would go with her. She would try to get Ali back.

Maggie felt that Lee should not go. Partly because he was still sore from recent hernia surgery and unable to lift heavy suitcases, and partly because she perceived the problem to be between herself and Joe. Her main fear was that his presence would be a further provocation to Joe. She remembered the sudden violence that erupted during their last face-to-face encounter. Furniture had been broken and Ali had gotten cut by flying glass.

Lee agreed, reluctantly. He did not want to see Maggie off on hazardous journey without him. Yet, somehow, to be truthful, he understood that this was between Maggie and Joe. Ali was their child. Lee loved her, to be sure, but not yet with the fervor that a father feels for his own. That would come with time.

How could they afford to leave work at the same time? How could Caridad and Jackie manage on their own? Jackie would go with Maggie and Lee would stay home.

They began to work and plan. There were so many details and problems to resolve. Lee was charged up with adrenaline and began to take various actions. He worked like a demon to make their lives right again.

They kept a log of their activities and phone calls to make sure they wouldn't forget anything. Lee made a list of all the things that needed to be done. A telephone call to Washington told the duty officer to cancel the "Welfare and Whereabouts" investigation. Maggie didn't want Joe to be stirred into further action by official inquiries. If Ali was in Bahrain, and if Joe feared trouble, he could send her back to his mother in Lebanon.

They called British Airways and made reservations for a one o'clock Monday afternoon flight to Bahrain via London and Frankfort. British Airways made reservations at the Gulf Hotel. Plane time was eleven hours away.

Lee called the U.S. Embassy in Bahrain and spoke to a Mr. Unger who was the chief consul. Lee told him to ignore the "Welfare and Whereabouts" inquiry on Ali Zayyat and asked him to recommend a good English-speaking attorney.

The official recommended two firms and gave them the telephone numbers. "You won't need a visa but you must have current typhoid immunizations before you arrive."

He called Bahrain again. The first law firm was closed for lunch, but he immediately reached the second, Alireza and

Associates. Mr. Salah Alireza spoke clear English. Lee asked if he represented Otis Engineering or Joe Zayyat.

He replied, "No." to both questions.

So Lee proceeded to explain their problem in a rather emotional and disorganized manner.

"Let me get this straight. You say that you're coming here tomorrow to rescue your five-year old daughter from her father who has just kidnapped her? And you want me to represent you? How can a father kidnap his own daughter? Who is this anyway?"

Alireza seemed incredulous. Lee spoke loudly and slowly and tried to enunciate each word more clearly to overcome the static.

"Yes, that is correct. Mr. Zayyat is in violation of the law here because my wife and I have legal custody. We have a court order demanding her return." Lee lied in anticipation of getting a court order later in the day.

"We will be happy to represent you when you arrive."

"Yes sir. But he could leave for Lebanon at any time. We need you to make sure that Ali doesn't leave the country prior to Mrs. Elres' arrival."

"Why would he go to Lebanon?"

They went over further details of their problem. Mr. Alireza was very courteous, but he indicated that nothing could be done until their arrival. Mr. Alireza said that a cable from their American law firm would be helpful.

They promised a cable to confirm the situation and gave him their flight information. "I'm sorry to trouble you with such a complicated story on the telephone, Mr. Alireza. It will be clear when my wife meets with you tomorrow."

"Don't worry Mr. Elres. We will do our utmost to assist you. Goodbye."

Lee was happy with the contact. At least they had the name and address of a real person, an attorney, who could help them get started. It also helped, Lee thought, that the American consul knew the story.

It was not yet light when the suitcases were repacked for Maggie and Jackie. Lee planned to call Mr. Gelb, who had represented them earlier, at seven o'clock to supply the needed legal weapons.

Lee wanted to leave as early as possible for the Dade County Department of Health to get immunizations for Jackie and himself. Should he want to follow later, he'd be ready at a moment's notice.

Lee thought about money. There was only a few hundred dollars in their checking account and less in savings. The airline tickets would have to be purchased using their American Express credit card.

As Maggie fell into a troubled sleep, Lee continued to make lists and schedules, trying to choreograph their morning activities into a workable timetable to make sure that Maggie got to court and then to the airport by one o'clock. It seemed possible.

He telephoned his boss very early in the morning. "Burt. I'm desperate. I need to borrow five thousand dollars." Lee explained their situation.

Dr. Arnold agreed immediately even though, as Lee and Maggie knew, the clinics had a cash flow problem. They agreed to take thirty-five hundred dollars right away and the rest as needed. Burt proved to be a good friend as well as a good boss.

Lee woke Maggie up at six A.M. She called her father to report the contact with Joe and her plans to go to Bahrain.

"Honey. What can I do? I'll take off work and help you."

"Daddy, don't. I just wanted you to know. I don't really know what you can do, but I promise I'll call you if I think of anything."

"I'll be praying for you sweetheart."

"Thanks, Daddy. That will help."

Mr. Gelb was called at home at seven a.m. He took charge. "We'll arrange an emergency hearing. The judge will be glad to sign an order under these circumstances. We'll ask for an order for his arrest. What's wrong with that man?"

Lee told Mr. Gelb about Maggie's one o'clock plane reservation. "Well, we'll try. But we're at the mercy of the court's schedule. Be in my office at nine thirty."

They all rushed out of the house at half past seven. Maggie's job was to get funds from Dr. Arnold and purchase traveler's checks at the bank. They would meet at Mr. Gelb's office. The plan was set.

Jackie and Lee went to the Dade County Health department to get immunized. Maggie had gotten hers a year ago and did not need to repeat the shot. Lee carried a package that contained all of the legal documents relating to the prior problem in Lebanon.

They were on time for their appointment with Mr. Gelb. They sat in his elegant office as he said, "Now don't worry about the court appearance. We'll get everything we need. But our petition can't be heard until noon. That's the earliest we can get in. My secretary is typing up the orders for a signature now."

It was apparent that with a noon court date and so many other details, they could not make a one o'clock flight. So the departure was rescheduled for seven in the evening. It turned out to be better actually, as the plane would arrive in Bahrain two hours earlier due to better connections!

Mr. Gelb handled everything with exquisite attention to myriad details and high energy. The judge granted orders that demanded the return of Ali and Joe's arrest. Attorney Gelb played a key role in shaping the rescue operation.

In the judge's waiting room, Gelb gave Lee a level look and said, "Lee. You ought to go with Maggie. Not your other daughter. Until Zayyat sees you standing together as man and wife, he'll never get over his problem. She's in no condition to go by herself. The Middle East is another world, and a woman alone won't be effective."

Maggie and Lee agreed immediately, she with relief, and Lee with a certainty that their lawyer was right. He felt a duty to go. Jackie had tears in her eyes, but she took the change of plans like a lady.

Again the mad rush in separate directions. Lee had to get the court documents certified by the clerk of the court and go to the office to clear his desk and calendar. Both tasks were complicated. People had to be notified that he was leaving. He had to be sure that the medical organization would go on with smoothly without him. He called his Army commanding Officer to ask for leave to miss reserve drills.

Maggie went home to pack his bags and make telephone calls. There was time for a last minute meeting with Caridad and Jackie; she gave them instructions as to who would give them the funds they'd need and made sure to give them all the appropriate phone numbers.

They left home, after a goodbye full of hugs, tears and promises of their safe return. There was a flurry of last minute details. Only one thing was sure-Maggie and Lee were going to do their very best to get Ali back to America, to her mother, friends, and family.

They were on their way to where? Bahrain? An old land perhaps but a brand new country. It was just a dot on the map situated between Qatar and the larger countries of Saudi Arabia and Iran.

Bahrain was soon to be "oil rich." That's what made it interesting for America and Europe. A country in need of skilled foreign workers and a land of opportunity for those who had the foresight, drive and skills to get there. Just the ticket for a guy like Joe.

At the Miami International Airport Maggie and Lee were alone again with two hours until departure. Since morning, they had been too busy to worry. Their ties to the everyday world were now severed, and there was that quiet time that can occur after the "goodbyes" are said and before a new episode can begin.

They were tired. They'd missed a night's sleep and were hungry because they'd missed four meals. Since there was time to grab a sandwich, they went to the airport lunch counter.

Surprisingly, there was a familiar face. Lee's fourteen-year old brother sat eating. Lee's father and brother were at the airport to meet his stepmother who was returning from a family visit to Texas. Lee had forgotten that this was the day. Even though Lee's folks lived only thirty miles away, they didn't see them as often as they'd like. The chance meeting served them well. It provided the opportunity to tell Lee's family about their problem and their quest in Bahrain.

They found Mom and Dad and gave them an outline of events. It was nice to have their good wishes while boarding their 747 for London.

Coincidences. Accidents of time and place play a part in everyone's life. Chance had certainly affected them. Miami International Airport is an enormous place. To find a friend there by appointment can be difficult. To find one's parents by chance seemed to be the best coincidence that could have happened under the circumstances.

Luck was on their side. Finding the ball-point pen and having the Louisiana telephone answered on a Sunday afternoon, seemed the equivalent of being dealt four aces in a poker hand. The fact that they were actually on the way to Bahrain so quickly awed them. "Joe is going to be surprised when he sees us in Bahrain Lee. We are going around the world faster than I can believe."

Lee smiled in agreement. "I'm proud of us."

Despite the stress, Maggie had performed very well. Once the decision was made, she had toughened up. Her tears disappeared and she did what she had do to get ready. Outwardly, she betrayed little of her internal strife.

Flying time to London is about five hours. That gave them ample time for reflection and sleep. Worry would be more accurate. Soon, the cabin lights were dimmed, and passengers began nodding off to sleep. Maggie and Lee spent most of the time talking. They felt very close to one another.

At one point Maggie said, "You know, honey, I can't believe that we're actually here. So much has happened."

"Yeah. We've had our share of trouble."

"No. It's not only that. I meant to say that we accomplished so much so quickly. Aside from finding out where Joe took Ali, we went to court, we've raised the money for the trip, and we did it so quickly."

"You're right," Lee agreed. "We've really been efficient. If we worked this hard and accomplished this much every day, we could be millionaires."

They were truly impressed with themselves. In addition to luck, they'd worked hard. A good team with every item on the long list checked off. In a night and a day they'd done a week's worth of work.

They worried together across the Atlantic. Then they rushed through Heathrow to catch another 747 that would stop in Frankfort and then roar off to Bahrain. More time, more meals, more worry. Sleep would not come. The Boeing magic carpet arrived in Bahrain only forty-eight hours after they had first missed Allison. They were hopeful but unsure that they'd be able to bring her back home.

CHAPTER 8 - BAHRAIN

JULY 8, 1975

Oh my God Lee! Look at that!" Maggie pointed out of the cab window at the human figures swaddled in dark robes as they moved about the streets. Everything seemed sinister.

Maggie and Lee were troubled by the remoteness of their destination. Their minds still overflowed with both trivial and important thoughts about this exotic place between Europe and the Asian continent. They'd learned a bit from their conversations with the state department and from the encyclopedia research they'd managed to accomplish.

"I look at this Maggie and I'm reminded of how grim Barranquilla, Columbia seemed when we got there at night."

Their noses were pressed against the glass of the taxi one minute and their necks were swiveling the next as they attempted to see every detail. Their thinking and perceptions were warped by more than a lack of sleep; they were burdened by preconceptions, misinformation and prejudices. They spent many weeks in Colombia and Mexico, mostly for work. There they'd encountered beggars, poor homeless children and thieves. They expected to face similar problems in Bahrain. "Lee, do you feel safe here?."

"I dunno Maggie. The airport seemed modern and new, but the people are so exotic and the night makes everything look dangerous."

"It scares me that I don't know exactly where Joe is Lee. Everything spooks me."

They were having a paranoid arrival, at night, in a strange and exotic city. They even worried about getting to the hotel unmolested.

The few people they saw on the street were olive skinned, and most wore Arab garb. Many women wore black robes with black shawls covering their heads. Faces were hidden by veils. Some women even wore masks, triggering out of place, out of time memories of the Lone Ranger movie serials. Maggie especially felt the cultural displacement as they wandered among these mysterious females.

The officials and clerks all spoke English and moved them courteously and efficiently through customs and immigration.

The plane that they'd just exited was on its way to Abu Dhabi. "Where, or what," they asked each other, "is Abu Dhabi?" Lee deduced, incorrectly, that it was a way station to Australia, probably in India or some other remote place.

They were given an automatic seventy-two hour visa. Extensions would have to be handled by the Ministry of Immigration offices in Manama. The suitcase containing Lee's best suit, for court appearance, was missing. A telegram was handed to him. For a moment he feared bad news from home. But it was the airline's promise to have the missing bag on the next possible flight. The fringe on the magic carpet had an ever-so-slight flaw.

Mr. Alireza had told them to go to the Gulf Hotel. They took a taxi, deciding to rest for the night and seek out their Mr. Alireza in the early morning. The ride to the hotel added to their tangle of impressions. It was very hot and the cab had no air conditioning.

The darkened streets were quiet and the buildings near the airport were modest.

As they crossed a bridge there were native boats of all sizes and descriptions pulled up on the shore. These boats were all of the type thought of as dhows and, in the dim light, the boats looked neglected. The driver spoke no English, so there were no answers to their questions about the sights.

Once over the water, they entered the main part of the city. Electric street lamps illuminated the main streets. Also, in favorable contrast to South America and Lebanon, there were no police patrols with machine guns and rifles.

They were still uneasy, however, because the neighborhoods they traversed seemed poor. In some of the Latin American countries there were masses of desperately poor people who might kill and rob a stranger simply for a few dollars. They whispered their impressions back and forth,

141

not wanting to share them with their driver. "Surely, if the city were dangerous we'd see police activity," said Lee.

Maggie nodded in agreement. Worried about everything.

Later, much later, they would come to understand the extent of their cultural bias.

They passed unpaved side streets and darkened buildings with bulbous roofs and slender towers. There were few vehicles.

There were mosques with minarets, and there were houses with unglazed windows and doorless entries. In Miami, even homes in the poorest districts are garnished with air conditioners and television antennas. Here, they saw none.

Street lights were everywhere in Miami. At home there were automobiles at every door.

Lee remarked as a joke to lighten their moods, "People at home don't wear sheets on the streets." Maggie didn't laugh.

The Gulf Hotel had a circular drive that rose to let passengers alight at the second floor level. The lobby was cool and presented an up-to-date appearance. They were pleased to find considerate and well-spoken personnel.

They were discomforted to find that there was no reservation for them. The clerk explained very carefully, "I am sorry to inform you sir, but there are no rooms available on the whole island. All of the hotels are booked solid for months."

That would have been an awful disappointment at any time. They, who had just come halfway around the world, were crushed. The clerk was civil and sympathetic. He agreed to get the manager.

The manager, Vincent Bartlett, an Englishman, confirmed the problem. "We have a very serious shortage. Due to petro activity and the Concord flights, which have just started, we've been packed for months. We hope that things will be better in a year or so."

Lee turned to Maggie and said, "I wish that Mr. Alireza had warned us about this. We could have..."

"Just a minute," The manager broke in. "Is your name Elres?"

"Yes," Lee said hopefully.

"Ah. Mr. Alireza told me that you were coming and, under great duress, he prevailed upon me to set a room aside for you. We had to do some doubling up in the aircrew rooms, but I do have a room for you." Their hearts sang praise for Mr. Alireza.

"But it is only for tonight. Perhaps you will be able to find a 'bed and breakfast' tomorrow."

Thank you very much."

"Yes," said Maggie. "I thought that we would have to sleep in your lobby. Mr. Alireza has saved the day."

"What's a 'bed and breakfast?" asked Lee.

"It is a kind of pension. A private home or small commercial establishment that provides a room plus breakfast. There are several that I could recommend. I'll make some inquiries for you tomorrow. Perhaps Mr. Alireza could help too."

They responded to his concern for their homelessness. "Thank you again. You are very kind."

Their room was blessed with a window air conditioner. They decided to eat in the hotel restaurant and go to bed as early as possible. Tomorrow could be a day for serious business. Lee telephoned to inquire, and learned that the hotel

143

kitchen closed at eleven. Since it was already past ten, they hurried.

Lee called the Alireza home and was told that Mr. Alireza was not there. Mrs. Alireza came on the line. She had a lovely clear British accent. "My husband is at the airport looking for you. I'll tell him that you called. Welcome to Bahrain." Lee was impressed by her gracious manner.

They converted dollars into Bahraini Dinars at the front desk. The rate of exchange was $2.50 to the dinar. Since they were used to getting many pesos for each dollar in South America, it seemed a little strange to get so little for a dollar.

Dinner was pleasurable. The restaurant was French and it was expensive; it cost at least twice as much as a meal in a similar hotel at home.

The food was good as was the serenade by a surprisingly talented Latin band with a pretty English singer. Under better circumstances it would have been a very enjoyable evening.

Later, as they passed through the lobby, they heard their name spoken. It was Mr. Alireza asking for them at the desk. He was a small man in his thirties, with prematurely graying hair. His demeanor was serious. He had olive skin, dark eyes, and was dressed in a white suit that was somewhat rumpled by the heat and cares of the day. To them, he looked like a lawyer. He was accompanied by a slender young man dressed in Arabian robes and a headdress.

Their mutual introductions were pleasant and they thanked him profusely for his thoughtfulness in obtaining a room for them. His companion was introduced as Jacob (pronounced 'Ya-cob'), his assistant. They took seats in a quiet part of the lobby.

"We must have missed you at the airport. I'm sorry that I was not there to greet you but, you see, I thought that you would be on the ten o'clock airplane." His English was formal and his manner gentle. There was a definite but mild, pleasing accent.

They realized that they'd forgotten to inform him when their reservations were changed in Miami, and that they had arrived two hours earlier. They apologized for their thoughtless error. "No matter," he said. "The important thing is that you have found your hotel. There is a big shortage of rooms here. I had to tell a big story to get you in tonight."

They began to relate the particulars of their problem, stressing the importance of preventing Joe from taking Allison to Lebanon. "He has a lot of influence with the government there due to family connections. At least that's what he would like us to believe."

Maggie reacted. "It's more than a claim, Lee. He really does have a lot of friends. And he understands the system. We would be like babes in the woods. When I went to Lebanon last year I felt absolutely helpless."

"We are concerned about the possibility of violence when Joe discovers we're here," Maggie said. "Can you arrange for a round-the-clock bodyguard to protect us from assault?"

"That won't be necessary," said Alireza with a certain disdain. "The law will protect you here."

Feeling that their point had not been made, they took turns explaining, "Joe is a violent man. Even though the law says not to attack other persons, he may do so in a fit of anger.

He took Allison in spite of a court order to the contrary. He won't abide by agreements, and he has a bad reputation. You see, Joe has a violent turn of mind. He may be ready to hire other people to do his dirty work."

Mr. Alireza solemnly declared, "I assure you that nothing like that could happen here. We have very strong laws that protect the rights of people. If he should try anything, he will be put in jail and punished. This is not the United States." He seemed to be warning Lee simultaneously; it seemed he may have had his own stereotypes about Americans.

They were taken aback. The reputation of the *Land of the Free and Home of the Brave* seemed to be tarnished. No doubt American movies and T.V. exports presented a distorted picture of the United States. Even though there were still misgivings, they could proceed no further on the subject of a bodyguard.

Jacob looked sad and worried.

Mr. Alireza expressed sympathy and concern about their difficult problem. He sat back on the sofa and began to smile. "When you called yesterday morning, I thought that it might be a joke. I was sure that some of my acquaintances had gotten together to have some fun at my expense." They laughed together. His eyes twinkled and they began to think of him as a friend.

"Please," he said, "call me Salah."

Jacob followed the conversation closely but had not contributed much beyond nods of understanding and friendly eye contact. He seemed to be sympathetic and they were comfortable in his presence.

Salah and Jacob declined Lee's invitation to join them in the lounge for coffee or a cocktail. Lee mentioned coffee also because he was afraid of offending them. Most Arabs, Lee thought he remembered, have religious scruples over drinking alcoholic beverages.

Mr. Alireza arranged to pick them up at eight o'clock in the morning. They said goodnight and went upstairs to their haven for the one night. It had been a long day for everyone.

They slept deeply but both Maggie and Lee had unpleasant dreams to tell in the morning.

Wednesday, July 9, 1975 – Bahrain

They woke at six-thirty to prepare for the day. The coffee shop provided breakfast. The cost surprised them. Lee realized that the people shipping these foods to the island needed to earn a living. He wondered where the flour, the bacon and the eggs came from: England? France? Lebanon?

Outside, the air was hot and clear. Salah was prompt. He wore a fresh and unrumpled version of yesterday's suit and a white shirt and tie. The car was his wife's, he explained, and the air conditioning was broken. The temperature felt like a hundred degrees. Perspiration began to flow. He seemed overdressed by Miami standards.

Maggie wore slacks and a demure white blouse. Lee wore a tie but carried his jacket.

Bahrain by daylight was not beautiful; however it was not unpleasant. Its waters were full of work boats and oil wells, its sun hot and bright. The sky was brilliant blue and the air was clear.

147

Mr. Alireza pointed out his home, which was close to the hotel. It was a nice two-story house on one side of a wide park. There was no grass in the park. It was just a hard-packed dirt playing field with goals set at the ends. "This is the football field. And not only for the children. In the season there are many adult teams and leagues." He meant in the winter, of course, when the temperatures were milder.

He pointed at a prominent building across the park. "This is the Sheik's summer palace. Foreign dignitaries often stay there."

The *Arabian Nights* mix of tiled roofs, domes and minarets made it an exotic structure. Lee wondered about a harem but did not ask. He did ask about his pronunciation of the word Sheik. "In the United States we use the word Sheik. Pronounced with a long 'E'."

Salah nodded. "Yes. Here, too, in the Middle East . But in Bahrain, it's Sheik, pronounced with a long 'A'. I don't' know why. Perhaps it has some connection with their history. My family is from Persia. It could be the Portuguese influence. They once ruled here."

"So," Lee thought. "Mr. Alireza is a foreigner here too." Maggie had the same notions. They exchanged glances, not knowing if this was a good thing or a bad thing. This law firm had not been the first recommended, just the first available.

The law firm of Alireza and Associates conducted its business in an office building next to the Arab Bank, on Government Road, downtown Manama. The city was not designed for the automobile, but then again many American streets are not either. They parked a few blocks away in a lot so rough it looked like a construction site. Salah liked to walk fast. They had a hard time keeping up due to Lee's recent hernia operation and Maggie's high heeled shoes. By the time they walked into the office, they were damp with perspiration.

The office suite consisted of three private offices without a hall, plus a single large room which served as a reception, clerical, and secretarial area. The rooms were bright and pleasant and all in a row, railroad fashion. One had to pass through each private office in turn to get to an office further from the entry. It must have been somewhat distracting to the partners.

There were three partners. The lawyers all wore western suits. An Englishman, Mr. Maurice Sellier, Legal Consultant, occupied the last and most luxurious office with a picture window and good view of the harbor. Mr. Alireza, the head of the office, occupied the middle room and Mr. Muhammad Murad, an Egyptian gentleman, had the other office.

They immediately gathered in Mr. Sellier's harbor-view office to meet with the partners and describe the situation. The meeting lasted for two hours.

These lawyers were understanding, sympathetic, and decent men. They had families of their own and seemed to relate personally to the problems Maggie and Lee presented.

As Maggie and Lee told their story, the lawyers seemed to acquire an aura of gladiators ready to battle for them. They really liked these men. They were soon on a first name basis.

Lee believed that the lawyers could picture themselves in their situation and that some part of their generous expenditure of time was due to personal empathy. "Also," he told himself, "Maggie and I were certainly not everyday clients."

149

A battle plan emerged, which hinged on keeping Joe from leaving Bahrain with Allison, if they were still there. They could sue in civil court to force recovery of the child, and for five thousand dinars in damages.

They had never even thought about the possibility of damages. Salah said, "You know, judgments are eminently collectable in Bahrain."

Lee figured that this would amount to over $12,500 U.S.

The legal costs were discussed with some apprehension on the part of the troubled couple. In Miami, lawyers generally require part or all of their payment up front. Their most recent day in court had required an advance payment of one thousand dollars. They hoped that sum would carry them through the end of the case. They'd also paid extra for the certification of their documents.

Mr. Alireza addressed the subject. "Let's see what's going to be involved and then we can decide on a fee. Don't worry about payment now, please."

Muhammad assumed charge of the case. They said goodbye for now to Maurice and Salah and moved to Muhammad's office. They quickly bonded with him.

Muhammad, the Egyptian, was a tall and lean. His speech was surprising because he spoke with the lovely Irish brogue so sweet to the ears of Americans. He seemed about sixty years old, smoked a pipe and had slippers on his feet and a twinkle in his eyes. His commanding presence was very reassuring.

"Several preliminary legal steps are necessary," he told them. "You must apply for visas to extend your seventy-two hour permit. Mr. Alireza must have Power of Attorney in order to represent you in court."

He picked up the file of papers they had brought with them and waved them for emphasis. "Your documents cannot be used here until they're certified by the U.S. Embassy. You must know that it is traditional for the courts to close during the months of July, August and September. But, since it's an emergency, it may be possible to get our case heard. Our work is cut out for us."

Their hearts fell in unison. They glanced at each other each thinking, "What if the court wouldn't hear their case until fall?"

Salah had made some phone calls on their behalf. He walked in and announced. "An informal interview is scheduled with the Minister of Immigration to ask him to issue orders preventing Joe from leaving."

"Very good Salah!" Muhammad beamed, as if addressing a bright student.

In addition to typing the preliminary work, they had to find a place to stay. The hotel could not accommodate them for a second night.

The hotel manager, was a friend of Salah's. He recommended the Shakar Bed and Breakfast as a suitable lodging.

Check-out time was noon and the appointment with the Minister of Immigration was set for four in the afternoon. Maggie was to go without Lee.

Lee called and arranged an appointment with Mr. Howard Unger, Chief U.S. Consul. They had spoken to him in their dark hours on Monday morning. He would see them at noon.

Wednesday, they learned, was an important day in Bahrain. Americans say, "Thank God it's Friday." whereas in the Middle East, the expression is, "Thank God it's Wednesday!" People work only half day on Thursday.

Friday, the Muslim Sabbath, was a day of rest. All government offices and businesses were closed. No one worked. So Thursday and Friday constituted the weekend. Oddly, Saturday and Sunday are regular business days.

If Joe was planning to take Allison to Lebanon, he might do it on a weekend, the Arab weekend of Thursday and Friday, in order to be back to work on Saturday morning.

Life is expensive in Bahrain. They found only two bargains: year-round sunshine, without cost, and taxicabs that cost one dinar to go almost anywhere in the city.

They took a cab to the Embassy. Mr. Unger turned out to be a pleasant man. Thirtyish, looking every inch like a career diplomat. Well dressed, well educated, well spoken, and well traveled, he exuded confidence.

Lee could not help but to admire Mr. Unger and the niche he had carved out for himself. There were flags on either side of his impressive desk and the Great Seal of the United States of America was emblazoned on everything. And the air conditioning was working great! It was one hundred-ten degrees outside.

They brought him up to date and presented their documents for certification.

"Look. As much as I'd like to help you, I can't certify these documents. There is a rather involved procedure to which I'm bound. They must be presented to the Chief Legal Officer of the State of Florida and be certified by him.

The Secretary of State of the United States will recognize his signature and certify the documents. Then, with the U.S. Secretary of State's signature, I can authenticate them to the Foreign Minister of the State of Bahrain, who, in turn, will then certify them for use as evidence in the courts here." He used his hands expressively.

"Do you understand? I hope that the explanation is clear enough." He looked at them earnestly. "I'm sorry, but it will probably take weeks."

The process made sense, but it came as a blow. All of their work to get certified copies of the relevant papers had been wasted.

"Look," said Lee, "this is an emergency. Couldn't you make some telephone calls to accomplish your verification. We'll be more than happy to pay for the calls. These documents are only two days old. The passport office is just across the street from the Dade County Courthouse. You could ask them to go across the street and check on their authenticity.

"No," he said, "I'm required to follow rules." He poured over several loose leaf bound manuals and directives. "I really feel for you. You're in a tough situation but the law is the law and I just can't change it for you."

They spoke at great length about their situation. He agreed to put some seals, stamps and red ribbons and signatures on their papers attesting to the fact that they had been examined at the Embassy of the United States on this day of our Lord, the ninth of July, one Thousand Nine Hundred and Seventy-five in the city of Manama, Bahrain. In other words, Mr. Unger would add to the official appearance of their papers, but he could not make them acceptable if they were challenged in a court of law.

Since that was the best he could do, the offer was accepted. The papers were very impressive when he handed them to Lee. A nice decorating job had been done with the shiny gold seals, ornamental red ribbons and embossed seals on every page.

He readily agreed to letting them use his telephone. They had to call Mr. Gelb at his home in Miami, due to the time difference, to ask him to begin the elaborate certification process on the necessary papers. Mr. Gelb agreed to initiate the process and he also volunteered to call Maggie's father and give him the status report.

A cab was hailed for the return to the hotel to pack and pay the bill. Lee's lost suitcase was at the hotel having been delivered by British Overseas Airlines.

Lee was thinking about how much they had done in the last few days, particularly the airfare to Bahrain. "Thank goodness for credit cards," he said. "You know Maggie, ten years ago we didn't use credit cards. No one used them much then. Boy! Do they ever make it easier to do this. Can you imagine if we needed cash for everything?"

Salah came to take them to their new address. Bab-El-Bahrain Road. There were no street signs or numbers on the buildings in Bahrain. Whenever they took a taxi to their Bed and Breakfast they would ask the driver to take them to the Al Nussar Club which was next door to the Bed and Breakfast. Salah taught them this as they drove from the hotel.

The weather in Bahrain is reputed to be the best in the Gulf. July and August were ferociously hot and the humidity is always high. It almost never rains.

The high humidity is the result of the island's position in the warm sea. They were all perspiring. Salah loosened his tie but did not remove his jacket. It was broiling hot as they labored with their luggage.

"Lee! Put that down." Maggie did not want Lee to carry a suitcase because she feared that his hernia scar would be aggravated. So he put it down.

Salah, Maggie and the house boy carried their bags up to the "first floor." In Bahrain, the floor one flight above the street was called the first floor, as is true in much of the world. The floor at street level was the ground floor.

An Irish lass checked them in to the Bed and Breakfast. She introduced herself as Catherine Griffin. "Now, then. You can stay only until the sixteenth of the month. We've booked the entire house to a wedding party from Saudi Arabia for three days. Saudi Arabia is dry, you see. So Bahrain is where they are allowed to have alcohol, and have their parties." Despite the negative message, her tone and her manner were warm and friendly, and she moved them in with a startling efficiency.

Their bedroom was pink. The coverlet for the double bed was pink and the plush carpet was pink. The room was sparsely furnished with a small bureau and chair. Neither Maggie or Lee had ever slept in a pension or boarding house. They'd have something to talk about at home.

There was no time to tarry. Maggie had an appointment with the Immigration official. So they climbed into the car and were off again. Salah said, "Do you know that the girl tried to give me three dinars?

"Really? What for?" said Maggie.

"Well I could not keep the money, naturally. But she thought that I was a taxi driver and that seems to be the usual finder's fee for a new tenant. I told her that I am an attorney and she went into shock. Apparently it's an illegal practice to pay such a fee. She was afraid that I would report her." He chuckled at her error.

They were driving again through the exotic back streets of the city. The strangely dressed throngs of pedestrians and the brilliant sunlight made it seem more like a movie set.

Salah was thoughtful. "You know, this Bed and Breakfast business must be very lucrative. My family owns several properties and I suspect that we could do better by converting them until this hotel shortage straightens out."

"How interesting." Lee said. "What would an ordinary apartment rent be?"

"Well," replied Salah in his slow and thoughtful way, "we get about one thousand dinars a month. They're getting four hundred and fifty dinars per room per month."

Lee was impressed. "Let's see. That would be two thousand five hundred dollars a month in American currency for an apartment."

He seemed to be embarrassed by Lee's comment. "Yes. That's true. But, you see, most of our tenants are expatriates, and their employers pay the rent as a part of their compensation."

"Oh, I see. I suppose that salaries are very high here. We find that everything here is more expensive than in Miami." Lee wondered about Joe's resources.

"That girl seemed very efficient," Salah remarked, back on the subject of business. They discussed the Bed and Breakfast business potential all the way back to the office.

Maggie's interview was very businesslike and official. Salah accompanied her and Lee remained in the office, reading the new bestseller, *All the President's Men*.

The report to Lee, later, was that the Minister was sympathetic. Maggie said that she had broken down and cried. The recital of the events was just too much for her. While Joe could not be arrested and Allison returned to them by police action, the Minister had said he would issue an order for Joe and Allison to be denied the right to leave Bahrain, pending judicial confirmation, which Salah promised for Thursday morning.

"Lee, the problem is that I am going to have to give them my passport. The idea is that none of us can leave the country until the authorities have a chance to evaluate the details. Oh Lee. I'm so scared."

Maggie said that she'd gotten a lecture on law from the official. He looked very serious when he said, in excellent English, "This action somewhat exceeds my authority. I could not justify it under ordinary circumstances. You must not depend on me for more than one day. We are a nation of laws and we cannot run our affairs by administrative edict. But I am sorry to hear about your troubles, and I pray that it will all be resolved in a just manner."

"Hurrah!" Maggie thought. They were promised that Joe and Allison could not leave. "Our first victory."

The Minister had been troubled by one thing. "There is no record of Allison's entry into Bahrain. Are you sure that she is here?"

Maggie explained the nature of her confirmation telephone conversation with a secretary. "Yes, I'm certain that she was here on Monday. I only hope that he hasn't taken her out again."

Back at Alireza and Associates, they discussed the interview while signing a blur of papers; all were written in Arabic, typed by Jacob on a modern electric machine that typed from right to left. Jacob was more than a typist clerk. Always dressed in crisp, clean white robes, with a nicely knotted camel hobble holding his headdress in place, he seemed to be an expert on Bahraini legal administration.

They were invited to make themselves at home in the office and to stay for the afternoon; although it was a better prospect for the moment than facing the heat outside, but they were anxious to go to their new quarters.

Bahrain did not operate on a nine-to five basis. Business hours were from eight in the morning till seven in the evening. But everything stopped in the heat of the day. Shops, offices and banks closed down from eleven-thirty until four. Despite having the best climate in the Gulf, it was just too hot to work then. Workers go home for lunch, to nap, and to change clothing.

They had used their siesta time for business, so they now returned to their B and B. They were exhausted by the time they crawled into bed. They awoke at seven p.m. refreshed and hungry.

"Life is so funny," thought Lee. "Despite their emotional problems, needs for food and rest, the ordinary pedestrian aspects of life continued." With nothing constructive to do, both looked forward to dining out and retiring early.

They went to the reception desk, just twenty feet from their room door, to ask for a recommendation on restaurants. They met another young woman at the desk, sitting with Catherine. She was introduced as Margaret. She, too, had an accent, but slightly different from Catherine's. She was from England.

Margaret recommended, "...Keith's Restaurant. It's just around the corner. People like it very much."

"How can we get a cab at this time of night? Is it possible to telephone for a taxi?"

"Oh, no! You can walk. It's very close."

"I see. But we're new here and we don't know our way around. Is it safe to walk?"

"Oh, for sure. You'll not have any problems with that. This is a very safe place. The police are very strict."

The Shakar pension was on unpaved Bab-El-Bahrain Street. The street was lined with rather shabby homes and apartment buildings, two or three stories high.

There was a "cold store" at either end of the street. These were small neighborhood shops where people can get cold sodas and canned goods and a variety of domestic necessities...a Middle Eastern version of a Seven-Eleven convenience store. It seemed to be a depressed neighborhood by American standards. It was dark out. For all they knew, the streets were filled with muggers. They explained their fears and asked the two girls to help them find a cab.

"It's so close. I hate to see you spend your money on a cab," said Catherine. "The streets really are safe. You won't be bothered."

Even so, Lee was only half persuaded that it might be all right. The two young girls were so sure that it was safe. But Maggie had doubts which showed on her face.

Margaret took pity on them, "Look. Our car's right out front. I'll drive you."

They protested that they didn't want to be a bother, but she prevailed and gave them a ride. It was an embarrassingly short ride. The restaurant was really very close. She convinced them that it was safe for them to walk back to the house.

"You'll never have any problems here. I've lived here for over a year and I can go anywhere, at any time of the day or night. There is virtually no crime." She elaborated. "The worst thing I've seen here is an occasional rat or two. You'll be fine."

The restaurant was charming, old world, candlelit, and decorated in Provincial style. Lee had lamb stew on a bed of rice and Maggie had steak. The food was good but not outstanding. They paid cash and trudged home, on the lookout for rats. And Joe. There was no sign of either. The streets were empty. All was calm and the evening was pleasantly warm.

Every moment brought new surprises. Back at the pension, they learned that the antique bathroom was not supplied with potable water. The water was salty. Not sea water, perhaps, but close. Margaret supplied bottles of water.

Water is short in Bahrain, and is conserved in many ways. At Shakar's there is no spray head shower, drain plug or curtain on the tub. You are forced to take a sit down 'spritz' kind of bath. It felt good anyway. They neither needed, nor were they provided hot water. The single supply, warmed by the daily temperature, was tepid.

The bedroom was warm, but they slept very well despite their feelings that the next day might be difficult. The enemy would have to be confronted. It was deadly serious. They had feelings of dread that they could scarcely express.

CHAPTER 9 - DECEPTION

JULY 10, 1975 – SEVEN A.M.

Maggie woke Lee early. She seemed frantic, crying a little as she shook him. "Wake up Lee!" she shook him again.

Lee groaned, "Why so early?"

"Lee. We've got to get going!"

"But Maggie. There's no way we can do anything until the office opens. Are you hungry?"

"No, honey. I'm too upset to eat. How about you?" She looked worn and sad.

"I'm not hungry either," Lee lied. "Why don't we go see what breakfast is like anyway. Just to pass the time."

Thursday was bright and clear as Maggie and Lee contended with Shakar's slow flowing and salty plumbing.

Lee led the way up as they climbed a flight of stairs to find a plain but cheerful room which contained three round tables, each of which might seat six people. Sunlight streamed through the windows and sparkled on the china and silver. The white tablecloths looked fresh and clean.

"Good morning."

"Good morning." They exchanged greetings with two men at the corner table. They were dressed in work clothing. Their skins were sun scorched. There were no other occupants.

They sat at the window table overlooking the street and the roofs of the houses across the way. The lovely aroma of frying bacon aroused their appetites despite their unhappy situation.

Margaret was both cooking and serving. She spoke to them through the kitchen door. "Hi. Coffee or tea?"

They opted for coffee. "What's for breakfast?"

"Oh. Anything your hearts desire. How about boiled eggs?" She was cheerful and brisk. The work seemed to please her.

"Yes, please. Bacon, toast, juice and jelly too."

They chatted with her as she passed in and out. "Are you here on business or are you tourists?" She poured coffee from a silver pot and left it on the table for seconds.

This was a loaded question. Joe could be living next door for all they knew. Discretion seemed to be called for.

"We're here on family business." Lee said this rather formally and stiffly and turned to Maggie, hoping to preclude further questions. "Coffee is good, huh?"

"Yes. It tastes like Colombian." Maggie understood perfectly.

"Excuse me." Margaret returned to the kitchen to tend to her cooking. Their strategy had worked for now. No further questions were asked about their business. Lee was a little embarrassed. He did not want to offend her.

The house boy, whose name was Abdul, made his appearance. Smiles and nods were exchanged as he presented a platter of toast and jams. Margaret followed with beautiful plates of eggs and bacon. Sweet orange juice flowed and their moods lightened.

The food was excellent.

"Thanks for a great breakfast Margaret," Maggie smiled and asked, "Now. How can we get a taxi? We need to go downtown. Near the Arab Bank."

"That's easy. You can find one on almost any corner. Abdul will get one for you when you're ready. Can I get you anything else? More toast?"

"No thanks. That was just enough." Lee said and Maggie nodded her head in agreement.

The cab appeared when summoned. The hot air blasted them as they stepped away from their Bed and Breakfast entrance. The outside air was slated to be broiling hot every day until December when the winter weather arrived.

"Lee. Look." She pointed at her skirt. "Can you see through?"

Lee studied the matter, discerning the outline of her legs as she stood in the strong sunlight. Maggie's white shoes gleamed in contrast to the packed dirt of the street.

"Yes. A little. It doesn't look too bad though. I think you might get by." Lee saw her point. Flashing legs wouldn't do at all here.

"You see how the women cover up in this country. I think that I'll need a slip and I don't have one. Otherwise people may stare and think that I'm a loose woman."

Two women passed, covered in black burkahs, glancing at Maggie. Their light burkahs billowed around. Each held one handle of a large market-basket.

"Perhaps there'll be a shop near the office. You can ask when we get there."

"Okay," she said. "But I'll need it before we go to court."

Mohammad was seated at his desk. He rose at first sight of the Elres' and said, "Good morning." with a broad smile. "And how did you pass the night?" His brogue pleased Lee's ear.

"Fine," they chorussed. "Thank you."

Maggie gave him a worried look. "And how are you feeling Muhammad."

"Very, very well," he said rolling his rrr's. "Is your hotel comfortable?"

"It's a bed and breakfast." She corrected. "It's not quite like the Gulf Hotel, but it's okay. It's nice and clean."

Lee chimed in. "The breakfast was first rate."

"Ah. I'm glad. Let us have a cup of coffee." He rang for the office secretary and placed the order.

"We have some work for you this morning. First, we must send you to the Ministry of Justice to record your Power of Attorney so that we can represent you in court. You must go now with Jacob and get this done. After that, our appointment in court is for eleven o'clock."

He looked at his wrist watch. "It's now five after nine. So there's not much time."

The troubled couple began to rise to leave but Muhammad stopped them with a wave of his hand, "I forgot. Here comes your coffee. Have some coffee first and then you can attend to business." He said this very kindly, as if he wished to please and make the Americans feel at home.

"Jacob!" Muhammad stood and waited.

Jacob hurried in. "Yes sir?"

"Jacob. As soon as Mr. and Mrs. Elres finish their coffee, go straight away with them to have their Powers of Attorney recorded."

Muhammad turned to Maggie and Lee. "Now. Tell me. Did you go to the Embassy yesterday?"

He paced the office as they filled him in. "...so we have asked Mr. Gelb, our Miami attorney, to get copies of the court orders legalized in the ways that Mr. Unger suggested. He promised to do so."

Muhammad was annoyed. "It is a shame that the Embassy won't help you."

Maggie agreed but Lee, as usual, defended the system that was frustrating them. "Well, you must understand. He has rules to follow. As far as I'm concerned, the rules make sense. And it is impossible to make regulations that cover every conceivable case. So I understand his position. Don't forget, he did put lots of stamps, ribbons and seals on the damn things."

"Lee. You're too kind. Mr. Unger could have been more helpful." Maggie was riled.

Mohammad made a face indicating that he thought that they should have tried harder.

Feeling the pressure of time, their coffee was gulped down.

Jacob seemed a very pleasant and able man. Among his abilities was a knack for somehow keeping his shoes shined and his brow free from perspiration while walking very rapidly through the dusty and hot streets of Manama. He had the speed of a New Yorker.

"Boy, does he walk fast," Maggie muttered between clenched teeth, struggling to keep up.

Lee agreed; tall and long-legged, he was accustomed to outpacing his friends. But that day, in that heat and with his hernia incision aching, he too worked hard to keep up.

The two-story government building was old and faded. It conformed to the image of a British Colonial structure. Uniformed police, robed citizens, employees and officials milled around in large numbers.

They made their way through a series of air conditioned offices as Jacob obtained directions to the proper officials.

They sat, finally, in a small and crowded room. Jacob negotiated in Arabic with an official at an old, battered desk.

The room, about fifteen by fifteen feet, was jammed with men. Maggie was the only woman.

Some of them sat quietly and talked. Others fingered worry beads; a ritual observed wherever Arabs waited. After a short wait they were invited to sign some official looking documents. The writing was utterly incomprehensible to the

Americans but they trusted that they were indeed Powers of Attorney papers.

They took off again, walking rapidly through alleys, squares and streets lined with shabby stores and stalls.

"Jacob. Please could we go a little slower?" Maggie was falling behind.

"Lee. Tell him about my slip. I'd feel so much better if I didn't feel so exposed. Those men must be staring at me."

Maggie was looking at women passing on the broiling street. They were covered from head to toe with black burkahs. Their eyes and hands were barely visible. Even those innocent features protected from the eyes of the men. Masks and veils made it seem to be an eerie 'other-world.'

"Jacob, Maggie needs to buy a slip. Is there a lingerie shop on the way back to the office? It will only take a moment."

His smooth young face showed concern. "Certainly sir. No problem at all. We must hurry though." He led the way to a general merchandise shop that displayed women's clothing in the window.

Maggie went upstairs with the proprietor while Jacob and Lee browsed through general merchandise on the first floor, closely attended by a solicitous clerk.

Maggie soon returned looking more relaxed.

"Everything all right?" Lee asked.

"Swell. I'm wearing it and it's fine. I took the cheapest one. It cost eight dinars." She seemed abashed at spending so much. She was worried about money. At home she would not have cared about the price and Lee would have never noticed.

Lee squeezed her hand to let her know that he didn't care.

Mohammad was waiting for them at the office. "Have you finished, then?"

"Yes sir." Jacob answered for them all.

"Salah." Mohammad called. Salah appeared at the door to his office.

"You must go straight-away to the court. Now with Madam Maggie." He handed Salah a folder containing the case files. "Do you have it all clear?"

"Certainly," said Salah with a hint of reproach in his voice, somewhat like a schoolboy might have answered when questioned about a completed homework assignment. "I know what to do."

"That's fine my boy! Good luck."

The clock on the wall said ten a.m.

Maggie and Salah moved to leave. Salah looked confident, a white knight in a fresh suit with Truth and Justice on his side.

Maggie, a little warmer but more confident in her new slip was not so confident of the outcomes that might arise in these foreign courts.

"Bye Dear." Lee kissed Maggie's cheek and gave her a one armed shoulder hug. "Give 'em hell!"

Lee felt a little depressed as he settled in to await their return. He couldn't think of one useful thing he could do at this point except cool his heels. He wished that he could go hold Maggie's hand but, with no standing in the matter he could not even attend the court session.

Salah and Muhammad had patiently explained that only Maggie had a formal grievance against Ali's father. Lee's relationship to Maggie, and strong feelings, counted for nothing.

Lee read and drank coffee in a corner of the outer office. He did not have a clue about how long the wait would be. Thirty minutes or five hours.

Lee continued reading his book, *All The President's Men*. He wished for a 'deep throat' in Joe's orbit to let them know what he was up to.

Maggie and Salah walked to court, some six blocks away. They entered through a rough wooden door built into a twelve-foot high, whitewashed wall. Beyond the door was a courtyard with a hard-packed and rather uneven earth floor.

"Is this the court?" asked Maggie brightly, inwardly quailing at the thought of being cross examined under a broiling sun in a language she couldn't understand, by men who would look upon her as an infidel, as well as an inferior female. She was intimidated by the fact that there were dozens of men milling about in the courtroom and because she was the only woman. Her head and arms were exposed and that was probably not acceptable here.

"Over here," said Salah, leading her to a doorway. He saw and greeted several men in robes, Arabic robes she guessed, not judicial. The courtroom looked like any middle American court built in the nineteenth century, except for the hum of a laboring through-the-wall air conditioning unit. It was stuffy inside but broiling outdoors with high humidity.

The lighting was dim; natural light entered through skylight windows high overhead. Maggie felt ill, probably from nervousness. Joe was not there. Joe had not been expected to appear, but she nonetheless was worried.

"We must wait for our turn," said Salah. "It won't take long."

They sat on pew-like wooden benches, arranged in rows. Soon, in response to some sign not perceived by Maggie, Salah said, "Let's go." He led her forward to stand before the bench but when she tried to follow him through the gate in the waist-high barrier wall, he said, "Sorry Maggie. You must wait on this side of the wall and do not speak to the judges directly."

Maggie groaned inwardly. She desperately wanted to tell her story.

His address to the three judges was in Arabic. He presented papers and lengthy interchanges ensued. Occasionally he asked Maggie questions and relayed her answers to the judges. "Is Joe a citizen of the United States?"

She explained his dual citizenship.

"You are divorced? What date?"

"January, 1974."

"What is your father's name?"

"Alfredo Alvarez."

"Where was he born?"

"Havana, Cuba." Silly questions, she thought, not related to the problem.

"Salah. Why can't Joe be brought in here and forced to give me my child?" whispered Maggie.

"Not now," pleaded Salah. "Be patient. Just answer their questions."

"Where were you born?"

"Havana, Cuba." Sigh.

The use of a language she did not understand drove Maggie wild. She strained to glean some understanding of the proceedings. Later, she told Lee, "Now I know how Americans feel when they don't understand Spanish in Miami," she said. "I've never been in that position before. It's frustrating!"

For Lee, now a loyal and happy citizen of Cuban-infused Miami, the language problem was a common occurrence. He shrugged it off. His Spanish was limited, and he was often at a disadvantage in the bilingual city.

Soon it was over and there was another walk for Maggie, back to the office. As they sat down in Muhammad's office, he bombarded them with questions. Salah gave his report, "Well, the court has issued an order instructing the Ministry of Immigration to prevent Mr. Zayyat and Allison from leaving the country. He will have to appear at court for a hearing. It went very well. The hearing will be on the thirteenth."

"The thirteenth! That's three days from now!" Lee protested. "We have to get this over with!"

"No. Don't be concerned." Said Muhammad. "It's fine. Just what I expected. Never fear. If she's here, you'll get her back." The time delay did not seem to surprise or upset him.

Maggie fretted, pacing back and forth, waving her arms in agitation. "Lee. We have to do something. I can't just sit and wait. Now he's going to find out that we're here. He'll get on a boat and disappear. He works with boats and ships and will know lots of captains and owners. I know him. He has no respect for court orders. Do you think I should call him again?"

Lee considered. "He'll know you're here if you call. So what's the point?"

"No. I'll pretend to be calling from the U.S. I've listened to so many of those calls that I think that I can fool him." Lee agreed, somewhat concerned about the wisdom of the ploy.

It was almost noon. Muhammad was told of the plan. He said, "Go ahead. Use Salah's office. It will give you more privacy." Maggie and Lee entered the room and Mohammad stood outside in the doorway.

The thin Bahraini telephone directory yielded a number for Otis Engineering. Maggie dialed. Her hands trembled and her mouth quivered.

Lee too was emotional and worried. Questions and images flashed through his mind. Good move or bad? Facing a tiger.

Maggie held her nose, and in a high and nasal voice said, "Hello. Bahrain, this is the United States calling for Mr. Joseph Zayyat." Lo and behold! Joe was called to the phone and Maggie began to speak in her normal voice. Fiercely, "Joe, where is Ali?" She motioned to Lee, indicating that he should share the instrument's earpiece and listen.

He was cold and distant. "Why are you bothering me again? I told you not to call."

"Joe, please tell me where she is!" This plea was uttered in a prayerful tone—not at all demanding. "I must know that she's all right." Tears began to flow.

"Look. She's all right. I'm taking care of her. You have what you want. You wanted to divorce me. I'm her father and she needs me. So don't come crying to me. Ali was very happy to go with me. I'm her father and I have a right to be with her."

"Please, Joe." Maggie was sobbing now. "Can't I just hear her voice? She needs me too. I'm her mother. Why are you doing this to me. You're going to hurt Ali."

"I'm not doing anything. Everything is all right. Don't you know anything?"

"Joe, I just want to talk to her. I want to hear her voice. How can you be so cruel? She'll think I've abandoned her."

The conversation grew more and more emotional. Maggie wept openly. Joe's voice was strong and clear to Lee as he sat close to the telephone.

Joe was cynical, superior, scornful, bitter. This was not the charming Joe who had asked Maggie to allow him to take Ali to Disney World. The conversation was taking its toll on both parties as emotional levels rose.

Lee scribbled notes to Maggie, desperate to keep the conversation going. 'SCHOOL. WHERE?'

"Joe, she has to go to school. She can't be put in a convent again." (There was no school in summer, but she didn't think of that.)

"She's fine. Don't worry about her. You have Lee to worry about."

"WHERE IS SHE? Joe, just tell me where she is! Is she in Bahrain?" Maggie was yelling.

"NO!" Joe shouted back.

"Please. Is she okay? Where is she? Who's she with?"

"She's not here."

"Then where is she?"

Silence from Joe's end. The conversation must have been getting tiresome for him.

"Is she in Beirut with your brother, Wadi?"

"No."

175

"Then, for God's sake, where is she?" Her voice was unnaturally high. "Can't you please let me know? I'm going crazy with worry. Who's taking care of her?"

"She's in the mountains with my family."

"In Bkassine?"

"Yes."

"Then I'm going there now to see her. Joe, please tell me I can. I'll do anything."

Lee was thinking with pride, "Maggie's emotions are always close to the surface. She can be terribly intense. When she's happy, she bubbles over and her laughter is infectious. When she's angry, she makes the earth seem to tremble and plaster walls turn to powder. When she's blue, her sighs rend the air and tears stain the carpet. And what a great act she was performing. No wonder I love her so."

Joe bore the full brunt of her emotional energy. Lee thought that Joe must have had an image of Maggie descending on his mother, because he changed his story.

"Look, stupid," he hissed. "She's just in Louisiana! You don't understand anything. She didn't <u>want</u> to go home to you! So don't make an ass of yourself by coming out here. She is well taken care of."

"Oh, Joe," she wailed. "Where in God's name is she? First you said that you were taking care of her. Then you said your family was taking care of her. Now she's in Louisiana. Who is taking care of her? Where? For God's sake, where is she?" Joe seemed now to be anxious to end the call.

"Look. I don't have anymore time to talk to you. I have to go to work."

"Joe. Please! Please! Please!"

"NO! I don't have to put up with this. I can't take these calls here. I'll tell you when I'm good and ready!"

"Joe! You're not telling me the truth. Is she in Louisiana? Please tell me where she is. I want to call her. I'll go there."

Joe hung up suddenly. Most of the staff had gone to lunch. He would make sure no other calls from Maggie got transferred to him. The rest of the staff made themselves scarce but his boss Ben Smith was still in his office. Joe was sure he heard him shouting at Maggie so he decided to step into the office and clear the air.

"Ben, I'm not taking any more calls from my ex. She'll get tired of calling and eventually leave me alone."

"Joe, this situation sounds like it could get out of hand. We're in a foreign country, the company cannot afford an International incident. If any of our employees break the law here in Bahrain we answer for it with the state department and the Bahraini government. Have you broken the law Joe? Did you take your daughter without permission? No, don't answer that. I'm not getting involved in any of this. Make sure that the company is not involved. We don't need that kind of trouble here."

Joe walked back to his desk in silence. He had to finish the work he started before Maggie's phone call, then he would go home for lunch to see Ali.

They sat and recovered a little.

"Maggie." Lee said. "That was brilliant! But where is she?" Lee wondered aloud. "Is she here? What can we do as a follow up to a phone call that emotional? Do we have to wait for the courts to settle our business?"

They looked forlornly at each other. Lee put his arms around Maggie and tried to soothe her. They thought for a moment, desperately trying to find the next line of attack.

"How about talking to his boss?" Lee asked.

"What good would that do?" Maggie moaned and covered her face with her hands.

"I don't know." said Lee. "But I can't think of anything else to do. Let's put his boss on notice. Tell him about the situation and ask for help."

They asked Muhammad for his opinion. He was standing in the doorway listening. "Why, certainly. It can't hurt. Do you know his name?"

They did not. Maggie went through her nose-holding, international telephone operator routine again. Lee sat by her side and listened.

"This is the United States calling Bahrain for the president of Otis Engineering." Her voice sounded ridiculously phony to Lee and herself.

"The manager is Mr. Smith. Do you wish to speak with him?" asked the secretary in a lightly accented voice. This was the same girl Maggie had spoken to on <u>three</u> previous occasions. Would she see through Maggie's disguise?

Maggie paused. To give the impression that she was conferring with the overseas caller. "Yes, my party will speak with Mr. Smith." She said this in an even more nasal voice.

"Just a moment, please."

Mr. Smith came to the phone. "Hello?"

"Sir. My name is Maggie. Joseph Zayyat is my ex-husband. He's kidnapped my five-year-old daughter Allison. I must know where she is and who's taking care of her. Could you please tell me if she's in Bahrain?"

Mr. Smith replied gently. "I see, but I'm afraid I can't help you. Joseph's here. Why don't you speak with him?" This was a reasonable response to the situation. He sounded concerned though.

Maggie cried again. Her tears must have been obvious even through the telephone wire. "Please, sir. He won't talk to me. He won't tell me where she is. I just want to know if you've seen her. I have to know if she's okay."

"Just a moment," he said, "hold on."

"Joe," she heard him say away from his mouthpiece, "I can't do this to this woman." We couldn't hear Joe's reply.

Then to Maggie, "Yes, she's here. I saw her yesterday. And she's fine."

"Thank you. Oh, thank God! She's all right. Where is she staying?"

"She's here with Joe. In Bahrain."

"Yes. But where in Bahrain?"

"Why do you want to know?"

"Look. Please. For God's sake, she's my daughter. He told me today, just five minutes ago, that she's in Lebanon. Then he told me that she's in Louisiana. I have to be sure. Where is she staying? Is it all right there?"

He said the magic words. Maggie grabbed a pencil and wrote, "Zapata Offshore Drilling Apartment."

"Oh, God! She's all right! Thank you so very much. I feel so much better but where is the Zapata Apartment? Is it a nice place?" She was pressing the earpiece to her head and I could not hear. She wrote the words 'Gold Souk'.

"Oh, thank you. Is she there now at the apartment? Who's taking care of her? Is she okay? Did she look okay?" Maggie continued to bombard him with questions.

Mr. Smith was talking to Joe again, "Look, Joe. I had to tell her. She's the kid's mother and she has a right to know." Back to Maggie. "Look, ma'am, she's all right. I did see her and I'm sure that Joe will take care of her and call you to straighten this out. Okay?"

"Yes, sir. Thank you very much. You have done me a real service. I just needed to know the truth. I can't bear to be away from her. God bless you! Goodbye." She hung up.

"Lee. She's here! Let's go get her!" A new energy possessed her. She was on her feet, gathered up her purse and headed for the door. Lee followed.

"Muhammad! Where is the Gold Souk?

"Jacob will show you. Did you find her? Is she all right?"

"Yes. Mr. Smith said that he lives in the Zapata Offshore Oil Apartment house in the Gold Souk. We know she's here. We'd like to try to see her. Could we go now?"

"Yes, of course. Straight-away. Jacob will show you."

The three of them rushed out of the office. Maggie in the lead, walking fast, almost running...

Lee and Jacob now struggled to keep up with her.

CHAPTER 10 - IN THE SOUK

THURSDAY, JULY 10, 1975,- twelve-fifteen p.m.

Maggie was hyperventilating. She felt that she could not breathe but kept moving anyway, driven by her need to find Ali. Jacob took the lead when they reached the street. His white robes billowed out behind him as he sped along. Maggie followed, striving to keep up.

Lee brought up the rear. He was lugging his briefcase thinking, "I hope Joe's not there because I couldn't lick a cream puff with my hernia operation still hurting." He had brought the briefcase to use as a club. Later, it seemed ridiculous to him. His "violent American" was rampant.

They outpaced all traffic, even the slow moving cars and trucks, which were seriously hindered by the narrowness of the streets. No one else hurried in the noon heat. They walked unpaved back alleys, used the side streets, and frequently changed direction as Jacob sought out the fastest route.

People in the busy street paused to gawk at their scurrying procession.

They came to the Gold Souk in about five minutes. It was a maze of even narrower streets and alleys, completely unmarked by street signs. Awnings were rigged in front of many shops as a sunshade.

The heat was intensified because there was enormous congestion and no open space for the wind to blow. The humidity was high as always. Strange odors, noise and heat hit them. Even unflappable Jacob perspired.

They moved slowly in the crowded souk. Jacob said, "I'm not so familiar with the streets here."

Still, they moved quickly enough to attract attention. Picture any movie of a Middle Eastern native bazaar. Pan the camera right. Enter two Americans, overdressed, following an Arab pellmell through the crowd. First Jacob, then Maggie, then Lee. They were all in a line. Everyone took notice of the passage.

Maggie gasped over her shoulder. "God. What if Joe's there?"

"Keep moving," Lee prodded. "Even if he's going home for lunch, we may beat him." They had no idea of the distance between his work and home, but it was time for the midday break.

They tried to examine every face and every automobile for a sign of Joe, his face or a company name on the side of a car. They walked purposefully along a narrow street.

Jacob slowed down and then began to backtrack. He looked puzzled. "I do not know the building. It should be nearby." They were now at the edge of the souk. The streets were a little wider and there were scattered residences and apartment buildings. The area looked a little seedy.

Lee spotted a small sign on a four-story building a block away. "There it is!"

The Zapata Offshore Drilling Company's apartment house was taller than its neighbors. The entry hall was dirty and the dingy, dark stairway was steep.

The first apartment was at the second story level. Maggie knocked, but there was no answer. She then banged on the door. A door on the landing above them opened and they ascended the steep stairway to encounter a balding, unshaven Englishman in his undershirt. He had opened his door when he heard the knocking below. "No one's home down there." He offered, in English.

"I'm looking for a little girl about five years old. Black hair. Her name is Allison." said Maggie. They walked to the man's door. Maggie boldly peered around him into his apartment. She was looking inside for signs of Ali. The room was trashy.

"Not here," he said, looking at them nervously. "I think she lives upstairs."

"What floor?" Lee said.

"Third floor," said the half-dressed man.

"Damn it! THIS IS THE THIRD FLOOR!" Maggie vehemently protested, more upset than ever at the thought of being near her daughter but not seeing her.

The man was startled by the outburst and ducked back into his apartment, slamming the door. The apartment interior she'd just glimpsed was shabby. There was no carpet and it was poorly furnished.

Then Lee remembered the European system. "The first floor was the floor above the street level," he said "We're only on the second floor."

"Upstairs," Lee commanded and they tromped, in a line, up to the top floor. Maggie, then Lee, and then Jacob, who was now following hesitantly.

Another floor, another door, and Maggie knocked again.

"Who is it?" Ali's voice!

"It's Mommy, Ali. Open the door." Maggie's voice was calm and low, just above a whisper.

Two latches snapped, the door opened, and there she was! She wore a light cotton play suit; just shorts and a top. Maggie had bought them new just a week ago for her trip to Disney world. No shoes. The apartment looked cluttered and dirty.

Maggie stooped and opened her arms. Ali leaped into her embrace and a wide toothless grin engulfed her face as Maggie murmured, "Oh, my baby. It's so good to see you." She quickly picked Ali up and began running. All done in a single sweeping motion. Lee let her pass to take up a position as rear guard.

Within a few seconds of the knock on Joe's door, they were pounding down the stairs. Jacob in front now.

A young sounding, female, American voice faded as they descended. "Ali. Who is it? Ali? ALI!"

The rescuers flew down the stairs and into the street. By the time they were a block away, they noted a young woman in pursuit. She was perhaps twenty years old. She frantically shouted after them, "Ali, is that your mother?"

Ali looked back over her mother's shoulder and called out, "Sherry, it's my Mommy. This is my Mommy!" Her face looked happy and excited to Lee who was just a step behind.

Maggie stopped and turned back toward the girl, her face contorted with rage. Lee tried to turn her away to continue their flight but Maggie resisted and shouted, "Damn you! This is my daughter and you'd better go back where you came from!"

Ali again shouted gleefully, "Sherry. This is my Mommy!" There was a big, gap toothed grin pasted on her tiny face.

Sherry gave up and turned back but they continued to race on as though the Hounds of Hell were on their trail. Their youthful pursuer turned and went back toward the apartment house.

A car slowly overtook them, creeping through the foot traffic. Jacob spoke to the Arab driver. They were being offered a ride!

The air-conditioned Mercedes was cool and quiet. The soft leather seats spoke of craftsmanship and luxury. There was no baby sitter and no Joe.

"Mag, I'm sure that there's no one chasing us," Lee offered reassuringly. But their agitation was as great as ever.

"Jacob. Ask him to take us to the American Embassy!" Lee said.

"Sir. He is taking us to my car. I'll drive you to the Embassy. It's on the way."

"Jacob, this is an emergency. Tell him that we'd be very happy to pay him." The white bearded driver smiled back at Lee but apparently he spoke no English.

"It is not necessary to pay him," said Jacob. "He said he'd be glad to take you anywhere you want to go. But my car is parked near the office and there is no problem. Don't worry. No one will harm you here."

Maggie and Lee were overwrought. She hugged and kissed Ali, crooning, "My baby. My baby. How are you? Were you worried that Mommy wasn't coming? I'm so glad to see you." Lee reached forward from the back seat to stroke Ali's hair and pinch her cheek.

"Mommy."

"Yes, my darling." Ali was planted on Maggie's lap.

"Daddy Joe said that we would go home on Monday, but when Monday came he didn't take me. Sherry and Daddy had a fight about that."

"Was that Sherry we saw in the street?"

"Yes, Mommy. I got lost in the souk and nobody would talk to me."

"Today?"

"No it was the other day. Daddy came in the car and found me. I was crying."

"It's okay honey. Don't worry about that now."

While Maggie and Ali talked, Lee pressed Jacob, trying to create a sense of urgency. He had visions of Joe storming after them, cutthroats in tow, to overpower them and take Ali away by force. He held out a roll of currency and said, "Jacob, please tell the man that he has performed an extraordinary kindness, and I'd like to show my appreciation." Jacob seemed disturbed by Lee's crassness.

"Please put your money away. He did not give us a ride for the money. He wished to do us a favor. He is happy to do it."

"Of course," Lee said, "But perhaps he would accept my watch as a gift." He took it off and held it up to the front seat. It was a silly, even rude gesture, but heartfelt.

Looking back, even years later, Lee recognized that this was one of the more emotional moments of his life and he can excuse himself. The driver, he thought, had saved them. He wanted, somehow, to communicate deep thanks. The watch was refused. He believed, and Maggie swears to it too, that even Jacob was embarrassed.

They soon came to Jacob's parking lot and proceeded to the embassy in Jacob's little car. It was a European-made vehicle and the air conditioner worked brilliantly.

They never saw the other driver again.

Ali continued to volunteer information and to answer questions.

She explained "Daddy and I went in the airplane to pick up Sherry. She was in Tampa. We saw Tio Wadi in Beirut, and then we came here. Daddy and Sherry slept in the bed and I slept on the couch. They had a lot of fights. She doesn't like it here!"

Her five-year old mind's sense of time was confusing. She could not relate the details of the story sufficiently well for them to fully understand Joe's future plans.

Now Maggie wondered aloud, "Does he intend to live here permanently?"

"Daddy promised me we'd go home on Monday. It's not my fault. Don't be mad."

"Of course not, sweetheart. Are you sure that you saw Tio Wadi?

"Yes, Mommy. He was at the airport."

"Did Daddy use your Lebanese passport?" Maggie showed Ali her American passport to demonstrate what she meant.

Ali took the passport and looked at her picture for a moment. "Mommy, Daddy Joe told the man at the airport to pretend that my picture was on this thing."

"Are you sure?"

"Yes, Mommy."

"So that's why the Minister of Immigration could find no record of Ali entering the country. That's Joe at his best," said Maggie.

Joe was walking to his car when he heard one of the secretaries call his name. "Joe there's an urgent phone call for you."

"I told all of you I didn't want to take any more calls from my ex."

"It's not from the states, it's local. The woman sounds frantic."

Joe came back to the office and picked up the phone.

"Joe, it's Sherry, I'm sorry I didn't know what to do, she's gone."

"Who's gone? Is Ali lost in the souk again?"

"No, no, Ali's mother was here with two men and she took Ali."

"Sherry stop this, Ali's mother is in the states, I talked to her just a half hour ago. What are you stupid?"

"Joe listen to me, Ali's mother has her. I ran after them to see who Allison went with and Ali shouted at me that it was her Mommy."

Joe was shocked. "It can't be Sherry…that bitch! That fucking bitch!!!"

"Joe, I'm sorry I was in the kitchen, I've told Ali never to answer the door. By the time I heard the locks open it was too late. They ran out of here with Ali, I didn't know what to do."

"Sherry, you stupid damn whore, I told you not to leave Ali alone for a minute. You've just ruined my life, you bitch."

"Joe let's go home. I don't like this place, you told me we would be here for a short time."

"There's no more us Sherry. Your ass will be on plane tonight. I don't need you any more."

Joe heard her cries as she was hanging up.

"God damn that woman, why didn't she just stay home and forget about Allison. She's always causing me problems!"

Joe looked around, the office was empty.

Some thirty minutes after Allison's recovery, Jacob's little auto approached the U.S. Embassy.

"Jacob. Can you park in the back so that we can go in without being seen?"

"Yes, sir." He parked in the rear of the well-kept building. Since it was after noon on Thursday, the day before the

Islamic holy day, Jacob remarked "I wonder if Mr. Unger will still be at work."

"What are we doing here?" Lee asked Maggie.

"Maybe we should have gone straight to the airport." She replied. "But I feel safer here."

"Me too. The Embassy is bound to help us. Mr. Unger will tell us what to do."

"I hope so." said Maggie feeling lost. There were no directions to follow in this scenario. They had no plan ready. They'd been operating on instinct and simply reacting as events unfolded. As their heartbeats slowed, their minds were beginning to function again. The burst of action only briefly replaced fear and doubt.

They entered the building, Ali in Maggie's arms. There was a U.S. Marine standing outside who readily admitted them.

The front office was deserted, but Mr. Unger was still there. He introduced them to an assistant, another Muhammad. Unger and Mohammad seemed pleased with the Elres coup.

Unger invited them into his office to sit and talk. "Well, well, well. You did it! Super. I'm very happy for you. What is your next step?" He made a fuss over Ali as she curled in Maggie's arms, smiling at him.

"Please Mr. Unger. Can we use your telephone?" begged Lee, who then proceeded to make reservations for a four-thirty p.m. flight to London via Beirut. He would have taken any flight out, but that was the earliest available.

Lee then called the Alireza law office. The lawyers were at lunch. The secretary expressed her congratulations when he told her that they had Ali. "Mr. Alireza will be back in a minute. I'll have him call."

"Well, we have our passports and we'd like to leave." Maggie said. "But Ali's has no entry stamp. The Minister of Immigration thinks that she came in without a passport, and Ali says that Joe played some kind of trick with the man at the airport. She said that Joe pretended with the man that her picture was on his passport."

"That's hard to understand. They're pretty straight here. The officials don't fool around."

"Joe will probably be looking for us. We felt that we'd be safer here. I wonder what he'll do first?" Maggie mused.

Maggie and Lee discussed the matter. Maggie emotionally declared, "Joe will probably go to the police. They'll be on the watch for us at the airport and maybe here at the Embassy too."

"And what about our court order?" said Lee with a catch in his voice. He was feeling pain in his groin from the running as well as emotional distress. "Remember, we were trying to keep Ali here. Is that going to jump up and bite us now?"

"I'm just thinking aloud now," said Unger. "It's up to your lawyers to advise you. But if you were to go for a taxi tour of the Island and arrive at the airport a few minutes before flight time, the chances of anyone finding you would be nil."

They discussed that gambit and decided that it was a good idea. Unger's secretary looked in. "There's a Mr. Alireza on the telephone for Mr. Elres."

Lee took the call and blurted out, "We have her!

"Salah. Uh. We're going to the airport and take the first plane out. We have reservations on the four thirty Middle East Airlines flight to Beirut and London. We want to leave right away."

"Wonderful news!" Salah then solemnly declared, "But Lee. They will not permit you to go. You can try it, but remember, we ourselves have asked them not to let Ali leave the country. It's a court order. I advise you not to try. You will probably be stopped and you may offend the court." He sounded deeply concerned.

"Hold a minute. Let me speak to Maggie." Lee said. He relayed the advice.

Unger, showing his involvement in the problem went beyond his diplomatic rule books, thought that they should try to leave. They talked about it again and in the end felt that they had to take the lawyer's advice.

It was a real dilemma. Finally, Maggie nodded, looking more troubled than ever. "Lee. I'm scared. Joe is a devil and he won't play by the rules. But we gotta do what we gotta do"

"Okay, Salah. We'll be there shortly." Lee hung up the telephone.

Ali, inevitably, picked up their fears and feelings on her sensitive antenna. She began to realize that her Daddy Joe had done something terribly wrong, and that her Mommy was very mad at him.

"Mommy?"

"Yes, my love."

"Did Daddy Joe do something wrong? Will he go to jail?"

"Don't worry about it honey."

"I don't want him to go to jail." Tears began to fall.

"Daddy""

"Yes, honey," Lee replied.

"Daddy..." she paused to gather her thoughts and be clear on who she meant, "*Daddy Joe* said that he was going to take me back to Miami on Monday, but he didn't. He was just playing a trick on Mommy."

"Daddy Joe loves you, honey. He wouldn't do anything to hurt you."

"I know. But Mommy said he did something bad, and I'm afraid the policeman will get him."

"Look, baby. The policeman won't get him. Mommy's mad at him, but she's been mad before and no one went to jail. Sometimes adults have problems. They usually fix them. Please don't be afraid. Daddy Joe won't go to jail. I promise."

She came to Lee and climbed into his lap.

"Daddy?"

"Yes, honey."

"Is your hernia all better now?"

Over a period of time, Ali learned the whole story. Maggie and Lee always tried to shield her from their problems but, bit by bit, she put things together by overhearing conversations.

"Mommy?"

"Yes, sweetheart."

"Will Daddy Joe try to take me away with him again? I don't want to leave you again. What if he comes after me? Should I hide?"

"We won't let him take you again. You'll be with us all the time. Please don't worry, sweetheart."

"Daddy?"

"Yes, honey."

"Can we go home now?"

"We'll go home soon."

"Can we go home tomorrow?"

"I don't know. We have to take care of some things here first. I don't know how long it will take but we'll go home as soon as possible."

"Daddy, I want to see my sister and Sandy and Laura. I miss them."

These conversations were to take place over and over again. Ali was developing a theme which she often voiced. "Daddy Joe took me away from Mommy two times. Please God, don't let him take me again."

The Alireza staff was enchanted by Ali. Her innocent face, gap-tooth smile, and outgoing manner captured their hearts without effort. Ali stayed in the waiting area to play with Tony, the young Arab office boy and messenger. They'd met him for the first time earlier that day. He was small and dark and seemed to be around eighteen. He was good with Ali. They looked at magazine pictures together.

"Congratulations, Maggie and Lee! You have done well." Muhammad was at his desk. Salah and Maurice were also in attendance. All three had returned even though it was Thursday afternoon, a time usually reserved for family and rest. They sat in a circle and related all that had happened since noon.

"You should have tried to leave," said Maurice. "I would have."

"But we couldn't," said Maggie. "Salah advised us to stay. Now, how do we stop Joe from taking her again? I know what he's like. He's quite capable of hiring bullies to overpower us, grab her, and leave the country by the back door. He has no respect for courts, laws and regulations. In his mind, only weaklings obey the law."

"Now, now. Never you mind." Muhammad's voice was soothing. "This is a very well regulated country. The courts are strong and just. Our court system is based on the High Court of Egypt. It cannot be circumvented."

His words were well meant, but a discordant note was struck. "My God!" Lee thought. "The High Court of WHERE? EGYPT! Isn't that the nation that keeps getting into wars they can't win with Israel every year? A fairy tale land of ancient pyramids and all those millions of poor people." Stereotypes were intruding again.

He continued, "We have a strong case. There is no reason for us not to prevail. Our task now is to present our case as soon as possible. Now, these papers are very good." He thumped the file which lay open on the desk. "But if Zayyat's lawyer knows what he is doing, we may not be able to use them. However, the perjury laws are most severe and he will not lie in court. Your testimony should be sufficient."

"How soon will we be able to go home?" asked Maggie. "We have had our lives turned upside down by this."

"Yes," added Lee. "That is a very important question." Now that Ali was back with them, time presented another, different facet. The mad pace had altered their sense of time. They had been so focused on a single objective that, for a while, even eating and sleeping had become automatic. The days since they'd first missed Ali had passed as quickly as hours. A jibber-jabber of events had rushed by like an express train in a tunnel.

Now time expanded again. They could sort out and deal with other more ordinary objectives.

"Well, you see," began Salah. "This is a very bad time of year. The courts close for the summer at the end of July. Since that time is near, they won't want to hear any new cases."

"That's right," agreed Maurice. "When it gets hot here, everyone wants to go off to Europe. I'm going in about two weeks. I'll leave for London as soon as I finish up a rather weighty commercial negotiation. That's the only bloody thing holding me here now. My wife and kids are waiting in London to take our annual holiday."

So time was going to be a crucial matter for everyone. "When can we get a hearing? How long will a judgment take?" Lee pressed. His questions were directed toward Muhammad.

"Lee, I understand perfectly. We will try to get the matter resolved quickly. There is really no question about the facts favoring us. Our hearing is scheduled for Saturday, the thirteenth. But Mr. Zayyat will be represented and we don't know what arguments he and his lawyer may present. The court will understand the urgency of the case. We will do everything possible to assure quick action. Their judgment may be made in a week," he paused, "or it may take longer."

"Oh boy!" Lee suddenly realized. "You mean no decision on the thirteenth. They'll hear the evidence and give a verdict later. We'll be here for quite a while." Muhammad nodded. Maggie looked stricken.

"Joe will have the best lawyer that money can buy ...," Maggie caught herself. "I don't mean better than you. But he will get a good lawyer and fight. He's sharp and he'll do anything to get back at me."

"We're not insulted." Salah said. "There are other good firms here. These matters will reveal themselves in time. We promise to do everything possible to get you home quickly."

Salah turned to Maggie with a serious face and said, "Maggie. The Foreign Ministry has told me that we must turn your passport over to the U.S. Embassy at once. They see this as necessary since they have arranged to not permit Mr. Zayyatt to leave. They have asked your embassy to hold your documents so that they will not be perceived as favoring one side of this dispute over the other. They must be impartial to all parties."

Maggie recoiled in horror. "Oh my God Lee! It's Joe pulling strings again. I know it's him."

Lee was also horrified. "Holding one's passport is a sacred thing Salah. We can't give them up!"

"I'm sorry Lee but we must comply. Note that we agreed only to giving Maggie's passport to your government. Lee, you can keep yours. They will not be held by the Bahraini authorities."

After a moment's silence Maggie and Lee looked at each other in defeat. "Honey. You gotta do it. We've got to cooperate if we expect fair treatment."

Maggie glared at everyone in the room as she reached into her purse and handed the passports, her own and Ali's, to Salah. She had a sense of foreboding.

"What should we do now?" said Lee.

Alireza smiled gently. "The thing for you three to do now is to have a day of rest. Everything is closed for the weekend. We'll go back to work on Saturday morning. I'll come around to fetch you at about eight o'clock in the morning. Would that be convenient?"

"No." Lee told him. "You've already been too kind. We'll be fine taking a taxi." Salah seemed puzzled by the refusal and, in fact, Lee's motives were somewhat mixed, even to himself.

By then, they'd used many hours of the firm's time. It was beginning to seem like an imposition. And the fee was still an uncertain matter. Lee wanted their case to take as little of the lawyers' billable and precious time as possible.

The Elres' were queried about their quarters again, given restaurant advice and bade, by all, a pleasant afternoon. They kept everyone's telephone numbers in pocket in case of an emergency.

Joe's reaction was still the unknown quantity to be reckoned with.

Joe opened the door to the apartment to find Sherry packing her suitcase. He stomped over to her, grabbed her shoulders and shook her.

"You stupid jerk, how could you let this happen?"

Sherry looked at Joe with eyes swollen and a runny nose and said. "Oh my God, I don't know who you are, you look like the devil incarnate. You never intended to marry me. You only needed me to take care of Ali. That's the only reason you brought me to this God forsaken place.

"You're right about one thing, I was stupid to have believed your lies. I'm glad Ali is with her mother. That little girl cried herself to sleep every night.

"You also lied to me about your ex abandoning Allison. You kidnapped her! That woman wouldn't have come half way around the world if she had done what you told me! You disgust me!!!"

Joe swung his arm out ready to hit Sherry but instead pushed her to the floor.

"Hurry up and pack. Get the hell out of here. I don't want to see your face again."

Margaret was at the desk looking somewhat harassed and exasperated when they returned. She was on the telephone vehemently saying, "...Shakar, you just can't do it! There's a limit, you know. People are not chickens!" They didn't hear his reply and had no idea what his offense was. Margaret seemed to be a take-charge person. "Hold on a minute," she said into the phone.

She put the telephone down, smiled and said, "Hello."

"Hi." They greeted her back.

She was eyeing Ali. "Well. Who is this?" Then, "Hi," to Ali.

199

Ali momentarily hid her face against her mother's legs. Then her shiny, dark brown eyes were on Margaret.

"Allison. Can you say hello?"

"Hello. I came here on a big airplane."

"You did! How nice. Was it fun?" Ali nodded shyly.

To Maggie. "Is she yours?"

"She certainly is." Maggie made a happy face at Ali. Not sure of how much to say, they retired quickly to their room. "See you later."

Now, for the first time, they were alone with Ali. Her play suit was a mess. Her feet were black. She was filthy. "Did Daddy or Sherry give you a bath?"

"No, Mommy."

"My God, Lee. This poor child hasn't had a bath since she left home!"

"Have you had a bath Ali?" asked Lee.

"But, Daddy, there was no bath tub." She was defending her father.

"Well, baby," Lee said, "How about taking a bath here? Would you like that?"

"Yes, Daddy, but what will I wear?"

"Maggie, we need to buy her some clothes and we have to tell these people our situation. Why don't you get her bath ready and I'll talk to Margaret."

Maggie looked at him warmly. "Honey," she said, "I never could have gotten Ali back without you. Thank you."

"You're the one who took all the initiatives," he said, looking down into her face. "It's all your doing. You're my hero. I'm so proud of you." He felt that she had pulled off an extraordinary coup that day. It seemed to Lee that they'd had a real life "Mission Impossible" situation, and that they'd carried it out without a hitch.

At the reception desk, not far from their door, sat Margaret. She looked at Lee curiously. "Hi." Margaret was a pretty girl - dark hair with hints of auburn and a light complexion. Her serious and capable air radiated. Her speech was delightfully accented with the tones of England.

"Hi yourself." Lee responded. "Do you have a few minutes to talk?"

"Sure." She looked at him expectantly. He walked around her desk and sat near her in a side chair, leaning forward on his elbows. He spoke rapidly, giving her a lightning sketch of the kidnapping and recovery.

She responded with a fervor that warmed Lee's heart. "Holy Jesus! What in hell is wrong with that man?"

Margaret's eyes were shooting sparks. "And to bring her here, of all places! She's such a tender thing. A girl needs her mother." This last thought was uttered with a sigh as if she had experienced times when she'd needed some mothering.

"Well, I can't tell you what's wrong with him. I just know that we're in a little jam here." Lee was underplaying the situation.

"What can we do to help?"

"Well. Two things, actually. I don't know how soon we'll be able to leave, but we need security. I don't think that he'll come here, but we don't want to take chances. Can we keep this door locked?" He indicated the door at his side. It separated the stairs from the reception area, Shakar's office from guest rooms and the bath. It had been closed whenever he'd observed it before, because of the air conditioning. But it was not locked.

"Yes, we'll keep it locked. That's no problem, but I don't think that he'll try anything. The police are tough." Lee was getting a little tired of hearing about the toughness of the police department.

"I know that it's Thursday evening and the shops will be closed tomorrow, but is there any place where we could get some things for Ali? We have no clothes or shoes for her whatever."

"You don't want to go out now, do you? Catherine and I could get some things for her." She saw Lee's pain and fatigue.

"That's the best offer we have had all day Margaret, but we really couldn't put you to that much trouble. Size and style are a mother's department and besides, we have time and you're working."

"Nonsense! We can get off now. You stay here and rest for a while. Get yourselves together. If you'll have Maggie give me a list, we'll pop off and be back in no time. We have the car and know just where to go."

"Well, thank you. You're awfully kind. Are there any stores open now?"

"Yes. Of course.

"Oh, I'd love to do it." She gushed. "The poor little thing has been through so much. We can probably go to Jashanmal's"

Lee went to tell Maggie and to make a list of things they'd need, feeling very happy about the offer of help. Maggie was lying down, tired after their exciting day. Ali was quietly playing tent with towels and a chair, content to be near her mother. She was clean again. She wore a towel like a sarong, wrapped around her slender body. Another towel was used as a turban around her damp hair. The room was dark and cool. The couple spoke quietly about what Ali would need. A knock on the door broke their concentration. Lee answered, "Who's there?" as he rose to open it.

"It's Catherine."

At the door stood Catherine, looking frightened. "There's a policeman here asking for Maggie - a Mr. Zayyat is with him.

"He's a mean looking fellow. Is this the guy?"

CHAPTER 11 - CONFRONTATION

Joe was moving fast. He was focused and furious at everyone. He left the apartment and hurried back to the office. "Ben should be back from lunch." he said to himself, "He'll help me fix this."

Ben Smith's car was in the parking lot. Joe went straight to his office and sat down.

"Maggie took Ali. She's here, she was here all the time we were talking this morning. Ben you have to make some phone calls to find out where they are."

Ben sat back in his chair and breathed to himself, "I'll be damned, she outsmarted Joe."

Joe stood and leaned against the desk in a threatening manner and said, "You gave her the name of the building where I'm living. You owe me."

Ben had heard from the men on the rig that Joe was forceful with them, that he had threatened some of them recently. He wasn't going to let Joe threaten him in any way.

"I'll make some phone calls to find out where Maggie is staying, maybe she went to the embassy. If so, the ambassador will know where they are. But Joe you were the one who started all this, you took your daughter, I didn't. Don't ever try to intimidate me again."

It only took one call to the embassy to find out where Maggie was staying. The ambassador wanted to keep the company happy. Having this large American company in Bahrain was good for the United States.

THURSDAY, JULY 10, 1975 – five p.m.

Adrenaline began pumping immediately. Maggie looked like she was going to faint.

Maggie and Lee stood, transfixed, looking at each other, eyes locked in a nonverbal communication. "What shall we do?" "Is it all over?" "Who should see him?"

Ali began to cry. "Oh Mommy. Don't go. I don't want to see Daddy Joe. I want to stay with you." Her towel-turban fell to the floor as she ran to her mother.

"Hush. It's okay Ali." She patted Ali without looking to Lee. Fear was clearly her dominant emotion.

Catherine stood nervously, just outside the door. "What shall I tell them?"

"I'll see them." Lee volunteered, unable to see any way to avoid the confrontation.

"Lee. Please be careful."

"It's okay honey. Don't worry. I'll be careful." He put on shoes and glanced in the mirror to be sure that he wouldn't look incompetent due to open buttons or mussed hair. "Keep the door locked," he ordered.

Catherine led the way down the hall. Lee followed her through the outer door, which was ajar, and she pointed up the staircase. "They're in the parlor. It's up the stairs, next to the breakfast room."

Lee climbed the stairs, slowly and carefully, taking time in an effort to firm up his composure.

There were three men seated in the well-furnished room. The afternoon sun streamed through the loose weave of the curtains.

Joe sat on one of the two sofas, stony faced, sullen, and looking fat. His stomach bulged under a dirty tee shirt. His grease-stained hands and trousers gave evidence that he had been hastily summoned from work. He stared straight ahead, his eyes fixed on the wall.

"Hello Joe." Silence. Joe did not move nor did he even look at Lee.

Lee said "Hello." again. This time to the policeman sitting next to Joe, an arm's length away on the same sofa. The officer looked at Lee blankly. Again there was no reply.

"Excuse me, Mr. Elres," said the third man. Lee took him to be Joe's lawyer. He sat on the opposite sofa.

The lawyer stood and offered Lee his hand. "I am Kahlill." Lee took his hand warily, attempting to keep Joe in sight. "I will interpret for you. The officer does not speak English."

Kahlill was a tall, strongly built man. Broad shoulders and deep chest. His round face bore a beard and mustache, Van Dyke style, not unlike Lee's. His robes were astonishingly white, obviously made of quality material. His turban and head cloth were tied with black silk cord.

"Mr. Zayyat says that he would like to see his daughter." Kahlill smiled at Lee. His large white teeth contrasted with his dark complexion. He seemed faintly amused and his manner radiated complete assurance.

Lee felt no assurance whatever. All his fears and anxieties were surfacing. His heart was palpitating. "No way," He sputtered. "She is in the legal custody of her mother and myself and we will not permit him to see her." Lee was standing awkwardly, shifting from foot to foot. All of his senses alert for an attack.

Kahlill relayed the message in Arabic. Joe and the officer spoke to each other in Arabic. The policeman then addressed himself to Kahlill for several seconds. His olive green uniform looked too warm for the climate. It was adorned with leather holders for handcuffs, a long black club and his other law enforcement paraphernalia. He wore no gun. His hands moved deliberately as he gestured in conversation.

Lee's turmoil increased. He did not understand one word, but imagined the worst. Joe continued to stare at the wall, even when speaking to the officer.

"Mr. Zayyat says that he must speak to Maggie. It is urgent that he do so. Very important." Kahlill quietly waited for a reply.

"No. Mrs. Elres does not want to see him or to talk to him!" Lee said this loudly. Anger and fear were affecting his control. "Goddamned stupid son of a bitch..." he began to mumble opinions, barely able to get the words out, wanting to break through Joe's icy, insulting silence.

"If you want something from me, you'll have to start speaking English..."

Kahlill calmly interpreted. Lee was hopping mad, still moving from foot to foot, on the brink of running or attacking.

"Please. Sit down and let's talk." Kahlill was taking charge. He led Lee to the other sofa and sat down himself. "There is no need to be upset."

Childishly, Lee did not want to sit with him. He was the enemy's representative. So he squatted on his heels, facing Joe and the police officer. He kept a little distance from Joe and rested his forearms on his knees. He was ready to attack!

Lee only squatted for a moment. The policeman stood, and Lee got up too. Angry exchanges broke out, voices filling the room. The three Arabs were fairly shouting at each other. Lee expected to be arrested.

Joe never moved his eyes from the wall. He sat rigid and unmoving. Suddenly, he jumped up and marched out of the room, brushing past Lee. The policeman followed, on his heels.

Lee whirled around to catch up with them, intending to prevent them from getting to his room. "Elres' Last Stand!" he thought stupidly.

But Kahlill stopped him with a softly spoken message. "Don't worry. He won't be back."

Lee was confused. He strode to the stair well and watched Joe and the officer descend down toward the street, away from the closed door to his floor.

"Boy! That is one nasty character." Kahlill remained comfortably seated. Smiling.

"Who are you?" Lee asked, perplexed, having expected him to leave with his client.

"Kahlill Ben Shakar. Catherine and Margaret told me the whole story and I thought that you could use a little help."

"My God! You own this place. I thought that you were Zayyat's lawyer." Lee's mental set toward Kahlill underwent a complete turn around.

He laughed. "No. I am Shakar's son. Did you understand what was said?"

"No. But look. I didn't realize what your role was, at all. I thought you were with them." Lee extended his hand and Kahlill took it and pulled to stand up. The two men shook hands warmly.

Smiling, Kahlill took Lee's hand in both of his hands and gave him a firm two handed grip. "Well. Thank you very much indeed." Lee had not yet guessed how helpful Kahlill had actually been. "What else was said?"

"Well, when you said, 'No,' he threatened you. He said that he would take...is her name Allison?"

"Yes. We call her Ali."

"Yes. Of course...Ali. He said that he would come back with friends and take Ali by force."

"My God. That's just like him."

"He said that no one was going to stop him from seeing his daughter. He was so mean that the policeman told him that he was going to take him to jail, 'NOW,' if he didn't shut up and behave."

Kahlill grinned, his big white teeth prominent, "I told him that he'd better not try anything around here." He pushed his loose sleeve up, exposed a hairy arm with an impressive biceps. "I told him that if he wanted to show us his muscles, we'd show him ours. And that I have a black belt in Karate to back me up."

Lee was practically dancing by this time. Their laughter rang off the walls. "Holy shit!" Lee thought. He said, "I thought that *I* was going to jail. I totally misunderstood."

"Well there's no problem now. He won't show his nose around here again. And don't worry about his threats. The police are on to him now. If there is any trouble, he's the one that will land in jail. He'll stay there too."

"Look. I can't thank you enough. You have been very kind. I have to tell Maggie what's happened. She must be worried sick."

They walked to the reception area. Margaret and Catherine were talking to an older man. He had curly gray hair and was wearing a white dress shirt with no tie and slacks. His sleeves were partly rolled up. He reminded Lee of his accountant in Miami.

"Hallooo." He sounded out the "ooo's" in a playful way. "I'm Shakar." His hand was extended.

Lee took his hand in greeting. "Hello sir. I'm Lee Elres. Nice to meet you. Kahlill and the girls have really been looking after us. Thank you very much."

"Pshaw. It's nothing. Glad to help you out."

They stood and chatted for a moment. Lee was moved to make a little exit speech because he was anxious to leave them and tell Maggie his news. "Thank you all so much for the support you've given us. We've been very worried about meeting up with Joe. After all, we're strangers and this is his territory...."

"The Hell it is!" interjected Kahlill. "Those damned Lebanese think that they can get away with anything. Nobody likes them." His father nodded approval.

Lee looked at their friendly faces and thought, "Wow. We have a little army of supporters!"

"I must excuse myself. Maggie must be worried. See you later."

"Hey! Don't forget the list," called Catherine to Lee's back. "We've got to get Ali something to wear right away. Jashanmal's will be closing soon."

"Okay." He called back to her over his shoulder.

A soft knock. "Who is it?" Maggie's voice was strained.

"Me. Lee. Open up, it's okay."

The door opened a crack and Maggie peered out, saw that he was alone, and opened the door wide. Her face was white and taut with fear. "What happened?"

"Fine. Every thing's fine." Lee was grinning from ear to ear. He told her about the scene upstairs and how Kahlill had helped. He told the story quickly. Over the next few hours, he would recall other details and relate them with relish.

"But, Catherine and Margaret are in a hurry to get Ali's shopping list. The stores will close soon and they're ready to go."

So Maggie finished the list and Lee took it to their new friends. The two girls were waiting with purses in hand.

Ali needed underwear, a dress, play shorts, T-shirts, sneakers, sandals and hair ribbons. They also included a coloring book and crayons in the list.

Maggie, Ali and Lee went to present the list. Lee offered the girls a ten Bahraini Dinar note. Maggie was annoyed with him. "Lee. That's not enough." He thought her wrong, but cheerfully doubled and then tripled the amount to thirty, sure that he'd get change.

Later, when the girls returned, Lee was glad that Maggie had spoken up. The little purchases had cost over twenty two Bahraini Dinars.

At dinnertime they dressed to take their first walk with Ali. They were watchful, alert for any sign of Joe.

The dark street was warm, but not unpleasant. The couple each took one of Ali's hands to sail her over potholes and curbs. Ali was happy to be out of the house and in the open air.

They walked in another direction, away from Keith's Restaurant, exploring new territory beyond the sedate Al Nussar Club and the dark apartment buildings.

At the corner, the cross street was thronged with foot traffic. An exotic mix of Arabs, Asians and Pakistanis. There were black people and Europeans too. There were few cars. Little shops lined the street, selling walkaway food, cold drinks and sundries. There was a tiny drug store. The sign said "CHEMIST" under Arabic lettering, but it sold a variety of merchandise, similar to drug stores at home, on a small scale.

A modern, but rather dingy, theater occupied one corner of the intersection. Hundreds of Pakistanis filled the lobby and the broad steps leading to the movie house. They shuffled forward to gain admission.

The Americans were fascinated by this scene. In Miami folks stood in lines to crowd into theaters the same way, but these people looked so different. Most wore turbans and white clothing consisting of a smock-like shirt, and trousers. All seemed to wear sandals.

As they circled the crowd, they strolled up a dark dead-end street, toward a red neon sign advertising "DOWNTOWN RESTAURANT." This was their destination, recommended by Salah.

For all of their initial fears of these strange streets and foreign faces, no one bothered them with even a curious stare despite their odd, foreign appearance. Lee's height and their clothing clearly separated them from the mob. Yet they felt perfectly at peace and comfortable in Bahrain.

The restaurant was cool and dark. Ali fell asleep in Lee's lap before the order was taken. Lee smiled and thought, "She's had a heck of a day."

The food was good and the restaurant accepted their American Express card.

Back in the room, still asleep, Ali was eased into bed. They shaded her by stringing a sheet across the room, using belts and Venetian blind cords.

The couple spread a soft bed cover on the fuzzy pink carpet to play a few hands of rummy before putting themselves to bed. It seemed cozy and private.

The hastily packed deck of cards was missing the seven of clubs, but it was a fun game nevertheless. It was the first of many such gin games; always played on the floor to allow Ali to sleep unmolested.

They discussed the events of the day. Snug in their little pink universe, they were happy in the knowledge that a keystone of their crumpled lives was back in her place and warmed by her nearness.

"How do you suppose he found us?" Maggie asked as she slowly dealt the cards. "We did tell the Gulf Hotel not to give our address, didn't we?"

"Yes. The manager promised to keep it a secret. But you know how those things go. Lots of people might know. There may have been slip-ups. Also, if the police were asking, he may have been required to tell the truth. But Joe found us a lot quicker than I expected him to."

They played their hands. The conversation was intermittent.

"Lee. These people here are very nice. It's not at all like I expected."

"Yeah. I like them too. I feel so, you know, grateful. The guy who gave us a ride when we were running in the Souk. Kahlill and his dad. Margaret and Catherine. The lawyers. Jacob. They have done a lot for us. And we're strangers. I can't believe how helpful everyone's been."

"Gin!" She cried triumphantly, displaying her hand. Her black hair gleamed as she leaned forward to put down her cards. They'd been playing automatically, enjoying the look and the feel of the cards and the little riffling snapping noises made as they were shuffled.

"I suppose that everything we know about the Middle East comes from TV, newspapers and books. I expected to see a lot of, oh, I don't know...like P.L.O. headquarters and anti-Israel and anti-U.S. propaganda."

"When I was in Lebanon," Maggie recollected, "there were soldiers everywhere. Tanks guarding the streets. Checkpoints. Cars were stopped and searched all the time. But here the people seem very friendly. The crowds didn't even bother me."

"Well Maggie. Maybe Salah and everyone else is right. This may be a very safe place. But, even so, we have to be careful. We have to be prepared for the worst. So let's keep a sharp lookout. All the time."

They played a few more hands and then retired. Ali slept between them in the bed. Maggie, as always, went to sleep quickly. That was her escape from trouble.

Lee's sleep didn't come immediately. His mind continued to analyze events. He thought about the meeting with Joe.

He was embarrassed by his behavior; how he'd squatted on the floor. How churlish! He'd had been ready to fight. Lee had not been the cool, rational adult that he wanted to be.

And thoughts about Joe, sulking off in defeat. What was he doing now? Berating and abusing Sherry for losing Ali?

He was proud to have faced Joe but he analyzed and picked the encounter apart. He decided that it was a key event in Joe's life too.

Joe must have been surprised by Maggie's first telephone call and wondered, "How in Hell did she find me?"

The Elres presence in Bahrain and recapture of Ali must have crushed Joe. He had been on top of the situation, first punishing Maggie for deserting him and for her ultimate refusal to come back to him. Then rubbing it in by telling her that she'd never see Ali again. He felt secure, no doubt, in the knowledge that thousands of miles and an enormous cultural wall insulated him.

Lee saw something else too. Joe lived in relative squalor. Shakar's B & B was much nicer than his apartment. Joe's giant salary and his cash in the bank hadn't yet allowed him to live in anything like the comfort and elegance he had seen the Erles' enjoying in Miami.

Not that they were rich. Newly wed with new furniture and decorating expenses, they lived from payday to payday, but with luxuries still not commonly available in other parts of the world. Their private swimming pool sparkled like a jewel through large glass doors.

Lee recalled a certain scary day in Miami a few weeks after Maggie had returned from Lebanon. Joe came by the house, uninvited and unannounced, to see Ali.

Maggie had allowed him to visit on the street, in front of the house. She stood nearby, expecting him to talk for a few minutes and then leave.

Suddenly he put a protesting Ali in the front seat of his car and was walking around to the driver's seat. Maggie began to yell, "Lee! Lee!" as she rushed to the car to stop him from leaving.

Lee rushed to the scene from the back yard but he was too far away.

Joe jumped in and began to drive away as Maggie reached in through the open passenger window and pulled Ali out of the moving car.

The car was creeping and Joe was pulling on Ali's legs. A terrifying incident. Lee watched helplessly.

Joe gave up. Ali came out through the window and was in her mother's arms and Joe went tearing off down the quiet residential street.

There was another rotten day in Miami when Joe had come to the house and demanded to see Ali. He was at the door.

Maggie had refused to let Joe in or to see Ali because he was too agitated. Frightened, she refused to go outside with Joe and Lee placed himself firmly in the doorway between them.

Joe had rushed at Lee and tackled him! Lee, astonished, grappled with Joe and they wrestled in the foyer.

Ali had run out and was now in her mother's arms while the men threshed around. Joe and Lee pushed hard at each other.

The glass etagere in the entryway was knocked down and broken glass flew, cutting Ali's scalp. Lee screamed at Maggie, "Call 911. Call the police!"

Joe left, tires again screeched on the street. Ali had to go to the emergency room for a couple of stitches. This incident left permanent scars all the way around.

These sorry encounters were a part of the history that shaped the meeting in the B and B parlor.

Lee felt that when Joe found them that afternoon in Bahrain, he saw them living well. The parlor was a nice room. He recalled the two white sofas, facing each other, on a white plush rug.

Persian rugs decorated the walls and expensive lamps were placed for comfortable evening light. There were French doors opening onto a little balcony, closed and curtained to keep the heat at bay. What a contrast to Joe's dirty apartment. He must have thought that they were doing a better job of caring for Ali.

But there was Lee. Big and acting ugly, refusing him permission to see his daughter, with Shakar as a black belt defense team member.

Lee had been enraged and frustrated. But he believed that Joe must have been even more ill at ease.

Lee also thought that Joe may have felt guilty because he had failed to keep his beloved daughter in decent surroundings, and he had exposed her to his relationship with Sherry.

Even worse, Joe had separated Ali from her loving mother, taken her away from her nice home, friends and summertime activities...viciously hurting Maggie.

Lee felt bad for another reason also. Because, in a better world, he and Joe would have been able to simply talk and resolve things without a hint of violence...violence which Lee abhorred.

Maggie never, never wanted to deny Ali and her father the pleasure of each other's company and love.

Not that Joe and Lee would have been friends. But they could have been rational enough to talk about what would have been best for Ali. Their behavior had denied Ali the benefit of adult decisions that concerned her welfare.

"What a mess," thought the guilt ridden Lee as he finally drifted off to sleep.

CHAPTER 12 - LIFE IN BAHRAIN

Bahrain was closed for the Islamic day of worship. The Alireza law offices were closed, shops were shuttered and Bahrain rested.

"Lee. This is such a waste of time." Maggie complained. "What in heck are we going to do with Ali today?"

"I don't know. Let's ask Catherine." replied Lee.

The Islamic holy day commanded a day of rest. The law office and the courts would not open again until Sunday. The Family Elres sat at breakfast deciding on the plan for the day.

They had dressed for a holiday. Maggie looked cool in light denim bellbottoms and a halter top. Lee was in a light blue seersucker leisure suit and Ali wore a brand new polka dotted pinafore with a ruffled blouse and white knee socks.

Breakfast was English style, good as before, beginning with a pot of coffee, bacon and eggs. A rack of crisp toast, butter and jam followed. Catherine's service was always cheerful.

Ali wanted cereal. Since they went to breakfast late, they were the only diners in the sunlit room. The third floor vantage gave them a view of the street and of the rooftop across the street. The building didn't look watertight but since it seldom rained, this was a matter of small moment.

"Catherine," Maggie asked. "What is there to do here?"

"Well, I don't know. Not much."

"Give us a suggestion," Lee prompted. "What do you do on your day off?"

"There is the Sheik's (pronounced "Shake's") beach. Only foreigners can go there, except the Pakistanis."

"Oh? What's wrong with them?"

"Nothing that I know of. Mostly they're laborers and servants. I suppose the Sheik feels that they're second class and he doesn't want to associate with them. The Gulf Hotel is the only other place to swim. You could go there."

As a gesture of good will, the hotel manager had invited them to feel free to use the hotel facilities. "What else?" they pressed, determined to catalogue the island's attractions.

"You could take a taxi to Awali."

"What's Awali?"

"It's a village. A lot of Americans live there. You can tour the island on the way."

"How far is it?"

"I don't know. Can't be too far, can it?" she said ironically referring to the fact that they were on an small island.

Lee cast his vote, "The pool sounds fun. I haven't been swimming since my operation."

"I don't know about that. What if Joe uses the pool?"

"That's right. Today's probably his day off, too. Better take a tour. We'll be sorry later if we don't see Bahrain."

They decided they'd better think about money too. Looking ahead, they couldn't be sure of a quick getaway from this place and wanted to have sufficient funds on hand to care for themselves. Having money in hand would allow for a greater show of strength should the need arise.

Lee used the house telephone to call a good friend at the Continental National Bank of Miami, Paul Rauschenplatt. It was late afternoon for Paul. The bank stayed open late on Fridays. An unusual conversation took place.

"Hello, Paul. This is Lee Elres. How are you today?"

"Hey Lee. How's it going?"

Lee cut straight to the chase, "Paul, I have a problem and you can help."

Lee eased Paul's mind into the proper channel, "Maggie and I are traveling and I'd like to have you wire me $1,000.00 and charge it to my checking account."

"Sure, Lee. Where are you?"

"We're in the Middle East in Bahrain. This is the little island in the Persian Gulf. We had to come here to get Ali. She was kidnapped by her father but we kidnapped her back and we may be stuck here for a while."

A short silence as Paul absorbed the words.

"Come on, Lee. Where are you really?" He chuckled over the 'little joke.'

"Paul. I'm in Bahrain. B-A-H-R-A-I-N. That's the name of the country. And I'd like you to wire the funds to me at the First National City Bank here. I'm not kidding. And there's something else you need to do. My mother-in-law is taking care of Jackie and the house and she'll need some money. Paul, could you charge my account if she needs to pay some bills like the electric or rent or groceries and such?"

Paul shifted gears. "My God! What did you say? How is Maggie holding up? Are you all right?"

Lee told Paul more about the situation. He explained how expensive things were and that their position was uncertain. He also told him that even if the account gets low, he should still pay whatever was asked since their paychecks would be deposited and that they'd have additional funds available to cover an overdraft should one occur.

"Sure, Lee. I'll handle it."

Lee thought that those were the nicest words Paul could have said.

"Hold it, Paul. Maggie wants to say hello." He handed her the phone.

"Hi, Paul. Thank you for helping!" She laughed at his reply, "Yes, all's true. We're really here. Lee wouldn't put you on. Ok. Thanks again. Bye."

They hung up, feeling better about the home front.

The next call was to Dorothy Buttersmith, one of the managers at work. Lee told her of events to date and asked her to speak with their folks and Dr. Arnold to give them a situation report. He asked her to act as a 'go between' for

Maggie's mother and Paul at the bank should they need help. She promised to do as Lee asked.

Feeling up at the prospect of getting more cash soon, they went in search of a taxi.

Taxi service in Manama was excellent. They had only to stand on the corner and wait. On this occasion, a taxi appeared in less than two minutes. About average for the location.

"Do you speak English?"

"Yes, a little bit."

"We want to go to Awali. We want to take a tour of Bahrain."

"At your service, sir."

Lee had hoped that he would volunteer the price. "How much?"

"Excuse me?"

"How many dinar?"

"Ten dinar."

"To Awali? The price is five dinar. My friend told me. Always five dinar."

"Yes, but today is Friday and I must charge ten dinar."

Maggie had opened the door. Now she closed it. "Ten dinar is too much." She addressed him. "Five dinar, your taxi is not air conditioned." That was a telling point. They began to look up and down the street for another vehicle.

"Very well, sir," he said in a cheerful way. "For you, madam and the little girl, seven dinars and I will give you a tour of the island."

As always, the local men were caring and respectful toward women and children. Maggie thought to herself, "This should only carry over into the courts."

"What the hell. We're rich Americans, right? Right! Let's go, gang!" Lee opened the rear door and held it for Maggie and Ali.

Once he began the tour, the driver's command of the language proved to be barely adequate. He managed keen fare negotiations very well but his descriptive and educational abilities in English were nil. The Elres' knew no Arabic whatsoever.

Awali turned out to be approximately fifteen long, hot, barren miles away and there were sparse points of interest in-between. They started by driving through the main thoroughfares of Manama, noticing restaurants. Some of the names were familiar.

There were groves of date palms at the western edge of the city. These trees were tall and straight, resembling Miami's royal palm trees. No other agricultural activity was seen. They slowed to a stop to view a spring that flowed into a large, natural pool. In the hot afternoon, it acted like a magnet that attracted nearby residents. The pool was called "Adari." The steep sides of the basin was swarming with men and children jumping, swimming and playing in the water. The canal leading away from Adari was also used for playing while mothers washed clothes and fathers polished cars on the shady parts of the bank.

"Mommy, I came here with Daddy Joe and we went swimming."

"I can't believe it Lee." The water suddenly looked polluted. "Joe couldn't have let her swim here!" She was offended by Joe's lousy child-care skills.

The driver commented on a little tower near the pool. It was, he said, in halting English, the most sacred place in the country. They were interested and sat forward in the seat, hoping to get more information. They passed it quickly and the driver could not enlighten them further as he seemed not to understand their questions.

"It looks like a little minaret." Lee observed. It looked abandoned, set in a little patio, a miniature plaza, old and ruined. It seemed poorly cared considering it was a a holy place.

"Perhaps," Lee thought, "the lack, of care reflects a religious attitude, not to interfere with the sacred past. Or maybe it's lack of interest or money."

The desert in Bahrain is harsh, as deserts are everywhere. A place of heat, rock, sand and emptiness.

Awali proved to be a company town, built for the expat employees of BAPCO (British American Petroleum Company). The small homes and gardens were reminiscent of Levittown of 1950, gone hot and dry. "Life must be more comfortable here than in town since obvious care had been given to westernizing the environment," Lee mused.

They visited the BAPCO club and refreshed themselves in its air-cooled spaciousness before they returned through the heat and glare to their Bed and Breakfast. Ali fell asleep on their laps at the Downtown Restaurant.

"Strange how soon this exotic place seems so familiar," remarked Lee. It was now Saturday, the first day of the new work week, July 12th. Maggie, looking grim, was nodding in agreement.

The morning bout with salt water in the pipes, breakfast in the dining room and the hot stroll in the brilliant sun in search of a taxi seemed normal. They arrived at Alireza and Associates' office a little after eight.

"Good morning," chirped Mary, the now familiar English secretary.

"Good morning, sir. Good morning, madam. Good morning, Ali," bowed Tony, the swarthy office boy. "Would you care for a coke? Coffee or tea?"

"Yes, coffee please," Maggie said. "Black for Mr. Elres. Ali, do you want a coke?"

"Yes, Mommy. Can I color now?"

They had gone to a 'cold store' and bought Ali another coloring book and crayons. Lee noticed that the items were made in China.

"Look Maggie. We never see anything made in China at home. Real Red China, not Taiwan." This pleased him somehow since they didn't ever see chinese products at home where communist goods cannot be imported. It made Bahrain seem even more exotic.

"Mr. Murad has a client. He'll be with you soon," said Mary. They settled down to peruse the Middle East Edition of Time Magazine and a local English language paper, "Gulf News". Tony looked over Ali's shoulder, intrigued by her activity. He seemed to be just a boy. He had a light mustache and Lee guessed that he was seventeen. Ali said, "Do you want to color with me?"

He nodded and soon they were head to head over the pages, industriously coloring the simple pictures. "This would make a great photo." Maggie thought.

Muhammad was soon ready for them. "Well, well, well. And how did you spend your day yesterday and where's Ali?"

"We had a very quiet day," Maggie replied. "Ali is coloring with Tony."

Lee volunteered, "We took a ride to Awali and saw some of the sights. Very pleasant."

"Fine. I'm glad to hear about it. Do you want coffee?"

"We just had some but I'm sure that Lee would take another cup."

"Very well."

"Tony!" Muhammad called sharply, and the summoned one appeared promptly to take their order.

"What is our program for today?" asked Lee.

"Today. Hmmm. Our hearing is scheduled for the 13th. We must prepare ourselves for that but the preparations do not involve you. We would like you to call us in the morning in case there is some fact or information, signature or whatever that we might need."

"It's very hard to do nothing to further our cause. Can't we participate in the work somehow?" Maggie pleaded.

"No. We will take care of everything. Go conserve your energy. Think of this as a vacation for today. There will be things for you to do later."

They were dismissed. So they picked up Ali and headed back to the B & B.

In the office elevator, Ali said, "Daddy. Are we going to go home now?"

"No, darling. We must stay a while longer to take care of some papers."

Ali looked up at him inquiringly, "What does 'a while' mean?"

"That means soon, but not now. We think we have to stay for a few more days."

"Mommy?"

"Yes, sweetheart."

"Do Sandy and Laura know what happened to me?"

"Mr. and Mrs. Garnet know. I'm sure that Sandy and Laura know too. The kids ask about you every day."

"How about Jackie and Grandma Carrie?"

"Yes, honey. Grandma knows everything."

"What about Aunt Jane and Grandma and Grandpa Alvarez?"

"Yes, honey. Everyone knows because we told Grandpa Elres and Grandpa Alvarez everything and they know just what's happening."

Out of the elevator, into the breeze-swept building entry landing. They led Ali to the busy street, hands locked together.

"Mommy. Where do babies come from?"

"Ali. You know that. You came from Mommy's tummy." Maggie looked amused.

"Yes, Mommy. What I mean is, how did I get into your tummy? Where do babies really come from?"

Maggie was no longer amused. She looked to Lee for such technical details. They were now on the hot street, looking for a taxi, eyeing the Arab street life, and the women dressed in black robes with either a veil or a mask covering the rest of their faces.

Happy to be of service, Lee said, "Well, Ali, the daddy must put a seed in the mommy's tummy and that grows into a baby. That's how everyone gets started."

Little Allison seemed satisfied for the moment. She'd have to think about it for a while. "Where are we going now?"

Lee waved down a taxi and they boarded; feeling "in" now that they could do simple things like saying "Al Nussar Club, please." The driver understood and off they went.

"What are we going to do today Mommy?" asked Ali

"I don't know, Ali. What do you think, Lee?"

Lee thought, "I'd like to be home where it's 30° cooler and the swimming pool is only ten steps from our bed. Home... where we earn a living instead of spending chunks of money we don't have."

Then said, "Let's go swimming at the Gulf Hotel. The manager had told us that we'd be welcome there even if we couldn't stay at the hotel."

The sun poured through the open taxi windows and their perspiration flowed freely.

"Do you think it's safe? What if Joe goes there?"

"Now that we're in court, I think it's probably O.K. Would you rather stay in the room?"

"No."

"Well."

"Mommy. Let's go swimming. Daddy Joe works every day and Sherry stays at home."

"O.K." Maggie was getting warmer.

Lee directed the driver to wait at the door and went up to get swim suits.

Once at the Gulf Hotel there was a moment of confusion at the front desk. The clerk informed them that the pool was only for guests and members of the club. Membership was 100.00 B.D.!

"We're only going to be here for a few days. We were only able to stay one night. The manager, Mr. Bartlett, invited us to come whenever we liked."

"Yes, but I must follow the rules," the clerk argued.

Maggie explained the situation in her usual, persuasive manner and Lee concluded with the brilliant argument. "Look. For us it's personal. We don't have a company to pay our bills. It comes out of our own pockets and they're not very deep."

The clerk willingly relented with a big smile and directed them to the pool. They soon were sitting in the shade of one of the little thatched shelters scattered about the pool. It was a beautiful place. But hot.

Behind the hotel, the Persian Gulf's waters surrounded the pool on three sides since the hotel is on a little peninsula. The bathhouse stretched along one end of the pool. There was an outdoor bar with stools and a kitchen behind it. The men's shower house formed one wing and the women's shower room the other.

Lots of people came to the Gulf's pool each day to swim, relax, have lunch, sun bathe and pass the time of day.

The pool itself was very large, irregular in shape, new, modern and clean. Pool attendants in uniform tee shirts seemed to spend long days marching to and fro with drinks and food in the hot sun.

The English and French dominated the scene. Some were flight crews for the airlines; others worked in Bahrain and spent some of their twelve-to-five lunch break there. They seldom saw any children.

Arabs, Pakistanis, Europeans and Asians were also present with a scattering of other Americans. The language or accent identified these diverse persons since, in swimsuits, one human is much like another.

Maggie sunned, Ali swam and Lee read *All the President's Men*. He was not supposed to swim yet because of his hernia operation. Temptation was too strong so he eased himself into the water and learned a thing or two. The water, pretty, clear and blue, was also warm; pleasant but not very refreshing since, in all the heat, a body really wants to cool off.

The highlight of the day were the toasted, crisp, ham and cheese snacks served pool side. The delicacies were served with potato chips on the side.

They looked over their shoulders for Joe constantly, always on the alert for any untoward activity. Nothing happened.

When the shadows grew long and their tolerance for the out-of-doors grew short, they showered, dressed and returned to the Bed and Breakfast.

Catherine handed them a message when they returned: 'Call Mr. Unger at 52936, the number for the American Embassy.

Lee dialed from the desk.

"Howard? This is Lee. You left a message. What's up?"

"Lee. I'm glad you called. How is your case coming?"

"O.K., I guess. Our lawyers seem hopeful but it looks like we'll be here for awhile."

"I see. My wife and I would like to invite you and Maggie to have dinner with us one night."

"Oh, why, thank you. What night do you have in mind?"

"We're quite open this week, but Tuesday would be good for us."

"Right. I'm sure that's fine. We really appreciate it. I'll talk to Maggie and call you if it's not a go. Where shall we meet?"

"We'll have you come to the house for cocktails first and go from there, O.K.?" He gave Lee an address and directions.

"Yes, fine. Thank you very much. We're looking forward to it!"

Maggie was also happy to be invited and had only one reservation. "What about Ali? Where can we leave her?"

"I don't know. Maybe here. We could pay one of the girls to baby sit."

"Lee, I don't think that'd be safe. Joe knows where we are and, if he knew that we'd left her, I'm afraid that he might try to grab her again."

"Look. We have until Tuesday to find a baby sitter. Let's table the matter for now, and if we can't solve it, we'll either cancel or take Ali with us. O.K.?"

"O.K., but I'm not going to let Ali out of my sight for a minute unless I'm absolutely sure that she's safe."

"Yes, of course. I agree." They embraced to convince each other of their solidarity on that point.

Saturday evening already. They'd been in Bahrain for four nights and four days. They were becoming oriented and knew a little about their pension's neighborhood.

There were two cold stores on their street as well as a chemist, a cinema, three restaurants, a theater with an open-air lobby, two carryout hot food shops. They had patronized almost all these places except for the movie house which seemed to cater to the Pakistani population. The films were Indian and they wondered if the subtitles would be Arabic, French or Pakistani.

The first day of the workweek the streets in this part of town teemed with people. Sometimes the sidewalk traffic was so heavy that they'd opt for the street in order to make their way to and from dinner. The people there, seemingly very poor, never made them feel uncomfortable.

When they stopped to buy something, a medicine from the chemist, a drink in the cold store or a sandwich at a brasserie, they'd have to point and gesture to make the transaction; yet they never felt unwanted, threatened or put down. People were very kind in Bahrain.

They were heading for the Middle East Hotel that evening. It had been recommended by Salah and would represent a change from the Downtown Restaurant.

Joe wanted to see Maggie. He knew he had been ordered to stay away but when had he ever done what he was told to do? The street where the Shakar Bed and Breakfast was located was dark so it was easy for Joe to wait in his car until Maggie came out. He had been lurking around for a couple of days to find out where they went and what times they left the B&B. Ben had told him to take a few days leave so he could cool off and take care of things. So yes, Joe was taking care of things. Today they went to the Gulf Hotel to swim.

Joe positioned himself in a comfortable chair in the hotel lobby. It afforded him a good view of the pool area. Lee stayed with Maggie and Ali all day, so there was no chance to talk to Maggie. What was he going to say? He had been thinking about this the whole time he was sitting in the car. What could he say? I took Ali because I knew you would come and get her and we could be together again. Joe didn't know Lee was going to come with her. So now what?

Now they were walking, the three of them, towards a hotel down the street. Joe got out of the car and followed about a block behind. He stood outside the hotel thinking of ways to get Ali back, but if he got her back, what would he do with her? Sherry had gone back to the states…good riddance to bad garbage. What good was she? She couldn't even keep an eye on Ali. Joe looked through the hotel's plate-glass window to the dining room. The threesome were eating dinner now.

He grew emotional and raged inside, "I hope they choke on their food."

"Oh no, not Ali she's just a baby. She's my baby. I have every right to want to be with my daughter. Maggie, why did you leave me? I would of given you the world. I just couldn't be a father to Jackie. I just want to be with my own kid."

When they got up to leave Joe saw that Ali was sound asleep, Lee was carrying her. "I can't keep doing this! I don't want to scare Ali. The police said they would put me in jail.

I have to find another way to get Ali back," Joe thought as he slid behind one of the columns outside the hotel until he saw them walking back to the Bed and Breakfast.

The Middle East Hotel was a three block stroll from the pension and proved to be a delight for Maggie and Lee. The building, lobby and restaurant were somewhat on the shabby side. This was a businessman's hotel now, probably forty years old. In Miami it would cater to the lowest trade. In Bahrain, a country loaded with visitors, it was a fourth or fifth best hotel and clientele seemed high class in comparison to the structure.

The dining room was rather large and had high ceilings. It must have been elegant a quarter century ago.

The maitre'd was a slender brown man with straight black hair. Perhaps he was half oriental. His smile and manner made them feel right at home. Especially Ali who was in flirt mode.

He seated her with a flourish. "How are you tonight, Miss?" He gave her a friendly pat.

Ali smiled shyly, very pleased, "I want spaghetti with no sauce. Just butter," she told him.

They all laughed. Allison was happy. The menu was presented and the adults felt at home too.

The prices were low. Maggie ordered shish kabob and Lee wanted Chicken Kiev which he'd never had but knew about the preparation. The food was delicious. They feasted and then Ali slept on Lee's lap, unable to go the distance.

Dinner over, satisfaction complete, Lee picked up Ali and nestled her head on his shoulder. Maggie reacted, "My God, Lee. Your hernia! Let me carry her."

He'd forgotten. But there seemed to be no problem. "I'm O.K.! If I get tired you can take her."

So, Lee carried her home to Shakar's. In the calm and quiet, they put Ali to bed, strung up the pink bedcover shades and played gin rummy until sleep came for a visit.

Joe lurked a while outside Shakar's before he went home to his empty apartment with the bare refrigerator.

CHAPTER 13 - SHARIA COURT

SUNDAY, JULY 13, 1975. "Lee. Do you know how much money we've spent so far?" Maggie was fretting over a list of expenses with a pencil stub in her teeth.

Their case would be heard at last! Now they had been in Bahrain for six days and expenses were piling up. They still didn't know what Alireza and Associates was going to charge.

"I know we've already spent over $6,000.00," said Lee. "And we'll have to spend $125.00 a day to live in our pension, travel by taxi and eat. I think things here are twice as much as they'd be for the same stuff at home."

They visited the office again that morning. Muhammad was in conference so they chatted with Salah in his office.

As they sipped coffee, he smiled and said apologetically, in his deliberately phrased English, "My wife and I are embarrassed that we haven't been more hospitable. There are so many obligations. Nancy said to bring Ali by the house one day to play with the children. And we would like very much to have you to dinner one night soon. Do you have a particular restaurant you've found that you like?"

The Elres' social life was picking up.

"Thank you," Maggie said. "Ali's sort of lonely and she'd love to play." She looked to Lee to continue.

"Yes, sure." Lee smiled. "We would love to unless, of course, it is possible to go home. But, meanwhile when can we get together?"

"Oh, I'll have to check with Nancy."

"We're free except for Tuesday night. Mr. Unger has invited us to dinner."

"Ah. Mr. Unger seems to be a very nice fellow. I spoke with him about your case and he's very sympathetic."

"Salah," asked Maggie. "When will our case be heard? When can we leave?"

"We'll know more this morning. You are to go with me to court at ten thirty. It would be better for Lee and Ali to stay here until we return."

"Will Joe be there?" Maggie asked apprehensively.

"Yes, he should be there. But don't worry about that. He can't do anything to harm you here."

Maggie and Salah left at ten o'clock to walk to court.

Ali and Lee kept each other company. Lee read and drank coffee. Ali colored and drank coke. She was patient and never complained or seemed antsy. Ali just wanted reassurance from time to time...a little pat, a hug or a kiss.

Joe got to court at ten o'clock to meet with his attorney. They needed to talk before the case began.

Attorney Essa Hussein was a tall slim, man in his thirties. He wore a custom made suit with a silk shirt, a silk tie and custom made shoes. Essa had studied in the U.S. at Yale University and got his early training at a large New York firm where he learned that the suit made the man. As the newest attorney at the Bahrain partnership he felt he had to dress better, know more, and win more cases.

Hussein had not been happy to be given this case. The more he learned about Joe Zayyat, the more he disliked him. The firm had been working with Otis for a couple of years but never on anything like this. What kind of a man takes his five year old daughter from her mother? No matter, he was given this case and he was going to win it.

Joe saw his representative coming down the hall and waved. "Hello Essa"

"Hello Joe."

Joe was not happy with this cold greeting but he was told this guy was good by Ben, who had set up the deal.

"Essa. I want my daughter back, and I don't care how we do it."

"I will not do anything against the law for you Joe. Everything has to be above board."

"Ok, ok I understand that but there has to be a way to get around this charge Maggie has made against me."

"I've been studying your case and the charges. You're ex has taken you to civil court, and if the case is heard there I think you have a very slim chance of getting your daughter back.

"However, there is the Sharia court. It has jurisdiction over religious and family matters. If you were a Muslim we could take the case to the Sharia court. In that court I'm very confident that you could get your daughter back."

Joe thought for a moment, "Mami would have a heart attack if I change my religion, but how would she know. Maggie will never see this coming and I could get Ali back. That will teach her who is in charge."

"Essa, I think that's the way to go. I will declare myself a Muslim today in court and ask if we can have the case heard in Sharia."

Essa looked past Joe to the entrance of the courthouse. "This man has no morals," he mused. "He just wants to hurt this woman no matter what. Well, I'm his attorney and I don't have to like who he is, I just have to win this case."

"Ok Joe," he said, "If that's what you want to do we'll declare you a Muslim this morning and the case will be moved over to the Sharia court. It will probably take a few weeks for the case to be heard."

"I don't care how long the case takes, Maggie is the one away from home, her family and her work. Maybe Lee will have a need to go back to the States for work, that will give me a better chance to reason with her. This place is very expensive. Let's see how long they can hold out."

Essa and Joe walked together to the court where the civil case was going to be heard.

Maggie and Salah arrived in court just as Essa and Joe were going in. Maggie noticed immediately that Joe's attorney looked very competent and sure of himself. Joe looked straight ahead followed his attorney into the court, and sat down at a table.

Maggie and Salah walked up to a gate and Salah opened it. Maggie went to follow. Salah stopped her. "Women are not allowed past this point Maggie. You are going to have to sit back here while I plead your case."

"There's no way I'm doing that Salah. This is my daughter we're talking about and I have just as much right to go in there and plead my case as Joe has."

"Maggie. Don't make a scene here in court, it will not look good for you to do that. Remember you are in Bahrain not the U.S. and you must follow our rules."

Maggie saw that Joe was looking at her with a grin on his face. "Oh Joe," she thought, "I know how much you are enjoying this day, but if you think you are getting Ali you are very much mistaken. I will do anything it takes to get out of this country with my daughter."

Salah said, "Maggie let go of the gate and go sit down please. The judge is here now."

The judge wore a white robe. He was not very tall, but up in his dais he seemed ten feet tall to Maggie. His beard was black and he had very light eyes. Maggie wondered if his parents were European. He rapped his gavel and the case was then under way.

Maggie sat as close as she could to see the proceedings. She did not understand a word of what anyone was saying. Salah was standing, arguing with Joe's attorney. The judge must of told them to sit down because they both did. The judge was talking to Joe now and asking questions. Joe was answering and Salah was objecting, saying something that Joe got angry at.

Joe's attorney got out of his seat and said something to the judge that made the judge sit back and think for a few moments. After about what seemed like a lifetime, he sat up again and said something that Joe and his attorney liked because they smiled at each other and shook hands. Salah was up on his feet saying something that seemed to get the judge angry. The judge pointed his finger at Salah and spoke for a few moments. He wrapped his gavel, got up and left the courtroom. Salah sat back down, he looked defeated.

Maggie thought, "My God, I wonder what happened. Will I have to give Ali back to Joe? Will we have to come back to court?"

Joe and his attorney left the courtroom but not before Joe caught Maggie's eye and gave her a tightlipped smile.

Maggie and Salah got back to the office just before noon. Maggie was visibly upset. Her face was flushed and she was perspiring. Out of breath.

"That bastard! He changed his religion to Muslim!"

"So what happened?" Lee asked. "What does religion have to do with this?"

Salah led them to Muhammad's office. Maurice joined up and the story was told.

Muhammad explained. "There are two court systems here. The civil court and the Sharia court. The latter is the

Islamic court with jurisdiction over religious and family matters for members of the faith. Now that Joe has declared himself a Muslim, the Sharia court will have to hear the matter."

Maggie wore a grim face.

Lee was astounded. His face reddened and he blurted, "But, it's a sham! He's not a Muslim. He's just doing it to obtain some temporary advantage!" He was outraged. "Which court takes precedence?"

"The question can't be answered yet," Salah said. "Your case is unique and we have no idea what the judges will do. The court understands the urgency but since this is the beginning of the summer recess, it is difficult for them to take new cases. So we'll just have to be a little patient," he concluded.

"It's very sad," Maggie said. "Joe's mother is a very religious person. Her home in Lebanon is full of religious statues, crucifixes and pictures. She would die if she knew what Joe has done."

Muhammad leaned forward, hands flat on his desk and glared at Lee. "Lee. One of Zayyat's claims is that you are a Zionist in league with the Jews. He says that you both work for a Jew! If that is true, that is a serious charge."

"No way Muhammad. We are not Zionists! In fact I'm not even one hundred percent sure I know what you mean by Zionist."

Muhammad thought this over.

Lee continued; he wanted to make sure that all his "t's" were crossed and all "i's" dotted. "It is true that the company Maggie and I work for is owned by a Jew. But he's an American, not a Zionist. He's not even religious."

Muhammad's face contorted and turned red. "Well that's a relief. You know I just can't stand those FUCKING KIKES!"

Maggie and Lee were stunned by this outburst. They maintained their cool however and tried to will the conversation in other directions. They were not Zionists but had great sympathy for all sides in that troubled part of the world. They cringed at news reports that cited pain and suffering on all sides of the conflict.

Muhammad spoke again. "I despise this man. He makes a mockery of the highest and most profound beliefs which are a part of the religious experience. If the Sharia court consents to this false conversion, all Muslims will feel ashamed." His passions were aroused.

"When will the Sharia court hear the case?" Lee asked.

"On the Seventeenth," replied Salah. "That's this Thursday."

Muhammad sucked his pipe and gazed at Lee, "Tell me. Have you ever thought of borrowing a Bahraini passport for Madam Maggie?"

"Yes," Maggie answered. "We've thought of it but from where and from whom? We don't know any Bahraini ladies."

Maurice said, "Damn! It's a first rate idea. You could probably pay someone a few dinars and because your coloring is just right, there'd be no problem. You know that these women here don't say much."

"And I could wear a veil and a black robe." Maggie was serious. "But don't just tell us it's a good idea. Help us find someone to borrow the passport from."

Alireza looked troubled. He said, with a Boy Scout's intonation, "It's against the law! I'm sure that such a step won't be necessary.

"Yes. Quite so," Muhammad said around his pipe. "The courts here are just." Lawyerly scruples were at work.

Although Lee and Maggie thought that it was a good idea, despite not knowing all of the ramifications, they didn't know how to find a person from whom to borrow such an important document. And, when they discussed it privately, they felt that few dinars might mean thousands. Cash! And American Express didn't cover that service!

They discussed everything at great length but there was no clear conception of what would happen.

They were shaken by the deviousness of Joe's actions: threats, assault, lies, kidnapping, a willingness to let Ali suffer. He had no respect for American courts and now he was making a mockery of this country's institutions.

Lee felt that Joe's character was warped. This guy was not a fit custodian for a child.

When their time in the office was over, there was a need to structure the hours until bedtime. High noon and the sun was blazing away. Ali wanted to go to the pool and, since they lacked an alternate plan, they decided to go.

Passing a Hertz sign in a shop window, they asked about a rental car and found that the weekly rate was about $70.00 for a small car. The rental could be charged to American Express and payment thereby deferred for at least a month. Taxis required cash.

Later Salah, who had acquaintances in every conceivable business, agreed to help them rent a car.

So again, they taxied first to Shakar's and then to the Gulf Hotel and again lounged away the afternoon.

Maggie and Ali were getting very tan. Ali was a deep nut brown. Maggie well done - almost toast. There were some people at the pool who seemed to be regulars. Since business stopped from noon until four in the afternoon, many people spent this time at the pool.

They made a friend, a slender gentleman who looked like an Iranian prince Lee had seen in the papers that attended Harvard on a foreign exchange program. He always smiled at Ali and nodded our way when he passed. Sometimes he and Ali talked in the pool.

"Hello," he said. "Your daughter is so pretty. She reminds me of my little one."

"Hello," they responded with a suspicion because he might be an enemy.

"May I introduce myself?" he asked politely.

"Of course," Lee stood up, reluctantly as he put his book down.

"My name is Shabir Hussein. I manage the United Bank Limited branch in Muharraj."

Lee offered his hand. "I'm Lee Elres and this is my wife, Maggie. You know our daughter, Ali, in the pool."

Maggie said, "Hi. It's nice to meet you."

Shabir sat and they chatted for a few minutes. He told them he was from Pakistan and that his family was at home in Pakistan, escaping the heat of the summer. He remarked that, "Their absence leaves me in a lonely way."

Maggie warmed slightly, but although she no longer felt that he was a spy of Joe's, she did not tell him of their situation. He left when lunch was ordered, but they were to see him almost every day of their sojourn in Bahrain and he quickly became a friend.

The day passed slowly. Lee confident that the healing from his hernia operation was going well, enjoyed the pool.

Joe left the courthouse a happy man. "What a brilliant idea to change my religion," he smiled as he thought, "Maggie won't have any rights with Ali now. She'll be given to me to raise here in the Middle East. She'll go to a boarding school, I'll be able to see her on vacations and she'll marry in my circle of influence. Who knows, if Maggie realizes that Ali can't go back to the States she might come back to me and leave Lee so she can be with Ali. Things are going my way."

Joe was driving back to the office when he saw the building that Maggie's attorneys occupied. He parked around the corner in the hope that he would see Maggie and Ali. Only a few minutes passed when he saw Lee walk out and hail a taxi, Maggie and Ali were close behind. Joe followed the taxi a few cars back. It looked like they were going to the B&B. Joe parked his car a block away and waited. A few minutes later, they came out with a bag, got back in the taxi and headed out of the city. Joe stayed close enough to see Ali through the back window as she played with her mother.

The taxi stopped in front of the Gulf hotel. Maggie, Ali and Lee got out and entered the lobby. Joe parked and got out of the car. As he opened the front doors of the hotel he saw the threesome going towards the pool. He waited a few minutes and then found a place to stand to see the pool. Maggie and Ali came out of the bathroom with their suits on.

"My God, Maggie is absolutely beautiful, she looks like a movie star, and look at Ali, she looks just like her mother. I pity the guy that falls in love with Ali. How could Maggie have left me? I tried to give her everything money could buy. I just couldn't find it in my heart to be a father to Jackie. That doesn't seem like such a bad thing."

As Joe looked at "his girls," one of the hotel employees came up behind him. "Sir may I help you?" Joe turned and said "No!!!"

The young man retreated back to his desk. Joe really looked mean.

Maggie and Lee sat in the chaise lounges to read their books. Ali went in the water immediately.

"Mommy, mommy come in, it's really warm." Ali knew Maggie didn't like cold water.

Maggie sat up in her chaise, put her book down to go in the water with Ali when she felt a chill up her back. She looked around and saw Joe looking at her from the hotel lobby windows.

Maggie jumped into the water next to Ali and took her into her arms. "Lee I saw Joe inside the hotel looking out here at the pool."

"Mommy is daddy Joe here?" asked Ali.

"I don't know honey, I thought I saw him." Then she called out to Lee, "Lee, please walk over to the hotel and see what you can see."

Lee, immediately alert, put his book down and walked over to the hotel. As he was approaching the doors that led to the lobby he saw Joe lurking and looking out at the pool. Lee quickened his step and was able to catch up to Joe as he walked away.

"Joe, what are you doing here? The police told you to stay away. I have a mind to call and tell them you've been following us."

Joe turned looked at Lee with hatred in his eyes and said, "You've taken my wife and my daughter. What else do you want?"

"I didn't take anything away from you that you hadn't already lost Joe. You lost Maggie on your own. Don't try to blame it on me."

The hotel manager heard them arguing and walked over. "Mr. Elres, is there anything wrong? Do you need help?"

"No thank you Mr. Bartlett, Mr. Zayyat was just leaving." Joe turned and stormed out of the hotel. Lee watched him climb into a small, red, four-door Mercedes Benz. One of the common cars in the country except for the color.

Vincent Bartlett remembered Lee from the day they checked into the Gulf Hotel and he had to tell them that they were full. He had also given them permission to swim in the pool.

"Mr. Alireza asked me to keep my eye out for your family, that you might have problems with the little girl's father. I hope I was of some help."

"Yes Mr. Bartlett, that was just right. Thank you."

Lee went back to the pool and motioned to Maggie that everything was all right. He didn't want to say anything in front of Ali. They soon packed up and left by taxi. They looked around for Joe or his little red car the whole way home.

Soon one day faded into the next. Their routine moved them from breakfast at the Shakar pension to coffee at Alireza's office to lunch at the Gulf Hotel to dinner at the Middle East Hotel and to a game of gin rummy before bed.

Lee went to the police center with Jacob one hot morning to apply for the Bahraini driver's license required to rent a car. Together they fought their way through a press of Arabian gentlemen gathered there on a miscellany of official business, spending hours in line, only to be defeated in their purpose. Lee could not qualify due to a six-week residency requirement and therefore could not rent a car.

Lee later told Maggie, "Oh my God, how those poor people were herded about! It was almost, but not quite, as bad as getting a driver's license in Florida. I felt at home there in that respect."

They had occasional need to buy things for Ali or themselves. The crayons did not work quite as well as the ubiquitous Crayola brand crayons at home but the fire truck and other toys were first rate. When wound up, it had a siren and the ladder raised automatically.

They sometimes shopped in Jashanmal and Sons, which was Bahrain's Neiman Marcus. The prices seemed astronomical but the surroundings were much like home. It was nice and they enjoyed whiling away time just browsing there. They bought a few books and a thing or two for Ali and Maggie.

Most importantly, they shopped at the <u>Beauty Store</u> which sold clothing for women and children. <u>Top class ladies and children's wear</u> crowed the sign. The Beauty Store was not small but they were attended by the proprietor, Mr. Mirza H. Kanian.

They purchased only a pair of socks for Lee and a shirt for Ali. Very small dealings. But Mirza was personable and somehow in conversation they told the kind gentleman of their impending need for a place to stay and of their complicated circumstances.

They had to leave their cozy B & B the next morning.

"Look. Your problem is solved. All you have to do is tell Muhammad, the manager of the Delmon Hotel, that I sent you. I'll make a phone call right away. He'll put you up for as long as you like."

He was sincere and serious, but already having been turned down at the Delmon's desk, and told by Mr. Shakar that he'd find a place for them, they did not pursue the matter.

Mirza gave them his business card. Another display of Bahraini kindness.

Tuesday evening, July 15th, was a social evening with Howard Unger and his wife Monica. Both Maggie and Lee thought that she was lovely and talented.

They presented themselves at the Unger home at the appointed hour with Ali in hand. Ali was taken over by the Unger's nanny and offspring for her dinner whilst Maggie and Lee settled into a comfortable evening. The Unger home was on a date palm shaded back street. A large home, nestled with others of similar rank, all hidden behind lovely old walls and gardens. The neighborhood was a surprise to them. It was not small town U.S.A. but it was comfortable and pleasing to their American tastes.

Howard and Monica were gracious hosts. Maggie and Lee admired the heirloom furniture they had gathered from around the globe during their consular career. The Ungers had spent twelve years in India and, in that time, had accumulated many interesting things.

Monica said that she loved to paint and the house was graced by her canvasses.

Maggie admired an enormous piece of furniture which occupied a place of honor in the parlor.

"That," said Howard, "was made for us by a carpenter in India. You know, it cost us the equivalent of eighty dollars and he worked about a year finishing it using the crudest tools imaginable."

The mighty object was ten feet long, five feet high and was inlaid with finely worked woods and polished brass hardware. "All made by hand," he said. "The chap who made this piece seemed satisfied with the price but to us it seemed a shame for him to devote a year of his life to it."

Maggie and Lee were duly impressed, both by the object and by Howard's stories about their travels and his career with the State Department.

The program was a cocktail at home and dinner at the Paradise Restaurant. They enjoyed both.

The Paradise Restaurant was Indian and the most exotic placed they'd ever been. Not at all fancy; rough tables, benches, floors, walls. The two couples sat in a coarsely curtained space and, thus, had a private dining room. Howard rattled a fusillade of Hindi at the waiters. An array of twenty or thirty small dishes soon arrived. There were curries, rice, chicken, fish, meat and vegetables, hot Indian dishes and sweet things. All, insofar as the Elres' were concerned, alas, without names. But, it was a fine meal and it ended too soon with four stuffed Americans.

Wednesday, July 16, 1975

This was the day! They had to leave the protecting walls of Shakar's Bed and Breakfast to make way for the wedding party that had booked the entire establishment. Salah had spent some effort on their behalf looking for accommodations.

They found only one hotel. It proved to be unacceptable too dirty, too poor and too broken down.

Shakar, knowing their plight, suggested a friend of a friend who was going into the "Bed and Breakfast" business. They packed and moved to the "Mechanical Constructions and Technical Services W.L.L. Company's Hostel" for twelve Bahraini Dinars a night. No good. It was not up to Shakar's standards and they were very unhappy with the facility.

The people seemed kind and hospitable enough, but they didn't have their act together. The inoperable plumbing, dirty, uncarpeted floors, and general shabbiness were not to their liking.

They had to be in Sharia court on Thursday for the presentation of the custody case and they were miserable.

The street was getting dark and, with trepidation, they decided to walk to the nearby and untried Sahara Hotel for dinner. They walked narrow alleys in the fading light and passed straying goats, staring children, mysterious adults and dark doorways.

"My God, Lee. Let's go back."

"Daddy. What's wrong?"

"Onward!" Lee urged. A regular Columbus, he reassured his troop.

They made it to the hotel without a problem and enjoyed the good meal in the room's opulent but deteriorating décor.

Lee wanted to take a different route back to their bleak pension. Maggie got spooked when she thought she spotted Joe in a darkened doorway halfway home. They hurried on as they looked over their shoulders but saw nothing on the dark street.

A most uncomfortable night passed slowly. "Nothing works in this damn place," Lee muttered to Maggie, "not even the door locks."

Thursday morning, July 17, 1975

Maggie and Salah walked to court. Lee passed the time in the office with Ali.

Salah set a fast pace through the busy sidewalks and Maggie had a hard time keeping up. The now-familiar streets were blazing hot.

As Maggie walked the dusty streets she thought about her life in the States. Being with her family, the kids. Coming home after a day's work. Sitting with her husband and kids by the pool with a cool drink. How easy it was to take little things for granted, like reading a book to Ali at bedtime and not having to look over your shoulders everywhere you went.

Their lives had changed the minute they found out Allison was taken, the minute they heard the name of this city, Bahrain, that was half way across the world. Maggie realized that Ali might pay the highest price and she could be forever scarred. She cringed inside as she realized that if the judge ruled against Maggie, Ali would have to stay in the Middle East to be raised by nannies and boarding schools. She would only see her father on his vacations and never see Maggie and Jackie.

On the other hand, if the judge ruled for Maggie, Ali would go back to the states, and not be able to be with her father for a long time. Every way you looked at the situation, for Ali it was a traumatic one.

Finally Salah paused in front of a rather plain building and told Maggie, "Here it is. Through the courtyard." Maggie heard her name, Salah was calling her. "Maggie, Maggie, where are you going? Court is this way."

"Sorry Salah I was lost in thought." They walked into the building and immediately Maggie saw Joe and his attorney. She wanted to go up to Joe and slap his face. She wanted to do something. She kept her eyes on Joe but felt totally helpless.

They stepped through an open arch into a large, walled yard which was full of men in white robes. Some, like Salah, wore western attire and some wore shabby workman's clothing. Many carried briefcases or clutched file folders. Serving boys circulated among the crowd offering coffee in little cups. There was some shade but most stood in the bright sun.

They entered a dim courtroom. The chamber was dimly lighted and cooler than outside. Salah sensed Maggie's mood and took her arm courteously to lead her through the courtroom. Before he passed through the swinging gate he paused and looked at Maggie for a brief moment. Then, satisfied that she knew her place, he took his place at the bench. Maggie was left behind.

Joe felt the hatred in Maggie's eyes. He had never seen her this way before.

Essa Hussein, Joe's lawyer, felt the awkwardness of the situation. "Joe, if looks could kill, my man, you would be a goner."

"I don't care what Maggie feels now. When I get custody of Ali here in Bahrain, we'll see how she will change and beg me to come back. As long as she can be with Allison, she'll do anything. I have the power now."

Maggie saw that it was standing room only. She wondered who all they were. As she glanced around she could see the back of Salah's head as he stood at a table.

Joe stood with two men who, she thought, must be lawyers. Joe stared straight ahead and did not look at her.

A judge in white robes came through a door. He wore an Arabian headdress with a silken black cord holding it in place. He sat at a high bench and the room became deathly still as he read papers on his dais.

Maggie stood as close to Salah as she could and whispered urgently, "Is this the place? How come there are no women?"

Salah turned and said quietly, "Women don't attend these hearings. Their lawyers speak for them."

Maggie was horrified. "So," she challenged her lawyer, "...if a Bahraini woman has to defend herself, she has to do it through a male attorney?"

"That's correct. A woman cannot approach the court."

"It's different for western women. Right? I can talk to the judge so he can hear me tell my side of the story?"

"I'm sorry we didn't make this clear to you Maggie, but you'll have to let me talk for you."

"No offense Salah. I know you'll present a strong case, but I'd rather speak for myself. I need to explain to the judge how much Ali needs me as her mother. You can't possibly understand how a mother feels about her children.

"My God Salah. This is 1975–not the 1700's. Women certainly have their rights!"

"Of course Maggie. No offense taken. But this court is in the Middle East and your case is being heard here."

Maggie sighed and her shoulders slumped. On the verge of tears, she felt deflated and defeated.

"You must stay behind the gate and not come to the counsel table."

Maggie sat near the front to see the attorneys and Joe. She was frustrated that she couldn't understand anything being said. The judge rapped his gavel to bring the court to order.

Salah was up first stating their case. Maggie saw the judge nod his head and ask him questions.

After a while Joe's attorney stood and spoke. Maggie could see him ask Joe questions and then talk to the judge. She wanted to go through that almighty gate, to stand by Salah. She wanted an even playing field.

Salah could sense that Maggie was restless and was ready to cause a scene. He glanced at Maggie with eyes that seemed to plead for patience.

The magistrate read aloud from papers he held in his hands. He appeared to ask Salah a question because Salah rose and spoke for a few minutes. Maggie writhed inside with the frustration of not understanding.

Joe's attorney took a turn speaking then Joe stood and spoke in Arabic. His tone seemed to be angry and full of venom. Maggie was more and more frustrated by the proceedings.

Salah rose and interrupted Joe with a little speech to the court. Maggie wondered if he was objecting or denying what Joe was saying.

The other attorney spoke again and suddenly they were done and all filed through the gate.

Maggie was stunned by the speed and urgently whispered to Salah as he drew near, "Is it over? What just happened in there? It can't be over. That was too quick!" She stood in front of Salah to make him stop. Fear, frustration and anger took turns making her heart palpitate. She searched Salah's face for clues.

"Maggie please let's wait to get back to the office so we can discuss everything." Salah looked tired and worried and for the first time since they had met Maggie saw a bead of perspiration running down his cheek. They walked in silence through the streets that Maggie had gotten to know so well and was now starting to hate.

Maggie knew it was not good. She felt so helpless not knowing the language and what happened in court. Her thoughts raged, "How can these women live like this? They don't have a say in anything. How can they be so submissive? I see them walking the streets with their veils, their heads down and children in tow. How can this be happening in today's world? I can't let Ali grow up in a world like this.

I want her to be able to make her own decisions and be her own person. If I leave her here with Joe she will never be free to be Ali. My God, give me strength to follow this through."

"Please Maggie. Let's talk about it in the office. This is not the place to discuss our case." Salah said. There were men everywhere so Maggie had to continue to acquiesce as they walked quickly back toward the office.

She had not seen Joe leave and wondered how he'd gotten away so quickly. "Salah. Stop and talk to me."

Salah found a patch of shade for them to stand in and said, "Mr. Zayyat changed his religion to Muslim, so your case will be heard in the religious court."

"How can he do that? How can someone just change his religion from Catholic to Islam? Doesn't the judge see through that? What happens in the religious court?"

Maggie was full of questions. Salah looked frustrated trying to figure out which question to answer first.

"Look Maggie, let's get back to the office, we'll talk about this change of venue with Muhammad and Maurice, and figure out what to do."

Maggie and Salah walked in silence through the streets of Bahrain. The sun was beating down on them, sweat was pouring down Maggie's face. Salah, as usual, was walking briskly on seeming not to be aware of the heat or the uneven streets. His suit still looked crisp Maggie didn't see any perspiration on his face.

"Salah, please don't walk so fast, I can't keep up with you."

"Sorry Maggie, I was thinking about the case and got carried away."

Essa Hussein got the news about the results and called Joe immediately. The sooner he could get this guy out of his hair the better. But he knew there would be an appeal and he would have to deal with this character a bit longer.

"What does this mean for me Essa," Joe asked.

"It means that your case will be transferred to the Sharia court as soon as I go back to court to file the papers. But don't get too excited because I'm certain that Maggie's attorney will file for an appeal and that will take a few days to sort out."

"What are her chances with an appeal?"

"Not too good I suppose, but we have to go through the motions. I'll keep you informed as the day goes by and I hear from the court."

Salah and Maggie arrived at the office to find everybody waiting for them, looking for news. Lee saw them first and jumped to his feet as soon as they arrived. He saw the stricken look on Maggie's face and said, "What happened?" She ran to him, unable to contain her tears.

"Joe was there Lee. But I did not understand one word. It was all in Arabic. It's made me very nervous. I'm scared."

Lee's heart sank as he heard her words and he hugged her.

Salah looked anxious. "Lee, Maggie. Come into the inner office so we can discuss what happened." By this time Muhammad had joined them. They filed into Maurice's office and sat.

Muhammad explained, "Under the law of Islam, when there is a divorce, the mother has custody of girl children until the age of thirteen. Then, custody goes to the father. But. Should the mother remarry, the father gets custody and it is with these principles that we must work."

"You mean that Joe might win the case?" They were astonished. "We must present evidence that he isn't able to care for her properly. He's like a nomad. No roots. Living in a dump with that girl. Breaking the law of the U.S. by taking the child from the mother and entering her into Bahrain illegally," Lee recited a list of Joe's sins.

He continued, "Look, if the court buys his conversion, we'll have to take equal measures. Can you arrange a divorce for Maggie and me? It would be just as real as his conversion and, by the logic displayed thus far, they'll have to accept it."

Muhammad did not like this proposal. It went against his sense of fair play. "Let's reserve that action for a later time and instead try to work out something. Can you get a duplicate passport from the U.S. Embassy?"

This was a departure in thinking. Maggie and Lee feared its ramifications.

"We don't know," Maggie said, "But we can try. But meanwhile, we need a place to stay. Let's go to the Embassy first and then let's try to find somewhere decent to stay. I don't want to spend another night in that pension. Maybe we should talk to the guy at the Beauty Store, whatshisname? He said that he would get us a room at the Delmon."

They left, hailed a taxi and went to the Embassy. Howard greeted them in a most friendly manner. He sat Ali down to color on the couch in his office.

"How is it going? Tell me what all you've been doing." His concern was evident.

They reported the present, new living arrangements and told him of the court appearance.

"Howard. We're really feeling stuck. Among other things, we don't even have Maggie's passport. Could you do anything about getting it back for us?" Lee pleaded without much hope.

"Well, as you know," Howard intoned, "It is being held by order of the court.

"Is it possible for you to give me a replacement passport?" Maggie asked.

"I don't think so. But I'll make inquiries."

Obviously, despite their friendly relationship, Howard was not able to go beyond prescribed limits. The visit seemed pointless. The U.S. Embassy was not much help in this situation.

When they were alone again Maggie began to complain about the lack of service from her government.

All their lives it seemed that, in books and films, people in trouble always went to the U.S. Embassy for rescue.

"Ah. Don't be mad Maggie." Lee tried to soothe her. "I think that the Embassy is not there to resolve family disputes between U.S. citizens. They just represent our government and help U.S. citizens in dealings with foreign governments."

Back outside in the blazing sun, they stood waiting for a taxi. Noon hour traffic was brisk by Bahraini standards (perhaps two cars passing every minute!) and they soon hailed a cab as it sped down the broad boulevard.

The Beauty Store was on Government Road, near the landmark First National City Bank. They directed the driver and soon arrived. As usual they were warm and sweating and it felt good to enter an air-conditioned building.

They found whatshisname's business card. Mirza. They asked for him and the gentleman appeared immediately. "Good afternoon. What can I do for you today?"

Maggie and Lee took turns explaining their position and needs.

"We really don't need any clothing right now but we have a problem and perhaps you can help."

"When we were in the other day, you mentioned that you could get us a room at the Delmon. We've been turned out of our Bed and Breakfast because of prior bookings and have no place to stay. Perhaps we should explain. We came here to pick up our daughter, Ali, who was brought here by her natural father and we're going through a custody fight in court. We just don't know how long we'll be here but we need a decent room."

Mirza nodded encouragingly. "Yes. I wondered what was going on with you. No problem at all. I'm glad to help. All you have to do is speak to the manager, Muhammad. I already called him. He'll see to it that you have a room.

"Tell me," he said, "You came all the way from the U.S. to pick up this angel? What is wrong with her father? A child's place is with her mother. Where does he stay?"

They described the building in the Gold Souk.

"He's crazy. That is no way to keep a child. I tell you. Bahrain is a wonderful country. The people here like foreigners and the government is very benign but to take a child here, away from home in America... well, it's wrong! You must let me know if there is anything else that I can do."

They parted as friends.

The First National City Bank was so close, they decided to stop there to see if the money had arrived before walking the three blocks to the Delmon. The $1,000.00 had arrived and was converted to Travelers' checks. The transaction took only a few minutes and then they walked to the Delmon, hopes high.

Muhammad turned out to be a young man, beautifully dressed in Western garb. About thirty, he was the epitome of courtesy.

"Yes, of course. For Mirza, I will give you a room."

"How long can we stay?"

"As long as you like."

What a relief! At last they had a home that wouldn't kick them out after a few days.

The Delmon was not a large hotel. It had three floors of hotel rooms above the lobby. It boasted a coffee shop, a restaurant, a bar, meeting rooms and service areas. It had a notably large lobby and public rooms with the biggest Persian carpets they'd ever seen.

While it wasn't new, it was well maintained. Their room turned out to be nicer than the room at the Gulf Hotel. They all loved the big and bright room. So, back to the awful B and B to get their things.

It was early afternoon by the time they had taken care of the move. Salah was told where they were and the threesome settled into new quarters.

The first thing that Ali wanted to do was go swimming in the hotel pool. This turned out to be a disappointment because, although the pool garden was very pretty, close up, the pool water was quite green and opaque and the garden full of flies. It wasn't long before they tired and went up for a siesta.

The phone awakened them. A call from the United States was coming in and Lee held the phone to his ear, wondering who it might be. Lee's sister, Jane, was on the line and he was overwhelmed with joy.

"Hi. How did you know we were here?" he asked. The connections was excellent.

"Dad called me. He's very worried about you guys. What's happening?"

"No, Jane. I meant, how did you know that we were at the Delmon? We just moved in."

"Oh. Alireza's office told me where to call. But what's happening with your case? Dad is frantic."

"Well, there's nothing wrong. We call as little as possible because of the expense."

"Yes, I can understand that."

"But here is a status report. Our case in civil court is stalled. Joe has converted to the Muslim religion and has sued for custody in the Sharia court, the religious court. The case was heard today in the Sharia court and until a ruling is made there, the civil court won't act. We've been promised an answer by the Sharia court on Saturday, the nineteenth."

"My God! I can't believe it. You mean he actually changed to Muslim?" Her voice was high-pitched here, a sign of emotion since her normal voice is rather low.

"Yep. But it's a sham, of course, and we're hoping that the court will recognize this and that we can settle things in the civil court."

"Lee. There may be some things that we can do for you on this end. There is a well-known law firm in Washington, D.C., which specializes in international matters. They were very successful in a similar matter recently that had to do with a child who was taken to Israel by her father. Art (Jane's husband) knows one of the partners, so we called to find out if they could be of help and the answer was that they can do things in Washington which may be of great help to you."

Lee thought of a number of things while they spoke. "Hold it a minute, Jane. Let me consult with Maggie."

"Maggie, Jane is recommending that we get a Washington lawyer. They 're recommending a firm which specializes in our kind of case. They've recently had a similar case where a child was recovered from Israel. What do you think?"

Maggie thought briefly.

"Honey. We've already spent so much money. I don't see how we can afford it. Do you see anything else could be done?"

"No, not really. Gelb needed $1,000.00 just to accept our case. These people would probably want even more. Let's say 'no' for now. O.K.?"

"O.K."

"Jane. I'm sure that this firm would be great but we can't see quite how they could help at this moment. Our legal fees are already three or four thousand dollars, some of which we've already paid. We have spent a fortune which we don't possess, and, unless things go badly here, we can't see another legal fee."

"Lee. I've discussed the fee with Dick Hooper. He's the lawyer. He needs $2,000.00 to take the case, plus expenses, of course. We know that you've been strapped by this trip. We'd be happy to take care of the fee. You can pay us back whenever you wish. In fact, (the pitch of her voice indicated pleasure) my boss, you remember Ed, will advance us the dollars out of the company so it wouldn't be any strain at all."

"Jane." Lee's voice reflected his emotional state. He was overwhelmed by her kindness and thoughtfulness. "We just can't. Please let's put Mr. Hooper on hold. We'll take advantage if we see that we need it."

Maggie gained Lee's attention with a gesture. "Lee, have her call Dad to ask him to call everyone in Miami."

"O.K."

"Jane. We have an awful lot to tell you but this is not a ten cent phone call. Would you take a few messages for us?"

"Of course. But first let me find out a few things. The folks are coming to Washington for a visit. They're arriving on either July 27th or August 3rd. Depends on when Dad takes his vacation. We want you to come, too, if you possibly can."

Pictures sprung in his mind. The Virginia countryside seemed like heaven. Green hills, blue skies and comfortable homes filled with family.

"Of course, Jane. We hope to be out next week. We would like to spend a few days in Europe on the way back. We've never been and it seems to be a real opportunity since we've already spent the money to be in the neighborhood anyway."

"O.K., Lee. 'Nuff said. We want you to come."

"O.K., Jane. The messages are to Caridad, Maggie's mom, and Jackie, to Dr. Arnold and to Maggie's dad Alfredo. Just tell them where we are and that all is well." He gave her the telephone numbers.

The phone conversation ended on a cheerful note. Ali was upset that they had not put her on the phone with Aunt Jane. She was cranky but determined to make her point.

"Daddy. The next time you talk to Aunt Jane, I want to say hello! And Grandpa and Grandma and Jackie and Grandpa Elres and Grandma Elres and...," she ran out of names of people she thought it reasonable to find on the other end of the phone.

Maggie and Lee were thoughtful. They had a waiting period to look forward to; the Muslim court's date of decision. There were some tasks to attend to but not many. They had to follow up with Howard to try again to get a duplicate passport for Maggie.

There was an invitation to spend some time with the Alireza family. Ali would be entertained by the children and Maggie and Lee would go out to dinner at a restaurant with Salah and his wife. But mostly, there was a need to structure the time and there wasn't much of a significant nature to look forward to. There was sleeping and eating. Visits to the pool. Walks to Alireza's offices.

During the next few days they ghosted around, continually alert for signs of adverse activity, Ali always in sight, always in hand or in the custody of Alireza's maid in the confines of his house.

Their new friend, Shabir, the Pakistani banker from the Gulf Hotel pool, called frequently and they became quite intimate with him. He was in the summer doldrums. His family was still not with him and he was lonely. They visited his home. Once they took a meal together. On another memorable occasion he took them for a ride to the Zoological Gardens. This proved to be a date palm grove with a few animals on display. It was a particularly hot day and the real treat was not the garden but his companionship.

They visited Shabir's apartment and found that he lived quite simply. Later they discussed his apartment and decided that his standard of living would improve dramatically should he ever take up residence in the U.S. They welcomed his friendship.

Lee told Maggie he was sure that Shabir spent a considerable sum of money for his lodgings, however for the same money in the United States he could have lived handsomely.

The next day they visited the Embassy about Maggie's duplicate passport. "No way. I'm sorry, Maggie, but I can't issue you a passport."

"Howard. It's such an injustice! We know that there are rules but there are also rule makers who have sufficient latitude in their positions to adjust for situations such as ours."

"It's not that we are going to use the passport. We know that we can't leave. We just feel so exposed without it. You know, for example, that Maggie is of Cuban birth. She'd feel more secure with a proper passport."

Howard excused himself. "Give me a few minutes please."

And he left for about twenty minutes. Maggie immediately spotted her passport sitting in the exact center of Howard's blotter!

"Look Lee. There it is! Get it and stick it in your pocket."

"No Maggie. We'll get in trouble." Lee looked at the document longingly but was afraid to touch it. Maggie apparently felt the same because she could have just as easily grabbed it.

They argued intensely in whispers so that Ali could not hear.

"Get it."

"No!"

"Pleeease! He left it there on purpose."

"Let's not do anything that could put us in jail or on the wrong side of the U.S. government."

"You're such a goodie two shoes!" she hissed and turned her back to him.

Lee was torn up over the decision to grab or not to grab the passport but in the end he did nothing. They would never know if it helped or hurt.

Howard finally returned with a thick loose leaf book. It looked like a manual of rules and regulations. After a few minutes of study, he said, "Once again, I've studied the rules and I have no way to help."

"But..." Lee resumed the attack.

"Look here, Lee," he interrupted. "To satisfy both of us, I'm going to wire Washington for instructions. I'll ask for permission to issue a duplicate passport."

This was a stopper. There seemed to be no further room for argument.

They said their goodbyes and again emerged into the hot day under the watchful eyes of the Embassy guards, on the lookout for Joe and a cab.

Maggie and Lee were getting homesick. Jane's call was a reminder that life was waiting elsewhere.

"Oh Lee," Maggie sighed, "What can we do? We're doomed!" ·

Lee for once had no words of comfort to add.

CHAPTER 14 - ON THE BRINK

The morning of the twentieth of July 1975 was passed in the usual manner.

Maggie was a little out of sorts. She'd had a fitful sleep with frightening dreams. She dreamed that Joe had taken Allison from their bed and she had woken during the night with tears streaming down her cheeks. Lee had slept like a log throughout her ordeal.

After breakfast at the Delmon Coffee Shop, they walked the few blocks down Government Road to the office, past the fenced in government administration building. Women on the street watched from behind black robes and masks. Workmen moved easily along the street. A policeman walked his beat down the center of the street, watchful and alert. The eternal sun was warming up for its daily extravaganza.

Maggie and Salah went to court.

Ali and Lee perched on the couch. She was coloring and Lee, still reading *All the President's Men.*

After a bit, Muhammad invited Lee to his office. Muhammad inquired, "Tell me, Lee, what did Mr. Unger say about Maggie's passport?"

He related Howard's position.

"I want you to go back today and see what you can do. They can really do whatever they want to. I don't understand why the Embassy isn't more helpful!"

Lee defended his country. "Joe is a citizen too. Mr. Unger said, a while back, that the Embassy received some criticism from Joe's company for being partial to Maggie."

"I see. Well, go back anyway and see what you can do, won't you?"

"Of course."

Maggie returned frustrated. "I didn't understand a damned thing," she said.

"What happened?"

"Honey, I just don't know."

"Salah. Tell us what happened."

"No decision Lee. They heard our positions and promised a decision later."

"When, later?'

"I'm sorry. I don't know. We'll stay right on top of it. Don't worry," Salah advised. "There are many avenues open to us should we not prevail here. But don't be negative."

Maggie looked scornful at these words. "Tell me how not to worry. I worry! She's my daughter and no one is going to take her away. There'll be a hell of a fight here if they try."

The Elres family trekked off, not calmed by Salah's reassurances. It was not yet lunchtime. They were not in the mood for food anyway so they decided to go to the Embassy to see if Howard had any word for them and to beg for Maggie's passport again. The receptionist at the front desk smiled and said, "Mr. And Mrs. Elres. How are you today?"

"O.K., thank you," replied Lee, trying to remember how many times his little group had walked through these doors. "Is Mr. Unger in?"

"No, but he's expected soon. Why don't you sit in his office?"

They sat in his office. Feeling a little presumptuous, the three settled down in two comfortable chairs. They read the worn out magazines and played with Ali.

Howard marched into his office about fifteen minutes later. He seemed surprised to see them. "Oh, hello. I'm sorry about your case."

"WHAT ABOUT OUR CASE? WHAT DO YOU MEAN?" Maggie wailed.

"You don't know?" Howard seemed astonished. "I thought you knew. I'm sorry. I didn't mean to speak out of turn. I just learned that the Sharia court has awarded custody to Joe!"

They were stunned. What did this mean? Even now, Joe must be looking for them with the police at hand to take Ali away from them.

"Oh, my God! Lee! What are we going to do?" Maggie was very upset. Ali was clinging to her leg as she stood and wrung her hands.

"I don't know Hon. We have to get in touch with Alireza now! Howard, may we use your phone?"

"Of course." Lee sat down, concern and pain played on his face.

Although Lee dialed all the numbers in his notebook, he couldn't find any of their lawyers. He called the office but there was no answer. The afternoon break had started and they'd not be back until four o'clock. He called the three home numbers but servants and wives indicated the men were out. He left urgent messages.

"Howard. What does this mean? What about our case in the civil court?" Asked Lee.

"I'm sorry, but I just don't know. You can stay here until you reach Alireza but I must warn you. This Embassy is not a sanctuary. By international agreement, should the civil authorities demand to arrest you, I would be powerless to protect you and, I'm afraid that, if they are looking for you, this is the first place they'd look."

Again, Lee tried repeatedly to reach their counselors but to no avail. After a brief discussion, they decided to go to the Middle East Hotel dining room and hide there, out of sight, until they could reach the lawyers.

"They're not going to take Ali without a fight!" Maggie was a tigress on this point, "They'll have to kill me first!"

"Howard. We came here to see about Maggie's passport. May we have it? Please!"

"I received instructions this morning. I've been authorized to issue you a duplicate passport, but," he continued, "I must give the government twenty-four hour's notice before I issue the document. It seems that our policy is that all citizens shall be documented but we can't go behind the backs of the government here."

"I think that that's a pretty shitty thing to do. Lee. Come on. Let's go. These people aren't here to help us." Maggie stomped out, Ali in tow. Lee could only agree and followed her out.

Lee was able to hail a cab after a few minutes of searching up and down the broiling boulevard. Frightened, Maggie and Ali lurked out of sight in the Embassy vestibule.

The destination was the Middle East Hotel. This was the one place where they felt at home away from their room. And they felt sure that no one would think to look for them there.

As they ate lunch, Lee used the dining room manager's phone to try to reach the lawyers every few minutes. The calls were fruitless. They ate halfheartedly. The meal stretched out and finally it became obvious that they were the only diners and that the staff was trying to close the room.

After paying the check the fugitives sat in the lobby, hiding between a forest of potted palms and a pillar, shielded from the hotel entrance. After an extended wait, Lee finally reached Salah at his office.

"Salah. What happened?"

"Well. The court decided in Mr. Zayyat's favor."

"Will they try to take Ali away from us?"

"No." The fear began to ease. "We have appealed the decision. Where are you now?"

"We're at the Middle East Hotel. We heard about the decision from Mr. Unger. When we couldn't reach you, we didn't know where to go or what to do. So we're hiding out here."

"Come to the office, please. We must discuss our next moves."

"O.K. We'll be there shortly."

Maggie was vastly relieved when Lee told her that there were still avenues of hope remaining and that Ali would not be immediately snatched away. She perceived a similarity to American jurisprudence. Things were not done hastily. Perhaps appeal could be tacked upon appeal, and the whole matter would be deferred until Ali was ready to marry. Then Joe could fight with Ali's husband. "All we have to do was wait in Bahrain for fifteen or twenty years!" she thought.

A new round of conferences produced a new timetable for court dates. An appeal had to be prepared and filed in the Sharia court. This would be ready in about a week. The matter must also be pursued in the civil court but not until the Sharia court case was fully resolved, one way or another.

Muhammad had only one clear theory of law which was discussed at great length.

"Maggie. The Sharia court follows all of the great religious principles as written in the Koran. The custody of children was of great interest to people of olden times when the laws were conceived. In the case of divorced parents, you already know that the father will prevail. There is another person at interest, however, and that is your mother."

"What about her?"

"I believe that you told me that she lives with you. Is she a widow?"

"No." They explained that she was divorced from Maggie's father many years ago, married, but separated, from her present husband.

"Very well," said Muhammad. "Here is the point of my question. If your mother is not married, she could claim Ali and her claim would prevail over Joe's until the child's thirteenth birthday."

"That's crazy!" Maggie exclaimed. "Not that my mother wouldn't help. On the contrary, she'd do anything for her granddaughter. But I just can't see any sense to that at all."

"Regarding her marital status," Lee interjected, "She is desirous of a divorce and could obtain one on short notice. Would she have to come to Bahrain to pursue the matter?"

"No. That would not be necessary. I don't want you to do anything for the moment. We will study the matter and consult with our experts."

Maggie and Lee were emotionally drained at the end of the day. Full of despair, depressed, unable to see their next step.

Despite the heavy expense, they decided to hire the lawyers sister Jane had urged. The prospect of losing Ali overshadowed everything. Jane was called at home without difficulty. Lee spoke. "Jane. How is everybody?"

"Fine. But the real question is," she said with instant perception, "HOW ARE YOU?" The pitch of her voice rose as she spoke.

"Well. Good physically and mentally but we are having legal problems and have decided that it's time to take an additional set of attorneys. We lost the case in the Sharia court and they awarded custody to Joe."

She interposed an "O-H–M-Y–G-O-D-D-D!" She stretched out the words.

"But," Lee continued, "We are appealing and we continue to have custody of Ali. But let me tell you more about our situation. Our appeal will be filed in about a week. Our case in the civil court isn't moving at all until we finish with the religious court. I think that your attorney...what's the name, by the way?"

"Lee, write this down."

"I'm writing, Jane. Go ahead." Lee had his ever-present pocket notebook in hand.

"The firm is Curry Cresak and Morris, and the lawyer who'll handle the matter is Dick Hooper." She gave him telephone numbers and the address.

Lee gave her Mr. Gelb's information and told her, "Jane, I don't quite know how we're going to proceed but there is something else you should know and a favor or two that you could do for us. Maggie has no passport. They have agreed to give her one but insist on giving the Bahraini government twenty-four hours of notice before issuing it and we've told them to hold off. I don't think it is a politic move under the circumstances. So the point is, can Dick Hooper get her a passport? We have mine and we have Ali's!"

"O.K., Lee. I'll tell him to try to get a passport for Maggie. What else?"

"Jane. Please call Dad and have him, in turn, tell Maggie's folks and the office too. Don't alarm them, though. We'll fix this somehow."

"O.K., Lee. What else?"

"Jane was anxious to go to war and mobilize the new troops," Lee thought.

"Jane. Call Paul Rauschenplatt at the Continental National Bank of Miami," He gave her the telephone number, "and ask him to debit our account and wire $1,000.00 to us at First National City Bank in Manama, Bahrain. He knows the routine because he's done it before."

"Lee, do you need help with money? This is no time to be shy."

"Jane. I promise to tell you if we need money. I won't be shy." To Lee it seemed that day was rapidly approaching.

Maggie signaled for the phone and Ali wanted to talk too.

Ali went first. "Hi, Aunt Jane. How is Morris?" (Morris is the red cat who owns Aunt Jane's house.)

Pause. "I don't know. Yes. Yes. Thank you. Here, mom. Aunt Jane wants you."

Maggie expressed her love and appreciation and said goodbye for everyone.

Lee said, "Well Maggie. Everything has been kicked up a notch. This is a tough game."

Maggie was in tears. "Oh Lee. Your sister is so wonderful. What would we do without her?"

They both realized that the costs of restoring their family had just escalated by thousands of dollars. They would never let the money be an excuse for not accomplishing their mission, but it had to be counted and obligations would have to be honored.

CHAPTER 15 - ON THE MOVE

They met Evelyn Barlow in Alireza's waiting room on the morning of July 21st. He was a middle sized man, well fleshed but not overweight. He had an open and cheerful manner. His ruddy face was punctuated by blue eyes and framed with well cut blond hair. He was about forty years old. His curiosity seemed thoroughly aroused. The little family must have looked out of place.

"Good morning," he said with a pleasant smile.

They greeted him in return.

"Oh, you're Americans." He recognized their accents. "What business brings you to this part of the world?" His question was so direct that they were left with few choices: to answer honestly, refuse to answer, or to equivocate.

Lee usually answered such questions curtly, saying only "Business." But Evelyn was such an attractive person that Lee couldn't help breaking the pattern that he and Maggie had agreed on.

"Oh, family business," Lee said as Ali stood at his knee, gazing at him in a friendly manner. "We're consulting with Mr. Alireza on some problems we're having."

"Oh, I see. Please. May I introduce myself?"

"Yes. Of course." Lee stood and offered him a hand. "I'm Lee Elres and this is my wife, Maggie, and this is Ali."

"I'm Evelyn Barlow. Just a neighbor here. My office is next door and I'm delighted to meet you all. Actually, I know something about your problem. You're the talk of the town. Isn't this the little girl who was kidnapped?" By this time, Evelyn and Ali were holding hands.

"Yes, that's our family business. We lost our case in the Sharia court yesterday." Maggie told him.

"Oh God, no! What the bloody hell, excuse my French, are you doing in that court! Is your former husband, the bastard, Muslim?"

"Yes and no." Maggie answered. "He's a Catholic but he converted on the day we filed our custody suit in Bahrain to take advantage of the local law. It's just a sham."

"And they bought it?"

"Yep!"

They found themselves talking freely with this likable Englishman. By the time he was ushered in to see Muhammad, he knew the general situation. Since they, too, were waiting to see Muhammad, they saw Evelyn again when he came out.

"Look," he said, "Pop into my office when you're finished here. I'd like to chat with you some more. Can you stop by?"

He was too charming to refuse. And, of course they had absolutely nothing to do.

"Sure. What's the office number?"

"It's just across the way. No number needed."

Muhammad was his usual charming and optimistic self, full of good spirits. "Ah, good morning, my friends." He stood to greet them. Lee's hand was shaken and Maggie's kissed. He patted Ali on the head and he ordered coffee from Tony, the office boy-cum-clerk.

Since this was Saturday morning, the Western equivalent of Monday morning, Muhammad was obviously busy. They had a very brief discussion relating to the strategy of the appeal.

Maggie was blue. "Muhammad. I wish that we could just jump on a plane and get the heck out of here. We just spent another $2,000.00 and there is simply no way that we can sit around here and fight this thing indefinitely."

"Ah. I too wish that you could do that, but alas, that day will have to wait a while longer. Maggie", he continued, "I just can't tell you how ashamed we are over this decision. It makes a mockery out of our religion. Don't worry. Please bear with us. We won't let them win." Then, in a very firm voice, as if to invoke powers awaiting in the wings. "They will never take this child away from you."

Oddly enough, even though the future was very unclear, his pronouncement made them feel better.

"Muhammad. We've just met Evelyn Barlow in your outer office. He's invited us to visit with him when we finish here. Do you know him well?"

"Ah, Evelyn. An excellent gentleman. I advise you to get to know him. He has many contacts and may be useful to you. He's an expat and does very well here. You can trust him."

"Well, we'll go to see him when we finish here. We have something to tell you."

"Yes." He was attentive.

"We have hired an American law firm in Washington, D.C. which was recommended by my brother-in-law. The firm is Curry, Cresak and Morris. Our newest lawyer's name is Dick Hooper, a partner in the firm.

"Now, we have no idea what they can do for us but we understand that the firm has experience in these matters. They were able, for instance, to recover an American child, in a similar case, from Israel."

Muhammad looked grim at the mention of Israel but he listened attentively.

"I asked them, through my family, to bring pressure to bear in order to get Maggie a new passport. They have good political connections."

"Ah, that would be nice, wouldn't it?" He looked at Maggie.

Maggie took over. "Yes, I'd love to see them <u>have</u> to give it to me. The point is for now, if you hear from Mr. Hooper or his firm, give them whatever cooperation you can. They'll work from the U.S. end and you'll work from this end."

"Well, I'm glad for you. We need all the help we can get. There is nothing for you to do here today. Why don't you meet with Mr. Barlow? Perhaps he can be of some service to you."

At this point, Salah and Maurice came through the office and exchanged greetings, Maurice with a wicked gleam in his eye, said, "If I were you, I'd be looking for a way to get out of here." He seemed to have less faith in the law than Muhammad and far less than Salah, who, by the disapproving expression on his face, said that he thought that this was a shocking idea.

Yet the notion had great appeal to Maggie and Lee. "Maurice" she said. "I don't see how we can trust this system any longer."

Lee nodded ruefully, "If there is a boat going out of here, let us know about it. We'd give anything to return to our normal lives. We live very nicely in the United States, but we are working people who must get back to work."

They left the office on a high note. Having spoken about their desire to escape this crazy situation made them feel good.

Standing outside the office in the breezeway Lee mentioned to Maggie the irony of thinking of a way to sneak out. "You know Maggie, we're talking about doing exactly what we criticized Joe for."

"Yes," she agreed, "but I don't trust this damn system. It is stacked against women."

Lee nodded in agreement.

They walked across the open air hallway to Evelyn's office. It turned out to be rather a large affair and seemed to be the focal point of a multifaceted organization devoted to import of industrial equipment and to the design of manufacturing facilities. He was alone in the back part of the suite.

They walked through somewhat timidly, calling his name until they heard his voice. He was on the telephone but waved them in to sit in his office. Lee looked around at his things as they waited and speculated on the nature of his business. Lee decided that he was an engineer.

Presently Evelyn hung up and greeted them warmly, "I'm glad you could come. Was there any progress in your case today?"

"No." Maggie answered. "Not really. We hired another American lawyer yesterday. We've gone crazy with this whole business. I guess that the next step here is our appeal at the Sharia court. That will be on the 27th."

Lee spoke. "Our American firm will try to get Maggie's passport back."

"What! She doesn't have a passport?"

They explained their documentation. And more.

"This must be costing you a bloody fortune. It's one thing to be here on business but to pay these rates for any other reason, that's just awful!"

Lee and Maggie nodded in agreement. More conversation followed. Evelyn was an engineer. He specialized in supplying a variety of industrial material to this rapidly developing part of the Gulf area. He represented a number of United Kingdom firms.

He thought for a moment. "Look. I have a proposition for you." His earlier directness seemed to be a hallmark of his personality. He gave them a warm smile. "I understand that you are living at the Delmon and prices are terribly high there. I'm living alone in a rather large house and I'll feel very put out if I can't talk you into staying with me for a while. My wife can't stand this place and she packed up and left two weeks ago with the children. Damned house is absolutely going to waste."

This was a real surprise. Maggie and Lee gaped in amazement. His generosity and compassion for strangers astonished them.

He continued, "It would be good for me to have someone in the house. No trouble, of course. My house boy does the cooking and cleaning."

"Well..." Lee began the customary and obligatory refusal but Evelyn wouldn't let him finish.

"Also, I'm hardly ever at home. You'd have your own rooms. Absolute privacy. You could use my other car and save on your taxi fares. In fact," he grinned, "I won't take no for an answer."

Lee supposed that there were cultural differences at work. He recalled that whenever he visited South America, his friends and associates looked hurt whenever he chose to live in hotels rather than in their houses. They, on the other hand, probably felt somewhat strange when Lee put them up in hotels rather than in their home when they visited Miami. Maggie and Lee, in the American way, didn't have servants to care for their home.

After a brief discussion, with much urging on Evelyn's part, the invitation was accepted. He seemed overjoyed at the prospect of becoming their host and arranged to pick them up at the hotel at one o'clock in the afternoon.

They walked back across the hall to the lawyer's office and informed Muhammad of the decision to move in with Evelyn.

"Splendid!" he approved. "I'm sure that it will work out very well for you."

"Look Muhammad," said Lee. "Please keep it quiet... about where we're staying. Don't tell anyone."

Muhammad agreed.

So off they went to pack, pay the final bill at the hotel and await Evelyn's arrival.

Maggie and Lee tried to be as inconspicuous as possible. They felt sure that Joe would be able to find them but they didn't want to make it too easy. And there was always the chance to slip out of sight altogether. That would be another safety factor for Ali.

They left by a side door. Evelyn appeared at the appointed time drove them to his home in a compact but elegant BMW sedan.

The house was in a part of town that they had not visited before on a new street which had not been paved or even graded. The street was remarkably rough and full of large bumps and potholes. The neighborhood seemed new and the street was under construction. Careful and slow navigation was required to prevent the car from being disemboweled.

Evelyn spoke rather sadly about his wife and children leaving. They were reticent about questioning him on the subject and never learned if their host's wife had left for the summer of if they were having a marital crisis.

The house was two stories in height and surrounded by a wall. It provided a large combination living room and dining room on the first floor in addition to kitchen, den and servant's rooms. The second floor contained four bedrooms and a number of baths. It was a nice house with comfortable enough furniture but seemed to be too new to have really been lived in. It lacked a woman's touch.

Ali was particularly interested in their new digs and was taking everything in with wide open eyes.

They were introduced to the house boy and to another gentleman who was a rather famous sportsman and adventurer, Robin Knox-Johnston. Robin's claim to fame was that he was the first man to sail solo around the world nonstop. And he had won major ocean sailing races.

In fact Robin, was an idol of Lee's and he was thrilled to meet him.

He was also a house guest. Lee and Maggie were very happy to meet him and to sit and have a drink with them. Maggie and Lee already felt very much at home.

Lunch was a curry on rice with a delicious salad. The house boy was an accomplished cook.

They spoke about the problems that Maggie and Lee were having at length. Both Evelyn and Robin opined that the simplest and cheapest solution would be to escape and they thought that anything could be had for a price. They promised they'd be alert for a means for the Elres' to flee the island.

Evelyn asked when lunch was over, "What would you like to do this afternoon? I'll be heading for the office and Robin is going to be occupied too. Here are the keys to my

Jeep. Feel free to use it as your own. I shall definitely not need it." He produced a set of keys.

"Thank you," Lee said. "but I don't have a license to drive. I tried to get one in order to rent a car but could not because of a waiting period."

Evelyn laughed. "That is no problem at all. No one in the entire history of this country has ever gotten a citation here unless there is a fatal accident. Don't worry."

"Evelyn," said Maggie. "I would love to cook a meal. I haven't been in a kitchen in weeks and I love to cook. Could I cook our dinner tonight?"

"Oh sure. That'd be great. It's the lad's night out. Can we invite Robin too?"

"Abso-friggen-lutly! It'll be a party!" said Maggie.

"Daddy!" squealed Ali when she saw the Jeep. "It's just like on T.V. Can you drive it? Can I sit in the back?"

There were no windows or doors and this was a real adventure for her. Lee used extreme care on Evelyn's street to avoid the holes, building debris and stones. The jeep, with its tough suspension, rocked, bumped and rolled. Ali was thrilled. Maggie was chilled.

"Be careful with this tent on wheels," she cautioned Lee.

They went to the Gold Souk neighborhood, driving on the left side of the roads. They parked by a grocery store which had a wide variety of merchandise crammed in a small space.

The array of foreign brands, mostly English, was confusing. Maggie selected basic items such as cheese, milk, eggs, tinned vegetables and a large canned ham. The prices were astronomical! Everything was imported.

They loaded up and went home to find that they'd forgotten the ham! "Oh, damn! We'll never get it now. Someone's sure to have picked it up," Maggie wailed.

But, hours later when they went by the store again, the clerk was glad to see them and had the precious ham wrapped and ready to go. "I'm sorry that I didn't know how to bring it to you," he said. The honest and open way of the Bahraini folk was again demonstrated.

They took great pleasure in preparing their own food that night. Maggie let Lee help.

They discovered an unsuspected side of the British penchant for warm beverages which Americans prefer to be amply iced. There were only two tiny ice trays in the small refrigerator. A round of cokes and a before-dinner cocktail would exhaust the supply of ice so Maggie emptied the trays into a small sauce pan and left the pan in the freezer section of the fridge while more ice was made. With careful timing they had a good amount of ice by the next day.

Later, Evelyn commented on the supply of ice, "As I live and breath! What a grand idea! That's how to do it!"

They didn't see much of Evelyn or Robin on Wednesday, the 23rd of July. They went to the office for a short visit and picked up a new supply of money at the bank, courtesy Paul Rauschenplatt and automatically deposited paychecks.

It was a great pleasure in having wheels. They spent a pleasant time at the Gulf Hotel pool, eating cheese snacks and visiting there with friends. Evelyn came by for a swim as did Shakar, their bank friend.

Home again they decided to splurge on a phone call to Jane to thank her for her help.

Lee dialed and soon had his sister on the phone. After a quick hello and a thank you for the help, Jane said urgently, "Lee. I just heard from Dick Hooper, your new lawyer and there's something you need to know right away.

"Here. Let me read a section of this paper...it's a memo from Dick and he faxed it to my boss."

Her voice was clear. "It's a little too long to read the whole thing so I'll paraphrase. It says the State Departments official position is 'Hands Off' your case. The American Ambassador to Bahrain is Joe Winesap and he's a personal friend of Dick. Winesap told Dick that your case is taking up a lot of his time.

"Winesap said that in the three years the Embassy has been there, he has never gone to the Foreign Minister's office. But he's been there three times in less than a week about your case. He's had a lot of official contact with the Bahraini Foreign Minister who wants it over and done with.

"The Foreign Minister says that, "he is sick about the case and sick of it.'

"But here's the big point I wanted you to hear. Now I'm quoting from the memo: 'Winesap has spent some time keeping Otis Engineering informed. He's been talking to two top executives of Otis who are in the area!'"

Lee's heart sank. He realized that the American Embassy was not in their camp and had even been talking to Joe's bosses!

"Thanks Jane," he croaked.

"Lee. There's a lot more here but nothing else you need to know right away. Your case is becoming a *cause célèbre*. We're working to get the State Department on your side since you have custody in the American courts. I'll tell you more later."

They said their goodbyes and Lee went to the kitchen to tell Maggie the news.

She took it calmly, saying, "I just knew that Joe would find a way to help himself here. He probably knows where we're staying now. That's how he found us so quickly at Shakar's."

Maggie, again, prepared a meal of scrambled eggs, a potato fritter and ham. It was shared by Evelyn and Robin. They vowed that they'd never tasted better.

Ali went to bed early. Their host and Robin departed for an outing of some kind. The rest of the quiet evening was spent reading.

CHAPTER 16 - THE PERSIAN GULF

FRIDAY, JULY 25, 1975

Robin brought Douglas with him to the house in the afternoon. He was an expat Scot seaman. A compact but ener-
getic man with curly red-brown hair. He was dressed in jeans
and work stained tee shirt.

Douglas, Robin, Evelyn, Lee and Maggie sat in the living
room with steaming cups of hot tea, enjoying the air conditioning. Douglas had a proposition.

"Look my friends," he addressed Maggie and Lee. "Robin
has explained your situation. I may have a solution for you."

"There·is a certain tugboat which passes near Bahrain.
My great friend Mohammad is the captain of this fine vessel.

The crew would welcome you as passengers to the United Arab Emirates. The U.A.E. There will be no formalities. It's just a ride over there and you would be put ashore in Sharjah, a small port, and taken to the local hotel. Then you'll be on your own to contact your Embassy and try to get home."

Here was the opportunity they'd been hoping for. They took turns asking questions. Where in hell was the U.A.E.? What kind of a place was it? Would they be sent back to Bahrain in disgrace? Could they trust the crew? Etc? Etc? Etc?

The fact that Joe's company had the ear of the American Ambassador to Bahrain was also in play.

It turned out that Douglas was full of information about the U.A.E. He began a somewhat rambling dissertation, punctuated with tidbits from Robin. Maggie and Lee were fascinated both by his lecture and by his strong Scot accent.

"The United Arab Emirates," he said, "is a new Middle Eastern country that we used to call the Trucial States. There are seven emirates there. You may have heard of some of them and others are a wee obscure. In total they're much bigger than this island but nowhere near the size of the neighbors like Oman or Saudi Arabia.

"As I said, before 1971," continued Douglas, "they were known as the Trucial States. They're sort of between Oman and Saudi Arabia. They've found tons of oil there and they're going to be very rich.

"I can't name them all," said Robin, "but I know a few like Dubai, Abu Dhabi and Sharjah. And I've actually been to Abu Dhabi."

"I saw that name Abu Dhabi at the Airport as our plane's next stop," said Maggie, "but I thought that it must be in India or someplace far away."

"And how far away is it? How long would it take a boat like that to get there?" asked Lee.

"Uh...I don't know?" admitted Robin, "but I suppose a couple of days."

Maggie and Lee both quailed at the thought of spending days at sea with Ali.

Robin was a bearded sailor and writer of books who drank a bit and told sea stories. He'd sailed around the world alone to win an "Around the World" sailing race. He was Evelyn's friend. Their lawyer, Muhammad, recommended Evelyn. Evelyn recommended Robin. Robin vouched for Douglas.

Not enough, by half, to bet their lives and liberty on foreign seas in a smuggling for hire operation!

Douglas was a handsome guy with a winsome, open face. He reminded Maggie of Robert Redford, the movie actor, and that was a point in his favor. "Look people," he said. "You obviously don't belong here in this money pit. It's different for those of us who work here. Our companies are footing the bills. If the courts go into summer recess here you will really be stuck.

"This guy Mohammad Hamad is a friend of mine. We've worked together for years on little deals." He winked as if to say "You don't want to know the details."

"He'll give you T.L.C. You'll understand when you meet him. A real good guy. A reliable family man. And he has good connections."

The price had been set at $1,500.00. Lee asked Evelyn if he thought it was a good idea.

"Damn right! Don't worry. The money here is not important to any of these people." (Meaning Douglas' captain friend). "They wouldn't risk their jobs and the boat for $1,500." Evelyn knew all about the people in question. "The money means very little. Mostly it's a gift for the crew. This is a very special favor to you."

He showed them a chart of the area and they realized that it was only a few hundred miles going around the peninsula that was the country of Qatar, across a stretch of the Persian Gulf. They'd be near the Hormuz Straits which narrowly divided Iran from the huge Arabian Peninsular.

They listened and believed. All of their questions were voiced: jail, return to Bahrain, etc. The answers were all along the same lines. "You won't be worse off."

And of course the money. This adventure they had calculated had already cost them more than twenty-thousand dollars. Ali's fare home would have to be paid and they'd even lost their twenty-one day excursion fare. Not to mention considerable time lost from work.

Later, Lee and Maggie spoke privately.

"Maggie, let's not forget what Jane told us. The fact that the American Ambassador is talking to Joe's lawyers. That scares me. What business do they have taking information about us and telling Joe's people?"

Maggie held her head in her hands and said bitterly, "Lee. That's probably how they found us so quick at Shakar's B and B. They probably knew every time we made a move. And they probably know we're here at Evelyn's house."

Suddenly Bahrain no longer felt safe.

They decided to go!

"Oh My God! Lee." Maggie wailed. "We're going to hell. We're going to jail! I'll never see Jackie again!"

Lee was full of trepidation too. He said, "The options are all bad. At least this way we'll be going down fighting."

They came up with a plan. The scheme was to take no luggage since they'd be leaving from Bahrain in a small boat and further, must not appear to be leaving.

Sunset, Saturday, July 26th, 1975, was the appointed time. Evelyn would inform the attorney Muhammad after the fact so as not to compromise his position vis-à-vis the Bahraini judicial system.

They did not know how to inform their families since Maggie and Lee did not feel free to speak about the arrangements on the telephone. They felt isolated from the world once the decision was made. They were adrift now, literally and figuratively, hoping to wash up on a safe shore again. No one would know where or when.

All fears and worries over their course of action sat heavily on their minds. They were full of 'what ifs' which could not be answered. Even by their new friends.

They didn't tell Ali for fear that she would fret excessively or ask questions they couldn't and wouldn't want to answer. The discussions and plans were always made when she was out of earshot, sleeping or otherwise distracted.

The hoard of cash was slim. Their remaining American cash, Bahraini Dinars and Traveler's checks totaled seventeen hundred and sixty-five dollars. After paying for the passage they would have only two hundred and sixty five dollars. The three of them so many thousand miles from home.

Joe, In fact had discovered their lodgment at Evelyn's house. He'd borrowed a car they couldn't know and parked near the Alireza law firm on Government Road. He spotted them leaving the office building with an unknown man. He felt proud of his detecting abilities as he followed them to a new two story home on a street newly hacked out of the desert sands in a good part of town.

There was a partly constructed house on the opposite side of the street with a tile roof carport. He backed his car into the deep shade and watched.

He had been at his post for two long hours now. The heat was unbearable, his water bottle was empty and he couldn't remember the last time he had eaten. Joe needed to urinate but there were no good options for this. He couldn't be seen! He thought about taking a break to go to Essa's office to check the progress of the case. But he waited. He suffered through the pain and discomfort.

Joe had devoted two whole days to lurking in the porte cochere with its clear view of the front door. No workmen appeared during his stake out. He noticed several European men came and went from the house where Maggie was staying. One of them was on a motorcycle. Twice Joe followed Maggie and Lee when they drove off in a small jeep. They did a little shopping once and the next day they went to the Gulf Hotel apparently to use the pool.

"Damn Them!" Joe thought. "They are living a good life while the Sharia court's decision process drags on. And I'm stuck in this filthy hot car." He dreamed about pleasant days in Florida and the good life they once had. "Damn her to hell!"

The days before departure were not easy ones. Sleep was fitful. Packing was difficult. The single bag they decided to take was the size of a large ladies' handbag and it was loaded to the bursting point. Papers, a change of underwear, a couple of paperback books, coloring books for Ali, and toiletries fit tight. They had a tiff over whether to take swim suits. Lee, ever optimistic, won and they jammed their suits into the bottom of the bag.

The escape must look like a local excursion. Just a little outing.

Everything else was in their luggage in a corner of Evelyn's spare bedroom. He would ship it to them when they were safely home.

Maggie wore blue, bell-bottomed jeans and a chambray blouse. Lee wore jeans, a golf shirt and sturdy white tennis shoes. Ali wore her shorts and a top. They were dressed for a twilight stroll.

Maggie, Lee and Ali walked out the back door and got in the car with Evelyn and Robin on the next street back. Lee thought the ruse unnecessary but Maggie insisted on stealth. They got in Evelyn's car. Douglas, their Scottish friend, met them on his motorcycle and Evelyn's car followed slowly, avoiding pot holes. The convoy moved more rapidly on the boulevard and across town, turning into strange streets.

The departure happened in full sight of Joe who had been in the street behind Evelyn's house and going in the same direction, ahead of them. He saw the motorcycle first, then the car, in his rearview mirror. He stopped the car well ahead of them, at the end of the street and ducked his head out of sight.

A half an hour before sunset Joe couldn't take it any longer. He pulled out and circled around the block just before the little procession formed up and began to move. Joe kept his head down and laid low as the motorcycle came up behind him. "I wonder where they're going," he thought. When the car passed he raised his head and saw Lee through the back window. Maggie sat next to him with Ali on her lap. The car followed the motorcycle.

Joe followed at a safe distance through the streets. Something was happening; he could feel it in his bones. He had never seen all of them driving together. Lee and Maggie usually took the Jeep and the others never went with them. Now they were driving across town in the direction of the yacht club. He kept them in sight until they stopped at the gate of the yacht club. He parked his car a half block away, got out, walked behind a delivery van, and peered at them from the shelter of its high rear end.

Maggie, Lee, and Ali stood at the end of the pier. They seemed to be saying goodbye. The one on the motorcycle climbed in the boat and was helping Maggie and Ali on board. There was another guy driving the boat.

"Where could they be going at this hour?" They must be taking a ride. The runabout is too small for a long journey and I didn't see any suitcases. Lee was carrying Maggie's purse. Joe watched as the boat motored away. The two men remaining on the pier waved, walked back down the pier. One got in his car, the other on the motorcycle, and they drove away.

"If I'm going to stay here and wait for the boat to return, I need to eat." Joe said to himself as he crossed the street to a little cold store. He used the bathroom, and bought bottles of water, candy bars, and some peanuts. "This should keep me going until they come back."

He moved the car to a better vantage point, sat back and waited for the runabout to return. It was dark when Joe spotted the running light of the small craft.

He sat up so he could get a better view. Two men tied the boat to the cleats. They were alone. No Maggie. No Ali. He walked down to the end of pier to confront them.

"Hey, he called. Where are the people and the little girl who left with you earlier?"

"What people? What little girl?" said Douglas. We went for a ride to test the motor. What's it to you anyway?"

Joe was agitated; he balled his hands into fists. He could feel his face getting red. He had to clam down, these men knew where Maggie was and he needed the information. "The little girl is my daughter,. Her name is Ali. I saw her and her mother leave earlier with you."

"Mister, I don't know who you are, and I don't care. We haven't seen anyone." The men kept on working getting gear out of the boat and ignoring Joe.

Joe was fuming. He knew they were lying. They were covering up for Maggie. He stood his ground for a few minutes glaring.

"I know you're lying, I saw them leave with you two. You'll be sorry if anything happened to my daughter!" he yelled as he walked off.

Joe got in his car, gripped the steering wheel and gave a guttural scream with the window closed, "Maggie, you bitch! Where in hell are you?"

After a few minutes, he regained his composure, and drove back to his old post by the two story house. The lights were on in the house, the Jeep, the motorcycle and the other car were in the driveway. He took his post in the porte cochere and waited.

"Where could they be? Maggie wouldn't put Ali in any kind of dangerous situation, he was sure of that. So where are they?"

"I'll have to wait here until morning to see if they come out of the house." With that plan, Joe settled back for a sleepless night.

The sun was coming up when Joe saw the house boy come out of the house with garbage. "Good, they're up. They'll be going out in the Jeep as usual." He waited.

Two hours passed. Now the two men who had been at the dock the day before came out of the house got in the car, and drove off.

"This is my chance, thought Joe." He knocked, looked through the side window to see the house boy walking toward him.

The boy opened the door and very timidly said "Yes sir, how may I help you?"

"I'm looking for the little girl and the woman that are staying here."

"Who may I say is calling, sir?"

"Tell the woman that Joe is here and needs to talk to her."

The boy closed the door, locked it, and hurried upstairs to the room where the couple was staying. He knocked on the door - no answer. He knocked again - no answer. He knocked for the third time, no answer. The house was very quiet and felt empty. He tried the doorknob gently. The door opened slowly and he saw the couple's bed was neatly made just like he had left it the morning before. Suitcases were piled in the corner of the room. The little girl's coloring books were gone. He closed the door, went down the stairs and opened the front door.

"There is no one in the room sir."

"Did you see them last night?"

"They went out yesterday afternoon with the master and his friends. I did not see them for supper or breakfast this morning. The bed has not been slept in. Their suitcases are still here so they must be coming back." The boy was starting to feel that he was in trouble. He could see this man who calls himself Joe growing angry at what he was saying.

"I'm sorry sir I do not know anything else, I have to close the door now."

Joe put his foot inside the door so the boy couldn't close it.

"Sir, I must close the door now, I will get in trouble with my master if I let anyone inside the house when he is not here."

Joe realized that it was useless talking to this boy. He didn't know anything; he was just a stupid house boy. He let the door slam and heard locks click as he was leaving.

Joe couldn't figure out where Maggie, Lee and Ali had gone. They disappeared from Bahrain, like they were never there, except the boy said their suitcases were still in the room. That really puzzled him.

"Would Maggie leave all her things behind?" "She can't leave Bahrain; she doesn't have her passport. Maybe they moved to another place." He would have to go back to the office and talk Ben into calling his contacts at the embassy to get information about Maggie. "They're here somewhere and I'm going to find them."

Confident that Maggie couldn't leave the island without a passport, Joe went back to Otis.

The yacht club in Bahrain had been guarded by red striped railroad crossing type barrier and a policeman. The guard waved them through without incident.

All of them; Douglas, Evelyn, Robin, Ali, Maggie and Lee, walked casually through the car park around the club's main building and then down the longish pier. Small sailboats and outboard runabouts were everywhere in colors of red, white and blue.

Maggie and Lee were scared out of their wits. Lee was swinging the bag casually, pretending that it was only Maggie's handbag. They felt as if eyes must be on them but they could see no one.

The sun was about to set but it was still quite light when they reached the end of the pier. A small runabout was tied there. It's outboard motor quietly idling. A dark skinned, dark eyed man at the steering wheel smiled up at them.

There was a stillness in the air. Everything else faded from their eyes. Just their immediate surroundings seemed real.

"Well. Goodbye, Evelyn." Goodbyes all around. A kiss from Maggie and a handshake from Lee. "Thank you for everything," said Maggie, "You are a real Samaritan and we'll never forget you." Evelyn looked misty-eyed.

"Good luck," from Robin.

Nimble Douglas jumped into the little boat and reached up to help Maggie down and then to lift Ali in. The helmsman was introduced as Jamal. Lee was the last to board.

What feelings Maggie and Lee had stepping into that little craft! The early evening air was warm and pleasant. The sky, still bright blue, was laced with fluffy pink clouds.

They roared away from the dock and had to hang on tight as Ali asked, "Are we leaving for good Mommy?"

"Yes, my darling," Maggie was a little quavery inside and seemed on the verge of tears.

Douglas, sitting in the front seat, produced pop top cans of cold beer. Maggie and Lee accepted and toasted the world.

Cold beer. Wind in their faces. Mixed emotions coursed through their souls! Fear was being trumped by action!

They drank deeply and then clung to each other's hands as Douglas pointed out sights to Ali. The receding shoreline bore the silhouettes of Bahrain. Seaward, the waters darkened and large ships appeared as dim shapes or little lights here and there.

As it became dark, the boat slowed and circled as Douglas got his bearings as he looked out at the multitude of twinkling lights on the sea. The air was no longer fresh. It was damp and warm. At sunset, when the winds stopped blowing, the air became oppressive. They could see flames billowing from the tops of the many oil wells that were sunk into the sea in the distance as they burned off the volatile gases.

"Jamal," said Lee, "what time are they due again?"

"Very soon sir. We're a little early." He looked at Maggie. "Don't be worried madam. We spoke to them on the radio this afternoon. Everything is routine." He stood easily at the helm, at home in his boat. Jamal's assurance calmed them.

Douglas sat, half turned in his seat. He too calmly grinned at them. "This will be your adventure of a lifetime. You'll be telling this story to your grandchildren one day." His Scot accent, though odd to their ears, was easily understood.

They sat quietly for a few minutes peering into the deepening dusk, looking at moving lights. Ali and Maggie sat quietly together, leaning on the gunwale. Maggie found a hairbrush in her shoulder bag and began to brush Ali's hair. She needed the comfort of this familiar ritual.

Still hot, the air had a special quality. It was like a warm black velvet curtain being slowly drawn over their faces, or like being underwater in a tub of slightly used bath water.

Pinpoints of lights were strewn on the black horizon. The flare of offshore oil rigs flickered in the darkness.

Foreigners want to leave the hot desert countries at this time of year. People begin to dream of green forests and home. Those who can, escape to cooler climates.

The Elres' escape attempt was afoot in earnest. They feared being sent back in disgrace even if they reached their destination. The authorities might even be in hot pursuit as the boat bobbed up and down.

Lee listened gravely as Maggie began to weep. "How the heck did we get to this point?" she moaned.

A steady red light came into focus and their craft slowly moved forward again and approached a tugboat. The boats were heaving up and down with the motion of the waves. A white light flashed amidships. This was the one!

The tug's deck was quite a bit higher than the runabout's gunwale so Maggie was boosted up first, then Ali and then Lee. The transfers had to be timed carefully as the surging vessels moved up and down in opposite directions.

The captain met them on the deck. He had a Brit accent and his crew seemed to be all Arabs, both by their mode of dress and visage.

"Welcome aboard! Glad to see you! I'm Muhammad. Come on in and let's have a look at you! Meet my mate, Abdul."

The faces were friendly and the handshakes hearty. The men, close up, had dark, sun bronzed skin and were able in appearance. Their confidence soared.

"Come. Come into the saloon and let's just have a bit of a chat." said the captain. He was tall and well into his middle years. He led the way from the deck, into a little doorway and through the galley.

The saloon was a miniature room. Eight feet to a side. It provided room for a formica table and padded benches on the sides which used the saloon walls as backrests. Brass ports, paneling all around, and book shelves with paperback books in several languages. The saloon had a cozy, nautical flavor. Compact though it was, seven or eight people could sit in comfort. If one wanted to get out, others would have to move out of the way.

Vibrating diesels and a faint odor of fuel oil combined with a well defined roll would have enabled a deaf and blind man to ascertain his whereabouts as being aboard a ship without the slightest difficulty.

The captain seemed concerned only with their welfare. "Have you had supper? No? Well, then, COOKIE!" he bellowed, in English, "What's on the galley?" The cook reported in Arabic, the captain ordered. Cans of cold beer were proffered for Maggie and Lee and a coke for Ali.

Lee mused, "Beer seems to be everywhere. It must be because we're Americans he must think we love beer. And of course, we do."

Lee explained the situation to the captain in a few paragraphs. He knew the story already but Lee wanted him to hear it first hand—a matter of getting to know each other.

The cook brought heavy china platters overladen with food. Maggie and Ali didn't eat much even though a noon lunch had been their last meal and it was now almost nine o'clock.

The captain volunteered his cabin for Maggie and Ali and their single bag was moved in. A snug affair, it had a narrow bed, an attached head and scarcely enough room for Maggie and Ali. Small but charmingly nautical, it was offered with a true spirit of hospitality since the captain would have to accept an inferior berth in the crew's quarters.

"When do we arrive in Sharjah?" Maggie pronounced the name with a flourish.

"We'll get in at about seven o'clock on Tuesday, the twenty-ninth," the captain replied. "With the barges we're pulling we only make about three knots."

Maggie looked worried. They'd have to sleep on the boat for three nights. She sensed that this might be a difficulty for Ali.

Just before Ali's bedtime Maggie and Lee took Ali to the small fore deck to catch a breath of air and see the night at sea.

Lee shifted his weight to wedge himself more solidly between the peeling paint of the deckhouse and a large coil of thick rope. Maggie leaned against him and Ali leaned on her mother. They saw in the light of the next day that the rope was the source of the black grease that now, indelibly, spotted Lee's clothing and shoes.

Maggie stirred against Lee and kissed his neck, the only spot she could reach without standing on tiptoe. The movement of the swaying deck made the embrace somewhat precarious. Her slender softness made him feel protective. He held her closer. She was so much smaller than him.

"Oh, my love. Poor baby. You didn't know that you'd have such troubles when you married me, did you?" She gazed up at him, a hint of a tease in her eyes.

"No way," he replied. "But I'd do anything for you. And for the kids."

This was their style. Lay it thick. Make it feel good.

"Mommy."

"What, my love?"

"I love you. Daddy too." Ali hugged her mother's leg. Lee reached around Maggie with his half free arm and stroked Ali's black hair. It is fine hair, just like her mother's, and cut very short. "Too short," Ali often complained. "It makes me look like a boy." She became silent then and smiled up at Lee without further comment. Her brown eyes glowed with the thrill of adventure. Her eyes were also like her mother's. Expressive. And lately, they had been troubled and full of pain. Bad things had happened. They had to run.

Lee blew Ali a kiss and lapsed into long moments of companionable silence. They could hear the control cables moving inside the wall on which they were leaning as the helmsman steered the boat.

The wash of white water against the stem produced a soothing sound. Dim navigation lights played on the water as the boat slowly forged ahead. Bahrain, their recent prison, showed faintly as a pale loom of light to the right and behind them.

Is it possible to appreciate how precious children are in the ordinary course of events? Lee thought not. Ali had almost been lost and he was intensely aware of his tender feelings for her. He was by no means certain that they'd still be Mommy and Daddy to her a week or a month from that moment.

So they held each other close. The three of them. The male and the females. The large and the small.

The outlandish circumstances required them to take great risks. All for the love of this child.

They would have to go ashore without visas, without proper passports, and without the official blessings usually required for international travel.

The chief consul at the American Embassy in Bahrain had warned them, "His Excellency, the Minister of Justice, wants all parties in this dispute to remain in Bahrain until the courts decide the matter." He had emphasized the official titles to impress them with the weight of his words.

Their families and friends, their support team, did not know that they'd slipped out of Bahrain. Maggie and Lee had a notion that overseas telephone calls were monitored and recorded. As lawbreakers in a stern land, they felt that it would be unwise to advertise their intentions.

So their plans had been made in secret, concealed from their legal friends in Bahrain. So they were on their own.

This was a source of unease. What if...?

It was a very special time. They were wrung out emotionally and physically tired. Ali was sleepy after the short time on deck and she went to sleep in the little bunk quickly. It was somewhat later than her accustomed hour.

Maggie and Lee broke out the worn deck of cards and played rummy in the saloon. Abdul joined them and he played enthusiastically. Maggie soon retired and the Mate and Lee passed a pleasant hour together talking about family and home.

Abdul's English was excellent and Lee found himself attracted to him as a man of gentle and serious nature, living a different kind of life in a different world. He spoke of his family and Lee admired photographs.

He had duties to attend and Lee, left to himself, picked up his book and read. He wondered how and where he would sleep.

Abdul opened the saloon door at midnight and announced that Lee would sleep in his cabin. Lee politely refused but the mate insisted and Lee soon found himself unable to resist the kindness.

Lee was in another compact, built-in bunk in an abbreviated cabin. There was room for the berth and a sink and deck space for one pair of shoes only. It was much smaller than the master's cabin. Before the bridge clock struck two bells, all had been rocked to sleep.

The time at sea was not all pleasant for Ali. She did not feel well. She suffered seasickness on and off. She ate little and Maggie kept her in the cabin. Sometimes she was nauseated and vomiting. She was pampered with light snacks in bed and lots of reading.

Maggie groaned after the first day, "Oh Lee. We've made a terrible mistake. This is making Ali so sick. What if she gets dehydrated or goes into a coma. What can we do about that out here?"

Lee, as always, tried to comfort her in her misery.

In between acute bouts of seasickness, Ali, sometimes, was able to walk about. She enjoyed exploring the boat. The bridge fascinated her as did the washing machine with an old-time hand wringer on the boat deck. The ship's boat was a salty Boston Whaler. Ali liked to sit in it and hold the steering lever. But mostly, she napped in the Captain's bunk.

They all loved to watch the dolphins at play under the bow. Early evenings were best. Daytime was too hot on deck and the ship's slow three-knot pace was usually not brisk enough to create a breeze. In a following breeze the air was foul with diesel exhaust.

The flares from oil rigs, planted at sea out of land's sight, made eerie orange and yellow glows on the horizon at night.

Conversation was limited to the captain and first mate since the rest of the crew either did not speak English or felt a cultural distance and did not go out of their way to make their acquaintance. Everyone on board was friendly but didn't converse much with the guests and they seemed shy around Maggie.

Maggie visited the galley and asked the cook to help her make mashed potatoes for Ali in the hope that this would be something she could keep down. Maggie knew how she liked them. This had some success but little Ali was anxious for the voyage to end.

Good food was the norm on the tug. English style. Heavy on gravy and potatoes. Both Maggie and Lee were occasionally queasy due to the unaccustomed motion. Sleep came easily at night. Maggie had to share her narrow bunk with Ali and that was uncomfortable for both.

They don't know where the captain slept but Lee caught Abdul sleeping in the saloon several times and felt guilty about having his cabin.

But Abdul always said, "Don't worry. I am up on watch every night anyway. I sleep very little so please, Lee, use my cabin. It makes me very happy to help you."

Their interlude on the boat was pleasant in one respect. They had solved the Bahrain problem. They did not have to think about future problems because they did not know what they might be. Their insular little world demanded nothing from them. They ate, read, played cards, talked world affairs and slept.

Since they had no changes of outer clothing, their wardrobes were a wreck. Lee's white shoes were the worst. They were soon stained with black grease. They only had the clothes on their backs.

On the third evening out, Lee found himself alone with the captain, drinking a beer in the saloon.

"Captain," Lee said. "We have a business matter to discuss. We must pay for our passage."

"Anytime at all," he smiled.

"Well. You know we're parting company tomorrow and this is as good a time as any." So he counted out fifteen one hundred dollar bills. Inured as he was by outrageous prices, and because the service was so valuable, Lee was actually glad to give him the cash.

"Thank you. Ya know, it's for the boys." He winked. "We'll give it to them." His words paralleled those heard before at Evelyn's table. He pocketed the money with a wink and a grin.

"Thank you," Lee said. "You and Abdul have put yourselves out and we're very grateful."

The last day at sea was calm and hot. Maggie and Ali were lounging in their bunk and Lee was reading in the saloon.

Suddenly the tug heeled unexpectedly, way over to the port side-perhaps thirty-five degrees. It felt even steeper to the landlubbers. It stayed heeled over and the regular throb of the engines went higher in pitch.

Maggie and Lee, each in their own places, froze. Not knowing what was happening. She thought the boat was sinking. Lee too was scared but he had a porthole and looking out, quickly saw that the barge they were towing was no longer in its regular position behind them. One half of the tow yoke had parted. Lee went to tell Maggie what had happened and then made his way to the deck to watch the crew re-rig the hawsers.

Toward five o'clock the shores of Sharjah came into view. It was a low coastline and not remarkable except for its lack of vegetation and lack of a skyline.

When close enough to make out details of the port, the captain and mate came on deck and asked them to lay low in the captain's cabin and not to come out until invited to do so. They explained that port officials would soon come aboard and that the passengers must not be seen. So the three waited in the tiny cabin, listening to a hubbub of activity outside as the ship was worked into its slip. A little over an hour elapsed. Not even a peek out of the curtained porthole.

Footsteps and voices frightened them. It seemed that the moment of truth was at hand.

On several occasions the captain brought men to the saloon directly opposite his cabin door, no more than five feet away. This particularly bothered them. They felt that they could be discovered at any moment.

Dusk began to fall and a light knock sounded on the door. They were afraid to answer.

"It's me," said the captain and Lee opened the door. He had a stranger with him who was introduced as 'Mike', a tall muscular man with an unruly bush of white hair. He was windblown.

They explained that Mike would drive them to their hotel now and that it was time to leave. Their hearts were in their mouths as they departed with warm handshakes from the captain and Abdul.

"Don't worry now," said the captain. The fear in their white faces must have troubled him. "You're on your way. Everything'll be fine here. They're good people here and I'm sure that you'll be home in no time at all."

Maggie carried her bulging handbag and Lee carried Ali. It was not quite dark but deep shadows were everywhere and the few small buildings in the distance were black. Stacks of construction and industrial material were everywhere.

Their tug was not tied to the wharf. It was tied outboard and alongside the massive barge that they'd towed for three days. They clambered up onto the barge and saw its cargo up close. Rusty pipes! Across the barge and down onto the land. They had to be careful because there was no ladder.

Lee went first, then took Ali and the bag. Maggie hesitated, fearing the water twenty feet below. However, with encouragement she made the leap safely.

They drove out of the port in an old white station wagon. There was little conversation. There were no guards or gatehouse. The place was deserted. Just a huge industrial store yard by the water.

The Carlton Tower Hotel proved to be quite close, less than a mile away. It was a brand new, fifteen story hotel rising out of a wasteland. There were no outbuildings, no neighbors and no neighborhood; just empty land.

At the desk, they were greeted in a routine matter-of-fact way which gave them great encouragement. Their hassles, if any, would at least be deferred until tomorrow.

The hotel was palatial and cold. Whoever set the thermostat liked his air temperature at about seventy degrees Fahrenheit. It felt like winter in the Rockies after the steam bath outside.

In prominent display by the check-in desk was a sign, "We do not accept credit cards or cheques." The rates were two-hundred-forty dirhams U.A.E. or seventy dollars U.S. This troubled them because of their cash shortage.

They were surprised to learn that there was no American Embassy in Sharjah. The desk clerk informed them that the U.A.E.'s embassies are all in Abu Dhabi.

Lee asked the clerk about transportation to Abu Dhabi. He said that a taxi would be best. It was a three hour ride and the cost would be modest.

"How much do you think it is?"

"Oh, sir. I don't know. Perhaps one hundred dirhams U.A.E." Lee did some calculating. He worked it out to be about thirty dollars U.S. Not bad for a three hour ride with the driver deadheading back to Sharjah but a significant drain on their store of cash. They'd be broke after the cab ride! He exchanged all of their U.S. Dollars for U.A.E. Dirhams.

The room was fine. Ali wanted to know if they were in America.

"No, honey," sighed Maggie. "We have a long way to go. Soon we'll be home again."

Their first need was to call home. Sister Jane was the obvious choice since she was the contact with the newly hired international lawyers. The eight hour time difference meant that they'd wake her up at about three a.m., but their anxiety was such that they could not wait. The call was booked through the hotel operator.

Jane's cheery voice greeted Lee, "Hi. Good morning! It's three a.m." She was alert and in good spirits.

"I know, Jane. I'm sorry to wake you up but we need to talk."

"It's O.K., Lee. Where the heck are you? We've been trying to reach you and the hotel said that you checked out a week ago."

"ane-Jay. E-way am-scrayed. Ane-Jay. Oo-day ou-yay understand-ay e-may? E-way uck-snayed out-yay."

"Yes. I think so." She was puzzled at first. But Lee had decided to use the pig Latin she had taught him as a child because he did not want to tell plainly about their crimes on an international telephone line. He was paranoid.

"E-way an-ray away-ay ith-way out-yay ermission-pay." (We ran away without permission.)

"I-ay ee-say," she responded. "Ou-yay uck-snay out-yay." (I see. You snuck out.)

"Jane. Write this down. We're at the Sharjah Carlton Hotel in Sharjah, U.A.E. U.A.E. stands for United Arab Emirates. Sharjah is a city. Spell S-H-A-R-J-A-H.

"We need money. It's urgent that we get at least one thousand dollars. Tomorrow. But we won't be here. We have to go to Abu Dhabi. That's another city. Spell A-B-U, new word, D-H-A-B-I. There is an Embassy there. Maggie will need her document. Do you understand?"

Jane's mind was in high gear even in the wee hours. She is a super-organized conspirator. "Yes, Maggie needs documentation."

It was clear that Jane had the essential facts:

- They'd Left Bahrain illegally.
- They needed a passport for Maggie.
- Money was a problem.

"Where shall I send the money?" She volunteered to provide the funds.

"Call Paul Rauschenplatt at the Continental Bank." Lee gave her the phone number.

"Tell him to send it to me at the First National City Bank in Abu Dhabi. And Jane, what can you do about the document?"

"Lee, don't worry. We'll raise heaven and earth for you. We have several senators and congressmen briefed on the matter and we're in contact with the State Department at a high level. There should be no problem about that."

Lee didn't know about all the political connections but it sounded good.

"I'm going to set my clock for six a.m., Lee, so that I can get the wheels going early. Don't worry. Can I speak to Maggie?"

"O.K. Bye now – Hold on."

Ali was jumping up and down. "I wanna talk to Aunt Jane. Pleeeease, Daddy."

So Ali took the phone.

"Aunt Jane. We were on a boat. A Big boat. And the captain let me steer it."

She spent a minute talking to Jane. Then it was Maggie's turn. "Thank you, Jane. I don't know what we'd do without you."

And then, Jane was gone.

They were hungry. Would the hotel serve them in such scruffy outfits. A call to the dining room confirmed the problem. A jacket and tie were required.

But the coffee shop allowed that they wouldn't need to dress for service there. So, they ate in the coffee shop and then left a wake-up request for six a.m. They asked for a taxi to come at seven in the morning.

Packing in the morning was no problem. Neither was choosing an outfit.

They paid the bill. Five hundred nineteen dirhams including the phone call and the coffee shop meal. They had a little over one hundred dollars left. Just enough for the cab ride and a few meals.

The taxi driver agreed to charge one hundred dirhams for the trip to Abu Dhabi. The drive took them through a sandy desert, complete with dunes and free ranging camels.

The driver spoke enough English to point out that the numerous wrecks along the road included his brother's car. Lee thought that he told them that his brother was killed in an accident, but they didn't understand why so many one car accidents occurred here. Six or seven abandoned and wrecked cars were passed along the highway.

The driver was wild. He careened along much too fast although the road was new and smooth.

Maggie and Lee never really saw Sharjah. Their only impression was of the rough port, the new hotel and a few utterly poverty-stricken hovels near the hotel. Little structures made from sticks, tin cans and rags. They never found out if it was an Arabian night's paradise or just an outpost in hell.

They arrived in Abu Dhabi at about ten-thirty. It was a large city with more construction in evidence than any city they'd ever seen. The Embassy was housed in a round ten-story building which appeared to be both commercial and residential.

Evelyn had been avoiding his friends at the law firm for two days. When Salah called he was told by the house boy that the family was out in the jeep visiting the area. It was time to fess up and tell them the truth. But not all the truth.

The Englishman walked into the office and asked to speak to Mohammad. As he was ushered in he couldn't keep the smile off his face. He said "Maggie and Lee are no longer in Bahrain." Mohammad sat back in his chair and with a smile he said, "I suppose you don't know where they went."

"No, I got up today and my house boy told me that the couple had left during the night, I have no idea where they could have gone. Their bags are still in their room."

"They were here everyday to check on their case so we missed them. Salah was worried about them when your house boy told him they were out visiting the area. Well, we better tell Salah so he can call Joe's attorney."

After his initial shock and many questions, Salah called Essa. "Mr. Hussein, I must report that Mr. and Mrs. Elres are no longer in Bahrain."

"What do you mean they are no longer in Bahrain? She was told to stay in the country until the case was over. Mrs. Elres doesn't have a passport. How could she have left the country?"

"We have no more information than what I'm giving you. They left the house they were staying at during the night and the host does not know where they went. Their bags are still in their room."

"The Elres' have broken the law. The judge is going to be furious. Mr. Zayyat will be down right uncontrollable. He will want to file charges against Mrs. Elres, so you'd better be ready for a fight Salah."

Essa hung up and sat back in his chair and thought, "How did they do it? How did they manage to outsmart Joe? Maybe they're hiding someplace until all this blows over. Joe is going to be up in arms. He will want to throw the book at the family. Well maybe this case will be over sooner than I expected."

He dialed Otis Engineering, after a few minutes Joe came on the line.

"Hello Essa, I hope this is good news. I'm tired of waiting for that judge to make up his mind. We know he's going to rule in our favor, what is he waiting for?"

"Joe I just received a call from Salah Alireza, Maggie's attorney, he called to tell me that the Elres family is no longer in Bahrain and he doesn't know where they are as of today."

There was silence on the other end, after a few seconds Essa said, "Joe are you still on there?"

"Repeat what you just said Essa."

"I said that Salah called to tell me that Maggie, Lee and Ali have left the country for parts unknown. They left the house where they were staying in the middle of the night and left all their luggage in their room."

"THAT'S IMPOSSIBLE!" yelled Joe. "HOW COULD THAT BE?" "Maggie doesn't have a passport, they don't know anyone here except their attorneys. Do you think those bastards helped them get out?"

"I rather doubt it Joe. This country is very strict with their laws and I don't think that firm would take a chance in loosing their license just to help them. Listen, I'll make some inquiries with the local police to see what I can find out. They couldn't have left the country legally without a passport. In the meantime, go to the house they were staying at to see what you can find out. I'm sure the ambassador knows where they were staying and so does your company. They've had plenty of information."

"What do you mean legally? How else would they have left?"

"I don't know Joe. I just found out just like you. Go out and look for them. Call me." Essa hung up with Joe and ran his hand up and down his face, smiling.

Joe held the telephone to his ear even after he heard the dial tone.

"How could this have happened? I was so close to victory. That God damned woman will be the death of me."

"Where in hell are they," he mused. He took a map out of his drawer and thought about where a small boat could go in the few hours he'd been watching for it. The closest land was Saudi Arabia but the round trip was over sixty miles over open water and that would have to be a risky trip.

"Aha! They must have met a boat outside of the Manama port and gone to Saudi Arabia that way. He pictured a white yacht with a uniformed crew and shiny, varnished railings and trim.

"But," he thought, "What about passports? Who would give them a ride? How would they proceed?" It baffled him and he took the only action he could think of - he called his brother Wadi who had a lot of connections throughout the region and who owed him big-time for many past financial favors and loans.

"Wadi. Maggie has escaped Bahrain with Ali and that bastard husband of hers. I need your help."

"Anything you want brother. Command me."

"Wadi you have police connections throughout the area. They left here, probably on a yacht, and I need to plant a bug in the ears of the police in a five hundred mile radius to be on the lookout for the names Elres and Zayyat. Maybe I can get ahead of them yet and drag them back here.

"I'm thinking Kuwait, Iraq, Iran, Saudi Arabia and the United Arab Emirates."

"Joe. That's a big job but I'll do it. I'd love to give Maggie a black eye. Mami is still not talking nice to me for over a year and even Joelle acts strange. It's all Maggie's fault."

"Shukran brother. Ma'a as-sal'mah."

"You're welcome Joe. I'll call you. Ma'a as-sal'mah."

July 30, 1975

A bright Wednesday morning. The Elres' straggled into the American Embassy in Abu Dhabi at eleven in the morning. They asked for the ambassador. He was not there. Neither was the chief consul. They settled for a Dr. John Boynton who was the highest officer available. To recount what followed represents the most satisfying contacts they'd ever had with their government.

Dr. Boynton was a young man in his late twenties or early thirties. He greeted them warmly and strove to put them at ease.

They were nervous. Lee stuttered and stammered as he began to tell the story. Dr. Boynton listened patiently for a few minutes and apparently felt sorry for them. They were sad sacks.

"May I call you Lee and Maggie? I'm John. We received a communication from Washington this morning. There are apparently a lot of folks there who are concerned about you. I've been instructed to issue a passport to Maggie without delay."

"Thank God," Maggie breathed. "I don't believe it. We've had so many frustrations." She was practically in tears.

Ali, who was still firmly fastened to either Maggie or Lee at all times, left Lee's lap to hug her mommy's leg.

"Don't worry, Mommy," she said. "Everything is O.K.!"

They all laughed because Ali was clearly mimicking the adults who had been mumbling kind assurances to her for the past month.

John offered coffee which was accepted eagerly. "Now. I find your story fascinating." he said, "Would you care to share the rest of it?"

They continued their tale, Maggie and Lee alternated. When the story was finished, John sat back and opined that they would be all right. "I don't think that the authorities here will give you any trouble. Once you have your passport, Immigration shouldn't care too much so long as you are just in transit.

"Your biggest worry is that they'll get it into their heads to contact Bahrain and that, if they do, the people in Bahrain might want Ali back since the matter is in their court system."

All agreed that that would be way too troublesome so they decided to cook up a story to tell the Abu Dhabi Immigration Department.

The concocted story line would involve the following elements.

1. They were on vacation in Bahrain and decided to take a boat trip to cap their holiday.
2. They found a dhow captain who volunteered to take them to Sharjah as passengers.
3. Maggie lost her passport over the side of the boat.

4. There was a big hurry to get home now because Jackie, their older daughter was ill. She was having pains in her stomach which might be appendicitis.
5. They'd have to sign papers to permit surgery.

John called the Department of Immigration and told them that he had an American family who had entered without going through Immigration and minus one passport. He tried to "grease the way" but he was, at last, informed that they would have to be "interviewed" by an immigration official before being allowed to depart.

An appointment was made for eight a.m. Thursday morning. The fact that their appointment was for the next morning seemed significant in several ways. Friday being the Sabbath meant that Thursday would be a half-day for government workers. If they let them go right away...fine. If not, they'd be delayed over the weekend.

"Oh my God Lee! We can't go to the police looking like this. Your shoes are so dirty and look at this." She pointed to holes and grease stains in her blouse.

Lee turned to Maggie. "We'll need time to get our money from the bank and to reconstitute our wardrobes so that we won't look like refugees."

While Maggie's passport was being typed (using passport photographs that they'd had made in Bahrain in hopes of getting documented there) Lee called the First National City Bank. Their money had not yet arrived.

They explained the lack of funds to John and he had no suggestions to make other than saying, "It would be a really good idea to dress up a little."

As to hotels, he recommended two. "The Hilton is really the best. It's new and has a fine reputation."

When called, the Hilton indicated that there was only one room available...the Presidential Suite!

After some negotiation, Lee said, "But there is only my wife and five-year old daughter!"

The clear kindly voice said, "Well, perhaps you would like to stay in the parlor of the suite. You could have it for three-hundred dinars a night.

Lee paused to do a calculation. That would be eighty-seven U.S. dollars a night. "That'll be fine. We'll be there in a few hours. Do you take credit cards?"

The answer, happily, was "Of course."

So a place to stay came off the 'to do' list.

John consulted with an aide and it was decided that it would be very much in their interest to have a letter from the Embassy attesting to their good character - a letter of reference:

July 30, 1975

To whom it may concern:

Mr. And Mrs. Liam Elres are well known to me and are of honorable character. Any assistance rendered to them would be greatly appreciated.

Special Counsel
Dr. John Boynton (Signature)

Embassy of the United States of America
Abu Dhabi, U.A.E.

They left John in rather high spirits. His interest and efforts to get them headed home gave them courage. They agreed to meet him at the Embassy at seven a.m.

Outside the Embassy, they made a discovery about Abu Dhabi. It was much hotter than Bahrain. It was one hundred twenty degrees Fahrenheit! This was a regular occurrence here.

A taxi appeared after a short wait. Luckily, since the Embassy was not in the heart of the city.

The driver was told City National Bank. After some initial difficulty in communication, he understood and they were treated to another tour of the city.

Abu Dhabi was a marvelous city! The roads were all brand new. Large buildings were being erected everywhere. Yet, despite the newness, there were still tents here and there. Desert dwellings with families living in the ways of the past.

The bank informed them that the money had not arrived. Lee asked for an officer and was introduced to a Mr. Ken Johnson. He was a young man from Brooklyn, New York. Lee established a rapport by speaking of his own childhood in Flatbush. They'd attended rival high schools. He told Ken of their problems and of the urgent need for cash with which to buy clothes.

To Lee's and Maggie's amazement, Ken allowed them to cash a check for one-thousand dollars! The arrangement was that he would hold the check until their funds arrived and then return the check by mail, using the wired funds to cover the cash advance.

His kindness was just that. He and his bank could not hope for any profit from this business.

They asked him about shopping. Where to go. What were the hours of business. He directed them to a shopping district and told them also to try the Indian Market which abutted the shopping area.

Maggie and Lee returned to their waiting taxi, no longer broke, and very anxious to buy decent clothes which did not have oil and dirt stains!

They visited several small shops and bought outfits. In Lee's case, the purchases were very difficult. Since he was very tall, and because the Arabian people are not large, there were few items from which to choose. But at last he had trousers, a shirt, socks and a tie, not a good fit but passable, under the circumstances. What he could not find were shoes. They decided to try the Indian Market and this proved to be a good decision.

Lee was struck by the way in which they could move among the throngs of swarthy, turbaned Indians and Arabs. People were courteous and gentle. If they drew attention because of the color of their skins, their worn and outlandish clothing, language or relative height, they were not uncomfortably aware of it. As in Bahrain, the people seemed to possess an urbanity of spirit and kind attitude toward foreigners.

The market was a bazaar devoted to clothing, luggage, shoes, toys, specialty food items and junk; but a good one! They trudged from store to store in the heat buying small items and a little airline bag to supplement Maggie's bursting handbag.

But, no size fourteen shoes! Vendors implored Lee to try the shoes but he was reluctant to do so because he didn't want to stand in the dirt to try on shoes which he didn't like and which he <u>knew</u> wouldn't fit. But at length, one persistent fellow found a pair of size twelve, brown suede shoes with crepe soles. Lee tried them on. They fit! Tightly, but, at this point the Chinese made shoes were a triumph. Lee had just learned that a British size 12 was about the same as the U.S. size 14. He muttered, "I should learn to listen."

While Lee was looking for shoes with Ali in tow, Maggie was looking at the burkahs the local women wore. They were being sold as an ensemble that included a head dress and mask that covered the face and with a hole for the eyes.

As Maggie browsed she thought, "When I tell my friends back home about the way these women dress in the streets, they are not going to believe me. I think I'll buy one so I can prove to them how controlling these men are making their wives dress like this."

Maggie paid for her purchase, spotted Lee and Ali at yet another shoe store, and joined them.

"Mommy, did you buy me a present?"

"No darling, this is for Mommy."

"What did you buy Maggie?" Asked Lee.

"A little something to take back home."

A cab was easily obtained and it took them to the British Airways office. The office was nearby so they had the taxi wait.

There were several people ahead of them and they took pleasure in waiting in the comfortable, cool waiting area. The glare and heat of the sun were ferocious but from their vantage on the right side of the insulated glass, it looked like any American city on a sunny summer day.

They learned that almost every plane leaving for the West passed through Beirut or Bahrain. They definitely didn't wish to visit either place - Bahrain for obvious reasons. Beirut was no good because Maggie and Ali were well known to many of Joe's relatives there. She had left them less than a year ago.

The only easy way out of U.A.E. which would avoid these two cities involved flights from Dubai, passing through Cairo or Athens. They considered going home to the east but this would have been more expensive and they'd hoped to go home through Europe. They opted to leave from neighboring Dubai and get to Miami via Cairo, London and Washington, D.C.

They reboarded their taxi and headed for the Presidential Suite parlor. The ride produced a blast of hot air but no relief from the heat.

The Hilton is located on the beach, quite removed from the city. The route to the hotel ran for several miles along the beach. White sand, blue sea, white foaming surf and no people.

"Wow Maggie. Look at this," said Lee, "Some year soon, when the earth is more crowded, the winter months could bring a million bathers to these beaches. You know supersonic SST jets already visit and when the flow of oil slows down, the locals may find treasure in their warm winter climate. These are really hospitable people."

Their Hilton reception was first rate. The parlor was a splendid room. As large as a house, it included a kitchen and a wet bar. It had everything but a bed.

The view from the balcony revealed miles of clean sand and sparkling surf finally fading away to the horizon.

The bellman said not to worry, they would sleep on the couch and Ali on a rollaway bed. The couch proved to be a super convertible so they lacked nothing.

They had brought their bathing suits from Bahrain, crammed into the very bottom of Maggie's bag. They went to the pool to eat lunch there. The pool-patio was elegant but hot.

While Maggie made a visit to the ladies room, Lee chatted up the waitress. She indicated that the temperature was 120 degrees. As a joke Lee asked if the pool water was refrigerated and she said, "Yes!"

He thought that she was kidding but when he and Ali stuck their toes in the water it was frigid! Maggie did not like cold water but Ali and Lee reveled in the idea of keeping it a secret from Maggie. So they did not tell her that the water was cold.

After lunch and coffee they decided to swim. When Maggie hit the chilled water, she shrieked and wriggled out as fast as she could. No amount of teasing could get her back in.

"I'd rather roast than be frozen to death." She lay in the sun for a while, getting darker by the minute.

They had nothing to do but pass the time. They relaxed in the suite, had dinner in the hotel restaurant and went to bed early in anxious anticipation of their appointment with the police.

Joe took the day off work on Sunday, the day after he saw the Elres' board the boat, and headed for the house. The house boy answered the door.

Joe growled, "I'm looking for the American couple with the little girl that was renting a room here for a few days."

The house boy stood to the side and motioned for Joe to come and wait in the parlor. He scurried away to find his master.

339

Evelyn and Robin were home for lunch so they went to face Joe. "How may we help you?" asked Evelyn.

Joe, who was pacing the room, turned and saw two of the men from the yacht club dock standing on the landing. He recognized Evelyn now as the owner of the house and some-one he'd probably met through his work.

"I'm Joe Zayyat and I'm looking for the couple that was renting a room here with the little girl."

"You mean the Elres family? Well they were not renting a room, they were here as my guests for a few days, but they left a couple of days ago."

"So they were your friends, and staying here as guests. Did you know them in the States?" asked Joe.

"They became our friends here in Bahrain, and I suppose you are the father of Ali who kidnapped her from her mother. That was not a very nice thing to do to your child, old boy."

"I'm not your old boy," Joe snarled. "And I have a right to know where they are so the courts can deal with them." Joe was visibly agitated; his hands turned into fists.

"You have zero rights here in my house. We don't know where they are. Their bags and all their belongings are still here in their room so maybe they will return soon."

"You'd better not have had anything to do with their dis-appearance or I'll…"

"Is that a threat then Mr. Zayyat? Because if it is, we can call the police right now to report this."

"It's not a threat, it's a promise. No need to call the police. I'll leave now but I'll be watching this house."

Joe left the house and slammed the door behind him. Evelyn looked at Robin and said, "This calls for a drink my friend. It looks like we'll have eyes on this house. Good luck to Mr. Zayyat, he's got a long wait."

Joe drove out of the driveway very angry. He muttered to himself, "How did Maggie and Lee make friends so easily?" I have never been able to make friends with anyone so fast. And to have this guy offer them a room at no charge, that's really something. It doesn't make sense..."

As he drove off he thought of the last time he had seen Maggie in court. She looked so angry at him. What was it Essa had said? "If looks could kill you'd be a goner.

Ambassador Joe Winesap read the Morning Journals which were wired to all American Embassies in the region; a name caught his eye - Maggie Elres. She was issued a new passport in Abu Dhabi. Curious he thought and wandered to his Consul's office to talk about it a little and see if he needed to take any action. "Morning Howard," he said as he politely rapped on the frame of the open door.

"Don't we still hold Maggie Elres' passport? What's happening with that case?"

"Morning Sir," replied Howard. I've got it here in my files awaiting developments. Have you heard something?"

"Yes in fact I have just learned that Mrs. Elres was issued a passport in Abu Dhabi yesterday afternoon. I think it's time to close our files and send her old passport to D.C. for destruction." He smiled a farewell and left for lunch at the British Club where he was an Associate Member.

CHAPTER 17 - ABU DHABI

THURSDAY, JULY 31, 1975

Maggie squirmed in her seat, uncomfortable with her emotions and the heat. Lee, sitting in the back seat with Ali, reached out to pat her shoulder. He whispered, "Maggie. We're going to be all right."

She touched his hand but could not speak, not wanting to vent in front of Ali.

The Elres family had met John as agreed and he drove them to a nondescript complex of government buildings some distance away. They made their way to a waiting area and found seats on a plain bench in a crowd of people who were no doubt doing business that involved the United Arab

Emirate's immigration or foreign department. John went off to see about their appointment.

For the first time they were served coffee Arabian style. A porter made his way from person to person, offering a small china cup without a handle. If a cup was accepted, a lightly colored coffee was poured from a steaming copper coffee pot. Lee accepted. Maggie declined.

The coffee was mild but not unpleasant. He finished it quickly and returned the cup to the porter saying, "Thanks." The man took the cup, refilled it and returned it to Lee.

Lee really didn't want the coffee but it was small so he tossed it down in a few minutes and offered the cup back again. This time he smiled and covered the cup with his hand to let the coffee man know that he didn't care for more.

The coffee man took the cup, refilled it and returned it again. Again Lee drank and returned the cup. This time he stood and gave the cup back upside down and made several gestures to say "Enough"! He patted his stomach, smiled and shook his head and pushed the cup away as he handed it to the man.

These bold steps had no effect whatever for when Lee sat down, another cup was pressed him. At this juncture Lee was feeling burdened. Maggie laughed and suggested that he not drink it but leave it under the bench. A neighbor, in the local mode of dress, spoke, "Sir. I see that you don't understand our custom. When you have had enough, you must move your cup like this." He waggled an imaginary cup by oscillating his hand from the wrist.

"Thank you very much. I'll do that now," Lee smiled. So, having learned the secret, he was able to refuse the fifth cup.

John returned and escorted them to a rather large and well furnished private office. Two men were introduced. The first seemed to be an army colonel in a turban and burnoose. John let them know that he spoke no English. They didn't catch his name. The man just nodded as he looked them over. Lee suspected that he understood and could have spoken had he wished.

The second gentleman was a complete surprise. He stood six-foot-six, weighed three hundred pounds and was dressed in a general's uniform. He was a ebony-skinned African and was introduced as Brigadier Al Bashir.

A conditioned reflex had occurred on the few occasions that Lee saw a black man in Bahrain. This phenomenon took place again. Lee had a strong feeling that the Brigadier was really an American. He supposed that this was because of the uniform size and appearance of the typical mid eastern male. And the headgear and cloaks further stamped the folks as Arab. But, anyway, Lee immediately related to the Brigadier in a very friendly fashion. They shook hands warmly and introduced themselves.

"How do you do?" said he in a strong British accent. "I am here as an advisor to the government of the U.A.E. I am from Sudan and I will interpret for you." So obviously not an American black man.

They sat around the colonel's desk in comfortable chairs and smiled at one another. John sat in the back of the room with Ali standing at his side.

The colonel took out a legal sized blank sheet of paper with a governmental seal on top and began to write. He asked a series of questions.

Names?

Address?

Dates of birth?

Parents' names?

Where had they gone to school?

Date and time of entry into U.A.E.?

Place of entry?

Reason for coming?

Mode of transportation?

Where had they come from?

When did they leave Bahrain?

How long had they been in the U.A.E?

Where were they staying?

Why did they not register with immigration officials in Sharjah?

Why had they not gone through official procedures when leaving Bahrain?

Why had they come by boat?

What was the name of the boat?

What was the captain's name?

What nationality were the crew?

How had the arrangements for passage been made?

Did they not feel afraid to trust themselves to an anonymous boat and captain in a strange country?

How had Maggie's passport been lost?

How long did they wish to stay in Abu Dhabi?

Did they not know that when entering a country, passports must be presented?

Where had they spent the night?

The night before that?

Where had they stayed in Bahrain?
Where were they born?
Did they have other children?
Were the children born in the United States?
Names and addresses of sisters and brothers?
What friends and associates in Bahrain?
Names and addresses?
How much money do you have with you?
Who do you work for?
What kind of work do you do?
How long have you been here?

The questions seemed endless. The Brigadier asked the questions and relayed the answers in Arabic to the colonel who painstakingly recorded everything in careful Arabic script.

The Brigadier was a thorough interrogator. He asked for explanations continuously. He seemed skeptical, yet maintained a friendly countenance. Lee did most of the talking with Maggie filling in information from time to time.

Ali had been told to "Keep very quiet! Don't talk." So she sat with her little lips pressed together.

Lee followed the story line they'd established at the Embassy, embellishing the answers as seemed appropriate under the circumstances.

When asked, "Why on earth did you choose such an unlikely spot as Bahrain for vacation?"

Lee answered, "Because it is unlikely. We wanted to experience a country and people that were off the beaten track."

"Did you enjoy your stay there?"

347

"Yes and no. We had difficulty in finding a place to stay but we made many friends and have come to deeply appreciate the friendly and hospitable nature of the people there."

Lee explained, "We wanted to spend a little time in other parts of the region. Before going home but we called home and our twelve-year-old daughter was ill. It may be serious. Appendicitis. And we must go home today!"

"Well. I share your concern. We must try to conclude our investigation as soon as possible."

"Investigation. Hoo Boy!" thought Maggie. That meant contact with Bahrain for sure and their lies would be exposed! The giant Brigadier stood and stretched. "Tell me, Mr. Elres. What do you suppose would happen if I were to enter your country and entered it as you have entered U.A.E.?"

That seemed a good question. Lee hadn't the foggiest idea. So he said, "Well, Brigadier, I'm sure that there wouldn't be any problem at all. We are accustomed to visitors from all over the world. If you wanted to become a resident, there would be a delay but a visitor in transit would not be troubled."

"I see. We, by the way, are awaiting the arrival of some boats from Miami. We have ordered Bertrams for use as patrol craft. Dhows come and go without being noted and we hope to prevent such occurrences in the future."

"If I can be of any assistance in Miami, just let me know. I'd be glad to help."

John spoke, "What, Sir, is the next step? We would like to proceed as rapidly as possible."

"There must be a police investigation. You will have to go to police headquarters and when they have concluded their work, then you may depart."

The word 'investigation' was a blow to the culprits. They imagined the worst scenarios including prison and losing Ali. They were again reminded that this was a high stakes game they were playing.

Joe couldn't get any information about Maggie. Wadi had not called him and his own contacts revealed nothing. It was like they had just floated off into thin air.

Joe pushed Ben. "Ben you have to try harder. Somebody has to know where they are."

"Joe, I've told you before I don't want to get in the middle of this, I've done everything I'm going to do. You're on your own. I gotta tell you buddy, you brought it on yourself. Stealing a little girl away from her mother takes the cake."

"You don't know anything about my ex, she's a bitch, and she deserved every bit of misery I've caused her. But now I'm worried about Ali. I can't sleep at night . I lie awake worrying about her."

"You're right, I don't know your ex, but I did see your daughter when you brought her to the office and she looked like a lost puppy. She'll be paying for what you've done to her for the rest of her life."

"I don't need your lectures Ben." Joe left Ben's office in a huff.

Ben wondered if he was going to lose a valuable employee over this mess. Even though he maintained a hard line with

Joe, he felt sorry for him. Practically all of his American and European staff, as well as himself, were enduring family separation problems. He was sympathetic to Joe as well as his ex and her daughter. They were all suffering.

When Ben ran into Ambassador Joe Winesap at lunch they exchanged pleasantries as usual and then, during dessert, Winesap dropped a tidbit that exploded inside Ben's head. "Maggie had gotten a new passport in Abu Dhabi yesterday afternoon! They were safe. Wow what a long way to go by boat. He wondered what kind of boat they made the voyage on but did not let the ambassador know how interested he was. He didn't want to be told to "Keep it under your hat."

Thus matters stood at an impasse until early afternoon when Ben decided to let Joe know that his daughter was safe in Abu Dhabi.

Joe was flabbergasted. He thanked Ben for his kindness and returned to his desk to make phone calls. The first call was to a travel agency and he learned that there was only one flight out of Abu Dhabi that made sense for Maggie. The daily flight to London with a layover in Beirut.

His next call was to brother Wadi in Beirut.

"Wadi. I found them. They're in Abu Dhabi. Maggie got a new passport yesterday. They're probably already at the airport but, just in case, I'll be on the five-thirty a.m. Middle East Airline flight tomorrow. It stops in Abu Dhabi and then goes to Beirut with a very short layover. I should arrive at one p.m."

"Joe. Wonderful news. What should we do? I've got a friend in the Abu Dhabi Police organization. He is a sergeant of police there and I interviewed him for a story about drug smuggling last year. I went to his house for dinner and we got along great. Let me call him and see what he can dig up. We may need a few hundred dollars worth of U.A.E. Dirhams to grease the ways."

Joe agreed that money was no object. "Wadi. Meet my flight tomorrow but see if you can keep an eye on the airport or find out what flight they're on. I'll fix their plan so that it will explode all over them!"

Evelyn and Robin were sitting at the bar in the English club when they spotted Captain Mohammad and his first mate Abdul back from their journey across the Gulf. Evelyn waved them over and offered them a drink.

"Well Captain, how was your trip? Did my three packages get across without a problem?"

"Our trip went without a hitch. I gave the packages to my cousin who took them to the hotel. The smallest package was very smart and loved being in the wheel house."

"Thank you Mohammad, we owe you one."

"No you don't, it was my pleasure and besides they were very interesting, very nice and told a great story."

Evelyn, Robin, Mohammad and Abdul raised their glasses and drank to the Elres family's safe journey wherever they were.

Maggie and Lee bade their interrogators goodbye and proceeded to police headquarters in John's car. He expressed disappointment. "I hoped that they would give you permission to depart. We must hurry now because it's almost eleven o'clock and we want to be there before the officials leave for the weekend."

The police building was of more recent construction than the government center housing the Immigration Department. The circular drive in front of the building passed under a marquis-type overhang. They parked in front.

The entry hall was a large, round, domed room, extending to the roof of the building. In it were twenty or so Indian or Pakistani men; they sat or squatted on the floor, silent, poorly dressed and looking dejected and rejected. Lee and Maggie had uneasy feelings. Some of them were handcuffed together.

Maggie and Lee didn't know why these wretched looking people were there, but images of the Black Hole of Calcutta were evoked in their minds. Maggie clung to Lee's arm with a claw-like grip. They were both terrified. A male receptionist guided them through a long hall which could well have been a police station in the U.S. Totally utilitarian, no pictures or windows lightened the mood.

They were escorted to the police chief's office, a large but plainly furnished room. The chief wore a western suit. They were asked to sit on a sofa while John spoke with him.

The chief approached and introduced himself. "Colonel Khouri will take care of you," he said. "Would you go with this gentleman, Mr. Elres?"

"Certainly," Lee replied. And he was led from the room to another office just across the long hallway.

Colonel Khouri was a smallish young man of swarthy complexion and he sported a thin mustache. He wore the typical Arabian outfit and remained behind his desk. There was another black gentleman who introduced himself as Mr. Sunawi, "Sudanese advisor." He wore a western suit and Lee again experienced the feeling of meeting someone from home. People are so alike in many parts of the world.

The procedure for this interview was a duplicate of that which was used by the Immigration Department. Lee did not feel that Colonel Khouri spoke any English.

The questions at first related to families. Lee had to write his father-in-law's address and name on a pad of paper because the interpreter was less facile with English than his counterpart at Immigration. Lee was questioned for ninety minutes.

Lee wondered what was happening with Maggie and Ali. He was troubled by the separation. In their innocence they had never expected to be questioned separately and they had not had a proper, detailed 'story conference.' The details of their lies had not been discussed. Only the broad outline and Lee recognized that there were many holes in the story.

Lee was asked to describe the boat, "Oh," He said, "It was a dhow about seventy feet long." He professed not to know the name since it was in Arabic. The color? "Mostly black with a green and white deckhouse."

"How much did you pay for your passage?" This was a zinger! The Brigadier had not asked this one and Lee had given no thought to the matter.

"Seven hundred fifty dollars." he lied.

"Do you mean Seven hundred fifty dollars American or Seven hundred fifty Bahraini Dinars?"

"We paid Seven hundred fifty dollars American."

"That is an outrage!" interpreted the Sudanese translator. "It was robbery! You must give us more information about the boat and captain so that we can help you get your money back!" This seemed to Lee to be a ploy of some kind. An offer of help?

At this point Lee had an opening to extemporize and did so heatedly. He even ventured to stand up and make his speech.

"Look. We have a real problem! I'm not interested in getting my money back. My daughter is ill and we don't know what's wrong with her. It's an emergency. We must go home as quickly as possible.

"I'm very sorry that we came to Sharjah improperly. I don't know how we could have been so foolish or ignorant. The captain said that it was O.K. No problem. No paperwork. At home we can go to all of our neighboring countries without passports and visas. We just get on a plane or boat to go to Mexico, Canada, the Bahamas, Jamaica, Virgin Islands or wherever. When the man said 'no problem,' I believed him.

"If Maggie hadn't lost her passport, we wouldn't have gone to our Embassy and if Jackie weren't sick, we would be happy to stay and visit here for however long we could. But now, we must go home! Could you please explain this to the colonel and ask him to expedite our departure. We would like to leave on the four o'clock British Airways flight from Dubai."

"How do you come to be so familiar with airline schedules?" the interpreter asked, somewhat taken aback by the tirade.

"We made a lot of inquiries yesterday and that flight would give us the best connections to Florida."

"We, too, are concerned and we understand how you feel about your child. We will try to be as quick as possible."

They continued their questions and Lee continued his lies about the reasons for their being in this hot and thorny situation.

At last the questioning was finished and Lee asked. "Well, you have all of the facts now. May we go? We must hurry to pack and try to catch our plane."

"Not yet. We must question Mrs. Elres and then we will decide."

"Uh-oh!" Lee thought. "They will surely find us out and return us to Bahrain in disgrace. Or worse, prosecute us for illegal entry and we'd join the sad people by the front door."

So Lee returned to the chief's office. John, Maggie, Ali and the chief sat there. Maggie was led away. Her face was white with fear.

Ali questioned Lee, "Daddy, where have you been for so long? What were you doing? Why is Mommy so sad?"

"Hush Ali. Mommy is very worried about Jackie." Lee said this aloud so that the chief would hear. He sat at his desk jingling his keys as if he were ready to go home. "I was talking to a man about going home."

After just a few minutes, Maggie dramatically burst into the room. The door was flung open and hit the wall with a bang. White as a ghost, she stood in the doorway with her arms spread apart. The Sudanese was behind her in the hall.

"Lee! Help me." She groaned. "I'm sick! Where is the bathroom?"

The police chief stood and pointed to a door in his office. A private bath. Maggie rushed in and, alarmed, Lee followed closely. "My God, Maggie! What's the matter?" She retched loudly as the door closed.

"Lee," she whispered, "What did you tell them?" So they were, belatedly, having a story conference. Maggie made loud, retching noises, "BLEAAHH!" every minute or so as Lee reassured her that he had stuck to the story line and gave her some details.

"I saw my father's name on a piece of paper written in your handwriting and I was scared. What does it mean?"

"Don't worry. They're just getting background information."

They ran the water and flushed the toilet twice. It was a loud flush. That Lee thought, would make them wonder. She returned to her interrogation.

Lee sat on the couch to hold hands with Ali. She was worried about her mom and he comforted her.

The chief continued to jingle his keys. It was well after noon and he was obviously anxious to go. "The Arab world's equivalent to Saturday afternoon." Lee thought. "He's anxious to get home to his family." He noticed that their passports were on the desk, stacked neatly near the corner.

No more than five minutes passed when Maggie again came through the door retching - "AARGHHH!" She went straight for the bathroom and called over her shoulder, "Lee! Help me!"

He followed her in, amazed at her flair for drama. She looked awful! "How much did you tell them we paid for the boat?" she whispered. "BLEAAH!"

"Seven-hundred and fifty-seven dollars. And they want to find the boat to get our money back. I told 'em that we thought that the price was O.K. for three people for three days because everything costs twice as much as at home."

They discussed a few more details, ran the water in the sink and flushed twice again, for effect. He helped her from the room and she was obviously very weak. Her fear, combined with her desire to appear ill, worked well.

"What's wrong with Mommy?" Ali was very concerned.

"Honey. Mommy is feeling a little sick. She'll be O.K. now. It must have been something she ate."

Ali and Lee continued to talk. John sat stoically and the chief, restless, kept his keys in hand and gave them an occasional shake.

It was after one o'clock. Lee had been grilled for more than one and a half hours. Maggie's questioning had been going on for more than an hour.

Finally, at one-fifteen p.m., Maggie was escorted back by the chief, after a phone call, presumably from Colonel Khouri, relayed word that they could leave. Needless to say, they felt relief from the tension. Their nightmare seemed almost over.

"John. We want to leave from Dubai. How far is it?"

The chief did not permit a reply. "You must leave from Abu Dhabi. You cannot go to Dubai."

"OHMYGOD!" thought Lee. "Colonel Khouri speaks clear English with an Oxford accent. Better than the Queen of England. A good thing to know!"

Nobody cared to argue his edict. "Very well. We will depart on the first plane out. Will you adjust our passports so that we won't have difficulty at the airport?"

357

"That won't be necessary," he replied. "The way will be cleared for you. Take my card and call me if you have any problems." He handed Lee the passports and a simple business card.

The happy couple thanked him and left the building in jubilant moods. "John," Maggie said. "Thank you from the bottom of my heart. You have been an angel!"

"We're very fortunate that it's Thursday," John said as we drove toward the beach. "On Thursday, everything closes by noon or one in the afternoon. Everyone there was ready to go home, tired from the week's work and all of that sort of thing. On a Sunday or Monday, the officials would have had plenty of time to check you out. It would have been very embarrassing to be caught in the lies."

They agreed that, as trying as it was, the end result was all that they could have wished for.

"I've never been so afraid in my life," said Maggie. "When they took you away, I felt so bad. I thought that I might never see you again." She patted his knee affectionately.

Ali took it all in and said, "I told you not to worry. Can we go home today?"

"Honey," said Maggie, "We'll leave as soon as the first plane goes."

In the suite, they could hardly sit still. Lee talked on the phone with British Airways.

Lee learned that there was a travel agent in the hotel and left to purchase tickets with their trusty American Express card and cancel the earlier reservation for a Dubai departure. He wondered what the credit card bill would look like.

The earliest feasible flight turned out to be at seven in the morning, B.O.A. to Beirut with a layover waiting for a British Airways flight to London.

Maggie announced that she would like to have a candle light dinner in the Presidential Suite. They decided to take a bath, have dinner sent up and go to bed early. They would have to leave the hotel at five-thirty a.m. and would have to rise by five a.m. to catch the seven o'clock flight.

They spent several hours lolling around the pool. Maggie again refused to enter the chilled water.

The room-service dinner was absolutely elegant. Cocktails arrived promptly at seven o'clock. The steaks with Bernaise sauce were consumed by the light of candles. The round dinner table was covered with a white cloth. Room lights were kept dim and their "high" made all the world seem like a better place.

Ali went to sleep right after dinner. Maggie and Lee played a farewell game of rummy on the game table and by half-past nine, they were fast asleep.

Essa and Salah exchanged a few phone calls and Salah was summoned to court to explain the disappearance of his clients. Joe attended the court hearing accusing Salah and his law firm of facilitating the escape, however it happened.

Salah vehemently denied the accusations and swore to the judge that he had no knowledge of the disappearance and had no idea what had happened to the Elres family. He said that he hoped they were okay wherever they were.

The judge believed Salah but ruled in Joe's favor giving him the custody of Ali, and decreed that the Elres family would be arrested and brought to justice if they ever appeared in Bahrain again.

Essa said to Joe as they came out of the courtroom, "Well Joe, you won. You have custody of Ali here in Bahrain, you have the victory you wanted."

"Yes Essa I have my victory without Ali and without Maggie. How am I ever going to be able to look my daughter in the face again?"

"Maybe you should of thought about that before you took Ali from her mother. Never underestimate the power of a mother's love Joe. It can move mountains, and it looks like Maggie did just that."

Lee woke up in a fog. The phone was ringing. He fumbled out of a heavy sleep and answered dully, "Hello."

"Is this Mr. Elres?" The heavily accented voice was not familiar.

"Yes. Who's calling?"

"Mr. Elres. This is the Abu Dhabi police. I'm sorry to wake you but I need to ask a question."

"Yes?" Maggie was up. The light was turned on. "Lee, it's 12:30. Who is it?"

"Wait a minute," he said with his hand over the mouthpiece. "It's the police."

"Oh my God! What do they want?"

Lee was too intent on listening to answer her. She sat up and began rocking and moaning, holding her face in her hands. Ali slept.

"Mr. Elres. Could you tell me when you are leaving?"

"Yes. Tomorrow. Why?"

"I need to have it for our records. Could you tell me what flight please?"

"Yes. We're leaving on the seven o'clock flight. B.O.A. for Beirut and then London."

"Thank you, Mr. Elres. Again, I am very sorry to have disturbed you."

"O.K. Goodbye."

"Goodbye." Click.

"Oh my God, Lee! What did he want to know?"

"Maggie. I don't know. He wanted to know when we were leaving. He was very polite but the only thing he said was that he needed it for the records."

"Geeze. What does it mean?"

"Shhh. Don't wake Ali." They sat up in bed, wrapped in blankets in the night. Maggie and Lee were spooked. Ali slept on.

Every aspect of the situation was discussed. They decided that the worst possible case was that the police had made inquiries in Bahrain, perhaps by Telex, thus explaining the lapse of time since they'd left headquarters, and learned that Maggie's passport was being held and that they had a case pending in the courts.

The best case was that the night shift had been left a number of assignments, one of which was to determine their travel plans. Since this was a relatively low priority matter, the person responsible had put it off and had gotten around to inquiring towards the end of his shift.

Lee decided to call sister Jane and let her know of the situation. It was a good time to call because she'd be getting up to go to work. So, the call was placed and she was soon on the line.

"Hi, Jane. It looks like we're leaving at seven this morning...our time."

"Oh, Lee. Wonderful! Tell me all about it. Nope...wait a minute. These calls cost like crazy. Let's be quick. Tell me what you want me to know or do and the story can wait till we get together."

"O.K. Here is the basic outline. We were interrogated by the police and Immigration Department today. They grilled us for over five hours this morning. We told them how we lost Maggie's passport at sea. We told them about Jackie's illness and of our need to get home quickly. We told them that we fouled up in leaving Bahrain without getting passports stamped and how we thought that travel between Bahrain and U.A.E. was similar to travel between Canada and the U.S."

"I see. When are you leaving?"

"Well, Jane. The best flight would have been from Dubai. It went via Athens or Cairo but we have to leave from Abu Dhabi. We have reservations on B.O.A. and have a two hour layover in Beirut. We should be in London by three p.m., London time."

"O.K. Sounds good. When will we see you?"

"Jane, it's one a.m. here now. We have to leave at five forty five. We finished at police headquarters at around one o'clock this afternoon. We went to bed early. The police woke us up a little after midnight. They telephoned to ask which flight we'd be on. Woke us up out of a sound sleep. It worried us so we're wide awake now and can't go back to sleep. So we said 'let's bug Jane'. Just wanted you to know, Jane."

"I see, Lee. You're worried about the phone call. What do you think you should do?"

"I dunno. I believe that we'll proceed as planned. We'll call you from London on August first. As soon as we check in. It'll be late tomorrow night. Or tonight. Jane. The time confuses me. I guest it'll be tonight. O.K.?"

"O.K. Good luck. Call me immediately if you have any problems."

"O.K., Jane. Maggie sends her love. Ali is asleep."

"Oh, Lee. One more thing. The folks are coming on the third. Kids and all. We want you to come too. Even if only for a few days. You can use us as an 'R&R' stop before going back to work. I spoke to Dad and he's bringing Jackie, subject to your approval, of course."

"Sounds great, Jane. Hold on while I ask Maggie." Maggie agreed to stop at Jane and Art's house. "O.K., Jane. I'll let you know when we'll arrive. Gotta go. Our dime. Love you. Bye." Click.

Maggie and Lee talked on and on as they walked around the room. They peered out of the shuttered windows at the empty dark road and beach far below. White breakers were dimly visible as the waves foamed against the beach. They were too alarmed and excited to go right back to bed. At length, tired, they turned off the light and tried to sleep.

Their wake-up call came promptly at five-thirty a.m. and they prepared for departure. Maggie and Lee were frightened. Their passports were not stamped.

The airport in the early morning light was magnificent in comparison to their expectations. Even more than Bahrain, the government was loaded with new oil revenue and had spent a considerable sum on it.

They lined up in front of a gate where a uniformed man, looking like a soldier, was examining passports, stamping them and allowing people through to the main waiting room. They nervously inched their way forward. A motley crowd from many nations created the hubbub characteristic of busy international airports.

Their passport inspector was silent as they smiled, said hello and offered their documents. He was an olive skinned man with a black, trimmed mustache. He poured over the passports, looking for an entry stamp as they stood with Ali holding on to their hands. Lee on her left hand and Maggie her right.

Back and forth the inspector leafed through the passports and finally, puzzled, he looked at Lee, for an explanation. "Why no stamp?" he asked in accented English.

Lee's answer was altogether spontaneous and, he thought, ingenious. "Because we came by boat."

"Oh," he muttered. He stood, looking at them, obviously not knowing what to do. Maggie and Lee were both smiling, explaining and 'making nice' at the same time. Lee handed him the police chief's calling card. The card seemed to be the deciding factor. He stamped the passports. Thump!

Thump! Thump! And turned to his next customer. They were in!

They found the boarding gate a half an hour early, took seats among hundreds of other passengers and waited. The B.O.A. Boeing seven forty seven would be full. So close to 'freedom', yet still worried. Hardly able to believe that they were there. Then a new problem arose.

The big plane arrived and parked outside in full view. As minutes crept by, they became aware of an activity on the other side of the large room. Two police officers with slung rifles were slowly and methodically moving through the room closely scrutinizing the waiting passengers. They seemed to be looking for someone.

"Lee! What are they doing?" Maggie whispered.

"I don't know, Maggie. They're only talking to women."

"Oh my God! They're after us!"

"Come on, now. You don't know that. We're a little paranoid. Let's be calm. We'll be on the plane in a couple of minutes." It was six fifty five a.m. Five minutes until take-off. People were lining up by the boarding gate but no one was allowed to pass. Most passengers remained seated.

The two policemen were moving very slowly. A little closer but still far away. Ali napped in Maggie's lap. Maggie's face was hidden by a straw hat she'd just bought and Lee had his face buried in a magazine, slumped down, trying to be invisible. Time ticked on slowly. The two officers approached, paused and then, to the Elres' relief, moved on.

They were finally forced to move when passengers were allowed through the boarding gate to straggle across the pavement and up into the plane. They planned their boarding move so as to stay within a crowd and to keep people between them and the still circulating officers.

Tense and wary, they boarded and found their seats. The boarding continued at a snail's pace and they still had not left at seven thirty. Finally doors were closed and the engines started. They were almost gone.

Then, the engines stopped. After a few minutes, the pilot announced, "Ladies and gentlemen." His accent was British. "I am sorry about the delay. We are being held up by Immigration. We should be leaving in a few minutes. The good news is that due to favorable winds aloft, our arrival will be on time."

"Oh my God, Lee! They're after us. I just know it!" Maggie whispered in a hoarse voice.

Lee's role has always been to say, "Don't worry. It's going to be all right. Calm down. Hey! Here's an idea. Why don't you and Ali go to the washroom and freshen up? You can stay there till we get going."

"Good idea. Come on, Ali. Let's take a walk."

"O.K., Mommy," Ali sighed. She was tuned in to their tension. She had become super cooperative ever since being found in Bahrain. Used to being led by the hand or carried, their three way relationship had grown ever closer.

The engines restarted after a short delay and the journey continued.

The Captain announced, "Ladies and Gentlemen, we are approaching the Beirut airport. We will be landing in a few minutes."

The flight attendant came on the speaker, "Ladies and Gentlemen, we will deplane in Beirut for a two hour layover. Passengers may leave the boarding area and stroll through the airport. Please return to your seat, fasten your seat belts, and get ready to land."

Maggie looked worried. "Lee, I thought we didn't have to get off the plane in Beirut."

"I did too. I don't know what happened. I'll go ask the her."

Lee got up and walked back to the area where the announcements were being made. "Excuse me. You said we would have to deplane in Beirut. I thought we were staying on the plane while other people get off or on as the case may be."

"I'm sorry sir but the Beirut airport wants all passengers to deplane while the plane is being fueled. You'll have a couple of hours to look around and enjoy the stretch."

"My wife and I would rather stay on the plane. She is not feeling well and our daughter is air sick."

"That's impossible sir, we have orders for everyone to disembark in Beirut. Now please go back to your seat, we are about to land."

Lee walked back to his seat to tell Maggie about the news, "Maggie, they say we have to disembark in Beirut. They have orders to have all passengers get off the plane."

"Oh Lee, do you think Wadi might be lurking around the airport?"

"No way Maggie, Joe has no idea where we are. What is his brother going to do? Stay in the airport for days looking for us?"

"What if the police called Bahrain to verify our story and they gave Joe our information? They called us to find out what time we were leaving and what airlines we were using."

The plane landed with a thump. The hostess was announcing again, "Ladies and gentlemen, welcome to Beirut."

Passengers collected their bags from the overhead compartment and proceeded down the aisle to the open door. Maggie, Lee, and Ali stayed seated waiting for the end of the line.

"Mommy, are we going to see Uncle Wadi?"

"I don't think so honey, he doesn't know we had to land at this airport."

"But Mommy he lives here, we could call him."

Maggie sat Ali on her lap and took her face in her hands. "My sweetie, I know you would like to see your uncle, but right now we can't do that. You are going to have to be very quiet while we're at this airport and stay with Mommy. I'll tell you what," she whispered, "we are going to play a trick on Daddy. When we get off the plane, you and I are going into the bathroom and when we come back out Daddy Lee will not recognize us."

"How are we going to do that Mommy?"

"You'll see; we'll have fun, are you ready?"

Ali nodded.

"Lee, please give me the package I bought at the market and as soon as we get off the plane I'm going into the bathroom with Ali."

"Ok. Honey, I'll be waiting outside." Maggie carried Ali off the plane and Lee followed close behind keeping his eyes and ears opened for problems. They spotted the restroom sign and Maggie and Ali walked in.

"Ali, come in with me, Mommy wants to show you something."

Maggie and Ali went into the small bathroom stall together holding hands, it was cramped in the stall but Maggie wiggled around so she could open the bag she was holding. Out came the black burka.

"Mommy this is the dress that the women in Bahrain were wearing in the streets. It looks very big."

"Yes honey this is exactly what those women were wearing. Mommy is going to put it on and you are going to go under the dress just like those children back in Bahrain."

"But Mommy I won't be able to breathe in there."

"Yes you will sweetie, there's a place where you can put your head right by my shoulder and you'll be able to breathe just fine. We need to play a game until we go back to the airplane. You can take a nap on my shoulder. I'll sing to you like I used to when we were in Miami."

Maggie put on the burka and the piece that covered her face, picked up Ali, put her under all the material, and walked out,

Lee waited dutifully outside the bathroom. He saw women in burkahs and women in western clothing go in and out of the bathroom. He waited. A few more women came out and still no Maggie or Ali. He was getting worried now. It had been fifteen minutes since Maggie had gone in. He started to pace back and forth in front of the door.

"I better not call attention to myself. I'll just stand next to the door and wait."

Lee saw a woman coming toward him. She was wearing a burka, all he could see were her eyes. It looked like she was carrying something under the black attire.

"Hello Lee. Don't you recognize me?"

"Oh my God. Maggie? Is that you? Are you carrying Ali under there?" His mouth had dropped open in surprise.

"Daddy I'm under here look at my hand." Ali giggled.

Ali stuck her hand out and waved at Lee.

"Where did you get this outfit?"

"Remember when I went shopping at the market? Well I wanted to bring one of these outfits home to show my friends what woman wear here. When I found out we had to deplane I thought that it would be a good disguise if Wadi shows up. I figured if I could fool you I could fool him too."

"Maggie, you are one clever lady. I don't know what to say. I'm stunned. I think you're overestimating the danger but it's better to be safe than sorry."

"Good, now we have to separate. They'll be looking for a family. I'm going to go sit down by the gate with Ali, and she's going to try and nap on my shoulder. As soon as they call the flight we'll be the first ones on. I can take this thing off on the plane after it takes off."

They each took a boarding pass and separated. Lee lounged near the automated arrivals announcement board enjoying the endless clicking it made as letters and numbers changed on their little wheels. He saw a constant stream of people walking by. People using telephones in the ranks of phones. Each phone had little wings to give the users privacy. He gazed absently at the arrivals board and became aware that there was a flight arriving from Bahrain at one thirty p.m. - fifteen minutes delay. "Oh God," he thought. If ever there was a moment for doubt this is it!

Maggie sat with Ali still wrapped in her garb and softly sang the Spanish song she used to sing to Ali at bed time. "Esta nina Linda que nacio de dia quiere que la lleven a la dulceria. Esta nina Linda que nacio de noche quiere que la lleven a pasear en coche. A roro mi nina a roro mi amor, a roro pedaso de mi Corazon." (This pretty girl born during the day, wants to be taken to the bakery. This little girl born at night, wants to be taken for a buggy ride. Rest my girl, rest my love, you are a piece of my heart.)

Maggie could hear Ali's even breathing.

"My sweet baby, you are such a good girl. I knew I could count on you."

As Ali slept, Maggie looked around the airport. It wasn't easy to see with this thing on her face. "How can these women wear this mask over their faces every day?"

It felt like time was standing still. Maggie could see Lee across the room trying to keep busy by reading his book. Every once in a while he would look up to make sure Maggie was still there. They had been in the airport for well over an hour when Lee saw two policemen and a man with sunglasses walking purposefully toward the waiting area.

Lee got Maggie's attention by jerking his head toward the approaching group. Maggie looked up to see Wadi. Lee strolled over to Maggie and took a seat right behind her. "Is that Wadi? What should we do?" he whispered.

Wadi was looking all around. He looked frantic. He got closer with the policemen in tow.

Maggie was a believer in omens and demons. In Miami, when things were worrisome for her she would go to a woman, she called 'The Lady,' for help in times of trouble. Lee suspected that chickens would die when Maggie saw 'The Lady.' She kept more than one talisman in her pocketbook including the pen that had helped her find Joe in Bahrain and the business card she got from the shopkeeper Nadia - the woman she'd met right here in Beirut the day she flew out with Ali almost a year ago.

"Lee. Take this card and call Nadia. She's the friend I made in Beirut. Tell her you are my American Husband and Ali's step dad. Ask her to arrange to page Mr. Zayyat to meet his party at the Saudi V.I.P. departure lounge. It's at the other end of the terminal from us. She was so smart and I feel like she'll know how to do this for me. Ask her to make it happen quick!" Maggie said urgently. Use the pay phones there. Someone will show you how for a few American dollars. Offer twenty bucks."

"Good idea." Lee got up and walked to the phone banks. Maggie didn't move, she looked straight ahead and held onto Ali for dear life. Ali stirred; she must of felt the tension in Maggie's arms. Maggie rocked back and forth still singing the little song. Ali went back to sleep.

"Do you speak English sir?" Lee asked a man standing at a phone. His hand outstretched, ready to dial.

"Certainly," came the reply. "How can I help you?"

Wadi was at the ticket counter speaking with the desk agent. He was hitting the counter with his fist and the agent was shaking her head. Now she was making a call. A few minutes passed; then she handed the phone to Wadi. The two policemen were standing by, waiting. Wadi ran his hand through his hair. He was agitated at the woman. He was yelling now. Maggie couldn't hear the words. She kept her head down. Ali slept. Out of the corner of her eye she saw Wadi and the two policemen looking at the passengers that were in the waiting area. Wadi walked right past Maggie and Ali. Maggie was looking down at the floor.

"Look," said Lee. I'm in big trouble. My wife and I are being harassed by her former husband. I need desperately to phone this number but I haven't got the right coins and I don't even know how to make a phone call here. Sir, could I pay you $20.00 to dial this number for me?"

The man, short and swarthy, with a thick German accent said, "Please put your money away. I'd be happy to call it for you. He took the card, dialed Nadia's number with the money he had already deposited, listened to the phone for an instant and handed it to Lee along with Nadia's card. "Let me know if it doesn't go through." He politely stepped back to give Lee privacy.

After making one more trip around the area looking at everybody, Wadi said something to the policemen and they stomped to the edge of the waiting area. The attendant behind the desk was crying.

Maggie held her breath and prayed "Holy Mary, Mother of God, please don't let them come back and look again."

The loudspeaker came on with an announcement, "MR. ZAYYAT MEET YOUR PARTY AT THE SAUDI AIR LOUNGE. MR. ZAYYAT. MEET YOUR PARTY AT THE SAUDI AIR LOUNGE."

Wadi's head snapped up when the announcement was made. He conferred with his companions and they began the trek to the Saudi lounge.

Joe heard the announcement as he came through the Middle Eastern Airline arrivals area. He stepped up his pace and headed for the lounge. "Wadi must be on to something," he thought. Both Lee and Maggie spotted him but Joe was on a mission and didn't look their way.

Lee sat down across from Maggie and said, "Maggie. Try to board the plane now. It's time." She struggled up to the gate and was the first one through. She was ahead of even the first class passengers.

Lee followed a moment later excusing himself for boarding early by saying, "Sorry to be in a hurry, but I have to help my wife with our baby."

EPILOGUE – PERSPECTIVE

After a few minutes, the doors closed, the big jets started and they began to taxi. Each foot of runway that passed by was a thrill. Their moods soared with the plane.

The takeoff for London was routine. Not an event to be recorded in history, but it was a huge event in their history. They were on the way.

They looked at each other. Maggie smiled and said to herself. "I think we might be home free."

Their spirits had been in the valley of despair and on the wings of ecstasy. But the odyssey was just beginning.

A week later, on another airplane, Maggie woke with a start. She felt the 747 descending. Lee was looking out the window and Ali was fast asleep between them. "Lee, are we getting ready to land?"

"Yes honey, we've just started to descend and I see the lights of the city ahead."

Ali opened her eyes and with a big smile said, for the hundredth time, "Are we there yet?"

"Almost baby," said Lee and Maggie in unison, they all laughed.

Maggie laid her head back, closed her eyes and thought about the journey her family had just taken. Maggie, Lee, Allison and Jackie were a family with bonds that could not be broken.

In a few minutes they would land and see Jackie. This has been a journey for Jackie also. The uncertainty of not knowing when and if her family would return. Jackie had not spoken to Maggie since they left.

Maggie knew her mother was taking good care of Jackie but she also knew that Jackie was afraid of Joe and what he was capable of doing. Jackie was also suffering.

All over the world children are being kidnapped from mothers and fathers, usually for hatred and revenge. There is a price paid by the innocent children involved.

The airplane made a smooth landing at Dulles International. The captain announced, "Ladies and Gentlemen, welcome to the U.S.A. Keep your seat belts fastened until we have come to a full stop."

Maggie and Lee were smiling; holding hands, looking at each other and smiling. Maggie thought "Those are the sweetest words I've heard in a long time."

Allison couldn't wait to get off the airplane; she held onto Maggie's hand and pulled her closer to the head of the line every time she saw the line move. "Come on Mommy, I want to see Jackie."

The family went through customs without a hitch but not before answering a series of questions from Ali..."Will the policeman take you and Daddy to ask more questions? Are you going to be sick again mommy? Ali was slightly confused.

The doors of customs opened, and the threesome walked through to find a dozen people in the welcoming party. Jackie, Lee's sisters and brothers, and Lee's parents held up a huge sign that said:

Welcome Home
Ali Maggie Lee
Bahrain - Bah Humbug!

Allison wriggled out of Maggie's arms and ran to her sister. "Jackie, Jackie! I missed you. Daddy Joe took me. I didn't want to go. Mommy and Daddy Lee came to get me. We came in a tugboat, and I threw up all the time. Mommy was sick and they were asking Daddy and Mommy lots of questions. On and on Ali was talking a mile a minute. Maggie's heart filled with joy to see the sisters together hugging and kissing and laughing together. Tears of joy welled in her eyes.

Jackie put her sister down and ran to hug Maggie. "Mommy, I missed you so much."

"I missed you too my darling." Mother and daughter held each other crying, but this time they were happy tears. Lee saw Maggie and Jackie hugging and went to get his own hug from Jackie.

After a few days of R&R with Jane and her family, the Elres family went home to piece their lives back together again.

Their lives changed forever. All the plans Lee and Maggie had made when they married were altered. They would not have a child together. They waited for decades to buy a house.

Economic times were terrible in the 1970's and 80's. Amidst the angst of declining income and high inflation, it took them years to recover financially and a lifetime to recover emotionally.

Maggie and Lee are still a devoted couple after thirty seven years of marriage. Senior citizens now, they count twelve grandchildren.

Allison was the focus of their existence. They constantly worried that she would be taken again. The worry and the anguish affected to whole family.

Maggie's mother had a coronary soon after they returned. The family moved five times, enrolled Ali in three different schools under fictitious names so that Joe couldn't find them, and got deeper and deeper in debt to pay for their attorneys and the trip to Bahrain.

Ali is a great mother and happily married to a wonderful husband who is like a son to Maggie and Lee. They have three smart beautiful children and a very successful business. Ali's relationship with Joe through the years ran hot and cold.

Jackie has a beautiful daughter who looks just like Maggie, a loving husband, and three step sons. She loves to cook, bake and entertain.

Lee's two sons are married and have five great children between them. Maggie and Lee have a close relationship with them and visit as often as possible.

Joe married and divorced three times and fathered five more children. The first three were boys who's care was given to Ali for a couple of years because, he said, their mother was incapable. Ali was a young married woman by then. It was not a happy time for her because the boys were hard to handle.

Years passed. He then had twin girls with his last wife. Joe took them away from her because, he said, she has a drug problem.

Joe didn't see Ali for two years after the kidnapping. Lee thought that it was because he was embarrassed to face Maggie. He was not able to be with Ali by herself until she was twelve years old, which was the age Maggie might have gotten Ali back if Joe would have kept her in the Middle East. Joe has never asked Maggie or Ali how they escaped or mentioned the kidnapping. As if it never happened.

Sister Jane and husband Art are alive and well. Maggie and Lee are very grateful for all the support they gave when they most needed it. Maggie always says, "Jane is an angel." Maggie and Lee have a very loving relationship with Jane and Art and visit often.

Maggie and Lee don't often talk about Lebanon and Bahrain. When they do, it seems that it all happened to someone else. Sometimes the images are clear and sometimes a little fogged over. They play the "what if...?" game. What if they hadn't been able to find Ali? Would she be walking the streets of some Middle Eastern country in a burkah? Would she have married a Sheik? What would their marriage be like if they had a normal start? Would they be richer and happier?

Sometimes, in their discussions, the urgency to tell the story was tempered by fear that Ali, as an adult, with children of her own, and their families would be offended or hurt by some of the things they needed to say. Ultimately they decided to tell the story as a novel and after many disagreements on how tell the tale, *Stealing Ali* is a real book. Life is crazy and some people are procrastinators. Lee said to Maggie, "What the heck. It's only been forty years."

The one thing they completely agree on is that they did the right thing and they would do it again.

###

Proof